Coming Up For Air

• • •

Simone Mondesir was born in England, but spent a peripatetic childhood in the Middle and Far East. After university she flirted with academia before moving into journalism and broadcasting, working for ITV, the BBC and Channel 4. She is married and lives in London when not travelling abroad. Her first novel, *Acquired Tastes*, was published in 1996.

Also by Simone Mondesir

Acquired Tastes

Simone Mondesir

• • •

Coming Up For Air

ARROW

First published in the United Kingdom in 1999
by Arrow Books

1 3 5 7 9 10 8 6 4 2

Arrow Books Limited
Random House UK Limited
20 Vauxhall Bridge Road, London, SW1V 2SA

Random House Australia (Pty) Limited
20 Alfred Street, Milsons Point, Sydney,
New South Wales 2061, Australia

Random House New Zealand Limited
18 Poland Road, Glenfield
Auckland 10, New Zealand

Random House South Africa (Pty) Limited
Endulini, 5a Jubilee Road, Parktown, 2193, South Africa

Random House UK Limited Reg. No. 954009

A CIP catalogue record for this book
is available from the British Library

Papers used by Random House UK Limited are natural,
recyclable products made from wood grown in sustainable forests.
The manufacturing processes conform to the environmental
regulations of the country of origin

Typeset by Deltatype Ltd, Birkenhead, Merseyside
Printed and bound in Great Britain by
The Guernsey Press Co. Ltd, Guernsey, Channel Islands

ISBN 0 7493 2256 X

For David

One
• • •

'Ohgodohgodohgodohgod oh *God* . . .'

The desperate entreaty to the Almighty rose to a shuddering crescendo before subsiding into a hoarse, croaking sob.

Further down the bed, the cause of Max Gordon's sudden religious conversion lifted her head from between his thighs and took a deep breath. It was the first warm day in late March and the air coming through the open windows of the flat tasted green and earthy, suggesting temptingly that spring had at last arrived in London. Pushing her tousled dark hair out of her eyes, Kate Daniels levered herself up from the awkward position she had been in and sat rubbing her shoulder, which had gone stiff. The only signs of life from further up the bed were the rise and fall of Max's massive chest, which was suffused with an angry red flush.

Feeling piqued at the lack of appreciation he had shown for her efforts, Kate clambered over Max and flopped onto her stomach beside him, her left hand fishing for the glass she had left on the floor by the bed. Her fingers found it and she brought it gratefully up to her lips, and gulped it down. The champagne had lost its chill, but sex was thirsty work.

Rolling onto her side, Kate propped herself up on one elbow and surveyed the supine body splayed

1

beside her. It was not the most romantic thought to have at a moment like this, but the violence of Max's orgasmic release sometimes made her wonder what she would do if he had a heart attack and died *in flagrante delicto*.

Max was at a dangerous age. He was in his forties and he was a large man. It was one of the things that Kate found so attractive about him. His frame had filled out considerably since they had first met at university. Twenty years ago he'd been rake-thin, and he'd had hair and plenty of it, worn in a flamboyant pony-tail together with a piratical single gold ear-ring. The ear-ring had gone along with the pony-tail. Max's hair was now greying and cropped short almost to the point of being shaved, but Kate preferred it that way.

She smiled indulgently as she remembered the Max she had known at university, the Marxist revolutionary who'd preached the downfall of capitalism from the corner table in the student union bar. The same table had served as the office from where he ran the agitprop theatre group for which he was writer, producer and director, as well as the desk on which was occasionally to be seen a beer-stained copy of his never to be finished Ph.D. thesis. In the intervening years Max had lost none of his flamboyance or his strong opinions on everything, but a successful screen-writing career had made him one of the capitalists he had promised to put up against a wall and shoot.

Kate knew there was no point in dwelling on the past and thinking about the 'what ifs' of life, but sometimes she could not help but wonder what if things had worked out with Max at university? Would they still be together now? Max was one of the few men she had met in her life with whom she might have settled down, although she was glad she hadn't. Her life was exactly the way she had always wanted to be and a man – particularly one like Max – did not fit into

2

it. Not full-time anyway. A man like Max needed a full-time wife, but she neither wanted, nor needed, a full-time husband.

Over the intervening years, as Max had made a name for himself in the film world and Kate had climbed her way up the television ladder, she had occasionally glimpsed him from the opposite sides of crowded rooms at media parties. But although she had felt Max watching her, Kate had always turned away. However, one day she had found herself seated next to him at lunch before an awards ceremony. She had pointedly turned her back and talked to her other neighbour, but Max was a difficult man to ignore.

'You haven't changed,' he had announced loudly to the back of her head. 'You can still freeze a man's balls off at thirty paces with those beautiful eyes of yours.'

Aware that everyone at their table was eagerly waiting for her response, Kate had been forced to turn round. 'Hello, Max. Still chasing lost causes I see.'

Max smiled ruefully. '*Touché.*' He draped his table napkin over his fork and waved it. 'Can we call a truce so I can plead my cause?'

'If it will stop you making a scandal and giving the gossips something to talk about, yes,' said Kate in a low voice, her eyes indicating the rest of the table.

'There's a quiet bar upstairs. We could talk there.'

Kate had hesitated.

His grey eyes had fixed hers. 'Please.'

What harm could one drink do? Kate could remember thinking. She hated awards ceremonies. The speeches always went on so long that she would have plenty of time to get back to her seat before the few awards which interested her could be announced.

But she never returned to her seat that afternoon. Despite her protests, Max had ordered a bottle of vintage champagne when they got to the deserted bar. 'This is my small way of trying to apologise,' he said, holding up his glass to Kate. 'I behaved like a right bastard at university and I've been regretting it ever since.' As Kate opened her mouth to agree, he put a hand on her arm to forestall her. 'Before you say anything I want you to hear me out. I do have a good excuse . . .' He paused and looked at her. 'You.'

'Me! What did I do . . .' Kate began angrily but then stopped, momentarily confused.

'All the men were in awe of you at university, Kate, not just me. You seemed so sophisticated in contrast to the other students. We were all terrified of you while fancying you madly at the same time. Compared with the other girls you had this aura of being a woman of the world and there was me, a little working-class boy from the Gorbals trying to impress you, and the first thing I do is get drunk and then not be able to get a hard-on.' Max leant forward. His voice, which was deep and still roughened by his Glaswegian upbringing, became even lower and huskier. 'Kate, have you *any* idea what it can do to a man's ego when, after lusting after a woman for a year, lying in bed, night after night, imagining what you intend to do to her, when you finally get her into bed all you can produce is this soft little thing which not only refuses to do what you want, but behaves like a shrinking violet? I was devastated. I just wanted to run away and hide.'

'Your devastation didn't prevent you getting married immediately afterwards, did it?' said Kate stiffly.

Max looked pained. 'Strictly on the rebound from you and Marianne was a very determined woman. In my experience, all American women are.'

His first wife, Marianne, had been an American film producer several years older than him. Max had met her while on a solidarity-with-the-workers-of-Nicaragua trip to South America. She had produced Max's first two films, as well as two daughters, before returning to Los Angeles after their divorce.

4

'But she wasn't determined enough to keep you, was she?' accused Kate.

Max shrugged his shoulders. 'It would have been different with you, Kate. Even after all these years I still have fantasies about making love to you and doing all those things I wanted to do then, but was too stupid and too young to get right.'

She could blame it on the champagne, thought Kate, but that would be unfair. She had gone upstairs to that hotel room with Max that afternoon because she had wanted to show him that she, too, could walk away without a backward glance afterwards, just as he had done to her. But she hadn't.

Kate bent forward and brushed her lips against Max's shoulder. Three years after what was supposed to have been a once-only bout of sex, she knew his body as intimately as she knew her own. He still had an intensely erotic effect on her, although not right at that moment. Aside from the sound of his heavy breathing, she could almost believe that he *was* dead, although his face was showing signs of at last returning to its normal colour.

She drained her glass. If Max were to die while they were having sex, how would she explain his presence in her bed? He was married, although no longer to Marianne, and quite well-known, too. The tabloids would love it. Perhaps she could dress him and drag him into the living-room before the ambulance arrived and pretend they had been having a business meeting. But how were you meant to dress a six-foot-six, heavily built, dead Glaswegian?

Smiling at the farcical idea, Kate reached across him for the champagne bottle, which was balanced precariously on the chair that doubled as a bedside table and a clothes horse. Not for the first time, she vowed that she would have to do something about buying some sensible furniture as her flat was seriously under-furnished.

She had fallen in love with her spacious flat, with its airy, high-ceiling rooms and floor-to-ceiling shuttered windows, the moment she had walked into it. The estate agent – a baby-faced twenty-something, driving an open-topped white GTi and wearing a shiny silver-grey suit – had not even had time to begin his salesman's patter before she had declared she would take it at the asking price. It had been far more than she had intended to pay, but she had made a pact with herself that she would economise on other things like furniture. A prohibitively expensive lunch with her accountant, accompanied by some outrageous flirting on her part, had ensured a set of accounts that, without resorting to certifiable dishonesty, suggested that she was able to afford the mortgage.

That had been five years ago. Since her promotion to Executive Producer at the Channel she now earned more than enough to pay the mortgage but no longer had the time to go shopping. Even finding a couple of hours every week to spend with Max was proving increasingly difficult and she had no intention of using her scarce, precious free time traipsing around furniture stores. Anyway, what more was needed in a bedroom other than a king-sized bed?

Kate refilled her glass and put the bottle on the floor beside her, then she arranged a pillow between her back and the wall, and sat up. There was a faint suggestion of movement of Max's eyelashes, then he groaned loudly, rubbing his eyes with the heels of his hands so violently he seemed in danger of gouging them out.

Kate bent down and kissed him on the top of his head. 'Is something wrong?'

Ever since he had called earlier on his mobile to say he was in his car and on his way over to her flat, she

6

had guessed something was bothering him. She could tell by his voice. Normally he entertained her with minute-by-minute reports of his physical arousal as he drove, rather like an erotic traffic report on the radio, but today he had just wanted to be reassured that she was there waiting for him. When he had arrived, his mood had been even more evident as he had trudged up the front doorsteps with his hands in his pockets – usually he was tearing his clothes off as he bounded from his car.

Max took his hands away from his eyes and stared up at the ceiling for a moment or two, a sheepish expression on his face, which was quite difficult for a man who looked like a prize fighter and a bare-knuckle one at that.

'There's something I should tell you before you hear it from anyone else . . . You know I don't want to hurt you, babe, but . . .' He looked at her, but his eyes slid away from hers almost immediately.

Kate felt a prickle of alarm. Max knew how much she loathed the term 'babe'. For one thing she was no 'babe' and for another it did not succeed in making him seem still youthful and street-wise, quite the opposite. 'But what?' she demanded.

Max reached for his glass and gulped some champagne. 'Harriet is pregnant again.'

The words hung in the air between them.

Kate could feel rather than see Max watching her. She found she could not look at him this time. She did not want him to know what she was thinking because she was not sure what she thought herself. She sipped some more champagne. It tasted sour. She put down her glass and pulled her silk wrap around her, tying it at the waist.

Why should she care that Harriet was pregnant? They had an agreement. Max's life with his second wife had nothing to do with her. Right from the start of

7

their affair, Kate had told him that she had no wish to step into Harriet's shoes and play happy couples. Even if she had wanted to get married – which she did not – Max would not have made it onto her short-list as a candidate for a husband. He was congenitally incapable of being faithful. Marianne had divorced him because he was having an affair with Harriet and Harriet had been only one in a long line of women. A man who could cheat on his wife and children with the alacrity that Max exhibited was not Kate's idea of long-term-relationship material. Just because she chose to remain single it did not mean that she was against marriage – far from it – it just wasn't for her. As far as she was concerned, she and Max had the perfect arrangement – great sex with no messy emotional complications.

'You know how women can be about babies.' Max's voice was both pleading and conspiratorial. He put his hand inside Kate's wrap, where it found her left breast. 'You don't mind, do you, babe? It wasn't my fault. Harriet got the idea into her head and there was nothing I could do about it. She can be very determined when she's after something. She said she wanted just one more baby before she was too old.'

Kate could feel her nipple hardening. She reached for the champagne bottle, putting her breast out of Max's reach. Her body always responded instantly to his touch, but just for once she didn't feel like sex.

Harriet, too old? She could only be about thirty-eight or nine, the same age as Kate, or maybe even a year younger. Since when had that been old? And what did Max mean: there was nothing he could do about it? Was he trying to claim Harriet had got pregnant by herself? Since when did a Scottish Presbyterian turned Marxist agnostic believe in the immaculate conception? If Max hadn't wanted another child there were ways in which he could have stopped it – that was, if he had wished to.

Kate could feel herself getting angry and not just with Max. She was cross with herself for being bothered that Harriet was pregnant. She had walked into the affair with her eyes wide open, knowing he was married and had two children – four, counting the two with Marianne – so why should another one matter? And why should the evidence that Max and Harriet still had sex be a problem? Although Max had implied he and Harriet had sexual problems, he had never actually said that they *didn't* have sex.

Kate prided herself on not being one of those gullible women who believed that a man could sleep in the same bed as a woman and not occasionally roll on top of her, however unattractive he claimed he found his wife. The attractiveness of their partners was not one of the overriding priorities in the male desire for sex and it came a lot lower down the list than availability.

It was at moments like this that Kate wished she hadn't given up smoking. What she really needed was a cigarette to help her think clearly. It was hard to explain to people who had never smoked how soothing it could be. Kate closed her eyes and breathed in the air, willing it to give her the same hit as that first taste of nicotine. It almost worked, but then she felt Max's hand parting her legs and the moist stirring of desire as her body responded to his fingers. Max felt it too and deftly pulled her down onto her back, easing himself between her legs.

He looked up at her with an evil grin. 'It's my turn now,' he announced before burying his head between her thighs.

'No!' Kate's voice was sharper than she intended, but the 'no' was meant as much for her as for Max. She put her hands on his head and forced him to look up. 'No, Max.'

Disappointed but not deterred, Max began to work his way up her body inch by inch, parting her robe and kissing the bare skin thus revealed. 'So what do you want me to do?' he murmured between kisses, 'and you know you can ask me to do anything, absolutely *anything*.' His lips closed around her right nipple and he began to suck hungrily like a baby.

'I want us to talk.'

Max's mouth was stilled.

He rolled over to the other side of the bed and cradled his head in his arms. Kate sat up again and hugged her knees.

'It's the baby, isn't it?' said Max after a moment or two. 'I wouldn't have told you if I'd thought it was going to upset you, but we've always been honest with each other. I mean, we both agreed this relationship was going nowhere, so I can't see where the problem is.'

Kate looked at him. Max was right. He couldn't see where the problem was. The problem was, neither could she. She just knew that there was one. She could feel it. It was like a hard, uncomfortable knot in her chest.

Max gave a short laugh. 'You're not going broody on me, are you, babe?' He held up his hands as he saw the expression on her face. 'Hey. I understand. It's only natural. I mean, you're a woman, aren't you?'

Kate swung her legs off the bed and sat up. 'Since men discovered the fact that women have hormones, they seem to think that everything we do is dictated by them, but some of us have brains too,' she snapped, 'and *stop* calling me babe.'

Max tried ineffectually to put a reassuring hand on her arm. 'You know I respect you ba . . . sweetheart. Hell, I love the fact you're so independent, it's a real turn-on.'

Kate walked to the windows and stood with her arms

10

crossed, looking down into the garden. She was reacting in just the emotional way she hated.

'Perhaps I ought to go. We can talk about this another time.' Max got to his feet.

There was no point in trying to reason with Kate, he could tell that just by looking at her back. It wasn't the way she usually behaved, in fact, he could not remember her acting like this before and it had unwelcome echoes of Harriet. Not that anything could ever be as articulate as Harriet's back when it was turned on him. That was one of the things he liked so much about Kate. If she had a problem she came straight out with it. There were none of the guessing games he had to play with Harriet. Kate was more like a man, really – or was it that she was less like Harriet?

He padded to the bathroom and ran the taps in the basin. Harriet's silences drove him mad and, the madder he got, the more silent she became. How *was* he meant to know what was the matter if she wouldn't tell him? Max began to splash himself vigorously with water. He'd worked out long ago that having a shower or using soap was tantamount to advertising his infidelity. Returning home with wet hair and smelling sweet and fresh after what was ostensibly a long day in the tiny room which he rented in order to write made wives like Harriet instantly suspicious. One whiff of another brand of soap on his body would be enough to betray him.

Not that she seemed to notice anything he did these days. If it wasn't the pregnancy, it was those damn cookery books she wrote. He rued the day that he'd joked about giving his agent a copy of a little booklet of her recipes that she'd run off on his computer for some school fund-raising do. Harriet had taken him seriously and he'd been forced to keep to his word. He had been embarrassed and expected his agent to laugh, but she had called a week later to say that she had a deal with a

11

small publishing house which was just setting up in business. Now Harriet's books sold around the world. But they were only cookery books, for Christ's sake, so why did she have to make such a fuss about them?

No one, least of all Harriet, seemed to understand the kind of creative pressures he was under. Yes, he had written a couple of well-received films, but they had been art house, Channel 4 movies and his last, three years ago, had barely made its investors their money back. None of the scripts he had written since had gone into production. At one time he had been such a hot property in the business that everyone had wanted to lunch him. Bitter experience had taught him that it was true what they said about being only as good as your last film. What made it even more galling was that his biggest successes had happened when Marianne was his producer. Since he had married Harriet, nothing had gone right for him and she never let him forget that it was her books that now made all the money. Not that she said it out loud; a woman like Harriet didn't have to.

That was why he needed Kate. He could talk sensibly to her about the problems he was having with his agent and his script. She spoke the same language and understood about the creative pressures a writer had to face. She also understood his sexual needs. Harriet didn't, or she hadn't, not since they had got married.

Max began to towel himself dry. If only, just once in a while, Harriet would do to him what Kate had just done. Remembering, he closed his eyes and felt a familiar prickle in his groin as he started to grow hard again. He opened his eyes and contemplated himself disconsolately. What was the point? He had seen that look on a woman's back too many times: it meant no sex tonight.

Hearing the water being turned off in the bathroom,

Kate hurriedly pulled on a shapeless grey sweat suit and padded barefoot down the corridor and into the living-room. Today she did not want to enjoy the intimacy of watching Max dress.

The living-room was over thirty feet long and had once been a magnificent drawing-room. It still retained all the proportions of its former glory, but now there was an open-plan kitchen of pale-green Shaker-style wood at one end, with more than enough space in front of it to have a dining-table large enough to seat twelve. But, like all the other furniture, Kate had not got round to buying it yet and made do with a small breakfast bar. She didn't have the time to entertain much anyway.

At the other end of the room there was a large, comfortable cream sofa and beside it a stack of glossy magazines, which acted as a table for an art deco lamp. Its base was a graceful silver girl, standing athletically on tiptoe, her slim arms held high and topped by a creamy gold glass lampshade. It deserved better than a pile of old *Vogues* to stand on, but it would have to wait for the right table, just as the books stacked along the walls would have to wait for shelves, and the television and video, which stood on the floor in front of the sofa, for a stand.

Not that lack of time stopped her spending money. She could have bought the furniture she needed and more for the price of yet another impulse buy – an antique silk Persian carpet of pale apricot and gold, which covered most of the centre of the floor. She had seen it on display in the window of Liberty's when she was stuck in a taxi in a traffic jam in Regent Street one day and it had seemed to pulsate with colour. She had gone back the next day and slapped her credit card down on the counter, refusing to look at the total on the sales slip as she signed it. The extravagance made its sensual feel beneath her bare feet even more delicious.

Kate walked across it now as she made for the kitchen and the whisky bottle. Although it wasn't advisable after champagne, she poured a large measure into a glass, then opened the refrigerator. The icebox resembled a set from a remake of *Scott of the Antarctic*. While global warming might be melting the ice-cap, it had yet to reach her part of Islington. After a struggle, she managed to wrench open the door and pull an ice tray free from its frosted tomb, only to discover that it contained one solitary ice-cube. She plopped it into her drink, threw the tray into the sink, then curled up on the sofa to wait for Max.

He did not take long. He emerged from her bedroom dressed, apart from his jacket. His broad shoulders filled the doorway. Kate felt another surge of desire. Why was she letting him go? She wanted him, right now, right there. They had never parted before without making love at least three or four times. *Damn* Harriet.

'Have you seen my jacket?'

Kate shook her head but made no move to look for it. 'You took it off as you came in. Maybe it's in the hall.'

He strode across the room and out into the hall. There was a loud Glaswegian '*Fuck*!' followed by a banshee howl and an outraged ball of grey fur, most of it standing on end, shot through the sitting-room, up onto the draining-board and out through the open kitchen window. Kate, who had half started out of her seat, found herself confronted by a furious Max, brandishing his jacket.

'That *bloody* cat was sitting on my jacket. I think it does it on purpose. It knows I'm allergic to it.' He sneezed loudly. 'Look at it! It's covered with hairs,' he continued indignantly.

Kate sank back onto the sofa and suppressed her desire to smile. The Marxist revolutionary had abandoned tattered jeans – the clothing of the workers – for the tailoring of Oswald Boateng and Paul Smith.

14

'I try to keep Hemingway out when you're coming over, but on a warm day like this I can hardly keep all the windows shut.' She held out a hand for the offending jacket but didn't make a move to get up. 'Would you like me to brush it for you?'

'It'll have to go to the cleaners now,' said Max bad-temperedly. 'I'll tell Harriet I spilt something on it. Have you got a carrier bag I can put it in, something with a nondescript logo so she won't be suspicious?'

Kate uncurled herself from the couch and went across to the kitchen where she rummaged in a drawer. 'Harriet shops in Marks & Sparks, I presume?' She thrust a green plastic bag at him.

Max did not appear to notice the sarcasm in her voice as he gingerly folded his jacket into the bag. 'Shall I give you a call when I can next get away?' He bent down to kiss her. Kate turned her face slightly so that the kiss landed on her cheek. 'There's a producer in town from LA who wants to talk to me about another of my projects, so I'm not sure when it will be,' he continued as he opened the front door.

Kate went to the window. In the street, Max was getting into his sleek black convertible. Harriet drove the family Volvo estate. He turned and blew her a kiss. Almost involuntarily, Kate blew him one back. He mouthed some words at her. Kate shook her head – she hadn't understood.

Max mouthed them again. He was saying: 'I love you.'

Two
• • •

'Well, I was going to say look what the cat brought in, but *girrl* . . .' Robert rolled his tongue with relish. 'You look like what the cat brought in last week and it was already well past its sell-by date then. Am I right in thinking that Hemingway here isn't the only little pussy who's had his nose put out of joint by some man?' As he spoke, he held up Hemingway who was draped languidly across his arms, purring like a supercharged formula-one racing car.

Kate squinted blearily round the door at Robert. She had buried her head under a cushion in an effort to block out the sound of the doorbell, but he had kept his finger on the button until she had finally stumbled to the intercom and yelled '*What*?'. Her anger had softened when she heard Robert's answering voice, but only slightly. The last thing she wanted was a social call and Robert's sharp eyes missed nothing.

'So what is this? Do I have to get on my knees and beg for the dirt?' demanded Robert, putting Hemingway down and walking past her into the flat. 'It'd better be good and it'd better be fast, as I have a cab waiting outside to take me to Heathrow.'

He stood with his hands on his hips, surveying Kate's flat. Through the door to her bedroom her rumpled bed was clearly visible, the champagne bottle and two glasses on the floor beside it. Kate could feel

Robert's eyes moving on to take in the nearly empty whisky bottle lying on its side beside the sofa where she had slept. She would probably still be asleep there now if it hadn't been for him. She ran a hand through her tangled hair. She had slept in her track suit and must look a mess.

Robert, on the other hand, looked as supremely elegant as always. His tall, slender figure was a confection of cream and white. Cream linen trousers; a white linen shirt; white, butter-soft leather slip-on shoes; and the palest of pale coffee-coloured cashmere sweaters tied casually around his shoulders. The contrast with his dark, golden-brown skin was perfect, just as he had intended it to be.

Robert had come to live in London from Alabama in the early Sixties. He was a fashion writer for a Sunday colour supplement as well as several women's magazines. According to Robert, where he grew up in the South the only long dresses a gay black man got to see close up were those worn by the Ku Klux Klan, so he had decided to get out of there. Thirty years of living in London had made him sound very English, but at times when he wanted to be camp, as now, he sounded like a character from a Tennessee Williams play in overdrive.

'Well? Am I meant to be reading the news in the bottom of your dirty glass?' he demanded archly, picking up the offending article between two long fingers. 'From the dregs in here I would say *that* man has been here again.'

Robert had never met Max, but had decided he was no good for Kate. He referred to him only as *that* man.

'Do you mind if I make some coffee first?' asked Kate. The cotton wool in her head was clearing and was being replaced by a dull but insistent pain in her left temple.

'From the state of you I'm the one who should be making the coffee, *and* I also make much better coffee than the pale imitation dishwater you English always serve up.' Robert waved an imperious hand at her. 'Off with you! Go and perform your morning ablutions.'

'Are you sure you have time?' asked Kate. 'What about your taxi?' It was only as she said it that her brain cleared and she remembered that he was on his way to the airport to catch a plane. She put her hands to her head. 'Oh, God! You're going to stay with Oliver today, aren't you? How long are you going to be away?'

Robert had his nose in a tin marked coffee. He was sniffing suspiciously. He looked up. 'The taxi can wait. I'm paying the man an exorbitant amount already *and* I've promised him a large tip if he refrains from regaling me with his opinions on politics, mad cow disease, Europe or race relations all the way along the M4.' He left the tin on the counter and reached into the cupboard for an unopened packet of coffee beans. He poured some into the grinder. 'I've made up my mind to go for the summer. Oliver and I have decided we're getting a bit too old for long-distance love affairs on the phone. My publisher has also been chasing me to finish my book, so the magazine has agreed to give me a short sabbatical.'

'For the summer?' repeated Kate faintly. She had thought that Robert was only going for a few weeks.

'Until the end of September,' said Robert and then, seeing her stricken expression, he reached across and put a hand on her arm. 'Come with me, dear heart. Surely that place owes you months of holiday. Oliver would adore to see you.'

Kate shook her head. 'I can't. It's the worst possible time to go. The weekly show runs until May and I'm planning some one-hour special documentaries for the summer. We're already behind schedule with them so I simply can't afford to be away.' She felt a sudden panic. Robert couldn't take off, not for six months. She needed him. He wasn't just her best friend, he was the one person she trusted enough to turn to when she was in trouble, like now. 'Do you have to go away for quite so long? I *need* you.'

'So does Oliver, but more than that, *I* need him.'

The look on Robert's face as he spoke made Kate feel wistful. He and Oliver had the perfect relationship. Just being with them could make her believe that there was still such a thing as true love. For a moment she allowed herself the fantasy of throwing a few things into a suitcase, grabbing her credit card and running away with Robert. Who could object? He was right, she hadn't taken a holiday – not a real one – in over two years, so she was owed at least two months' leave, but she couldn't leave London, not right now.

Robert's hand was hovering over the grinder. 'If you don't want to feel a lot worse than you already look, dear heart, I suggest you go into the other room while I do this.'

Kate closed the bathroom door just as the grinder screamed into action. She washed her face with soap and water, then dragged a comb through her hair, cursing at the tangles. As she looked at her face in the mirror she imagined how it would horrify her mother to see her now. It was her mother's proud boast that she had never let soap and water near her face since she was fourteen, and she had attempted to inculcate a similar respect for their complexions in both her daughters, constantly warning them of the dire consequences to their marital prospects if they took no heed of her advice.

But then, her mother was French and, aside from the obvious superiority of French culture, language and cuisine, Cecile blamed everything from the high divorce rate to juvenile delinquency on the English-woman's failure to use the right face-creams. But despite her mother's Cassandra-like predictions, Kate did not think she looked *too* bad for an old woman of thirty-eight, although her eyes were distinctly puffy.

When she went back into the other room, the rich aroma of coffee brewing made her feel a little better. Robert was opening a tin of salmon for Hemingway who was rubbing appreciatively against his legs.

'Why you have to feed this cat best salmon is beyond me. Why can't he eat horse meat like the rest of the poor mutts out there?'

'Because I can't stand the smell of whatever it is they put in those tins, it makes me want to heave,' replied Kate, bending down to take a pot of eye gel from the fridge where she kept it for emergencies like these. 'Anyway, I have no intention of looking like one of those sad women who walk around Sainsbury's with their trolleys piled high with Kitikins or whatever it's called.'

She perched herself on a stool and, scooping a copious amount of cooling gel onto a finger, smeared it across her eyes. According to the sales girl, the gel should be applied with the gentlest of pats using the tip of her little finger so as not to drag the delicate skin around her eyes, but she had neither the patience nor the time. Kate sat for a moment or two with her eyes closed, relishing the coolness of the gel. When she opened them she found that Hemingway had leapt up onto the breakfast counter and was sniffing hopefully at the pot of eye gel. Disappointed that it was not edible, he sat back on his haunches, fixing Kate with a disapproving golden-eyed glare. She swept him off the counter with her elbow. What right had a cat to disapprove of her? He was the one who had not come home last night.

She had a whisky-hazy memory of walking up and down the street until after midnight calling Hemingway's name, although why she had bothered she didn't know. She didn't like cats and certainly had never had any intentions of owning one. But she didn't own Hemingway, did she? *He* seemed to be the one who thought he owned *her*.

He had casually breezed past her legs and taken up residence in the flat soon after she had moved in and, right from the start, seemed to consider both Kate and her home as his personal territory. He was prepared to fight any male interlopers of whatever species to the death, with the exception of Robert.

When Hemingway had first moved in she had tried everything to get rid of him, including throwing him bodily out of the flat, but he just waited on her doorstep to be allowed back in and, when that failed, slipped through any window she left open. A call to the RSPCA elicited the information that they would take him in, but as he was a mature cat and not a cuddly kitten it was unlikely he would be offered a home and, after a decent interval, would probably have to be put down.

The voice on the other end of the phone had been gently accusing, cowing Kate into saying that, in that case, she would keep him. Her last-ditch stand had been to place notices in local shop windows and even on trees where she had seen pitiful posters pleading for the return of lost pets. But when all her attempts to find a distraught owner failed, she had reluctantly decided that she was stuck with him and, once it was clear she had become a cat owner by default, she bowed to the inevitable and decided to give him a name other than 'you'.

Thinking of an appropriate name proved more difficult than she had imagined. The usual feline appellations like Fluffy or Sooty seemed incongruous. Although he must have been a handsome cat once, he was now missing half his right ear and his badly scarred nose was testament to numerous testosterone-fuelled battles. However, he still had a certain charm, in a battered, macho sort of way, and he considered it his duty, if not his right, to impregnate every female cat within a square mile. The name Hemingway had somehow seemed apt.

But now Kate was beginning to wonder whether her grudging fondness for him proved that she had indeed become what her mother had always threatened she would – namely, a spinster.

Lonely, childless women and cats had always gone together in Kate's mind since she had been taken as a child to visit two elderly maiden aunts who had a house full of them. She and her younger sister Claire had screwed up their faces in disgust and giggled, holding their noses at the smell of cats, which started on the front doorstep and sourly pervaded every room. Enraged at their rudeness, their mother had shaken them by the shoulders and told them it was unkind to make fun of those less fortunate than themselves. Having no husband and no children was one of the saddest fates that could befall a woman, she had warned them – or was it threatened? – and if they didn't behave it would happen to them.

Other mothers frightened their children with bogey-men, only a Frenchwoman would scare her daughters with becoming spinsters, thought Kate wryly. Well, her mother had been proved right. She hadn't behaved and here she was, heading fast for forty, unmarried, childless, and condemned to running up and down the street late at night calling hysterically for her cat.

She looked with disgust at Hemingway whose whole body throbbed with a deep-throated purr. For some reason he was not only prepared to tolerate Robert, but he also allowed him to pick him up and scratch him behind the ears, as he was doing now, an intimacy he refused even Kate.

Robert put him down in front of his bowl of salmon. '*And* you won't pick up the right sort of man with cat meat,' he declared, straightening up. 'They say the late-night shopping aisles of certain branches of Safeway are simply *heaving* with hunky men desperate to find someone to sample their crab cakes with salsa.' Robert rolled his eyes expressively. 'Unfortunately, as an old married man I can't sample their wares, but I just don't understand why a single sexy girl like you isn't out there having more fun instead of wasting your time on *that* man.' He poured some rich, dark coffee into two mugs on the breakfast counter. 'Now, come along, dish the dirt so I can run.'

Kate perched on a stool opposite him and drank a scalding mouthful. Then she took a deep breath: 'Harriet is pregnant.'

Robert raised one eyebrow. 'You've always known he had a wandering dick, dear heart, what did you expect? Exclusivity?'

Kate cradled the coffee cup in her hands. 'I know. You're right. I'm being stupid.'

'Not stupid. Blind maybe. Blind to what *that* man is *really* like and blind to your feelings towards him.' He put his cup down and looked serious. 'Sex, wonderful though it may be, does not by itself keep a relationship going for three years. I *know* when you're just after sex, my girl, I've seen that gleam in your eyes. Trust me, this one is different, although what you see in him is *totally* beyond me. Hemingway possesses more morals in one of his paws than *that* one has got in his entire body.'

Kate opened her mouth to protest, but Robert got in first: 'I know, I know, you're just good friends who have sex together.' He snorted derisively as though it was a mantra he had heard a million times before and still didn't believe. 'But if you really *are* just good friends, tell me why you slept with a bottle of whisky last night and why my usually beautiful Kate resembles such shit this morning?' He looked quite stern. 'I know this is the last thing you want to hear from me right now, but I'm going to tell you anyway. For a highly intelligent and honest woman you are displaying a remarkably overdeveloped capacity for both stupidity and self-deception over this man and, when it comes to self-deception, believe me, you are looking at one of the greatest living exponents of the art so you can't fool me.'

He wagged his finger at her, then looked sorrowful. 'But even more important, Kate, don't fool yourself. Is this – is he – what you really want?' He stared hard at her, then his face softened and he reached over and touched her cheek. 'Dear heart, come with me to Majorca. Give yourself time to think and let Oliver and me tend your wounds. It's always going to be a bad time for you to leave the office, but if you don't take care, one day you'll wake up to discover that you have no time at all.'

Kate suddenly found her eyes filling with tears. She fumbled for a tissue. Robert handed her a beautifully laundered linen handkerchief. She blew her nose.

'Maybe you're right about Max. I just don't know any more. I thought I had it all under control.'

Robert came round to the other side of the counter and enveloped her in a hug fragrant with the light, flowery Penhaligon cologne he always wore. 'Nature didn't design hearts to be under control. Believe me, I of all people know that.' He held her for a few moments before drawing back. 'I wish I could stay, as it worries me to leave you this way, but my chariot awaits. I'll call you later this evening. Here are my keys just in case of emergencies.' He laid them on the counter. 'But *do* think seriously about coming to join us. You could get on a flight tomorrow. Just give us a call and we'll be at Palma airport to meet you.'

He gave her another hug and kissed her on both cheeks. Kate followed him to the street door. She felt a keen sense of loss at his departure. But since Oliver, his long-time lover, had retired to Majorca, Robert had begun to spend more and more time in Spain. Although Kate knew she could always telephone him there, it wasn't quite the same.

For nearly fifteen years, Robert had been the one constant in her life. They had met when she was a young newspaper reporter writing an article about drag queens and Robert was performing as his outrageous *alter ego* Greta in the evenings, while trying to establish himself as a serious fashion writer during the day.

They had been prepared to dislike each other. He expected an ambitious journalist wanting to write a flashy exposé. She expected to meet a man who performed an exaggerated parody of women because he hated them.

But Robert had seen beyond her undoubted ambition while Kate had seen beneath the make-up – or the slap as Robert termed it – and they had become what, to Kate at least, seemed like more than just close friends. Robert often joked that it was because, if he had been a woman he would have wanted to be like Kate, but Kate knew it was more than that. She trusted Robert further than she had ever trusted any man, or any woman friend for that matter, and the thought of him not being around to talk to and to share a bottle of wine with when she needed advice or, even more important, to laugh, made her fight hard to keep back the tears.

Hemingway brushed past her legs and she bent down and picked him up, hugging him tightly as she waved Robert goodbye. Outraged at this infringement of their no-sentimentality rule, Hemingway squirmed desperately to be free and leapt out of Kate's arms, before stalking off down the road, his tail twitching angrily.

Kate walked slowly back into her flat and surveyed

the mess. Was Robert right, was she in love with Max? Was that what had reduced her to such a maudlin state that she had consumed half a bottle of whisky on top of most of the bottle of champagne and fallen into what could only be described as a drunken stupor on the sofa? She stripped off and stepped into the shower, turning it on full so that the force of its jets stung her skin.

As far as she was concerned, love was not part of the arrangement she had with Max. He had said he loved her, but she didn't believe him. He was behaving exactly like Hemingway. Metaphorically speaking, he had just been rubbing his head against her legs and purring because he wanted something.

Kate soaped her loofah and began to scrub her body vigorously. Robert was wrong for once: she was not deluding herself about Max. Any woman who was foolish enough to believe that a man meant the same as a woman did when he said the words 'I love you' or 'I'll call you' needed her head examined – particularly if the former was said either before or during sex and the latter when the man was walking out of the door after it.

When Max said he loved her, what he *actually* meant was: 'I know I've upset you although I'm not quite sure how, but if I say I love you I know you won't be mad at me for long; then things will get back to the way they were and we can carry on with our affair.' It was simply a matter of translation from male to female speak.

Feeling refreshed, Kate towelled herself dry. Robert was a romantic. He wished her to be in love. But that was not what she wanted. Being in love took time and energy, neither of which she could afford. Love suggested need and she did not need Max, she *wanted* him, and there was a big difference between need and want. Need suggested dependence, while wanting was

26

a question of choice. She had battled hard to win her independence and would fight even harder to protect it.

Kate glanced at her watch and hurriedly began to search for something to wear. She would barely have time to get to the office before having to head back across the river to Soho for lunch. She threw a charcoal-grey single-breasted Agnes B jacket onto her bed and then began a frenzied search for the matching pair of trousers. All her clothes were either black or grey, the theory being that dark colours always looked good and were easy to match – but not when you had a hangover.

Her search finally located the matching trousers and a slip of a black top, which she had forgotten she had bought and which had lain undiscovered beneath a pile of clothes in its original carrier bag for months, to go underneath. Kate checked her watch again and dialled her office.

Her secretary, Ruby, anticipating trouble, had already rescheduled her first meeting that morning for later in the day. She cheerfully assured Kate that everything was under control and that the rest of the morning's business, including checking the first draft of the week's script for the weekly current affairs series, could be done by e-mail if Kate didn't want to come into the office until after lunch.

Satisfied, Kate put some more coffee on to brew, switched on her computer and emptied the contents of her make-up bag onto the bed. Last night had been just a momentary hiccup, she decided, as she swiftly dabbed some concealer on the dark shadows under her eyes and applied mascara. She had over-reacted to Harriet's pregnancy. There was no need for anything to change. It would be months before the baby arrived and even then, why should she let it affect her and Max?

Three

• • •

'Mystical . . . that's the only way I can explain it, it was the most . . . well, the most *mystical* experience I've ever had. You see . . .' Jessica paused and concentrated on spearing a creamy scallop with her fork, her brow furrowing as she sought the right words. 'It's so difficult to describe. No one who hasn't been through it could possibly understand.' She looked across the table at Kate. 'Don't you feel even the tiniest, *weeniest* urge to try it?'

Kate raised a quizzical eyebrow. 'There are many things in life that I have, on occasion, had the urge to try, like sky-diving or having sex while swinging from a chandelier. However, spending nine months looking like a beached whale and suffering from backache, wind and incontinence, only to be rewarded by hours if not days of excruciating pain is not one of them.'

'Oh, but it's not like that,' protested Jessica. 'Well, I suppose it is . . . but *only* just a bit. The rest is . . . well . . . it's this hormone thing. They sort of take you over so that you forget about everything else.'

'That's *exactly* what I want to avoid,' said Kate vehemently. 'If I ever needed proof that not only is God a man, but that he is the God of the Old Testament – all brimstone and fire and everlasting damnation, not the wimpish, kindly God he is being re-branded into in order to be more in keeping with the caring, sharing

Nineties – I would use pregnancy as my incontrovertible proof. Not only does he make sure that women have to go through agony, he also turns them into quivering masses of hormones for months, even years, either side of the birth, which in turn reduces their brain function to that of a gnat, and an immature one at that.'

Kate suddenly realised she had been speaking both very loudly and very fast. She stopped and gulped her wine. It was Australian Chardonnay and not really to her taste, but as copious cups of black coffee had proved ineffectual at clearing her head, she had decided she might as well try the traditional hair-of-the-dog remedy.

'Whether it was hormonal or not, I remember sobbing myself to sleep on my thirtieth birthday because I thought that was it, I was past it,' said Jessica defiantly. 'I never saw men after that, all I saw were gigantic walking sperm. Every time I met a new man, the only thing I could think about was what our children would look like and that was before he had even asked me out.'

'Well, I suppose seeing men as gigantic sperm is one stage better than seeing them as big pricks,' said Kate drily.

'You are wicked, Kate. Sometimes I wish I could be a bit more like you.' Jessica giggled, but then, putting down her fork, she suddenly looked unaccustomedly solemn.

The transformation made the warning bells that had been dully clanking through the fog of Kate's hangover ring true and clear. Jessica looked like a woman with a mission and Kate had a sinking feeling that the mission might once again be her.

As long as Kate had known her – which was since they had shared a house as students – Jessica had believed it was her vocation in life to make everyone happy and to her, happiness for a woman meant marriage and motherhood. She considered Kate's obstinate insistence on remaining single as a personal affront and, despite Kate's objections, went through periods of trawling her copious address book for what she deemed 'suitable' men.

It did not seem to matter to Jessica how much Kate insisted she was happy and that she did not need a man or a child to make her feel fulfilled, or that, in her experience, the last thing men and babies made women feel was fulfilled. Jessica continued to insist that, as Kate's best friend, it was her duty to find her a man.

Kate put down her glass. She was aware that Jessica meant well. Jessica always meant well – it was one of her endearing qualities. But she knew what was coming next and she did not want to hear it, especially today.

Jessica put her elbows on the table and clasped her hands together. 'But seriously, Kate, don't you *want* to have children before you're too . . . well, you know . . .'

Kate raised an eyebrow. It usually acted as a warning signal, but today Jessica did not flinch. 'Old?' she demanded.

'Well, not old *exactly*.' Jessica's face screwed up with her attempt to explain. 'But you know what I mean.'

'I don't think being thirty-nine next birthday means that I have to go out and buy a Zimmer frame, do you?'

Jessica pouted prettily. 'I didn't mean it quite like that. Anyway, it's all right for you. I'm an actress and actresses can't be, you know . . . nearly forty.' She lowered her voice when she said forty as though it was an obscene word. 'Actresses have to be either young and twenty-something, or simply ancient so they can play character cameos. Women aren't allowed to be . . . well, *our* age. So I've decided I'm going to be twenty-nine, at least for the next five years.' She screwed up her face with disgust as she delicately beheaded a prawn and then concealed the offending head under a piece of lettuce before popping the pink body into her mouth. She munched contentedly for a moment or two. 'But how can you be so sure you don't want babies, Kate? Perhaps you haven't met the right man yet. It would be simply awful to wake up in a few years' time and regret not having children. Having Thomas was such a . . .'

'Mystical experience?' snapped Kate.

Jessica gave her a hurt look. 'It's not just me who says it, you know,' she said defensively. 'I mean, just *everyone* has babies these days, nobody is single any more. Parenting is such a Nineties thing.'

Kate fought to keep her irritation under control. It wasn't Jessica's fault that the last subject she wanted to discuss today of all days was babies, but it was at times like this that she wondered why she and Jessica were friends. They had not had much in common when they were students and they had even less now.

When they had first met, Kate had dismissed Jessica as frivolous, while Jessica later admitted that she had been terrified of Kate. This impression was strengthened when Kate had resolutely refused to be drawn into the endless round of parties, love affairs and consequent emotional traumas indulged in by Jessica and the other occupants of the house, preferring to work hard for her degree. But all that had changed when Kate found Jessica weeping in the bathroom late one night.

Jessica was pregnant and the father was a married lecturer. He had no intention of divorcing his wife and marrying Jessica, and she could not face having a baby on her own. Several long nights' talking into the early hours later, Kate had accompanied Jessica first to a doctor and then to an abortion clinic.

No one apart from Kate knew about it, not even Jessica's husband Hugo. During the nearly two years it had taken her to conceive their son, Thomas, Jessica had been haunted by the fear that she would be punished for the abortion by not being able to have another baby. Kate had been the only person Jessica could and did turn to – in long, anguished phone calls often in the early hours of the morning, while Hugo slept. Perhaps it was this shared secret that had given their friendship a depth that had outweighed the disparity of their lives and personalities.

But while she knew Jessica's secrets, Kate had not told her about Max as Jessica found it hard to keep other people's confidences. She was not a malicious gossip – Jessica would be appalled if she thought she might hurt anyone – but her indiscretions were legendary and, added to that, she knew Max and Harriet.

Jessica had performed in several of Max's plays or street 'happenings' as he called them, when they were students, but she had not enjoyed it as her talents were more suited to Oscar Wilde or Noël Coward. She had also been tested, although rejected, for a part in his second film.

Jessica still cherished ambitions to act, and had an agent and her picture in *Spotlight*. Unfortunately, calls from casting directors were now few and far between. To her chagrin, she had what they perceived as a period look – a pre-Raphaelite cloud of orange-gold hair, pale, almost translucent skin, which seemed to reveal every milky blue-green vein, and wide-set hazel-green eyes. During her twenties her looks as much as her acting talent had helped her to achieve modest success in supporting parts in Sunday evening BBC classic drama serials. She had also played small but significant parts in two Merchant Ivory films, which had earned her calls from a couple of Hollywood casting agents, although nothing had come of them. But the gritty contemporary roles, which would have won her the recognition she craved, had always eluded her. The nearest she had got to contemporary fame was to play Erica, the girl next door who never had anything to flavour her casseroles, in a long-running series of commercials. Even though the campaign had finished four years ago, people still occasionally recognised her as the bouillon cube girl, which was at least fame of a kind. It was how she had met her husband, Hugo, who had directed one of the commercials.

Hugo was a successful director who harboured ambitions to make Hollywood films. Kate had disliked him from the moment she met him and could not understand why Jessica stayed with him. It was often on the tip of her tongue to say so, particularly during one of Jessica's lengthy phone calls, which were invariably about Hugo's latest wrongdoing. The calls always began: 'You know how much I love Hugo but . . .'

He seemed to have reduced Jessica's already fragile self-esteem to nothing. The fact that he was three years younger than her did not help. To Jessica, those three years were a lifetime. She lived in constant fear of him leaving her for someone younger. She had always been thin, but these days she looked as though the slightest whisper of wind could blow her away, yet she had confided to Kate that last week she had lived on low-fat diet yoghurts for three days because Hugo had made some comment about hating fat thighs.

But it was during Thomas's birth that Kate's dislike of Hugo had turned into barely concealed loathing. It was she, not Hugo, who had been at Jessica's side during most of the so-called mystical experience, although mystical was the last thing Kate remembered it being. When Jessica had been screaming for Hugo in the delivery room, he had been directing a commercial for disposable nappies featuring a hundred dancing babies doing a Busby Berkeley-style number. It had won him several awards but, as far as Kate was concerned, he deserved none for being a father.

It had been a protracted and difficult labour and it was Kate's hand Jessica had clung to tightly through the long night until Kate was asked to leave the room and the doctor suggested a Caesarean to avoid further complications. But Jessica had read every natural birthing book ever published and was determined to give birth without medical intervention. Eventually, exhausted and nearly hysterical, she had been forced to agree but without Hugo there at her side. He had phoned in his congratulations on his mobile phone.

The Caesarean had left Jessica with a sense of failure. In her eyes she had not really given birth and she wanted another child. Kate suspected that this was at least partly to prove she could have a baby naturally and partly because she still felt guilt over her abortion. However, Hugo was adamant that he did not want more babies. Jessica had produced a son and heir, and that was enough.

Kate chased a crouton around the edge of her plate with her fork. She had ordered a Caesar salad but had not really wanted it when it arrived. The waiter had made such a performance of mixing and tossing it in a large bowl beside their table that it had irritated her. Either it was freshly dressed or it wasn't. It wasn't necessary for her to have to sit and watch. Anyway, it looked far too green and healthy. She reached for her wineglass.

The restaurant had been Jessica's choice. It was new and owned by television's latest star chef. It had therefore been hard to get a table although it was unlikely he was cooking in the vast kitchen Kate could see on the floor below, fashionably open so that the clientele could see where their food was being pre-pared. He was probably too busy making his next series. Kate thoroughly disliked the current vogue for large, canteen-like restaurants that was sweeping London. They reminded her of nothing so much as a school refectory, and she attributed the fashion to men reaching a certain age and developing a sudden misty-eyed nostalgia for their boarding-school days. The menu seemed to cater for Lower School tuck-shop tastes too, including bubble and squeak and bread-and-butter pudding among the Mediterranean roast vegetable salad with couscous and harissa, and purple figs with Mascarpone drizzled with warm Acacia honey.

Kate poured some more wine into her glass and topped up Jessica's, although she had barely touched her first. Studying her face, Kate noticed blue shadows under her eyes and a tightness around her mouth. Her blond eyelashes had not been dyed recently, which made her face look washed-out. She was still very pretty, but it was as though some inner light had gone out.

Kate felt penitent. 'I'm sorry, Jessica, I shouldn't have snapped at you. I'm afraid I had too much to drink last night and I'm a bit hung-over, but you look tired, too. Is there something the matter?'

It was the wrong thing to say. Jessica's hand went to her cheek in alarm. 'I look truly awful, don't I? I try hard, I really do, but sometimes Thomas is such a handful. Hugo says that I must learn to control him, but it's so difficult. You'd think because they're so small they would be frightened of anyone bigger than them, but Thomas won't do anything I tell him, but he will do anything Maria asks.' She looked tremulous and her eyes brimmed with tears. 'Sometimes I think he loves her more than me.'

Maria was Thomas's nanny. She was Filipino, small and slim and doe-eyed. Kate had a feeling that Thomas wasn't the only male in the household who was enamoured with Maria, but she had kept her suspicions to herself.

'Actually, I was thinking how pretty you looked today,' Kate lied. 'Is that a new dress? The colours look wonderful on you.'

For a moment Jessica looked happy as she fingered the gossamer-light green and gold material of the dress she wore, which made her look as though she should be wandering through Sherwood Forest. The high-busted and virtually transparent style would have suited few women, including Kate, but it looked perfect on Jessica's slender figure.

'I'm glad you like it. *I* thought it was beautiful, but Hugo says it makes me look like a suburban house-wife.'

'Well, he's wrong,' said Kate sharply. 'I think you look lovely and so did a lot of men when we walked in here.'

Jessica brightened up. 'Did they? Which ones?' She looked eagerly around.

It was not a lie. Quite a few heads had turned when they walked in the door and, despite her hangover, Kate had noticed that they had both been receiving appreciative glances from other tables.

Having satisfied herself with winning a few admiring looks, Jessica turned back to Kate. 'I *do* wish you'd let me fix you up with a man. I've got several very definite possibilities. They're all attractive, available and, most important of all, solvent.' She produced her filofax and started to leaf through it. A folded-up piece of newspaper fell out. Jessica smoothed it out. It was a page from that morning's *Daily Mail*. She pushed it across the table. 'I thought you might be interested in this. Max and Harriet are doing awfully well. They've got a weekend house in Cambridge now as well as their home in London. Of course, these days Harriet is the more successful one. Her cookery books sell by the thousands and her last one on vegetarian cooking for children was on the best-seller list for simply *ages*, although when I tried some of the recipes on Thomas he spat them out.'

Kate looked reluctantly down at the cutting. There was a photograph of Max with his arm around Harriet, smiling confidently into the camera lens. The headline read THE PERFECT COUPLE.

'Don't they look happy?' continued Jessica wistfully. 'I'm so envious of Harriet. She's really got it all *and* she's pregnant again.'

Kate forced herself to read the first few sentences of the article:

Harriet and Max Gordon are that unusual phenomenon in the divorce-ridden media world – a happy and successful couple. Harriet combines being the mother of Emma, 9, and Fleur, 7, with writing hugely successful vegetarian cookery books, while Max writes films that manage that rare combination of being popular with audiences and critics alike. His first film, *Gorbals for Tea*, was described variously as searing social comment and a two-Kleenex-box story of adolescent love.

Kate looked up.

'I'm not meant to say anything,' said Jessica confidentially, 'but Harriet is absolutely desperate for a boy this time. I don't think she would have got pregnant again if it hadn't been for Max wanting a son. She had such problems last time and this time it's taken nearly three years. Both she and Max had to have fertility tests and then she had to go backwards and forwards to the clinic for months before anything happened. She said it made her feel absolutely awful and nearly ruined their sex life, but she kept going for Max's sake.' Jessica looked around and then lowered her voice. 'Harriet says there have been a couple of times when she thought Max was going to leave her. He's had loads of affairs. But she says that a boy will make all the difference. Marianne, his first wife, only had girls and Max left her. It's special for a man isn't it – a son?'

Kate heard Jessica's question, but it was as though it came from a thousand miles away. She felt as if all the air had been sucked from her body.

'Kate? Are you all right?'

She willed herself to find a voice. 'I'm feeling a bit sick.' It was a voice of sorts, even if it didn't sound much like hers. 'Probably the whisky I drank last night. I'll be fine. I'll just go to the loo.'

She pushed back her chair and got to her feet. They felt heavy but they seemed willing to carry her. She could hear Jessica's voice floating behind her, asking whether she wanted her to come with her, but she carried on. A waiter danced round her, three plates in each hand, held perilously aloft. Someone at a table she passed seem to know her. She answered the unheard question with what she hoped resembled a smile. It seemed to take for ever to get across the room, swimming against a tide of voices. It was with a sense of reaching a semblance of safety that she pushed open the door to the ladies' cloakroom and found herself in its cool chrome and grey interior.

Kate clutched a hand basin and tried to steady herself. She wanted to kneel on the tiled floor, put her head down a toilet pan and vomit up everything that was inside her until there was nothing left. Instead, she ran the cold water tap until it was freezing, then leant down and splashed her face. She stood up and pulled some paper towels from the dispenser to dry herself. There were some dark damp patches on her jacket where she had been careless. She dabbed ineffectually at them and permitted herself to look in the mirror. Jessica was right, her normally healthy skin looked white. It did not help that most of her lipstick had worn off. She scrubbed away the rest with a trembling hand and applied some more. Now she knew why Max had told her about the baby. He had been worried she would see that article. What was it he had said about having nothing to do with Harriet getting pregnant? Kate waited a few moments more, steeling herself to face the room outside. She took a deep breath and opened the door.

From the other side of the restaurant Jessica watched Kate thread her way back through the tables. There was something wrong with Kate and it wasn't just a hangover – she knew her too well for that – but she also knew better than to push her for information. Kate would say nothing or, even worse, withdraw and become cold and closed off. Kate thought her a bit of an air-head, which she knew she could be, but she could also be a good listener, if only Kate would trust her. She didn't seem to have the need to talk about her emotions in the same way as other women did, although how she managed it Jessica did not understand. She herself would simply die if she didn't have her girl-friends to talk to. On the other hand, Jessica rather admired her for it. Kate always seemed so strong and so in control, at least until a few minutes ago.

As Kate neared the table, Jessica lowered her head and pretended to study the bill. She looked up as Kate sat down. 'Are you feeling better? I was worried about you. You were in there for simply ages,' she asked anxiously.

'I'm okay. Really I am. What's the damage?'

Jessica pushed the bill across the table. 'I'm hopeless at maths. Can you do it?'

Kate made the necessary calculation, noting that they had already included a fifteen per cent service charge. She hated it when restaurants did that. She liked to leave a tip according to the service she received. She made a mental note not to return.

'Well, what did you think of the place?' asked Jessica

as they stood outside on the pavement in the Soho sun. 'Hugo brings all his clients here. He thinks it's a real find.'

'I like my restaurants a little more intimate,' said Kate shortly, looking for a taxi. She couldn't face the Underground. It depressed her enough at the best of times. Right now, it would make her suicidal.

Taxis were backed up down the street, but none had their signs lit. It was mid-afternoon, restaurant coming-out time in Soho. They began to walk slowly towards Old Compton Street. Jessica stopped to gaze into the window of a patisserie shop, full of impossibly rich creamy confections.

'I was thinking of getting a personal trainer. Everyone has one these days. What do you think?'

To Kate's knowledge, Jessica was already a member of at least two health clubs. She shrugged. 'If it makes you happy . . .'

Jessica pouted. 'I know you think I'm obsessed by my looks, but an actress has to be, they're her investment.'

Kate kissed her lightly on the cheek. 'I know. Don't pay any attention to anything I say today, I'm just an old grouch. Do you mind if I grab the first taxi?' She had seen one heading towards them and was already holding up her arm.

Jessica returned her kiss warmly. 'You go ahead. I like to wander around theatre land occasionally and imagine my name up there in lights one day.'

'And it will be,' promised Kate as she opened the door. She waved as the taxi drew away and Jessica blew her an exaggerated kiss, looking every inch like the grand actress she wanted to be.

Four

• • •

A chill blast of air whipped Kate's jacket away from her body as she ran from the taxi across the wide open concourse to the tall building where Channel 22 had its offices. She had allowed the bright sunshine and prematurely blue sky to lure her into leaving home without a coat that morning, but while she and Jessica had been in the restaurant it had clouded over and now it was raining, and felt distinctly raw and March-like again. For once she was grateful for the overheated blast of air which greeted her as she pushed her way through the swing doors into the foyer, and she stood for a few moments, catching her breath and warming up.

The receptionist, a bouffant blonde with a perma-tan, beckoned her over. 'Miss Daniels, Mr Carson's office has been trying to reach you. He's left a message asking you to go and see him when you come in. Shall I let him know that you are on your way?'

Kate felt her heart miss a beat. Almost automatically, she reached for her mobile phone and then realised that she had turned it off when she sat down for lunch with Jessica, and had been so wrapped up in her thoughts since that she hadn't checked it for messages. She silently cursed herself. Leo Carson was the Channel's Controller of Programmes and when he called, everyone jumped. Ruby must have been frantic, trying to reach her.

'Miss Daniels?' the receptionist enquired again.

'Let him know I'll be right up.'

As the lift doors closed behind her, Kate tried to check her reflection in the steel walls but all she could see was a blurred outline, which was probably just as well for the rain would have turned her hair into a frizzy mess and she had no time to do anything about it now. As the lift sped up to the twenty-second floor her stomach gave an uncomfortable lurch. Kate grabbed the rail to steady herself. She had to get control of herself, put Max out of her mind and concentrate on what was important – her career.

She had a pretty good idea why Leo wanted to see her. The post of the head of the Factual Programmes department had recently become open and it was the obvious move for her. In the ten years since she had joined the Channel as a reporter from a regional newspaper group, she had worked her way up to Executive Producer in the Documentary and Features department, where her main responsibility was the Channel's prestigious weekly current affairs programme. Since she had been running it, it had won the Channel a clutch of awards, as well as newspaper front pages and even the occasional question in Parliament.

The head of department post would mean a significant increase in her salary and a company car, as well as her elevation into the ranks of management. Leo had taken her out to lunch to discuss it and she had got the impression that she would be his favoured candidate for the post. Kate had asked for time to think about it, as she enjoyed making programmes and the step up would take her away from her day-to-day editorial role, but although she did not want to be tied to a desk, she knew it was a move that she had to make. If there were any doubts in her mind, they had largely been scotched by the number of industry acquaintances who had called her assuming the job was already hers. Everyone knew that Leo was her mentor and that what he said went at the Channel.

Even though the post had not been officially advertised, she had begun to prepare her pitch for it. Like other terrestrial broadcasters, Channel 22 had been gradually but significantly losing its audience to various forms of broadcasting such as satellite and cable and, with the prospect of many more channels soon coming on air, the audience would splinter even further. The Channel needed a new direction; it could no longer continue to try to win audiences across the board. She wanted it to concentrate more on those areas of programming which it did well – news, current affairs, documentaries and high-quality drama. The audiences would be smaller, but they would be drawn from the middle- and high-income groups, and particularly from the decision-making classes. Advertisers would love a profile like that. There were already signs that they were moving away from their obsession with youth and beginning to concentrate on the post-fifty generation who were by far the largest group in the population. Narrowcasting rather than broadcasting was the way of the future, even traditionalists like the BBC were finding it hard to keep the broad audience share they had once enjoyed.

Kate had not quite honed all her arguments yet, but she had decided she would push the idea that this was not about broadcasting for old age pensioners but a focused product for the new age. She thought it a pretty good slogan and said it to herself several times so that she was sure of it.

As the lift reached the top floor, she ran her hands through her hair, wishing too late that she had tied it back. She pushed it behind her ears but it immediately sprang forward again so she abandoned it. There was nothing worse than a woman playing with her hair. At best it looked as though she was trying to catch masculine attention, at worst that she was insecure. But that was exactly how she felt today – insecure and indecisive – and she hated herself for it.

The lift doors slid open, revealing the glass-sided eyrie of the twenty-second floor with its panoramic views over London. This was where the Channel's senior management exercised their power. When Kate had first arrived it had seemed like Mount Olympus – wreathed in myths and the seat of the gods – but now it was familiar territory. Squaring her shoulders and forcing herself to smile confidently, she stepped out of the lift.

The reception area was divided into two, the larger part of which was occupied by the Controller of Programmes' personal assistant. In the smaller section, just far enough away for private conversation but near enough to be observed at all times, were her two secretaries, both of whom were tapping away industriously on computers. Neither of them looked up as Kate came in, but the Controller's PA uncrossed her long, elegant legs and came out from behind her leather-topped desk to shake her hand.

Dorothy Mackay held sway over the Controller's diary, which gave her a power even greater than that of any department head. Fall foul of her and access to the Controller could suddenly become very difficult, if not impossible. Dorothy had survived three of them and her loyalty to whoever occupied the seat of power was absolute. No computer could compare with the megabytes of information about people who worked in the industry filed away in her memory banks. It was rumoured that she could write a curriculum vitae for every major personality working in television, but not the kind of CVs they might write for themselves. Dorothy's version would reveal not only where they had worked, but whom they had worked with, how they had got on with them, whom they had argued with and, most important, whom they had been married to, lived with, slept with and even whom they had kissed drunkenly with intent one night after a Christmas party twenty years ago.

Information like that was worth a lot of money and, from the clothes Dorothy wore, Kate assumed she was paid what she was worth. Dorothy was very tall and thin, with ash-blonde hair cut in a sleek bob, which seemed moulded into place. It was hard to guess her age. She could have been anything from her early forties to her mid-fifties. Nobody knew for sure because, while Dorothy seemed to know everything about everybody, nobody knew much about her life outside the office. Whatever her age, she always wore the skirts of her designer suits cut briefly enough to display her slim legs, but not short enough to provoke.

'Hello, Kate. You're a hard person to find.' The rebuke was clear. 'Luckily Leo was able to make another window in his diary to see you. Would you like tea or coffee, or perhaps some Evian while you wait?'

Kate resented being told off by someone who, after all, was only a glorified secretary but she knew better than to show it. She shook her head. 'No, thanks. I'm fine, Dorothy, and I'm sorry about earlier. I was unavoidably delayed.'

Why was she apologising to Dorothy? Irritated, Kate plumped herself down on one of the large squashy leather armchairs in the waiting area. It gave out a loud sigh and she smiled weakly at Dorothy, but Dorothy's expression gave new meaning to the word inscrutable.

Just at that moment there was a discreet buzz. Dorothy looked up. 'You can go in now.'

Kate stood up, straightened her jacket, pushed open the heavily padded door opposite Dorothy's desk and stepped into the Controller's office. It was a vast, lushly carpeted area bounded on two sides by glass walls, which opened out onto a terrace looking eastwards down the Thames to St Paul's Cathedral and the City skyline. To reach the Controller's desk, visitors were forced to walk across what seemed like acres of floor to where he was seated, his back to the light so that it was difficult to make out his face. It was old-hat psychology and it worked every time, but today the Controller was walking across the floor to meet her.

He held out his hand. 'Kate. Welcome.'

His grasp was warm and bearlike. It always made her feel that Leo really was pleased to see her, unlike the empty air-kissing employed by most media people. He indicated an armchair and sat down opposite her. Kate smiled expectantly at him. Leo had a reputation for being a tough boss, but she had always found him fair as well as supportive.

'I'm sorry no one could locate me earlier, Leo,' she began. 'I'm afraid I got delayed while meeting a contact and I was in a bad reception area for my mobile phone.'

Even as she spoke Kate regretted it. There was no need for her to lie. But Leo's approval was important to her.

Leo nodded. 'Your secretary said.'

Kate made a mental note to buy Ruby an extra-large box of the continental truffles she adored.

Leo stretched his long legs out in front of him, and thrust his hands into the pockets of his baggy corduroy trousers. He still wore the casual uniform of his early days when he had worked at the BBC. He had refused to adopt the new uniform of designer suits worn by most TV executives these days. It was another of the things that Kate admired about him. She looked at him expectantly, but he seemed to be contemplating the tips of his shoes.

'I've been thinking about what you said over lunch about the job, Leo,' Kate began, 'and I've decided . . .'

'Before you say anything, Kate, I have something to tell you.'

The interruption was rough, abrupt; totally unlike Leo. Kate stared at him but he was not looking at her.

'I think it only fair to you to let you know that we have been forced to move quickly in the matter of Factual Programmes head. The board met yesterday and I wanted you to know their decision in advance of the official announcement this afternoon.'

'But I thought . . .' Kate protested and then stopped. However friendly, men – especially Controllers – did not like being interrupted. It had been one of the many lessons she had learnt in a male-dominated industry.

Leo cleared his throat. 'As you are aware the Channel hasn't been winning its percentage share of the ratings recently, so when we considered the candidates for the job the board's over-riding criterion was someone who could perhaps inject a more populist and sponsor-friendly feel into our schedule, particularly our early-evening one.' Leo cleared his throat again. 'As from next week, your new head of department will be Caz Jordan.'

Kate stared at him, not believing what she had just heard. '*Jordan*! But you can't! He's a jumped-up little media studies student who's never made a programme in his life.' It was not the way she would have described Jordan to the man who had just appointed him in a more rational moment, but Kate was not feeling rational.

Jordan had begun his rise in the television industry on the back of a much publicised thesis on the iconic status of *The Golden Shot* game show. The publicity had catapulted him from student to media pundit and since then, everything he had done had won him notice. He had a knack for self-promotion, like the time he had been asked to address a major television conference on his favourite subject – game shows – and had walked onto the stage with a bikini-clad blonde on either arm. When accused of exploitation and sexism, he had argued that the half-naked girls were an ironic post-modern statement and that feminists had no sense of humour. The tabloid newspapers loved him and had dubbed him the wunderkind of television. He was still only thirty-four.

Kate had thought Leo disliked Jordan as much as she did. In his day, Leo had been a legendary documentary maker. A man known for balancing his journalistic zeal with a fierce humanity, which manifested itself in real sympathy for the subjects of his films. Some people considered him old-fashioned, but Leo was the main reason Kate had wanted to work for the Channel and why she had remained there for so long. But perhaps she had been wrong. Maybe making television pro-grammes which could provoke people into thinking more deeply about the world around them, and possi-bly even change the way things were, did not mean much to him any more, or not as much as it still did to her. She had heard the rumours that Leo was under a lot of pressure from the Channel's shareholders about the falling ratings, but she had not thought it was serious enough for him to forgo his principles in favour of a greater market share. For the second time that day she felt betrayed.

'Kate . . .'

She looked across at Leo. She hadn't noticed before, but he was beginning to look old. His hair, although carefully brushed, was thinning on top and now completely grey. Even in winter he always had the ruddy complexion of a man who had lived much of his life outdoors, but Kate could now see clearly, as though for the first time, that his skin was deeply lined. Even the very blue eyes, which were now looking hard at her, were beginning to show the milky edge of age.

'I'm sorry. I know this must be disappointing for you, Kate, but the shareholders – and they are the ones that matter in this business now – wanted someone who has a public profile and whatever else you can say about Jordan, he has that.' He gave her a wintry smile. 'We have a fight on our hands to keep our audience and with them our advertising revenue. Being a fine programme maker doesn't matter any more. It's all about image and who are we to argue with that? We are responsible for creating our own monster and, like Frankenstein's, it's now uncontrollably loose on the streets and woe betide anyone who gets in its way.'

'Does that include you?'

Leo shrugged. 'I was thinking of retiring anyway. This is a young person's business. It has no need of old men like me any longer.'

'That's not true, Leo, and you know it,' said Kate fiercely.

'I wish I could believe you, but time and tide . . .'

Leo looked so beaten that Kate felt like putting her arms around him to comfort him, but she stayed where she was. He was not the only one whom Jordan's appointment affected. What about *her*?

As though hearing her thoughts, Leo made an effort to pull himself together. 'Your position is safe, Kate. I have Jordan's word on that, although I fear other people will not be so lucky. The Channel is heading for a big-shake-up. But I said I could not countenance the appointment of a non-programme maker unless he was balanced by experienced ones like yourself in senior positions.'

It was Kate's turn to look away from Leo. 'I'm not sure I would want to stay in the circumstances, Leo. Perhaps it's time for me to consider moving on. I have some wonderful people working for me and I could not sit still and see them fired.'

'Please, Kate, I know it's a hard thing for me to ask, but I want you to stay and work with Jordan. That way I will know at least *some* of the things I have fought for will continue. If there aren't at least a few people like you around, who care about the passion and integrity of programme making, what will happen to the Channel?'

Kate looked over Leo's shoulder at the sullen grey expanse of sky beyond the terrace for a moment or two. It was so unfair. She felt as though her life was spinning helplessly out of control. 'Of course I'll stay, Leo,' she said wearily.

Five

• • •

'Shit!' Kate announced loudly. 'Shit. Shit. Shit. Shit. *Shit*!' she repeated, banging her hands down hard on the steering wheel in time to her expletives. She was not going anywhere in her car today.

Her anger exhausted, she sat staring hopelessly out of the windscreen, oblivious to the fact that even if the engine had started, it would have been dangerous to drive with the Jackson Pollock-like splattering of multicoloured bird droppings which covered the glass, courtesy of the pigeons who infested the plane trees that lined her road.

Kate had congratulated herself on getting a bargain when she bought her car, a bright-red convertible MG midget. But it had not taken long to discover why its former owner, having waxed long and lyrical about its virtues, had accepted her first offer with such speed. It had spent more time off the road than on it since she had bought it and had cost her a fortune in repairs. The danger signals that yet again something else was wrong had been evident for weeks. On the rare occasions she had driven it, it had stalled at traffic lights and road junctions. But Kate had ignored the signs, nursing it along, hoping whatever it was would go away so that she would not have to face the condescending smile on the face of the garage mechanic as she tried to explain what was wrong. What made it worse was that what he was thinking was right – she didn't know the first thing about what went on under the bonnet of her car. She just wanted to put the key in the ignition and drive fast to wherever she was going, preferably with the hood down. Was that too much to ask?

Defeated, Kate took the car keys out of the ignition and dropped them into her bag. She thumped the car door with her fist to open it – the lock was yet another thing that needed fixing. Clambering out, she gathered up the assortment of carrier bags she had dropped onto the passenger seat and reached into the back for her weekend case. Bags in both hands, she kicked the door shut. She would have to take a train to her parents' house for the weekend.

Half-way down the road she remembered that she hadn't locked the car and turned back, but after a few paces she moved resolutely in the direction of the Underground. What was the point of locking it? No one could steal it as it wouldn't move and if anyone could get it going they were welcome to it, she thought grimly.

The failure of her car to start was the fitting finale to a wretched week at work. The official announcement of Caz Jordan's appointment at the beginning of the week had made the office grape-vine sing. All semblance of programme making seemed to have stopped as groups of low-voiced people huddled in corridors or congregated in toilets. Kate had tried to swallow her own disappointment and concentrate on producing that week's edition of the current affairs programme. But her telephone lines had blinked continually, with people wanting to know about Jordan and to commiserate with her, even though she had never officially announced she wanted the job.

The universal consensus appeared to be that Jordan was a bad appointment and that everyone would have preferred her to have been given the post. But Kate had been too long in the business to let the talk go to her head. If she had been appointed, many of the same people now telling her how much they wished she could have got it would be sitting in somebody else's office complaining that she didn't have the experience to do it and, as now, forecasting disaster for the Channel. It was the way the television industry worked.

Everyone was dying to know about what changes Jordan was likely to make, particularly in staffing, and wanted Kate's reassurance that their jobs were not at risk. She had tried to be confident although it was hard when she no longer felt that way herself. How could she be? She had been sure that she had known Leo and look how wrong she had been proved.

She had called Robert, needing his advice, but he had sounded so blissfully happy to be back with Oliver that she had not had the heart to tell him quite how wretched she felt and had instead made light of Jordan, joking about him. It also had not helped that Robert had been quite so pleased that she had not seen Max again. She knew he was probably right but that did not stop her wanting him desperately.

So her sister Claire's messages on her answer phone, virtually threatening her with excommunication from the family if she didn't come home that weekend, had not been welcome. Kate hated family gatherings and usually tried to avoid them, claiming pressure of work as an excuse, but for once Claire need not have worried. It was their father's seventieth birthday on Saturday and Kate would not have missed it for anything. However, she had not told Claire that and had not replied to her messages until the last minute to let her know she was coming.

Kate knew her behaviour towards her sister was childish, but it irritated her that, although Claire was younger than her, she seemed to think that marriage and children had elevated her to the status of elder sister, which gave her the right to lecture Kate on what she considered her irresponsible behaviour. Top of the list of Kate's sins was her neglect of her parents, closely followed by her failure to marry and produce more grandchildren for them and cousins for Claire's three boys.

But while Kate knew it was probably true that she didn't visit her parents as often as they would have liked, Claire refused to take into account the demands of her job, probably because she had never had one. She had gone straight from school to being a housewife and mother. How she could stand it, Kate did not know. The monotony of knowing, like her sister, where she would be weeks and even months ahead, filled her with horror. Perhaps it was because Claire had so little to think about that she was determined to turn their father's birthday into an occasion that was a cross between a royal wedding and the millennium night celebrations. It was not even as though their father would enjoy all the fuss. Kate doubted whether he had even been consulted about the plans. No doubt Claire had just ploughed ahead, regardless of anyone else's feelings, sure that she knew what was right for everyone. Sometimes it seemed to Kate that her sister was so obsessed with her children that she appeared to have forgotten how to deal with adults and treated everyone as though they had the mental age of a ten-year-old.

When she had eventually called Claire, Kate had made it very clear that she was coming home for her father and not to fit in with Claire's social plans. Luckily, the programme that week, a specially extended interview with the Foreign Secretary about the situation in Yugoslavia which Kate had been pursuing for months, had, at his request, been recorded on Thursday evening and she had been able to get away. Normally, the programme was a series of up-to-the-minute reports, some of which weren't edited until Saturday morning and some of which could even be sent down the satellite line live on the Saturday evening, so she had to be in the studios to check for any last-minute editorial problems.

On this occasion, although they were waiting until Saturday midday to record the opening commentary, in case there were any sudden changes in the situation in Yugoslavia, Kate had already approved the draft script and had left her deputy, Tim, in charge. He had promised to call her on her mobile if he had any problems.

Not that she had explained any of this to Claire when she phoned to say she would be coming home on Friday. Claire had never shown any interest in her work. As it was, Kate was going home a day earlier than she had originally planned as she had intended to arrive on Saturday evening and stay until Sunday lunch-time. As much as she loved her parents, one night of their company was enough. However, Claire had not sounded particularly pleased. The tone of her voice made it clear that Kate was doing no more than she ought to.

It was only after she had put the receiver down on her sister at lunch-time that day that she remembered she had not bought her father a present.

Kate had promised herself that this birthday she would find something extra special well in advance so she would not have to do her usual last-minute dash to the shops but, like so many of her good resolutions, it had come to nothing. As it was her father's seventieth, she had wanted to buy him something other than the bottle of malt whisky and box of Havana cigars she usually gave him, but the question was what?

She had asked her secretary, Ruby, to take all her calls for the next two hours, putting no one through to her and allowing nobody through her door unless it really was a question of life and death, and had worked through the most pressing things in her in-tray. Then she had taken the unusual step of leaving the office early, planning to go home by way of Simpson of Piccadilly. She knew her father liked to shop there when he was up in town as he loved to go to a lunch-time concert in St James's church next door, followed by an afternoon spent at the Reform Club. It was his idea of a day out in London, although not her mother's. She much preferred Harvey Nichols and Sloane Street.

It was only when Kate found herself staring at the empty display windows and a barred door that had once led into one of London's shopping institutions that she remembered her father telling her how sad he had been at its closure and how he wasn't sure whether he wanted to come to London any more since it had changed too much.

In desperation, she had crossed Piccadilly and headed for the Burlington Arcade. This was not her usual shopping area but she was determined to buy something special. A shop selling cashmere caught her eye and she threw herself on the mercy of a sales-woman who suggested that madam would find a cashmere cardigan a very suitable purchase. Kate expected her father would never wear it unless he knew she was coming to visit, but she was convinced he would appreciate the gesture and she enjoyed watching it being carefully wrapped up in layers of tissue paper before being laid in a box and elegantly bound with ribbon.

With her sister's words about her neglect in her ears, she also bought a Cacharel silk scarf for her mother from another shop and, as a peace offering to Claire, she crossed Piccadilly once again and got her a large box of handmade continental chocolates in Fortnum & Mason. Her sister was always on a diet, but Kate could not think what else to buy her and if she didn't want them she could always give them to the boys.

As a result of her last-minute shopping foray, Kate was carrying more than she intended as she left home. So when she turned into the Caledonian Road and saw a black cab, she flagged it down. It got her to Waterloo just as a train was about to leave. Abandoning dignity, she sprinted from the ticket office to the platform, leaping aboard as it drew out.

As it clanked slowly out of the station Kate was reminded — as if she needed to be — of how much she hated travelling by train. The carriage was scruffy and smelt sour, as though something unpleasant had been left mouldering under a seat, which no doubt it had. It was four fifteen and the evening rush-hour had not yet begun, but the carriage was reasonably full as it was Friday and many office workers seemed to be beginning their weekend early.

Kate placed her bag on the seat beside her to deter anyone from occupying it and looked around at her fellow passengers. They had the blank expressions of regular commuters. People who were travelling to a real destination had an air of expectation — even of hope — about them. It was hard for Kate to picture her father, Gerald, among these expressionless faces, yet he had done this journey daily for nearly forty years, not counting holidays and business trips abroad. An hour there and an hour back. Two hours a day, plus the drive to the station from the house and the journey on the Waterloo and City line to Bank. Forty years. That was a lifetime spent on a train. Kate's lifetime.

He had retired ten years ago when he was sixty. He had not wanted to, but his company had been taken over by an American multinational and the older directors had been encouraged to leave with generous golden handshakes. He still had shares in the company, which were worth about ten times what they had been when he had been on the board, but Kate knew that none the less he would prefer to be working.

Kate rested her head against the seat and stared out of the grime-streaked window. Her sister had organised a dinner party for fourteen on Saturday evening and a drinks party on Sunday for other friends, numbering around a hundred. She could imagine Claire and their mother – Cissy as everyone called her – planning the guest list for Sunday. Each would have drawn up a list of a hundred or more names that they absolutely *must* invite and they would have spent hours of good-natured bickering, trying to combine their separate lists, arguing the merits of those one of them wanted to ask whom the other didn't. Even when they had agreed on a final tally there would be numerous telephone calls to say that, on second thoughts, if Mr and Mrs So-and-So came, Miss Somebody-or-Other would *have* to be asked and the list would start to grow again.

The discussion would continue while they descended together on the local Waitrose supermarket where, as they filled two, or maybe even three, trolleys with food, they would no doubt bump into someone they had forgotten. They would then giggle like schoolgirls in the car-park about the white lie they had told to the unsuspecting first wife of the man they had invited with his new girl-friend as they loaded their booty into Claire's Range Rover.

Kate's sister and mother were very close. People often said they seemed more like sisters than mother and daughter. Her father joked about setting up a satellite link between their two homes to save on telephone bills as Cissy and Claire called each other at least three or four times a day, although what they found to talk about Kate could not understand. She tried to phone her mother once a week, although it was more often than not once every two weeks, and even then they never seemed to find much to discuss. She never rang Claire. She never had to. Claire always called her. Usually for a one-sided conversation about one, or all three, of her sons' latest exploits, or to deliver yet another lecture on how Kate was neglecting her filial obligations. According to Claire, it was unfair that she was the one who had to do everything for their parents. She had family responsibilities of her own, what with a husband and children, and she never failed to point out that Kate demonstrably lacked both.

Kate did not think her parents were neglected. Claire just liked organising other people's lives and then acting long-suffering when they refused to be organised. Their parents did not need Claire's help any more than they needed Kate's. They adored each other and lived a full social life – always entertaining or being entertained. Both of them were still healthy and strong, and they were more than able to manage their own affairs. Although her father would be seventy tomorrow, her mother was only fifty-eight, which was still young.

They had met when her father was twenty-nine and her mother seventeen. He was on a business trip to Lille and she was the daughter of the factory manager he went to visit. Despite the opposition of her family, who were staunch Catholics, Cissy was determined to have Gerald and they were married within a year. Kate was born almost exactly nine months to the day after their wedding and Claire two years later. Her father fondly referred to all three of them as his 'pretty girls'.

Cissy had never wished for anything else but marriage and children, and she had wanted the same for Kate and Claire. When Claire had announced she intended to abandon her A levels and get married, Cissy had been like a tigress, fiercely pouncing on any opposition to the idea. As usual, she got her way and Claire had been married on her eighteenth birthday. The wedding took place in the local Catholic church, with a reception for two hundred and fifty in a marquee in their parents' garden. Roger, her husband, now ran a successful computer software company, and they and their three sons, Philip, eighteen, Jonathan, sixteen and Matthew, ten, lived in a large, mock-Tudor detached house which was barely a quarter of a mile from the large, mock-Tudor detached house occupied by Kate's parents.

The rhythm of the train changed as it approached a station and Kate looked out. It was unmistakably her stop. When she was younger she had indulged in a silly fantasy that there was a band of fairies, not the usual gossamer-winged blond sprites, but tiny men dressed in white overalls with rosy red cheeks and brightly coloured scarves knotted around their necks, who came out every night while everyone was asleep and repainted the town so it was fresh and clean each morning. After retouching the flowers in the gardens and washing the lawns and fields with a particularly green shade of green, they then sprinkled dew drops everywhere so that the town's inhabitants would wake up to a sparkling new world. It was the only explanation that Kate could find for why this part of Surrey always looked so perfect. To complete the illusion that she had gone back in time to an Ealing Films version of England and had left the reality of Nineties London behind, when she stepped down onto the platform, a smiling ticket collector touched his peaked cap and wished her good-afternoon and, outside on the forecourt, a taxi driver leapt to attention, took her bags and respectfully held the car door open for her.

The journey from the station to her parents' took ten minutes. Although Claire had demanded to know what time she intended to arrive, Kate had kept it vague, merely saying that evening. Kate understood her mother well enough to know that if she had said a time and was delayed by more than two minutes – a frequent occurrence on that particular railway line – her mother would report her missing to the police. However, as the taxi turned into the road where her parents lived, Kate checked her watch and realised that she had mistimed her arrival. Her father liked to watch the early evening news bulletins – first on ITV then on the BBC – in order to compare them. He usually came to the conclusion that the BBC had been better in its selection of the most important stories.

Her father had taken a much keener interest in television since his retirement. Before that he had never had time for it. But now he said it was important that he still had something to say and, as most people watched television, he should understand what they were talking about. He also liked to talk to Kate about her work, although she knew it was to his lasting – but unspoken – disappointment that she did not work for the BBC.

The crunch of the gravel on the drive as the taxi drew up outside had alerted her mother. Even before the driver could race round to open the door for Kate, Cissy rushed out of the house. Calling Kate's father as she came, she threw her arms around Kate and hugged her tightly. Kate bent down to receive her mother's kisses. It never ceased to surprise Kate to find how tiny she was. As she looked up, Kate saw the tall, rangy figure of her father appearing on the doorstep, his glasses on the end of his nose from his television watching. His face lit up when he saw it was Kate.

'Pay the taxi, Gerald, darling,' commanded her mother, slipping her arm through Kate's and walking her into the house.

As they came level with her father, he bent his head to receive Kate's kiss. Then he dutifully paid the taxi driver, returning with Kate's bags. Her mother led the way through to the large, airy kitchen which opened out into a small conservatory filled with comfortable colonial-style cane seating. This was where Cissy spent most of her time, as a needlepoint frame and basket of tapestry silks beside her favourite chair testified. She fussed around Kate as though she had been on some long and arduous journey, making sure she was comfortably seated before putting the kettle on. Kate's father hovered uncertainly in the doorway, still holding her bags.

Cissy waved him out of the room. 'Leave them in the hall, Gerald, darling, and go back to your news. Katherine won't mind, will you, *chérie*? It will give us a chance to be alone, mother and daughter. It is not something Katherine and I can do very often.'

Kate gave her father a rueful smile, which he returned before disappearing, leaving her to settle back and watch her mother make the coffee. At fifty-eight, Cissy still had the gamine quality that had entranced Kate's father all those years ago. There was a framed pencil portrait of her up on the wall, sketched the year before they met, and she had not changed much. The dark eyes upturned impishly at the corners; a small, retroussé nose; determined lower lip, jutting out just as now, as she concentrated on making coffee; and the unmistakable, imperious arch of plucked eyebrows so familiar to Kate. Her hair was still cut boyishly short as in the picture, a single kiss curl on either side reaching out to the corner of her eyes. Only a wide, silver-grey streak running from the crown of her head to her forehead betrayed the passing of time since the portrait and even that added to her air of incontrovertible French chic.

Kate had inherited her mother's olive, Mediterranean colouring, but not her neat-boned figure. She had her mother's thick hair, too, but unfortunately, she had inherited her father's curls, which on her had a tendency to frizzy wildness. She also had Gerald's height and his long-legged, broad-shouldered build.

Claire was physically more like their mother. She was much shorter than Kate but, while she had Cissy's petite build, she put on weight very quickly, particularly around her hips, so she was constantly dieting. As a result, the last time Kate had seen her she had thought she was too thin.

Her mother brought over the coffee and sat down opposite Kate. 'It's so good to have you home, *chérie*. I was so happy when Claire called to say you were coming this evening rather than tomorrow, although I could not see why you did not phone to tell me yourself. Such a small thing.'

Kate remained silent. Her mother was right, of course, she should have called her, not Claire. As usual, it had made her look bad and Claire look good. There was no point in saying that she had intended to call her, but it was Claire who had insisted Kate should not phone as she was going to speak to their mother anyway and would let her know.

Her mother pressed down the plunger in the cafetière and poured the coffee. 'Your sister is so thoughtful about these things, but then, she is not the busy career woman.'

Kate took the cup and saucer her mother held out but refused to rise to the bait that was being dangled in front of her. She had too many other things on her mind. She had promised herself that she would not quarrel with Cissy that weekend and she intended to stick to it. Anyway, there was no point. They had gone over this ground a million times before and she knew she could not win. She sipped her coffee before looking up at her mother.

'Claire tells me that Philip has been offered places at three different universities for the autumn. That's wonderful.'

'Such a brilliant boy. He will go far. Claire is blessed to have such clever sons.'

Kate swallowed hard. Her mother had not thought her brilliant when she had been offered places at all five universities of her choice. In her eyes, boys were still different.

'How is Father? He looks well and so do you.'

'His doctor says he should cut down on alcohol and cigars, but what do doctors know? He is as handsome and as strong as the day I married him. Seventy is not old.'

Kate looked at her mother. Had she imagined it, or had she heard fear in Cissy's voice? Her parents were inseparable. After forty years of marriage they still sometimes acted as though they had fallen in love yesterday. It was a lot to live up to, almost too much at times. Other people blamed the failure of their relationships on divorced parents and unhappy childhoods, but she didn't have that excuse. Her childhood had been idyllically happy. She and Claire had basked in the glow of their parents' love for each other.

'Of course seventy isn't old. People have become prime ministers and presidents in their seventies,' insisted Kate. 'It's a pity Father was forced to retire so early. I think he would have been happier if he had been able to carry on working.'

Her mother's eyes flashed and Kate realised she had ventured onto dangerous ground. The only time she had ever known her parents argue seriously was over the boardroom coup which ended in his retirement. He had wanted to fight it as a matter of principle, but Cissy had been delighted. Not only was he being offered a substantial financial settlement, but he would not have to travel up to London every day and she would have him all to herself. Cissy had even gone so far as to telephone some of the other directors to make sure they would vote in favour of the take-over. Kate's father had been furious at her interference and had spent several nights staying at his club in London.

This had terrified Cissy. Although they had quarrelled many times before, she had always been the one who had done the shouting and the walking out. This time she had run crying to Claire who had gone up to London and, by her account at least, read the riot act to her father. He had returned home loaded down with gifts and repentance, and had quietly accepted early retirement.

Although Cissy and Gerald had then launched themselves on what seemed like an extended second honeymoon, Claire and Kate had not spoken for months after this incident, which had caused yet another rift between them. Claire had wanted Kate to go with her to see their father but Kate had refused. She did not believe that Claire should interfere in their parents' relationship and she thought it was wrong to take sides in their arguments. Particularly as, if Kate was going to take anyone's side, it would have been her father's.

'Why is it that people think work can bring happiness? What happiness has it brought you? Where is your husband? Your children? You always talk about being free, but free for what? What is this freedom?'

'It's a bit early for existential philosophy, isn't it?' asked Kate's father, walking into the room and kissing Cissy on the head before sitting down beside her.

She gave him a playful tap on the arm. 'Why do the English always make fun when the subject of emotion comes up? One would think you do not have any, except I know you do.' She leant over and kissed him on the cheek. 'Talk to your daughter. Tell her she must find herself a good man and settle down.' She shrugged her shoulders. 'It is probably too late for many more grandchildren now, but she must have a husband. A woman without a man ... pah!' She stood up. 'Talk some sense into her, Gerald, darling, while I prepare dinner.' She went into the kitchen.

Kate's father put his hands on the arms of his chair and levered himself up. 'If we are to have a father-to-daughter talk, I think a small pre-prandial drink would help. Would you care to join me, Kate?'

'I'd love to,' she replied promptly and got up to follow him, feeling her mother's disapproval trailing after them down the passage to the small front parlour, which served as her father's study and television room.

Cissy did not like television. She said it stopped people doing useful things. So Kate's father retreated to his study where he could happily sit staring into space for long periods of time and where he could watch his small portable from the comfort of a battered leather armchair which Cissy refused to have in her drawing-room.

Kate knew where her father kept his supplies of whisky and sherry and, in a ritual she had practised many times although not lately, went to the cupboard and poured two dry fino sherries. She handed one to her father before stretching herself out on an ancient wooden steamer chair which was the only other seat in the room.

Her father lifted his glass. 'Welcome home.'

They sipped in companionable silence for a few minutes.

'How's work?' Her father broke the silence. 'There was an article in the newspaper today about the changes going on in your world. It didn't sound too healthy to me. This new boss of yours, does he know what he's doing?'

Kate felt a rush of affection for her father. Although he knew very little about the television industry, he made a point of reading anything he could find. He had probably mulled over the article for ages, considering its possible implications for her. He had always supported her in whatever she had wanted to do. He had overruled her mother's objections when Kate had chosen to go to a university that would mean she had to leave home and, when she had decided to become a journalist rather than going into law as he had always hoped, he had still stood by her and encouraged her. However, Kate did not want him to worry needlessly. Her problems with Jordan were for her to work out, so she chose her words carefully.

'There are a lot of people who think Jordan is very talented.' She didn't add that there were a lot of people who thought he wasn't, including herself.

Her father looked hard at her. 'Everything is still all right? I thought at one time you were considering going after this job yourself?'

'Things are fine, Dad, really they are. Just an overdose of office politics, that's all. I thought about the job,' she said carefully, 'but it would be desk-bound, which isn't for me. I still like being able to get out into the field occasionally.' Kate found she could not meet her father's eyes and for once she was glad when her mother interrupted them to call them to the dinner-table.

Over dinner, she made herself chat animatedly, managing to avoid both her mother's pointed questions about the men she was meeting and her father's questioning looks.

Cissy began to clear the pudding dishes to the sink and Kate stood up. 'Can I help?'

Both her mother and her father motioned her to sit down.

'The machine handles the dishes,' said her father. 'I think it's time for the port as your mother has bought some rather good Stilton.' He winked at Kate. 'It's only taken me forty years to convince her that we British can produce a cheese to rival anything the French make, but it's been worth the wait.'

He went into the hall where he kept what he jokingly referred to as his wine cellar in the cupboard under the stairs and returned with a bottle. He picked up a tea-cloth and began to dust it. Cissy took it away from him and handed him a duster. 'I laid down some bottles of this a few years ago. I was saving it for tomorrow night's little shindig. Yes, I know all about it,' he said as Kate's mother's mouth formed a little disappointed 'o'. 'Couldn't fail to the way you and Claire have been carrying on.' He set down the bottle and took a decanter out of a cupboard. 'But there'll be plenty left for tomorrow and anyway, Kate will appreciate this a lot more than some of the surprise guests I hear are coming and I want to give her a proper welcome home.'

Not for the first time that evening, Kate was angry with herself for not coming home more often. She felt like a little girl again, warm and safe within the circle of her parents' love, as she watched her father decant the port. His hair was now completely white, although thick and wavy, and his back was still ramrod straight. She had always got on better with him than with her mother. He was not physically demonstrative, but then, neither was she. It was more their ability to sit happily in shared silence that she enjoyed and which drove her mother mad. Cissy considered silence a challenge, something to be filled with noise, which was what she was doing now, humming some light operatic aria to herself as she stacked the dishes into the washing machine.

Kate didn't really want anything more to eat or drink. As always, her mother had cooked a wonderful meal, but it had been rich with cream. Cissy still preferred the dishes of her childhood France – *nouvelle cuisine* had passed her by – and they had also drunk a bottle of excellent Burgundy. However, Kate did not want to spoil her parents' obvious delight at her homecoming, so the least she could do was to let them spoil her. She prepared an appreciative smile to greet their return to the table, her mother bearing a truckle of ripe-smelling Stilton, her father a tray with the decanter and three lead-crystal port glasses.

'I should really have decanted this earlier,' he said, holding the port up to the light, 'but I think we may just get away with it if I'm careful.'

As he held up a glass and began to pour, Kate saw a tremor in his hands. A single drop of port escaped down the side of the glass and dropped onto the white linen table-cloth, leaving a perfect ruby-red circle. Kate looked at her mother and once again saw fear reflected in her eyes. But it was only for a moment. Her mother's eyelashes veiled her eyes as though shutting out something unpleasant.

Kate helped herself to a water biscuit and scraped some Stilton from the centre of the truckle. It never ceased to amaze her that such opposing tastes – both creamy and rank – could be married together within one cheese and yet taste so wonderful and, with the added deep sweetness of the port, reach perfection. Stilton and port would forever be the taste of family Christmases. Port was the first alcohol she had been allowed to sip when she was a child.

Her mother reached across and patted Kate's hand. 'I'm feeling a little tired this evening, *chérie*, would you mind if I went to bed early? Your father will be out tomorrow morning so I shall have you to myself and we can have a long talk then.' She went round the table to kiss Gerald. He caught her hand as though to stop her leaving and she kissed him again. 'Now I'm trusting you both not to stay up too late and not to drink too much port.' And with that she left the room.

Kate's father offered her the decanter. She poured herself another glass. He would normally light a cigar at this point, but there was not one to be seen. Perhaps he had at least heeded this part of his doctor's warning. Kate was glad she had not bought him her usual box of cigars. There was a gentle silence as they both sipped their port.

Then her father put down his glass. 'Your mother is worried about you, Kate. She thinks you have man trouble.' He looked at her. 'You don't have to tell me about it unless you want to. You're a grown woman and I trust you to run your life in the way you deem fit.' He gazed ruminatively into his glass. 'Cissy hates not knowing about things, but some things are best left unsaid. She'd just worry more. The only measure of happiness she has is of marriage and children. That's what she wished for herself and she's always wanted the same for you and Claire. It's hard for her to understand that you might find happiness in anything else. I don't mind what you choose for yourself, Kate, as long as it is the right choice and it makes you happy. I have a beautiful wife, two beautiful daughters and three grandsons. What more could a man want from life?' He looked at her. 'What worries me, Kate, is that you might feel pressured into something that would be against your principles. A woman of your age without children is faced with some difficult decisions. They say things have changed, but certain basic facts of life haven't and they probably never will. It's not just your mother who thinks that a woman without children is no woman at all.' He sipped some more port and waited.

Kate wanted to say something, but she sensed that if she did, her father would stop talking and he had never talked to her like this before. She had not thought that he considered her a grown woman, at least not when it came to her personal life. She had supposed that, like all fathers, he preferred not to think about his daughter's sex life.

'When your mother and I married, women did not

70

have much choice. Not that it mattered to your mother; all she wanted was children. Once she had you and Claire, a side of our marriage died, not completely at first, but I knew that the physical side of it was for my benefit, not hers, and I never pressed it. But when it finally died, many years ago now, a part of me died too – an important part.'

Kate found that she was staring at her father, but he was looking somewhere into the distance. The knowledge that her mother and father had not had a sex life for years stunned her. Her mother was forever making arch comments or giggling at some sexual innuendo. She had always believed that they had the perfect marriage, but suddenly a crack had begun to appear in it. It was as though she had been standing in a slow-moving queue to see a beautiful work of art, only to discover when at last she had got to the front that it had a flaw in it.

'It wasn't your mother's fault,' her father continued as though to himself. 'Maybe it was mine. She was too young when I married her, little more than a child. But she was a woman in every other way and a strong-willed one at that. When she wants something, she usually gets it.' He looked at Kate. 'Don't think your mother doesn't love me, she does. It's just that her way of expressing love is not necessarily always the same as mine. However, one of the benefits of age is that I can comfort myself with the thought that I probably couldn't do the things I want to do anyway.' He smiled wistfully. 'But that doesn't mean I don't still occasionally think about them.'

Her father finished his port. 'I have no regrets, how could I? I love your mother more than life itself. But I sense a lot of me in you, Kate, and I don't want you to have any regrets. Don't rush into a relationship and children just because you feel you might be missing out on something. As wonderful as you and Claire both are, children aren't everything.'

Kate went round to her father and, putting her arms around his neck, placed her cheek next to his. He suddenly seemed less like her father and more like a man. She wasn't sure if she could speak. She had come to her father for protection, now it was he who seemed frail and in need of nurturing.

'Don't worry about me, Dad,' she managed at last. 'I'll be all right.'

Six

• • •

'Uh?' The pair of brown eyes belonging to her middle nephew Jonathan regarded Kate warily around the door, then dropped away. 'She's in there.' He jerked his head at some indeterminate inner region of the house and loped off.

Kate was left standing at the front door, the warm greeting she had ready dry on her lips, her arms piled high with containers of food that her mother had asked her to deliver to her sister.

Of her three nephews, Kate had always got on best with Jonathan. Philip, the eldest, had suffered badly from asthma as a child and Claire had been overly protective towards him. He had repaid her by taking after his father and turning to computers for refuge, shunning human contact.

In contrast to Philip, Matthew, Kate's youngest nephew, was loud and brash, his tough, street-wise persona more in keeping with the Bronx than green-belt Surrey. Although he was at the same prep school that his elder brothers had attended, there was some question as to whether he would be admitted into the upper school when he was eleven. He showed a complete disregard for learning anything other than the name of every footballer who had ever played for Manchester United. He knew with unerring accuracy the years when the team had topped the league or won the FA Cup, or both, as well as the names of the players who had scored the goals in the Cup Finals. Yet he steadfastly refused to learn those of the Tudor kings and queens. As his despairing teachers pointed out, there was no question but that there was a brain inside the baseball cap he insisted on substituting for his school cap once he was out of Claire's sight, but nobody seemed able to reach it.

Claire had followed the advice of the school counsellor and tried to learn something about football so that she could talk to him. But her suggestion that he support Wimbledon, because it sounded so much nicer and was at least a southern team, had been met with the kind of unremittingly stony stare that only a ten-year-old can inflict upon its parent and she had conceded defeat.

Jonathan, on the other hand, had been a lively child, and affectionate and demonstrative in comparison with his brothers. While Philip had inherited his father's tall, gangling body and sandy-haired colouring, Jonathan had taken after his grandfather and was a handsome brown-eyed boy, with a shock of curly dark hair. Or at least he had been the last time Kate had seen him.

The physical change in him since then had quite startled her. He had grown tall and, if he had not already reached it, he was well on his way to six feet and beyond. But instead of the round-shouldered, self-effacing tallness of his brother, Jonathan was hulking – almost threatening. His hair hung long and lank to his shoulders, and his face bore the evidence of acne.

As she stepped into the hall, kicking the door shut behind her, Jonathan leapt up the stairs two at a time. There was the thunderous sound of some heavy metal music as a door opened and then it became muffled again as it was slammed shut.

Kate made her way down the hall, balancing the

plastic containers one on top of the other. She was not able to see what was ahead of her, so she could not avoid the body that came hurling out of the kitchen with a cry of fury and cannoned into her. The air was knocked out of her body as she was slammed against the wall, boxes flying in all directions. Matthew hesitated long enough to be open-mouthed in awe at the chaos he had caused, before he thought better of staying around to suffer the consequences of his actions and took to his Nike-shod heels with a speed that would have shamed Carl Lewis.

'*Matthew*!'

Claire appeared, ineffectually brandishing a wooden spoon just as the front door slammed shut, making good her youngest son's escape. '*Bugger* that child,' she announced to no one in particular.

'And it's delightful to see you again too, Sister,' said Kate, recovering her feet.

Claire pushed a floury hand through her hair, which was now cut short, making her look more like their mother than ever.

'I'm sorry, Kate, but there are times when I could murder him. Do you know he just walked in and helped himself to some money from my purse? I don't know where he's learning these habits. I swear he hangs around with the children from that awful council house estate.'

'I thought there weren't any council house estates left. Isn't that what you and Roger voted for?' asked Kate mildly.

For once, Claire did not spring to the defence of Maggie Thatcher as she was staring horror struck at the containers that were strewn all over the floor.

'Oh, lord! That little *bugger*! One of these days I'm going to forget all my principles and beat the hell out of him.'

Kate got down on one knee and started to pick them

up. Claire watched her, seemingly frozen into inaction at the disaster.

'Are those Mummy's contribution to the party?'

'I think the operative word is *were*,' said Kate, carrying the remnants through and placing them on the large central island in Claire's kitchen. Suspended above its marble-tiled surface, like instruments of torture, was a large selection of cooking pots and utensils. Kate cautiously opened one of the containers and peered inside. 'Although there may be some that can be saved,' she added.

'Would you be a dear and take charge of the rescue operation while I finish preparing the main course for tonight?' commanded Claire, tracing a floury finger down the page of one of the large pile of open cookery books at her elbow. She considered the recipe for a moment, then busied herself with a large mound of puff pastry. Two enormous fillets of beef stood ready to one side. 'I do hope another trip to Waitrose is not going to be necessary. I do so *hate* going there on a Saturday afternoon. They never have anything left and it's full of horrid people.'

Kate looked round at the ranks of fitted antique pine cupboards which marched round the walls and floors of Claire's large kitchen. She opened the cupboard door nearest to her – it concealed a fridge. The next one revealed a dishwasher. 'Where on earth do you keep your plates?' she demanded.

Claire nodded to the other side of the room. 'Large plates for entertaining are over there, three cupboards from the right, second shelf down. Oh, on second thoughts,' she said as Kate started to reach up, 'next cupboard along, bottom shelf. My Royal Doulton would be wasted on the hordes coming tomorrow, use the stuff that Gran left me.'

Kate took down some large oval cream-ware dishes

with basket-weave edges. 'These are very pretty, are you sure you want to use them?'

'They've withstood many a bun-fight in this house and they'll withstand many more,' said Claire. 'Just save what you can of the food and chuck the rest away. Or better still, stick it on a plate and give Jonathan a call. That boy's always complaining he's hungry and he'll eat anything. He's a human dustbin.'

Kate began to pick through what was left of the dainty little cocktail titbits her mother had prepared. 'Jonathan's changed a lot since I last saw him, which can only have been a few months ago. He looks as though he's going to be the tallest of the boys.'

'A year,' Claire corrected sharply. 'It's over a year since you last saw him and change is hardly the word for it.' She deftly divided the pastry into two and began rolling the first lump out on a floured marble slab. 'More like an instant Jekyll and Hyde transformation. One moment he was dear, sweet little Jonty, the next he was that . . . that . . . *thing* you met in the hall. It's a pity you haven't been around much. If you took more of an interest in him it might help. You *are* his godmother after all.'

Kate had never been sure exactly what was expected of her as Jonathan's godmother, other than to buy him presents at birthdays and Christmas, which she did for her other two nephews as well, although she suspected that she was expected to bequeath her money to him when she died. She had a theory that the reason why childless women were so popular as godparents was that it was assumed they would have no one else as heirs. Perhaps she was being cynical, but she had found the number of requests for her to be a godparent had increased with every year since she had passed thirty and remained childless. Yet few, if any, of the people who asked her to assume the role of godparent believed in God and some would have danced naked smeared with sacred oils at the temple of Mithras if that was the current vogue and it allowed them to display their progeny – although, no doubt, the sacred oils would have been purchased at the Body Shop and come from an Indian tribe in the Amazonian jungle under a fair-trade deal.

'Philip was never like it,' Claire continued. 'If he had an adolescence *I* didn't notice it. He's always been just Philip. But since Jonathan turned fifteen, he appears to have gone into some kind of hormonal overdrive. The worst thing is, Matthew seems to be hitting adolescence at least three years early.' She stood back and looked at her handiwork for a moment or two, then rolled it a little thinner. Satisfied, she began work on the second piece. Then she tipped some fried onions and mushrooms into a bowl of goose liver pâté and mixed them together. Using her hands, she began to apply the mixture as a thick crust to the fillets of beef. 'Don't let *anyone* ever tell you that bringing up children is easy.'

'I never thought it was,' said Kate drily. 'That's why I wonder why everyone is in such a rush to do it.'

Claire didn't reply. She was intent on placing the first piece of beef exactly in the centre of the pastry and folding it up into a neat parcel. Her tongue stuck out pinkly between her teeth as she concentrated, just as it had always done since she was a child.

Kate watched her sister as she painstakingly cut out pieces of dough in the shape of leaves to form a pattern on the top of the wrapped beef. How was it possible that two people of the same gender, who had been born to the same parents, brought up in the same house, gone to the same schools, even been taught by the same teachers, could have so little in common apart from the facts of their upbringing?

Claire stood back and looked at her handiwork, then changed the position of one leaf so imperceptibly that it made no difference but seemed to satisfy her. 'There! What do you think?'

'It looks wonderful. I'm sure it will be a triumph,' replied Kate.

'Well, Daddy will like it and that's the main thing. I could put spam fritters in front of my lot and they wouldn't notice. They'd just guzzle them down. Sometimes I think they would only realise I was dead if the fridge were empty. Do you know I can go days without having a conversation of more than two grunts with any of them, even Roger.' She looked wistful. 'In some ways I wish I'd had at least one daughter. That way you'd know what they got up to in their rooms and it wouldn't be like entering a foreign country when you go in. Daughters talk to their mothers.'

'Not *all* daughters,' interjected Kate. 'You're the one who talks to Mother, not me.'

'And whose fault is that?' demanded Claire. 'It isn't as though we've ever excluded you. *You're* the one who has always had something better to do, even when we were children. Anyway, I always thought you preferred being Daddy's girl.'

They were back on old familiar ground again. Kate could almost hear the high-pitched querulous voices of two little girls trading insults: 'Mummy's favourite!' 'Daddy's girl!' It was one of the reasons she avoided coming home. In London the present was the only thing that mattered and it was possible to walk away from the past, but not in Surrey. Here the past seemed to have as much reality as the present.

'I admit that I have always got on better with Dad. But the way you paint it, it's as though he and I take sides against you and Mother. It's never been like that,' she replied.

'Not even when I got married?' Claire demanded.

Kate had wondered when Claire would bring up her wedding. At some point she always did. 'I simply thought you were making an error,' she said wearily. 'I hope you would do the same and try to stop me if you thought I was in danger of making a mistake that might ruin my life. Isn't that what sisters are for?'

Claire had barely had time to stop playing with dolls before she exchanged their parents' home for her husband's and began playing mothers and fathers for real. The idea had horrified Kate. She had been convinced that Claire did not know what she was doing. Blaming their mother, she had come home from university, determined to talk Claire out of getting married. A terrible family row had ensued, or rather Kate and her mother had shouted at each other while Claire had cried. Their father had refused to take sides, acting like a UN peace-keeping mission, braving the cross-fire to mediate between them, patiently standing outside slammed doors until they were opened.

Kate seemed to remember that she had accused her mother of brainwashing Claire and selling her into a life of domestic and sexual slavery. Equally melodramatic, her mother had declared that feminism was the root cause of Kate's ruination and would be the ruin of all women. She had demanded that Kate's father stop paying her grant, cut off her allowance, and force her to leave university and return home.

Kate had stormed out, vowing that she would never come back, especially not to attend Claire's wedding for which her bridesmaid's dress had already been ordered, although no one had consulted her about it. Equally resolute, her mother had declared that she did not want Kate to come to the wedding as she was no daughter of hers.

It had been left to Kate's father to follow her to London when, for once, he had been firm. While agreeing with Kate that Claire was too young, he had pointed out that he could hardly forbid her as he had married Kate's mother when she was a year younger than Claire and that, for Claire's sake, he expected her to come to the wedding.

So Kate had walked down the aisle behind her sister although she had gelled her hair into outrageous spikes and had insisted on wearing Doc Martens under her peach satin Empire-line dress rather than the matching satin pumps that had been made for her and the four other bridesmaids. She had also steeled herself to go to the reception, where she had nodded mutely as beaming friends and relatives congratulated her on what a wonderful wedding it had been. Under her father's watchful eye, she had gritted her teeth when they had mistaken her silence for being upset at not being married first and had reassured her that her time was sure to come soon.

She had comforted herself with the thought that it was unlikely the marriage would last. But she had to give her little sister credit – she had known what she was doing. Not many marriages of Claire's and Roger's vintage had lasted so long or so happily.

'Silly me, and *I* thought sisters were meant to support each other through thick and thin,' retorted Claire peevishly. 'But then, *I'm* only a suburban housewife, so what do *I* know?'

'I've never called you suburban,' remonstrated Kate.

'No. But you've thought it, haven't you?'

Kate was silent. Was that what she thought?

Claire took off her apron and began to wash her hands. Why did she always let Kate rile her? Kate had probably never suggested that she was suburban, but she had a way of making her *feel* suburban. She picked up a tea-towel and dried her hands. It wasn't anything that Kate said, at least not directly, it was just the way she was. Her presence was a reminder to Claire of what she was not. Kate had always been able to make her feel that whatever she wanted to do was silly.

It was ridiculous, now, looking back, but while all

Claire's friends had been worried about taking their boy-friends home to meet their parents, she had been worried about her boy-friends meeting her elder sister. Kate's disapproval somehow made whichever luckless boy incurred it – and that was most of them – a lot less desirable.

Kate still managed to make her feel as though her life in some way was not worthwhile – as though she had failed at something. Although at what, Claire had never been quite sure. She had not been clever at school, not like Kate, so she could not have had a career even if she had wanted one. The most she could have done was to be someone's secretary and since when had that been worthwhile? No, she was 'only a housewife' and she had the hands to prove it, thought Claire ruefully, looking at her dry, reddened skin. But what did Kate have to show for her successful career? What woman in her right mind would choose to reach forty and still be alone?

In some ways she could feel quite sorry for Kate, thought Claire. For all her cleverness she had never learnt how to handle men, or why was she still living alone? In that way at least she could teach her older sister a thing or two. She would be celebrating her twentieth wedding anniversary that year, something none of her friends from school could do. They were all separated or divorced and one was even on her third marriage. When Kate could say she had been happily married for as long as her, *then* she could act superior, thought Claire and, with a sense of satisfaction, squeezed some moisturising cream onto her hands and smoothed it in. Someone had to make Kate see sense on the subject of men and, as usual, it looked like it would have to be her.

Filled with resolve, she switched on the kettle. 'Time for some coffee, don't you think? At least one good thing about the boys staying in their rooms all the time is that we have peace to talk.'

'Where's Roger?'

'He's gone to the office. Not that he needs an excuse to go there, but for once I was glad to get him out of the way as he'd only get under my feet when I have so much to do and I thought it would nice for us to have some time to ourselves. It's not very often we get the chance.'

So that was why her mother had insisted she brought the food over this afternoon, thought Kate. Her mother and her sister had decided on a two-pronged attack: her mother that morning and her sister this afternoon. Cissy had probably called the moment she left the house to come to Claire's and reported what she had said, which had been very little.

For once she had steadfastly refused to allow herself to get irritated by her mother's litany of who, among the daughters of her many acquaintances, was getting engaged, married or having babies. She had merely said how nice it was for them, ensuring that she had survived the morning with a semblance of equanimity, which she was determined to maintain, no matter what her sister said.

'Would you like some choccy biccies with your coffee?' asked Claire, turning round. 'I know I shouldn't really, but the boys insist on having them in the house, so an occasional indulgence won't hurt.'

'Not for me. I've been non-stop eating since I arrived, you know what Mother's like. But you don't have to worry about your figure, you look awfully thin to me, too thin.'

'Thanks, but I have to be careful. I wouldn't like to feel I was letting Roger down.'

'Why on earth would you think you were doing that?' Kate waved her arm at the room. 'You've given

83

him three sons, you keep a perfect house. What more can he want?'

'Oh, it's not Roger, he wouldn't say anything,' said Claire quickly. 'He probably wouldn't even notice if I put on weight. But when you live in an area like this and move in the circles we do, these things matter.' She brought two mugs of coffee and the tin of biscuits over to the table and sat down. '*You* look good, though. I've always wished I had your bone structure and hair, rather than mine.'

The conversation had been brought swiftly back to her, Kate noticed.

'However, looks, at least for us women, do not last for ever. We have to take advantage of them before it's too late.'

'Too late for what?' Kate's voice was dangerous.

Claire held out the tin of biscuits. 'Are you sure you don't want a biscuit? They're awfully moreish.'

Kate shook her head but Claire took one and munched for a while.

'Is there anyone special in your life at the moment?' Claire's question was casual, but she was stirring her coffee with unnecessary vigour. 'You live such an exciting life up there in London. You must meet loads of gorgeous men.'

'If this is to be yet another inquisition about my love life and marriage prospects, you might as well stop now. I am not prepared to discuss them either with you or with Mother. There are more important things happening in the world, like war and floods and famine, although you would never know that judging by you two.' Kate sounded pompous and she knew it.

Claire bridled. 'Oh, we know our little concerns are nothing compared with meeting prime ministers and changing the way the world works, but they matter to us. *You* matter to us, although we don't appear to matter to you. You seem conveniently to forget you have a family until you want to come and visit.'

'That's not true . . .' began Kate, but Claire was not to be stopped.

'Have you any idea what it means to Mummy and Daddy, him especially, to see you happily married and to have grandchildren? But no, you selfishly put your career before everything and everybody. Well, one day your precious career will let you down and what will you do then?' she demanded.

For a moment it was on the tip of Kate's tongue to tell her that it had already happened. That the job she had thought was hers had been given to someone younger. The desire to tell someone was almost overwhelming. But she wanted neither her sister's sympathy nor to see the tight little smile she wore which meant 'I told you so'.

She looked across at Claire. 'This weekend is meant to be about Dad. For once, let's try not to quarrel, for his sake.'

Claire opened her mouth but then thought better of it and closed it again. She nodded. 'Pax?' She crossed her fingers in the sign they had agreed on when they were children to signal a truce.

Kate held up hers, crossed in the same manner. 'Pax,' she agreed.

Seven

• • •

Kate gazed down into the sluggish brown Thames with pleasure, then held up her face to catch the watery April sunshine. She felt her heart lift. It was on days like this that she loved London. Dirty, crowded and polluted though it was, she felt she belonged. Surrey and the weekend seemed a long way away and almost in another country.

Never had she felt less at home than during the last couple of days. It wasn't the quarrel she had had with her sister – they always quarrelled – but the sense that her parents had somehow cheated on her. She had watched them as they presented the perfect picture of happiness, arm in arm, greeting their guests, though she had known it was not real. It was absurd, but she had found herself feeling angry. Not so much at them, but that she had measured the rest of the world up against a symbol of perfection that had never existed. If she had needed proof that love meant compromise, she had only to look at her parents' marriage. If this was what was meant by growing up, then she was doing it a little late in life, Kate thought ruefully.

She looked along the river, it was in full flood, as was the dark tide of commuters hurrying across Waterloo Bridge towards the Strand and Covent Garden. It was eight thirty and Kate was earlier than usual for a Monday morning. By an unwritten agreement, any production team that was in the studio at week-ends did not come in until lunch-time on a Monday, but she had programmes other than the weekly current affairs series to deal with and she wished to be early in order to gather her thoughts.

No doubt at some point today she would be called in to meet her new boss and she wanted to have her strategy planned before she did so. Last week she had allowed everything to run away with her – Max, her job, her family – but today was the beginning of a new week and it was time to wrest back control of her life.

She had resolved to end the affair, a decision she had reached on the tedious journey back from Surrey on a slow train that had taken nearly twice as long as scheduled because of engineering works on the line. It was not just that Harriet had suddenly become a creature of flesh and blood whom she could no longer comfortably ignore, but the compartment of her life which had securely contained Max had begun to leak. And not just in one place. As soon as she thought she had it under control it started to leak somewhere else. She had always prided herself on never bringing her personal life into the office, but last week her feelings for Max had caused her to react with Leo in a way that was out of character. She had to get the affair under control again and the only way to do that was to end it.

Grasping her *Guardian* and her briefcase in one hand, and the rapidly cooling double espresso she had bought from the little Italian café where she went every morning in the other, Kate walked resolutely towards the Channel. There was a more direct route but she had a sneaking liking for the South Bank.

Most people thought the concrete maze of theatre and concert hall buildings which squatted along the river beside Waterloo Bridge was a monstrosity, but although they were large, brutal and ugly, the build-ings had a kind of primordial strength which rather appealed to her, a bit like Max, thought Kate, unable to suppress a smile. In rare quiet moments in the office she also liked to escape to browse among the second-hand book stalls which nestled in the shelter of the bridge, or to linger over an espresso in the National Film Theatre café, promising herself that she would book tickets for a retrospective of the films of Tarkovsky or the new, unmissable neo-realist film by a first-time Serbo-Croat director. She never did, but she liked to think that one day she would.

She was even fond of the multi-storey car-park, dank and evil-smelling though it was. Once, when Max had only been able to get away for an hour and they had been desperate to see each other, they had met for a drink in the National Theatre bar, but it had proved impossible to sit there, side by side, without touching and they had rushed out, laughing, and made love in his car in the car-park. It had been crazy, even dangerous, but they had not been able to stop themselves.

Sex with Max had always been like that: two bodies tearing at each other with hands and mouths and legs and teeth, exhilarated beyond caring about the consequences. It was like a drug, which blunted all sense of responsibility and which delivered a physical rush that made Kate feel high and always left her wanting more. But no longer, she thought, hurrying towards the glass edifice of the Channel, which glinted in the sunlight like a beacon ahead of her. It had all become too messy, too out of control.

Kate pushed her way through the swing doors and, with a brief nod at the receptionist, made her way towards the lifts, only to find her way barred by a newly installed turnstile. Behind it stood a uniformed security guard. He unfolded his arms and, with practised boredom, pointed her back to the reception desk.

'But I *work* here,' she protested.

'There's a new system. *Nobody* gets through here without a pass.' As he spoke, he caressed the shiny metal gate as though it were a lovable animal.

Kate reluctantly turned back. Behind the receptionist's desk a wall-sized bank of TV monitors flickered soundlessly with pictures from TV channels around the world, like a silent tower of Babel. This, too, had been installed over the weekend.

'Sign your name, print it here, put your time of arrival and state who you're going to see and the number on your security pass,' the receptionist intoned, jabbing a blood-red-tipped finger at five separate columns in a large book on the desk. 'I'll issue you with a temporary pass for today, but you must report to security and have your photo taken for a permanent pass before the end of the week. If you lose the pass it will cost you five pounds so I suggest you keep it with you at all times.' She handed Kate a blue plastic strip. 'Oh, and this will only permit access to the administrative sections of the building. If you want to get into any of the technical areas you need one of these.' She held up a red plastic strip. 'However, if you need access to both, you must have one of these.' She held up a yellow plastic strip.

'Since when did we become part of MI5?' asked Kate sarcastically.

'Management says there have been too many losses,' the receptionist replied darkly, nodding at two more security men positioned impassively on either side of the front entrance. Kate had not noticed them when she came in.

'Should I prepare myself for a body search when I leave the building?' asked Kate, signing an indecipherable scrawl where she had been instructed. She received a bright but humourless smile for her sarcasm.

Carrying her pass, Kate went back to the turnstile, ready to take on the security guard too. But when she looked at the face above the dark serge suit with its military buttons and epaulettes, it was the pale scrawny visage of a youth barely out of his acne-ridden teens. She relented on her intention to make a comment about *Mein Führer* – from the look of him it was unlikely that he had got as far as history GCSE to learn about Hitler before being thrown onto the dole queue.

She held up her pass and offered him a friendly smile instead. 'What do I do with this?'

Her smile won her a grateful blush. He pointed at a small screen. 'Hold it against that, Miss, and it will let you through.'

Kate did what she was told and the cylindrical metal gate turned to allow her past.

The guard followed her to the lift. 'Which floor, Miss?'

'The ninth.'

He called the lift for her and when it arrived he held the door and pushed the ninth-floor button before letting it go with a shy smile.

Kate's room was one of the few partitioned areas at either end of a vast open-plan office. Each of the many desks in the open area also had low partitions around it, creating a maze which seemed to change daily as desks were added or taken away according to the needs of the different production teams that operated from the office. As Kate had expected, she was first in and with luck would have an hour, possibly longer, before her telephone started to ring and people began to demand her attention.

Pushing the door to her office closed behind her with her foot, she dropped her briefcase on the floor and, discarding the top of her cup in the waste-paper basket, sat down and put her feet up on her desk. After a mouthful of blissfully rich coffee, she glanced over the front page of her newspaper. She liked to skim through the headlines before turning to the feature pages, although on Mondays she normally flicked immediately to the media section to catch up on the latest television news. This time, however, her eye was caught by a headline at the bottom of the page: TROJAN HORSE DELIVERS *COUP DE GRÂCE* IN TV BOARDROOM TAKE-OVER.

Kate swung her feet off the desk and sat up. She spread out the newspaper. The story went on:

The TV industry, already surprised by the appointment of media pundit Charles Jordan, to the post of head of Factual Programming at Channel 22 last week, woke up this morning to the shock news that Jordan is now Controller of Programmes. This follows the take-over of Channel 22 by one of the world's largest newspaper and publishing groups. According to industry sources, Jordan was the Trojan horse who opened the gates to the take-over of one of the youngest, but already ailing, terrestrial commercial TV channels. As new technology bites deeper into the audience share of all traditional terrestrial broadcasters, more take-overs and mergers are forecast.

Leo Carson, the much-respected former Controller of Programmes who announced his retirement yesterday, refused to comment further apart from saying that Jordan was an able and ambitious young man whom he wished well. More news and analysis in the media section.

Kate stared at the paper. She did not have the heart to turn to the other section. She had read all she needed to know. Part of her wanted to believe it was not true, but the evidence had been downstairs in reception. Although she knew it was hopeless, she dialled Leo's private office line.

Dorothy Mackay's brisk tones answered: 'Charles Jordan's office.'

'Dorothy, it's Kate Daniels. I've only just heard the news. Is Leo coming into the building today?'

'Mr Carson flew to his villa in Italy yesterday. I believe he's expecting to take an extended holiday.'

'Oh.' What else was there to say? Kate knew she would get nothing further out of Dorothy, whether about Leo's departure or Jordan's appointment. She could feel Dorothy's impatience on the other end of the line, but she couldn't resist asking a further question: 'Are you remaining with us, Dorothy?'

There was silence for a moment or two. '*No one* is indispensable, but yes, happily I have been asked to retain my present post and, in that capacity, Mr Jordan has instructed me to set up meetings with all heads of departments today. As the senior executive producer in your department and in the absence of a head, he has asked that I arrange one with you. Would ten fifteen be suitable?'

'I have a production planning meeting scheduled for ten thirty, but in the circumstances I could postpone it.'

'I suggest you do. Mr Jordan will be a *very* busy man for the next few days.'

'Ten fifteen it is, then,' said Kate in a light-hearted tone, although light-hearted was the last thing she felt as she replaced the receiver.

As she did, her office door burst open without a preliminary knock. It was Ruby, her secretary. What Ruby lacked in height she made up for with her outrageously high platform shoes, whose colours and variety never ceased to amaze Kate. Today's were red with large purple flowers on the front. The rest of her clothes lived up to the promise of her shoes. A tiny black ra-ra skirt displayed formidable thighs and a tight white-and-gold T-shirt left little to the imagination about breasts that defied every law of gravitational pull. Ruby's round pretty face was made even rounder by her close-cropped hair, which this week was bleached white in contrast to her black, velvety skin. She was the best secretary Kate had ever worked with, calmly dealing with the conflicting demands of a busy department and the often histrionic behaviour of some of the people in it, but today it was her turn to be angry.

'Have you heard?' she demanded in an outraged voice.

Kate nodded. 'I've been summoned to present myself to our new leader at ten fifteen. Can you reschedule the planning meeting?'

'Postpone it more like. Have you read your e-mails this morning?' demanded Ruby.

'No.' Kate switched on her computer.

'I'll save you the trouble. As far as I can see, almost our entire output has been put on hold. Only programmes which are already on air or due to be on the air within the next two months are allowed to continue in production. Everything else is cancelled.'

'*Cancelled*. Are you sure?' Kate stared at her, shocked.

'Or as good as.' Ruby came round to Kate's side of the desk and took her mouse, clicking into the e-mail programme. She pointed a long silver nail extension at the screen. '*See.*'

The message said that all new programming was suspended until full consultation with all departments had been completed.

'But they can't *do* that,' said Kate. 'What are they going to put in the schedules?'

'Repeats. I've been asked to deliver a full summary of our last three years' programming by the end of tomorrow.'

Kate's telephone line began to trill. Ruby made to

pick it up but Kate motioned her to leave it. Whoever it was could leave a message on her voice mail. Almost immediately, the line began to trill again. Kate could guess what the calls were about. Everyone would be desperate for information about the take-over.

'Ruby, would you mind fielding all my calls until I get back from my meeting with Jordan and if anyone wants to see me I'm busy. I don't care who it is.' It was already past nine o'clock and she needed time to prepare herself.

Ruby left the room, closing the door behind her, leaving Kate to stare at her computer screen. What was she meant to be preparing for? She needed someone to talk to and at moments like this, only one person would do. She reached for the telephone and, after checking the number in her filofax, dialled Majorca.

Robert's voice answered. '*Sí?*'

'Robert, it's Kate.'

'*Dear* heart, how are you?'

'Wretched. Do you know any tall cliffs I can throw myself off?'

'Now, now, I won't have talk like that. Tell auntie all. Is it *that* man again?'

'No. Yes . . . well partly. I've decided it's over with him.'

'Good! You've never made a better decision in your life.'

'I know. You're right.'

'You've told him?' demanded Robert.

'Not quite . . . I'll tell him when I next see him.'

'Why can't you just call? You know what you're like when you see him.'

Robert was the only person Kate had confessed to about the physical effect Max had on her. How she could not be near him without wanting to make love to him.

'It would be unfair just to end it on the phone after all this time.'

'*Unfair*!' Robert's ejaculation forced Kate to hold the receiver away from her ear. 'Unfair is a man who sleeps with two women at the same time and lies to both of them.'

'You're right. I know you're right,' she agreed reluctantly. 'I'll just call and tell him.'

'Good. Now what else can your agony aunt offer you advice with?'

Kate explained about Jordan.

Robert's voice became serious. 'It sounds to me like you've got a fight on your hands. But make sure you know what you're fighting for and that you really want it. Remember the old saying: be careful for what you wish – it just might come true.'

Robert's words echoed in Kate's head as she rode the lift to the twenty-second floor. What *did* she want? Until a few days ago she had been so sure that she had everything she wanted, now she was sure of nothing. Not even of what she wanted.

The lift doors opened to reveal a floor denuded of carpet. Dorothy Mackay was not at her desk, but her two assistants were. One of them looked up as Kate walked in. Kate knew her slightly as she had worked briefly in her department before moving up to the management floor, her name was Tina.

Kate indicated the floor. 'What's going on?'

Tina grinned. 'It seems we've got a new company logo which is going to be printed onto the carpets as though we don't know where we're working. The office is being completely redecorated too. We've had a Feng Shui expert in here this morning telling us that we're all sitting in the wrong places and that there's too much negative chi or something like that.' She started to giggle but stopped and immediately began to tap away on her computer as the door to Jordan's office opened and Dorothy appeared.

'Ah, Kate, you can go right in. Mr Jordan is expecting you.' She held the door open.

As it closed softly after Kate, Jordan got up from behind his desk and came forward, his hand held out. She had seen him before, but it had always been at a distance at some crowded television function. Kate's first impression on meeting him up close was how small he was and he was made even more diminutive by his casual dress – a dark Brooks Brothers button-down shirt and khaki chinos. A suit and tie might have given him greater bulk.

His handshake was brief and soft. 'Kate. I'm pleased to meet you. I've heard a lot about you. Shall we sit down?'

He indicated that they should sit together on a pair of hard white leather-and-chrome sofas which offered little in the way of comfort. They were new to the office since she had last been there. Leo had favoured deep old-fashioned leather furniture of the sort common to gentlemen's clubs. Kate recognised the sofas from a spread in an interior design magazine about industrial post-modern chic. They were comfortable enough if you had short legs like Jordan, but if you had long ones like her, you were left with the option of sitting awkwardly splayed, or stiffly upright. Kate opted for the stiffly upright and offered a prayer of thanks that she was wearing trousers rather than a short skirt.

She looked around, waiting for him to speak. Jordan had not wasted time in changing the office and getting rid of all signs of Leo. Not only had the sofas been replaced, but the place had been redecorated in shades of pale-blue and lavender which toned with the new lavender carpet. Kate wondered if this colour scheme was the work of the Feng Shui expert. She suspected

Jordan would have chosen a brasher one, judging by the fluorescent-soled trainers he wore. They were the kind which had been designed to shoe the feet of tall American basket-ball players, but had become the expensive trade mark of young men who made their living on the streets – usually by illegal methods. Kate's opinion must have registered on her face, as Jordan crossed his legs, bringing the trainers into even plainer view.

'I do hope you are going to be at one with me in introducing a new style of informality into the Channel, Kate. I want us to work together as I am an admirer of your work, but I think it's only fair for me to begin by putting my cards on the table and saying that I have a philosophy about programme making and, while other people have their own way of doing things, which may be as good as mine or even better, at *my* channel we do things *my* way. Anyone who wants to do otherwise had better consider their position now.'

There was no mistaking the implied threat in his pronouncement, but Kate could not help but feel she was being lectured by a self-important schoolboy. She attempted to concentrate on what Jordan was saying, trying to avoid looking at either his feet or his outsize Buddy Holly glasses. She settled for a point in the middle of his forehead.

'I am an unrepentant populist and I make no apologies for it,' he continued. 'The television industry has been run for far too long by Oxbridge-educated BBC types who think they know what's best. I'm the first of the new breed to reach the top. One of the *true* sons and daughters of the television age. We suckled television at our mothers' breasts. It is *our* heritage. The heritage of the common man not the privileged few and we must grasp it back from their hands.' He reached out and grabbed a handful of air, which he contemplated for a moment or two. Then he released it and looked at Kate, an almost messianic glint behind the lenses of his glasses. 'Would you like to hear my vision for this company, Kate?'

There seemed nothing else to do so she nodded.

'*Feel Good Family Values.*' He pronounced this slowly, as though talking to an idiot. 'No more sex or violence. No innuendo. No more knocking programmes.' He looked hard at Kate when he said this and she felt a faint sinking sensation. 'I want our audience to be as sure of our brand of programming as they are when they pick up a tin of baked beans in the supermarket. It will be wholesome nourishment that they can serve up at tea-time to the whole family. Every time they pick up the tin, or in our case turn on the channel, they will get exactly the same. No surprise ingredients that can give them indigestion or worse. Are you with me, Kate?'

Kate cleared her throat. The sinking feeling was rapidly turning into a sensation of drowning. 'I'm not sure that I am, Mr Jordan. I'm an investigative journalist. I can't quite see how I would fit . . .'

'Charles to you, Kate. I want none of that crap hierarchical stuff in my company.' He stood up and walked over to his desk. 'Come over here, Kate,' he commanded imperiously.

Kate followed him. Jordan's desk was large enough to stage a football match on and still leave room for some spectators. She stood in front of it, but he beckoned her impatiently round. She went and stood beside him.

He pointed to a large collection of frames on the desk. 'What do you see there, Kate?'

She looked. Each frame contained a photograph of the blonde weather girl who had so famously given up her successful career to marry him, surrounded by an assortment of three equally blond young children, all under five.

'Your family?'

'Absolutely. And who is there at the centre of it all?'

'Your wife.'

'*Exactly*!' he said triumphantly. 'A woman. The mother without whom nothing would be possible. The icon of the post-modern woman is the madonna and child. Not *the* Madonna of course.' He gave a dry little smirk at his own joke. 'Although she, too, has entered into the spirit of the *Zeitgeist* and reinvented herself as a mother with child.'

Kate was just about to say that Madonna's personal trainer had had something to do with her reinvention but thought better of it.

Jordan picked up one of the photographs of his family and gazed fondly at it. 'Do you know that when I turned on the television yesterday at mid-morning the BBC had a discussion on homosexual marriage, while on ITV they had a single mother talking about having a baby by artificial insemination. I don't want my children to be tuning into those kinds of things.'

He put the photograph down and stood looking out of his vast panoramic window at the London skyline. He waved a hand at nothing in particular. 'We're coming to the end of the millennium, Kate, and it's time to ring the changes.' He paused significantly. 'I want programmes which are life-style oriented, which are aspirational and inspirational. But most of all, I want you to deliver me ideas for programmes which are upbeat and promote old-fashioned family values, particularly those of motherhood. The mother was once sacred in our society. She was the protector of hearth and home, and I want to put her back there again.' He reached up and placed his hand on her shoulder. 'Are you with me, Kate?'

Eight

• • •

'*Balls* to sacred motherhood! When he's had his legs up in stirrups and had an episiotomy performed on him, then had a nine-pound lump of bawling flesh dragged out of a hole that's barely big enough to take even a small prick like him, *then* he can talk to me about motherhood,' declared Anita in a voice that caused heads in the open-plan office beyond Kate's to look up with interest.

Anita perched herself on the edge of Kate's desk and, in a dangerous manoeuvre, swung her legs round so that her feet rested on the window-sill. She defiantly lit a cigarette, ignoring the Channel's no smoking rule, and rested her elbows on her knees. It was her favourite position when she wanted a gossip with Kate.

'What *is* it about these men that they can't just let women suffer in peace? They talk as though they've just invented the whole process of pregnancy and birth. *Them*, mark you. They declare that they are this thing called a "new man".' She made apostrophe marks in the air with her fingers. 'Then they walk around with baby sick on their shoulders as though it's a medal received for courage in combat. Idiots like that one' – she jerked her head at the ceiling as if Kate could have any doubt as to whom she was talking about – 'would even turn birth into a spectator sport if they could have their way. It would be like the Romans and the Christian gladiators, with the women as the gladiators, bleeding and suffering, while the men urged them on. Push, breathe, no push *harder*. Well, *bollocks* to him!' she finished roundly.

Kate liked Anita. They were the same age and had first worked together as junior researchers nearly twelve years ago. They had done so on and off over the years, and by now Anita should have been an executive producer like Kate. She had more ability to spot a good story than anyone else Kate had ever worked with, but she had taken time off to have children – three of them – and as a result she was only an associate producer, which was barely a step up from being a researcher.

'Are you sure you won't join me?' Anita leant back and offered Kate a cigarette, grinning seductively and waggling the packet under her nose so she could smell the tobacco.

Kate smiled back but shook her head. Anita was not attractive in a conventional sense. She was short and broad-hipped. She didn't seem to care about clothes and usually wore a man's shirt and the kind of unflattering trousers that fitted the word 'slacks'. Her make-up was a gash of inexpertly applied lipstick, which transferred wholesale onto her first mug of coffee in the morning, and she wore her brown hair scraped back into a semblance of a French pleat which unerringly began to unravel from the moment she pinned it into place, until by the end of the day it formed a halo of untidy tendrils around her square freckled face. But Kate thought she had an earthy, sexy quality about her that was heightened by her deep voice, roughened by forty cigarettes a day for over twenty years, pregnant or not pregnant.

According to Anita, smoking had not affected the size of her babies – she only wished it had. If she ever got pregnant again – which she had no intention of doing – she would smoke sixty a day if it meant she could produce a small one. As she cheerfully announced to Kate after her third child, yet another bouncing boy, giving birth was not so much like shitting a brick as shitting Mount Rushmore.

Anita lit another cigarette and exhaled a long stream of smoke. 'So, have you any idea what's going to happen? There are rumours of redundancies and I've been asked to report to personnel.'

'I just don't know,' said Kate. 'After all that stuff about motherhood he talked another load of management gobbledegook about rationalisation of resources and right-sizing, but when I pressed him to tell me how it would affect this department he just fobbed me off with the excuse that nothing was certain. I've got to present proposals for what he calls life-style and aspirational programming by the end of the week, although exactly what he's looking for I'm not sure and I don't think he is either. The only thing I know is that he's not interested in serious journalism.'

Anita glanced at her watch and swung her feet down onto the ground, reluctantly stubbing out her cigarette. 'I guess I ought to go to personnel and learn the worst.'

'I'm sure it's probably just to discuss the renewal of your contract.' Kate tried to sound reassuring. 'If I'm going to have to make programmes about motherhood I need you around. You're the only sacred mother I know.'

Anita pulled a face and made a rude two-fingered gesture over her shoulder as she walked away.

'Good luck,' Kate called after her and reluctantly began to leaf through her contacts book. There were a number of people she had approached about a new investigative consumer series on multinational companies she had been developing, some of whom had provided her with confidential information at risk to themselves. She would have to tell them that the series was not going to happen, at least not yet. There had to be *something* she could rescue from this mess.

Tim, her deputy on the weekly current affairs show, knocked tentatively at her door, an offering of a mug of black coffee in his hand. Kate smiled at him as he placed it in front of her. He was still only twenty-eight and Kate thought it disgraceful that he should have been promoted over Anita. But he was keen and methodical, and she could not help liking him, even if he was a little earnest and a sense of humour was not his strong point. It amused her that he was in such awe of both her and Anita. He was a self-declared feminist and wanted desperately to be in sympathy with them, but at times he did not know how to deal with their less than politically correct views, particularly when Anita baited him, something she could not resist doing.

'There are hundreds of e-mail edicts,' he announced pointedly.

'Saying what?' asked Kate, gratefully sipping her coffee. She had no intention of reading them yet. She already had too much to think about.

'Well, the purge has begun and the first of those false "with sympathy" announcements have begun to appear. You know, the ones that begin "we are sorry to announce the departure of . . .". Why can't they just say that some poor sod's got the chop,' said Tim angrily. 'Then, after the roll-call for the execution, come the scraps for the reprieved: a list of cost-cutting measures which seem to suggest all we are allowed is one phone call, two sheets of paper and a return bus journey to central London a week, anything more being punishable by instant death. How on earth do they expect us to make television programmes?'

He was joined by Jenny, one of Kate's researchers. She looked worried. 'Are our jobs safe, Kate?'

Kate shrugged her shoulders. 'I wish I could put my hand on my heart and swear to you that they are,

Jenny, but I can't. All I can promise you is that I will fight to keep you all on.'

'I *know* you can do it, Kate,' said Jenny. 'Tim and I have been talking about it, haven't we Tim, and we agree that we're both right behind you whatever happens, aren't we, Tim?' She looked adoringly at him, two bright-red spots on her cheeks.

Jenny was a pretty blonde, a year younger than Tim. She was hard-working, if not particularly bright. She had also been in love with Tim for at least the last year, although he appeared to be the only person in the office not to have noticed. Kate felt almost motherly towards the two of them and had considered whether she ought to take Tim aside and tell him. But, as she also had a feeling that Jenny was the wrong girl for him, she had decided to say nothing. She was hardly a fit person to be offering advice on relationships.

Kate felt two sets of trusting eyes on her and tried to smile confidently although she almost resented them for putting their trust in her.

'Look, I'll do my best, but . . .' she began, but was interrupted as the entire floor was wished a cheery: 'Morning all.'

Kate glanced at her watch. It was after twelve but Ken, the senior director in the department, did not believe in starting his day until nearly lunch-time, at least when he wasn't filming. He was a portly, grey-haired man, somewhere in his mid-fifties, who sported a bushy beard and prided himself on being something of a bon viveur. He had started off in the industry as a runner when he was seventeen and constantly reminded everyone that he had seen, heard and done everything there was to do, so nothing could surprise him. He refused to direct any programme which meant he had to work between June and September, the months he spent in his beloved France where he owned a house in the Dordogne. He had bought it as little more than a cowshed twenty years before and had been renovating it ever since.

There were plenty of people at the Channel who did not like working with Ken as he could have an acerbic tongue. But Kate had always found that his acid remarks were reserved for those who did not know their jobs and always asked to have him on her team. Ken was particularly dismissive of what he termed the 'computer kids' – young directors who thought everything could be done with computers in the editing room. Kate had worked with that sort of director and understood exactly what he meant. They believed that if they missed a shot, or if it was not quite right, there was no problem, as it could all be sorted it out in the edit with the computer. But Kate, like Ken, believed that computers were no substitute for good journalism, although she was beginning to wonder whether this was a mark of growing older.

Ken was the only person in the office who could outshine Ruby in the brightness of his dress and today was no exception. He was wearing a sweater that was unusually colourful even for him. It was a combination of canary yellow and kingfisher blue, and with it he wore a white shirt, a lilac and yellow bow tie and rust-coloured trousers.

He held his arms wide as though to gather the whole room in his embrace. 'Well, me old chinas, your Uncle Ken is going to take you *all* out for a drink and I will brook no rejections. I don't care even if you're booked to lunch at Buckingham Palace. *Cancel* it.'

'And to what do we owe this honour?' Kate called.

Ken came and stood in her doorway. 'I have just been up to the ivory tower on the twenty-second floor to see the fair Dorothy, or as I prefer to call her, the Wicked Witch of the West. There I made my humble obeisance' – he swept a low bow at this – 'and placed my carefully composed resignation in her beautiful

105

white hands. But do not let those immaculately manicured digits fool you. Those hands have been stained by the blood of many a good man and I should know,' he added darkly. Ken had always hinted that he was one of the few people in the business who knew something about Dorothy Mackay's past.

Kate was shocked. 'Ken, you can't possibly mean it.'

'I do, my dear Kate,' he said with mock sorrow. 'I do.'

'But what will I do without you?'

'Like all faithless women, you will find a younger, better-looking man than me and forget that I ever existed.'

Kate got up from her desk and hugged him. 'Forget an old rogue like you? For a start your jumper is indelibly seared onto the back of my retina. I may never be able to see properly again.' She kissed him. 'But why?'

'Yes, *why*?' wailed Jenny and blew her nose loudly. She had started to cry.

'*Why*? I think a question that might more fruitfully be asked is: why not? The news this morning was enough to convince me that I have tarried much too long in a place that is meant for young men, *not* that I am old. On the contrary, I have a lissom young bride who urgently awaits me.' At this he winked knowingly. 'So I am going to carry her off to my chateau in the Dordogne and have my wicked way with her until these limbs are too weary to do more.'

Jenny blushed through her tears and blew her nose again to cover her embarrassment.

Ken's first wife had left him twenty years ago and he had been devastated. No one thought he would ever remarry. But two years before he had fallen in love with Beth, a production assistant some thirty years his junior. Much to everyone's amazement, they were married within six weeks.

Kate hugged him again. 'Although I will miss you

106

terribly, Ken, I can't think of a more wonderful thing to do.'

He raised a bushy eyebrow at her. 'Then it's about time you did it, my girl.' He wagged a finger at the other two. 'And that goes for all you youngsters. I lost my first wife, God rest her soul wherever she is, because I thought that television and my work was everything. Well, take it from an expert, it's not. There's a great big wide world out there and, although there are a lot of people in this building who think they run it with a flick of a switch, they don't. Get a life for yourselves before it passes you by and that's an *order*. Now.' He straightened his bow tie although it did not need it. 'Uncle Ken has given the lesson for the day, so let's go out and eat, drink and be merry, and get comprehensively pissed.'

'Yes, let's,' announced Anita's strangled voice from behind them.

They all turned round. Her face was drained of colour and her clothes, rather than eccentric, looked dowdy and ill-fitting.

'Anita?' asked Kate.

'They've fired me. The bastards have actually fired me.'

'But they can't . . .' protested Kate.

'Yes, they can. My contract finishes in less than a month's time and I'm surplus to requirements.' Anita put on a whining voice. 'They would have liked to keep me, but my work record shows that I have taken too much sick leave.' She returned to her normal voice. 'What they mean, of course, is that because this company is too miserly to have a crèche or flexible hours, so that working mothers like me can work, I'm being canned because I put my children first.'

'You ought to take them to an industrial tribunal for discrimination,' urged Tim.

'Yeah, right,' said Anita drily. 'If it were that easy,

almost every mother in the country would be suing her employer.' She lit a cigarette and Jenny, who had put a sympathetic arm around her shoulders, moved away. Kate noticed that Anita's hand was shaking as she put the cigarette to her lips. She inhaled deeply.

'Well, if ever there was a need for a drink I think it is now,' announced Ken. 'Shall we go forth?'

It was still early and Kate knew she should stay in the office and start working on ideas for new programmes, but right at that moment she didn't think any ideas that were suitable for broadcast in family viewing time would occur to her.

She took her jacket off the back of her chair and swung it around her shoulders. 'Okay, let's go.'

But before she could follow the others out of the door, her telephone began to trill.

'Shall I take that?' asked Ruby who was busy applying some glossy plum-coloured lipstick.

Kate looked down at the number of the caller which was registering on her telephone. It was Max's office number.

'No, you go ahead and I'll meet you down in reception in five minutes.' She pushed the door shut and picked up the receiver.

'Max?'

'Hi, sexy lady. Why don't you jump into a taxi and come over here for lunch? I'm hungry for your body.'

Kate felt a familiar fluttering in the pit of her stomach. 'I'm sorry, Max, but I can't. I have to go to a farewell party.'

'Can't you slip away?' Max sounded disappointed. 'I was planning a three-course meal but hey, I can live with fast food. I don't care what's on the menu as long as it tastes of you.'

Kate closed her eyes. She still wanted him. The memory of the animal scent of his body when he became excited filled her nostrils.

'Please . . .' It was Max. 'Have you any idea what just sitting here thinking about what I want to do to you is doing to me? I want to lay you across my desk and then . . .'

'Max, I'm sorry.' Kate had to fight to control her voice. 'I just can't.'

He groaned. 'How about tonight? I could get away for about an hour but no longer. There's something on that Harriet is insisting on going to.'

'Okay. Tonight. After six thirty. I'm sorry, Max, but I have to go now, my team is waiting for me.'

Kate put down the phone and walked slowly to the lift. She'd just had the opportunity to tell Max that they were finished and she had blown it. What had possessed her? She was behaving like a love-sick adolescent who had hormones for brains. But at least she could now tell him their affair was over to his face. It would be better that way. It was her chance to show that she was back in control.

Nine

● ● ●

Kate sat naked on the edge of her bed in the gloom. As she heard the front door close behind Max she pulled the bedclothes towards her and buried her face in them, inhaling the strong scent of his skin. The knowledge that she still wanted him swept over her like a tidal wave and threatened to drag her under.

After they had made love, she had lain in bed as he dressed, watching the subtle changes in his body as he unconsciously prepared to become a father and husband again. With every button he did up the lover who had arrived at her flat barely an hour ago, already aroused, his hands and his lips rough on her body in his urgency to possess her, slipped further and further away. Those same hands which had lifted her and carried her to bed would soon be playfully cuddling his daughters and the lips which had been greedy to devour her body would shortly place a dutiful kiss on Harriet's upturned cheek. By the time Max bent over the bed to give her a farewell kiss, Kate could tell from his eyes that he had already left her.

She closed her eyes to block out the memory. Why couldn't she have him. Not just for a snatched hour or two, but always? If he *really* loved Harriet and his children, how could he continue coming to her bed, especially when Harriet was carrying his child, the baby that Jessica had said he wanted as badly as

110

Harriet? Surely no one would risk losing so much unless it was for love?

Kate opened her eyes, aware of another presence in the room. A grey shadow padded softly across the floor and leapt up onto the bed, sniffing suspiciously at the tangled bedclothes. She had thrown Hemingway out before Max had arrived, but she must have left the kitchen window open.

She reached out and began to stroke him. Hemingway stiffened for a moment, his tail twitching, then he relaxed, sitting back on his haunches and regarding her quizzically.

'You know you're not allowed on the bed,' said Kate, making no move to push him off.

Hemingway lifted one of his back paws and vigorously started to scratch behind his ear.

'Wonderful. You're probably giving me fleas.' Kate tossed the bedclothes over him. Hemingway thrashed madly around before bursting out into the fresh air and leaping like an animal possessed onto the floor, where he set about smoothing his ruffled fur with his tongue. Every fibre of his body indicated outrage at this indignity.

Kate watched him for a moment or two, then reluctantly stood up and stretched. When she had come home there was a message on her machine from Jessica, reminding her that she had promised to go to her drinks party that evening and that Jessica would never forgive her if she didn't come.

It was just as well that it had been there. With everything else that had been happening, Kate had forgotten all about it. She was tempted to ring and say she had too much work to do, as she hated parties and Jessica always forgave her after a show of being hurt. But with Max gone, the flat suddenly seemed very empty and she felt in need of company.

Wrapping herself in her oversized towelling robe,

111

she picked up the bottle of champagne which Max had brought with him, as always, but which they had barely touched that evening, and headed for the kitchen, turning on lights as she went. Hemingway padded at her heels, his nose raised expectantly in the air as he sensed the possibility of food.

She poured herself a glass of champagne and opened the cupboard where she kept Hemingway's tins of salmon. It was empty. Between Max, work and going down to her parents for the weekend, she had not been near a shop for days. She bent down and peered into the fridge. The glacier in the icebox was beginning to threaten the rest of the compartments. She would have to defrost it soon.

Kate sniffed cautiously at a carton of milk. Two minutes more and it would be sour, but it would do for Hemingway. She had no intention of going to the corner shop tonight. She could manage with black coffee. She poured the milk into Hemingway's bowl and considered the rest of the contents of the fridge. There was a packet of smoked salmon, past its sell-by date. Kate slit it open with a knife and sniffed it warily. It smelt all right. Smoking preserved food for months and supermarkets were always over-cautious. Last year she had made a programme showing just how much food was wasted because of sell-by dates. It had provoked a lot of newspaper articles.

Kate cut the thin slices into even smaller pieces. Dividing it into two equal lots, she scraped one onto a plate which she placed on the floor for Hemingway and, after a cautious lick, he began to devour it as though starving. Then she broke two eggs into a bowl and, after beating them rapidly, melted some butter in a small pan and poured them in, adding the remainder of the smoked salmon. In a few minutes she had a creamy mound of scrambled eggs, which she piled onto a plate. She would have liked some bread to go

112

with it, but her bread-bin had revealed a growth of mould that would have made a piece of gorgonzola proud.

There were some rice cakes in the biscuit container, which she had bought in a momentary fit of healthiness, but one bite had been enough to convince her that good for her though they might be, they were akin to eating polystyrene, although the latter probably tasted better.

Kate stood, leaning against the kitchen cabinet, and wolfed down the scrambled eggs. She was hungrier than she had thought. She had only had a salad sandwich for lunch and it wasn't good to drink on an empty stomach. She put her empty plate in the sink and, after drinking another glass of champagne, drained the bottle into her glass and headed for the shower, sipping as she went.

It was nearly half past eight when she climbed out of her taxi and walked up the steps to Jessica's house. Before she could ring the bell the front door opened to allow an early guest to leave and Kate found herself face to face with Jessica's husband, Hugo.

He stood, blocking her way, a wineglass held indolently in one hand. 'Well, hel-*lo* there, sexy,' he drawled, his eyes sliding up and down her body.

Kate had never understood why Jessica found Hugo so attractive or, for that matter, why he had once featured as one of the ten most handsome men in London in an evening newspaper article. He had come fifth, after two actors, a chef and a hairdresser. Blonds had never been to her taste and, while his curly hair, blue eyes and almost girlishly rose-bud-shaped lips might have been much appreciated by the older boys at the public school the Hon. Hugo Hemsley-Green had attended, Kate found them vacuous. Never more so than when the eyes that the over-enthusiastic woman journalist had dubbed cornflower-blue in the article were glassy and bloodshot with drink, as they were now. Hugo had the appearance of a man who had started his own personal party early.

'Do I stand here for the next two hours or am I going to be allowed to come in?' she snapped.

'Only if you are prepared to pay the entrance fee, which for you is a kiss.' Hugo thrust his head forward to present his lips, but in doing so he lost his balance and tottered down a couple of steps, giving Kate the chance to brush past him into the entrance hall.

'A lucky escape, but you won't get away so easily next time,' Hugo called after her.

The hall, which was the size of most people's front rooms, was full of people and Kate looked around for someone she knew to talk to, *anyone*, just so long as she could keep away from Hugo. But a quick glance revealed no one she knew, or wanted to know for that matter. All she could see were identikit versions of Hugo – blond, tousle-haired young men wearing bored expressions and expensively crumpled linen clothes who seemed more interested in themselves than in the pretty young girls in bottom-skimming mini-dresses who clung to their elbows like that season's fashion accessories.

She forced her way through the crush and looked through the door into the main living-room. The central dividing panelled oak doors had been opened to create a room nearly forty feet in length, which was predominantly a rich, dusky pink – Jessica's favourite colour. Extravagant displays of white lilies graced the mantelpieces of the ornately scrolled fireplaces, made of pale-grey marble shot with pink, which dominated both rooms. The warm, vanilla-like scent of the lilies permeated the air, completing the feeling of opulence.

A good-looking waiter, with impossibly white teeth and perfect bone structure, offered Kate a tray of drinks. There were several other similarly young and handsome waiters wandering round with trays and artistic-looking snacks arranged on silver platters. Kate decided that the catering company Jessica had hired for the evening must employ out-of-work actors. Such well-honed beauty would not have been acquired merely for the task of serving drinks. She avoided the cocktails on the tray that was being offered to her and helped herself to a glass of red wine. She took a sip, then looked around for Jessica.

Unlike the homogeneity of dress in the hall, in this room anything went: from pin-striped suits to jeans and T-shirts, and from logo-laden fashion victim to frilly, born-again hippie. That, combined with the low but animated hum of conversation peppered with laughter, indicated that this was where Jessica's, rather than Hugo's, friends were gathered. While all his cronies worked in advertising, Jessica's were a diverse group. She acquired friends in the same way some people accumulated foreign coins – everywhere she went she came back with a handful of them. And rather like souvenirs, at the time she probably imagined they might be useful, or even decorative, which some of them undoubtedly were, but mostly they had a vague curiosity value. However, they could always be relied upon to turn up at her parties.

Kate spotted Jessica's slender figure at the end of the room. She had abandoned her medieval look for the evening, no doubt at Hugo's request, and wore a calf-length sheath dress of antique gold silk. She looked lovely, her hair a halo of paler gold around her shoulders.

Jessica was deep in conversation and had not spotted her, so Kate made her way over. As she reached her, Jessica's face lit up in recognition and the woman to whom she had been talking turned around. Kate sensed the blood draining from every tiny vein and artery in her face until it felt like a tight mask. It was Harriet.

'Kate! I'm so glad you managed to make it.' Jessica brushed Kate's cheek with her lips. 'I was just telling Harriet how well she looked, don't you think so?'

Kate managed to nod, her mouth dry. She had not seen Harriet in years. At university she had been small and slim, with long, thin, dark hair parted in the middle and reaching almost to her waist, strands of which she constantly twisted around her hands as she stood or perched at the edge of groups. Harriet had never joined in or voiced her opinion, she had always been on the edge of things, silently waiting. Sometimes a man would get up and leave the group and Harriet would follow him, although there had been no communication between them that anyone else had noticed. She had irritated many of the other women students – Kate among them – with her passivity and her willingness to wait patiently on men. But all her waiting had paid off. She had got the man she had wanted in the end, thought Kate – Max.

She had not changed much since their university days although she looked far from the 'well' that Jessica claimed – quite the opposite. Her stomach seemed far too large for her slight frame, and her face was pale and drawn. The purple shadows under her eyes resembled bruises. She looked as though she had made an effort for the evening, but it had not helped. Her make-up had been applied with a careless hand. Her foundation was too dark and stopped at her jaw-line, and pink shiny blusher had been streaked uncompromisingly across her cheek-bones. The dark-red lipstick which she had applied in an attempt to make her lips look fuller had transferred itself to her teeth and to the rim of the glass of orange juice she was twisting around in her hands. She was dressed in what looked like a little girl's party dress. It was made of deep-blue velvet and edged with white lace around the neck and wrists, and was high-busted to allow for her stomach. Just like a little girl, she also wore thick blue tights, black shiny ballet pumps and a black velvet Alice band in her hair, which was now cut to shoulder length. Kate automatically held out her hand, even though every instinct was screaming at her to turn and walk out. At that moment she hated Max. Why hadn't he warned her that he and Harriet would be at Jessica's party?

'It's nice to see you after such a long time,' she heard herself saying. 'Jessica's right, you are looking well.'

The hand that briefly took hers felt as though it was made of parchment. From touching Kate, it went to rest on the child in her belly. 'Thank you. I was just telling Jessica that I've been having a bit of a rough time with this one, but thankfully things have settled down now and I'm feeling fine.'

Harriet's voice was light and little-girlish. It forced the listener to stoop towards her to catch what she was saying.

'I'm just so pleased that you decided to come,' said Jessica. 'Hugo and I are always bumping into Max at parties, but you're never with him. I consider it quite a coup that you've come tonight.'

Kate dimly remembered that Jessica had mentioned something about trying to get Harriet along to one of her parties. Harriet had recently become one of the parent governors at the nursery school Jessica wanted Thomas to attend. Failure to get into the school was tantamount to being considered a social leper, at least in Jessica's eyes.

'Honestly, darling,' she had told Kate, 'attending a parents' meeting at that school is like being at the BAFTA awards. Anybody who is anybody has a child there. Hugo thinks I'm being silly, but if he wants to make film deals he ought to take more interest in

Thomas's education. When I went round there the other day, Jerry what's-his-name, you know, the one who produced last year's top-grossing film, was delivering his four-year-old to the school in person. I nearly went up to him and introduced myself but I thought it might look a bit gauche, so I smiled and he actually smiled back. Next time I will make some comment about how his son and mine are going to the same school and how nice it would be for his son to come to tea some time and get into conversation that way. It will be so much better than just coming out and saying my husband is a director who has a film he wants you to finance, don't you think?'

Harriet flipped her hair back from her shoulder although it did not need flipping. 'I don't like leaving the children. You know how it is.'

Kate caught a passing waiter and exchanged an empty glass for a full one. Had she sensed the hint of a maternal rebuke passing between Harriet and Jessica?

'Oh, I know *exactly* how you feel,' said Jessica quickly. 'I simply hate leaving Thomas too. But Maria is so wonderful with him and Hugo does so like having me beside him on certain occasions that I feel it's my duty, although, of course, one does feel torn at times.'

'I only came along this evening because of Max. He said that there was some American producer in town who is interested in one of his scripts and that he would be here tonight,' said Harriet. 'Max thought it would look good if I met him too. A united front, so to speak.'

'Oh, that must be Chip or is it Chuck Cline? I can never get those sorts of names right, he's a big player in LA,' said Jessica disingenuously. 'Hugo's agent set up lunch the other day, and Hugo and Chuck got on so well that Hugo invited him here tonight, but he hasn't arrived as yet.'

Now Kate understood why there were so many

people milling about in the hall rather than near where the drinks were kept. Word travelled fast on the media tom-toms when there was a Hollywood producer in town.

'Max and Chuck have had several long transatlantic telephone conversations,' said Harriet competitively. 'It's just that their diaries haven't allowed them to get together yet, but I gather lunch is in the offing.'

'Well, I'm sure Chuck will be along soon. In the meantime, can I leave you with Kate while I make sure all my other guests are all right? I'm sure you two have a lot to talk about after not seeing each other for so long.' Jessica gave them both a gay smile and departed, trailing a waft of floral perfume in her wake.

A waiter arrived in the silence she left behind. Kate took another glass of wine. Harriet seemed to be waiting for her to say something. They had had nothing in common when they were at university together and had even less now, unless you counted Max. 'Congratulations on your cookery books. I gather they are very successful,' she managed after an awkward moment or two.

The reply was almost an accusation. 'You're not a vegetarian, then?'

Kate shook her head. 'No. Neither am I much of a cook.' She attempted to lighten the conversation. 'Thank God for my local Italian deli and the food counters of the blessed St Michael. Where would working women like me be without them?'

Her reward was a frosty smile. 'You obviously don't have any children.'

Kate could not think of anything more to say, at least nothing that would not betray what she was feeling. She had become aware that her whole body was charged with the expectation that Max was somewhere nearby. She always felt the same around him and not even having his pregnant wife standing in front of her could alter that. She knew she had to find some excuse to get away from Harriet. But it was too late. From the look in Harriet's eyes she sensed that Max was behind her.

Before she could move, Kate felt the palm of his hand on the small of her back as he kissed her lightly on the cheek. Such a casual gesture and yet so intimate. How could it be construed as anything other than a friendly greeting between old acquaintances? So why did it feel as though the outline of his hand had been branded onto her skin?

'Kate. Where have you been keeping yourself? I never see you these days.'

The corners of his eyes had crinkled up just enough, his mouth was composed in precisely the right smile of surprise and pleasure. How could he be so casual, lie so easily? Just two hours before, their naked, sweating bodies had been grinding together on her bed.

'You know how work is . . .' It was lame, but it was an answer.

'Kate and I were just discussing cooking, weren't we?' said Harriet.

'Were you?' said Max, his right eyebrow lifting slightly as he looked from her to Kate. 'When I saw you two together I wondered what you were talking about.'

'And the baby, of course,' said Kate. 'Harriet was saying what a hard time she's been having with this one.'

Max looked at Harriet. 'But that's all over with now, isn't it, love?'

He had used the word 'love' but it did not sound to Kate as though that was what he meant. Nor was he asking a question, it sounded more like a command.

Kate felt the pressure of his hand on her back again and she almost jumped, but Max was looking at Harriet.

'I've just seen Sheena in the hallway, she was asking

where you were. She seemed very excited about your idea for your next book; she said it sounded like another best-seller,' said Max. Sheena was Harriet's agent. He looked at Kate. 'Harriet has had this idea for a vegetarian cookbook for expectant mothers, starting with preconception and ending with weaning.'

'How clever,' said Kate faintly.

Harriet's demeanour suddenly became brisk and businesslike. 'I really ought to talk to Sheena. I want to get this deal tied up as soon as possible. The last time we got bogged down with the illustrations and I'm not prepared to allow *that* to happen again. I want everything signed and sealed before the baby arrives.' She marched off determinedly.

Kate found herself guided into the corner with Max's powerful frame blocking her view of the room. There was a group of people nearby, but they were involved in a lively discussion which prevented anyone over-hearing what Max was saying. All the same, he kept his voice to a husky murmur. 'You look so sexy in that dress I could eat you. Starting with your little toes, working my way up slowly to your gorgeous knees, then to your luscious, oh so tasty thighs and then . . .'

The proximity and scent of Max's body was making sensible thought hard. Kate drained her glass of wine. 'This is neither the time nor the place, Max.' She wanted to stay angry with Max; she *should* stay angry with him. But she could already feel her rage draining away and being replaced by desire.

He bent his head, so that his lips were close to her ear. She could feel his warm breath stirring the tiny delicate hairs on her cheek. 'Then let's go back to your flat. I want to fuck you again, right *now*.' He straightened up, his eyes searching hers. Daring her.

A waiter hovered at Max's elbow. Kate reached past him and took another glass of wine. 'You're crazy.'

'About you, yes.' He turned and took some whisky

from the proffered tray. 'Harriet will soon be tired and want to go home. She always does. I'll play the good husband and take her, then say I'm coming back to the party to talk to this producer but instead I'll meet you at your flat. No one will be any the wiser.'

Kate drank some more wine. Max wasn't crazy, she was. It was idiotic, but in spite of his pregnant wife standing a few yards away and a room full of people, any of whom might at any moment guess what was going on right at that moment, more than anything else in the world, the only thing she wanted to do was make love to Max. If he reached for her now and kissed her she would respond, not caring what anyone thought. She could see the same thought in his eyes.

'*Max!*' Jessica's voice cut between them like a cleaver. Their heads drew back.

Jessica's eyes were wide as she looked from one to the other. 'Sheena asked me to find you. Harriet is feeling unwell, so she's taken her upstairs to lie down and Chuck Cline has arrived. Do you want me to order you a taxi so you can take Harriet home?'

Max straightened his jacket. 'Let Harriet rest. Where's Cline?' He was gone almost before Jessica could reply.

It was Kate's turn to meet Jessica's questioning eyes, but Jessica spoke first, almost as though she wanted to forestall anything that Kate might say. 'Max can be a very naughty man at times, particularly when he's had a few whiskies. You ought to be careful, Kate.'

'I know.' Kate looked down. There was no need to tell. It would be unfair on Jessica. 'We've always flirted, ever since university. It never comes to anything, of course.'

The lie smoothed everything over. Jessica smiled happily. She linked her arm through Kate's. 'Well, I've got *just* the man you *ought* to flirt with. He's perfect for you. His name is Paul, he's fifty-two, unattached, divorced, no kids, *very* solvent and I know he will adore you. Oh, and I also ought to add that he's *seriously* gorgeous. Men like him aren't available too often, so come on, no arguments.'

Kate let Jessica lead the way but they made slow progress as Jessica stopped to talk to everyone, introducing Kate to the people she did not know, occasioning a polite exchange of civilities which Kate had even less of a heart for than usual as she was straining to see Max.

When they emerged into the hall she finally saw him. He was towering over a short, overweight man, wearing tortoiseshell glasses of the type she always associated with Americans. Kate assumed this to be the eagerly awaited Chuck Cline. He had not got much further into the house than the front doormat where he now stood patiently, sipping his mineral water and nodding his head as he listened to Max. There was a disconsolate crowd of people milling at Max's elbows, trying to get to speak to Cline, but Max had used his physical advantage to get between them and the American, and looked as though he intended to remain that way for quite some time.

Jessica led Kate to a smaller sitting-room at the back of the house, which had french windows and steps down to the garden. Its predominant colour was a pale, almost translucent green, although there were occasional touches of pink. Comfortable rattan furniture and an old pine dresser that stretched the length of one wall made it feel more lived-in than the rest of the house which, while beautiful, reminded Kate of a carefully staged set.

There were four or five people comfortably ensconced in armchairs and several more in the garden. Standing at the top of the steps leading down to the garden was a tall, slim man with thick, greying hair. He was dressed in a lightweight, well-cut suit, that immediately stood out by not being linen. He was alone and appeared to be contemplating Jessica's garden, a glass of white wine in his hand.

Jessica released Kate's arm and went up to him. 'Paul, there's someone I'd like you to meet.'

He turned. Kate noted that he was wearing a tie, something else that marked him out from the conscientiously tieless media people. It was grey silk, perfectly understated, just like his suit.

'This is Kate Daniels. Kate, Paul Hegley.'

He held out a hand. It was firm and smooth to the touch, its grip perfectly judged. Blue eyes held hers for just the requisite length, but long enough for Kate to know that she had been checked over in the same way she'd checked him, and both liked what they saw.

In any other circumstances Kate would have been interested in him. The men Jessica decided were perfect for her were usually the exact opposite. Eager to play Cupid, Jessica had a habit of building Kate up into a combination of Helen of Troy and Marie Curie. *And* she promised the men that Kate was dying to meet them because she had heard such wonderful things about them, thus guaranteeing that they would be over-eager and manage to embarrass both Kate and themselves within moments. But not this man. Kate could not imagine him being over-eager about anything or embarrassing himself.

'I really must go and see what the caterers are up to in the kitchen – you can't trust the hired help these days,' trilled Jessica. 'But I'm sure you two will find *lots* to talk about.' She gave Kate a knowing glance and left.

It was Kate's turn to feel embarrassed. To her horror she could feel a dull red blush spreading to her cheeks.

Paul grinned. 'Don't worry. I think I have a pretty clear idea of Jessica's intentions.' He held his hands up in mock surrender. 'You can leave without saying a word and I won't hold it against you.'

Kate couldn't help smiling. 'Jessica loves to play the matchmaker. She's forever trying to set me up with the perfect man.'

'At the risk of embarrassing you again, this less than perfect man can only say that he is honoured to be among the chosen ones. Although he thinks the rest of them must have been mad to let you get away.'

'Maybe I'm the mad one.' She had not meant it to sound that way, but Kate's words sounded bitter even to her own ears.

Paul raised a quizzical eyebrow. 'Why do I get the feeling that I have just walked into the middle of something?'

'I'm sorry. It's not you. Another time . . .'

'There's an old-fashioned song, but then, I'm an old-fashioned man, which goes something along the lines of "It's the wrong time, and the wrong place, though your face is charming it's the wrong face . . ."' He looked at her. 'Would that be near the mark?'

Kate nodded. 'Something like that. And I like that song too.'

'My disappointment grows with every passing minute.' He smiled ruefully. It made him look boyish.

And he did have a charming face, thought Kate, mentally damning Jessica for finally producing a man she could really like but at just the wrong time. 'I really *am* sorry,' she said.

'So am I. Dare I say another time?'

His eyes held hers for a moment or two. They were very blue, not like Max's which were sometimes grey, sometimes blue.

'I hope so.'

Kate turned and left, taking another glass of wine from a passing waiter as she went. It was her fifth, but she was fine. In fact, better than fine. She felt she could

125

do anything. Now was the time to confront Max. He had to make a choice – Harriet or her.

There was an even greater crush in the hall as many more people had arrived. Jessica's 'few people for drinks' had, as always, turned into at least two hundred. Kate pushed her way through, looking for Max's broad shoulders, but she could not see him anywhere. She reached the bottom of the stairs and climbed up the first few steps so that she could have a better view.

As she sifted the faces below her in the hall for the one she sought, a blonde woman in a red dress that appeared to be held together only by a few laces rushed down the stairs, knocking her elbow. She did not stop to apologise, but pushed her way through the crowd to the front door and ran out, leaving it open. Kate had just put her hand to her mouth to lick the red wine which had splashed over it when her elbow was jogged once more, this time by Hugo.

He stopped and turned. 'Did you see where she went?'

'Who?' asked Kate, knowing precisely whom he meant.

'The girl. The blonde girl in the red dress. Debbie.' Hugo's voice was impatient.

Kate looked at him. His hair was even more tousled than usual and the buttons of his shirt had been done up wrongly. 'Some blonde just rushed out of the front door. She looked as though something nasty was chasing her. You perhaps, Hugo?'

'Fuck and twice fuck,' declared Hugo running his hand through his hair. 'Look, Kate. You wouldn't mind going upstairs and talking to Jessica, would you? She's a bit upset. I've tried to explain it was nothing, just a bit of harmless fun, but she gets so hysterical over these things.'

Kate stared at Hugo, her eyes glittering. 'You *bastard.*'

Hugo snorted. 'Don't come the innocent with me. I'm hardly the only person around here indulging in a bit of extra-marital bonking, am I?'

'Fuck you!' said Kate, throwing the remains of her glass of red wine down the front of his white shirt and cream trousers. She turned and marched up the stairs.

'I wish you would, Kate. Oh, how I wish you would,' she heard him calling after her.

Ten
• • •

Kate reached the first landing where she hesitated, unsure of herself. All the doors were closed to deter guests making themselves at home and the last thing she wanted to do was to open the one of the room where Harriet was lying down.

She looked around. She had been in the house so many times that she should know it nearly as well as her own flat, but thinking clearly was difficult as she was still in such a rage with Hugo. The knowledge that he knew, or had guessed, about Max made it worse. The nursery, the nanny's room and bathroom, and another bathroom plus a guest bedroom were on this floor. Harriet was most likely to be in the guest-room.

Almost as though to confirm this, the door at the end of the passage opened and Sheena, Harriet's agent, came out. 'Were you looking for Harriet?' she enquired. 'She was beginning to wonder where the taxi had got to.'

'No. I was looking for Jessica. I don't know what's happened to the taxi. You know how undependable minicabs are.'

Sheena heaved an irritated sigh. 'I suppose I'll have to go and chase it up, and Max too. That man is absolutely impossible. He doesn't give a damn for his wife, like all bloody men. Tell me, why do women bother with them?'

Sheena had famously come 'out' as a lesbian some years ago. She chose a book launch to announce her divorce and introduce a seventeen-year-old, shaven-haired girl called Finn, who had a Chinese dragon tattooed on her right shoulder, as her lover. Her former husband, who had also been her partner in their literary agency, had run off with their eighteen-year-old secretary. However, Finn had not been much in evidence recently and Jessica had giggled to Kate that Sheena had drunkenly propositioned her at her last party.

Sheena did not seem to require an answer to her question, so Kate stood back to let her pass. She was just about to go up to the next floor when she heard a snuffling sound, which sounded like someone crying, from behind the nearest door. Kate tapped lightly and, when there was no reply, pushed it open. It was a bathroom and it was occupied by two of Hugo's friends. One was snorting a line of cocaine from a mirror with the help of a twenty-pound note. Kate slammed the door shut and headed up to the next floor. This time she did not need to guess where Jessica was, the door to the main bedroom was ajar and Kate could hear loud sobbing. She went in. Jessica was curled up in a foetal position on a *chaise longue* near the window, her shoulders heaving.

'Jessica?' As Kate crossed the room she noticed that the bedspread on their king-sized bed, which was draped in green and gold silk from a wedding sari, was rumpled.

Jessica looked up. Her eyes were red-rimmed and swollen. 'How could he? And on *my* bed, too.'

Kate sat down beside her. 'I'm so sorry.'

Jessica sniffed and reached across for some tissues, which were in a mother-of-pearl container on a small table. She blew her nose.

'He says it's just a drunken flirtation, but it's been

going on for ages. I know. I can always tell.' She looked at Kate, her eyes glistening with tears. 'You can, you know. It's the little things. They always give him away. But he's never invited one of them to our house before. Not to one of my parties.' A tear rolled down her cheek.

'Why do you put up with it? Hugo's a bastard.'

'But I *love* him,' wailed Jessica and began to cry again.

Kate put her arms around her and held her.

Eventually Jessica took a deep breath and dabbed her eyes. 'I knew what he was like when I married him. It's difficult for a man like Hugo. He's surrounded by pretty young actresses all day and they'll do anything for a part.' The tears began to well up in her eyes again. 'I was a pretty young actress once, so I know all about it. That's how I got him.'

'You're *still* a pretty young actress,' said Kate fiercely, 'and what he was like when you met him is no excuse for what he does now. I really don't understand why you stay with him.'

Jessica dried her eyes and, with one more sniff, stood up and began to smooth her dress. 'I wish I could explain, Kate, but you've never been a mother. It makes everything different. Hugo is the father of my child. We're bound together by blood, our son's blood.'

It was like ripping a scab from a festering wound.

Kate stood up and took Jessica by the shoulders. 'I've never heard such utter rubbish in my life. Hugo's ability to ejaculate seed merely qualifies him as a wanker, not as a good father and certainly not as a decent husband. It's about time you stopped acting like a martyr. The man's an utter shit and if you can't see it then maybe you deserve him.'

She turned and walked away, leaving Jessica open-mouthed, tears once more welling up in her eyes.

Half-way down the stairs Kate sat down heavily. She put her head in her hands and let out a loud groan. She should go back. Jessica hadn't meant what she said any more than she had, at least not the bit about deserving Hugo. Nobody did.

But before she could move she heard Max's unmistakable voice above the clamour of the party: 'Clear the way, please. My wife needs air. She's pregnant.'

Kate lifted her head and peered through the banisters. Max had one solicitous arm around Harriet's shoulders and the other was gesturing that people should stand aside so that they could reach the front door. It was a performance worthy of Laurence Olivier. Another movement just below her caught Kate's eye. It was Paul Hegley putting on his coat.

She stood up and leant over the banisters. 'You're not leaving already, are you?'

Paul looked up, his face creasing into a delighted smile when he saw it was Kate. 'I'd just about given up looking for you. I wanted to give you my telephone number before I left and hoped it might be in order to ask for yours.'

Kate came down the stairs to where he now stood at their foot. 'I can offer you something much better than my telephone number.'

'If it's a date, consider it in my diary. Just name the day, the time and the place. Wild horses wouldn't keep me away.'

'How about now and my flat.'

Paul's face registered surprise, if not shock, but he quickly recovered his composure. 'I assume we're not talking about dinner.'

'That depends on what you like to eat.'

His eyes narrowed. 'I wouldn't like to get this wrong.'

'You're not.' Kate kissed him full on the lips. 'Is the message clear enough?'

He nodded.

Spotting Max looking at them, she kissed him again,

this time putting her arms around him and making her kiss long and lingering. Paul returned the kiss in kind, although she could feel uncertainty in his lips. Before he could change his mind she took his hand, led him past Max and Harriet and out of the front door.

The taxi ride to her flat did not take long, which was just as well. Having invited Paul into her bed, Kate could think of nothing more to say to him. Thankfully, he seemed to feel the same way and was content to sit in the other corner of the taxi.

The ride was completed in silence and when the taxi drew up outside her flat Paul scrambled out ahead of her and held the door.

On the pavement Kate fished in her bag for her keys and some money. 'I'd better warn you that I have a cat who doesn't like visitors, especially of the male variety,' she said, opening her purse.

Paul waved her offering aside and paid the fare. He looked at her rather oddly in the light of the street lamp. 'Beware of the cat?'

Kate nodded. 'He's very territorial.'

'I think I can manage a cat.' He smiled and took the keys out of Kate's hand, his fingers closing round hers for a second as he did. He opened the front door to the flats. 'What's he going to do, whisker me to death?' he asked as they walked down the hall. Kate indicated the door to her flat and he put the key in the lock. 'Anyway, animals like me. It's just a question of showing them who's boss.'

As they walked in there was no sign of Hemingway. Kate relaxed and turned to joke that they were in luck as it was probably a night he had gone looking for sex, but before she could say anything a grey ball of fur shot across the room and stood looking up at them, his yellow eyes flashing dangerously.

Kate bent to pick him up, intending to put him out of the front door, but Paul brushed her aside and reached out a hand. 'Here kitty, kitty. *Nice* kitty, kitty.' He turned and looked up in triumph at Kate as Hemingway appeared to be sniffing his fingers. But his look of triumph turned to one of agony as Hemingway hissed and raked his claw along the back of Paul's hand.

Paul snatched it back and stood up, clutching it. 'That *damn* cat. *Look* what it's done.'

He held his hand out to Kate. Blood was beginning to well up from the scratch. Kate fished out a tissue and dabbed ineffectually at the wound. Paul winced and pulled his hand away. 'That cat is a menace.' His voice shook with outrage. 'I think I should get this checked at a hospital. I might need a tetanus booster.'

Kate advanced on Hemingway who was sitting, nonchalantly cleaning his paws. 'Out!' she shouted, pointing at the door.

Hemingway backed away. Kate made a lunge for him but he turned and raced across the floor and leapt up onto the breakfast bar where he knocked over a mug of cold coffee that Kate had left there earlier. Using a stool as a stepping stone, he leapt from the bar onto the kitchen work top, sending a pile of dirty crockery crashing into the sink. Pursued by a yelling Kate, he leapt back onto the breakfast bar via a cupboard top, skidded through the large pool of cold coffee, off the other side and down onto the Persian carpet, where he added coffee-coloured paw prints to its intricate age-old design, before leaping onto the cream sofa and racing along its back, dripping coffee as he went.

Frustrated, Kate bent down, took off one of her high-heeled shoes and hurled it at him. But her aim was blurred by alcohol and the shoe went wide, hitting her art deco lamp instead. For a moment it seemed to have survived the shock, but then, almost in slow motion, it fell forward, its glass shade shattering with a loud crash on the wooden floor.

There was a moment's shocked silence, then Hemingway, sensing that this was probably a good opportunity to make himself scarce, shot past Paul's legs and out of the door.

Kate raced after him, brandishing her other shoe, but all she found was a madly flapping cat door where Hemingway had escaped from the hall into the street.

She walked slowly back into the flat. Paul was holding his hand under the kitchen tap.

'I think I have some plasters in the bathroom,' she offered lamely.

'A strong drink would help heal my wounded pride,' he said, smiling ruefully at her.

Kate put down her shoe on the breakfast bar and, finding two tumblers, half filled them with whisky.

'Whoa!' exclaimed Paul. 'I'm not much of a drinker when it comes to the hard stuff.'

'I'm really sorry about Hemingway,' said Kate, cradling her drink in her hand. 'He has this stupid macho thing. He thinks I'm his property and he doesn't like any other men coming near me.'

'I can understand that,' said Paul. 'And I'm not sure about machismo being all stupid. There's something to be said for a man standing his ground, don't you think?' He flashed her a crinkly smile.

Kate smiled back. She had nearly finished her drink and she was beginning to feel very relaxed and very sexy. Jessica was right. Paul was a *very* attractive man.

She put down her glass and reached for his hand. Lifting it to her lips she gently kissed where Hemingway had scratched. 'There, does that help?' she asked huskily.

'Mm. But there's still my badly wounded pride.'

'That might need more radical treatment, but I think I know just what to do.' Still holding his hand, she led him to her bedroom.

It took her barely a couple of moments to slip out of

her dress and she stood in front of Paul's appreciative eyes in her bra and pants. Starting with his tie, she began to undress him, pushing him back onto the bed to remove his socks and shoes and pulling off his trousers. He made no move to help her, just lay watching, his arms cradling his head. When Kate slipped off his underpants, he already had an erection.

Kate reached for the condoms she kept beside the bed, but when she turned back, Paul already had one in his hand which he swiftly put on. Removing her bra and pants, she climbed onto the bed and knelt astride. Looking down at his expectant face, Kate gently slipped him inside her, and began to move her hips backwards and forwards to his evident pleasure. His back started to arch up to meet her.

Sensing he was not far off orgasm, Kate quickened her movement. But as she did, the room began to spin around her and she could feel perspiration breaking out on her face. She tried to swallow, but the ominous feeling in the pit of her stomach was not to be ignored. Clutching her hand to her mouth, she scrambled off Paul. She stumbled as her feet touched the floor, which seemed to come up to meet her. Around her, her familiar bedroom walls had taken on a strange liquid quality, bulging inwards to meet her and then mysteriously disappearing as she reached out to touch them for support.

She reached the bathroom only just in time. Sinking to her knees she lowered her head to the toilet bowl and threw up.

The awful retching seemed as though it would never stop, but finally it did. Kate remained kneeling for a few moments more, then staggered to her feet and, running some cold water into the sink, splashed her face and washed out her mouth. It was only then that she was aware that Paul was hovering uncertainly at the door, her bedspread wrapped toga-like around him.

'Is there anything I can do?'

'No,' said Kate shortly, still hanging onto the basin for support. She could not bring herself to turn and face him.

'Do you want me to go, then?'

Kate nodded. Whether he could see her agreement from behind she didn't know, but the sound of someone rapidly dressing confirmed that he had.

Kate pushed the door shut and, wrapping herself in her bathrobe, perched on the side of the bath, waiting for him to leave. After another minute or so there was a cautious knock at the door.

'I'm going. Are you sure you'll be all right?'

Kate didn't answer.

'I'll call you.'

As the front door closed behind him, Kate stared into the darkness. She felt exposed. Not because she had allowed a stranger to look at her naked, but because she had permitted him to observe her so vulnerable. Her only consolation was that they would never meet again. Who would want to see her after her drunken exhibition? To add irony to her humiliation, Paul Hegley was the only man Jessica had introduced her to whom she had not intended to frighten away. When she had tried to shake off some of the others, they had proved irritatingly persistent, calling her until she had been forced to be blunt. Perhaps she should have thrown up over them, mused Kate with a grim smile.

At the thought of Jessica, Kate closed her eyes. Paul Hegley was not the only person to whom she owed an apology. She had not been kind to Jessica. The first thing she would do in the morning would be to call and apologise. What she had said was unforgivable.

Kate suddenly felt very thirsty. She should have felt ill, too, but vomiting had the advantage of clearing most of the alcohol out of her system. She stood up very cautiously. The room wavered a little but then settled down. Pulling her wrap around her, she padded through the living-room to the kitchen where she poured herself a glass of water. She drank it quickly and, having poured another, started back to the bedroom. Her eyes were now more accustomed to the gloom and as she came through the living-room the sight of broken glass reminded her that among all the apologies she would have to make she also owed one to Hemingway.

This time the fault had not been entirely hers, as Hemingway, too, had behaved badly. But there had been no reason for her to retaliate in a manner that could only be described as that of an inebriated fishwife.

Kate winced as she turned on the light. Disregarding the danger the broken shards of glass posed to her naked feet, she looked at the remains of her lamp. The graceful, long-limbed girl had lost one outstretched hand. It could probably be repaired but the delicate lampshade was in a thousand indistinguishable pieces.

Kate stared at the statue for a moment or two and then, slumping onto her sofa, she began to cry. Almost silently at first, like someone gasping for air, a loud sob forced its way out of her throat and after that she could not stop, her whole body shaking with the force of her weeping.

She must have cried herself to sleep because she woke, her throat dry and aching, with the silvery light of dawn filtering between the cracks in her shutters. Kate climbed stiffly to her feet. It took nearly an hour before she was satisfied that she had picked up every last tiny piece of broken glass. It seemed to have got everywhere: under the sofa, between stacks of books, lodged dangerously down the cracks between the floorboards. When she had finished clearing the glass, it only seemed sensible to continue and clean the whole flat – it was long overdue. She even decided to defrost the fridge, using her hairdryer like a blowtorch to melt the Arctic waste that had taken the place of her icebox and forming a large pool of water on her polished kitchen floor.

Three hours later she had the flat cleaner than it had been in months, if not since she had moved in. Feeling exhausted, but suitably chastened, Kate decided to make the first of her peace offerings. Pulling on some jeans and a sweat-shirt, she went to the corner shop at the end of the street and bought a pint of milk and a tin of Hemingway's favourite salmon, which she placed in his bowl on the wide ledge outside the kitchen window.

Bowl was a misnomer. It was actually a large, ugly cut-glass crystal ashtray that someone had once given her for a present and which she hated, although no doubt it had been expensive. She had used it as a doorstop, but Hemingway had adopted it.

To show the extent of her repentance, rather than plain milk, Kate poured some long-life cream from a carton she kept for emergencies into his water bowl and put that beside the salmon. She then banged the side of the dish with his fork and waited. He was usually there before she could count to ten, food taking preference over everything – even sex.

Kate had a good idea where Hemingway might be. He had been taking a lot of interest in a Siamese cat which had been acquired recently by the people who lived in a house two doors down. She had seen it preening itself in its owners' front window. It was the nearest feline equivalent she had seen to Eartha Kitt and she could quite understand why it was driving all the males in the neighbourhood mad, among them Hemingway. Very wisely, its owners did not allow it out of the house, so it amused itself with what Kate could only assume to be the cat version of prick-teasing. Sitting in the safety of the front window bay, it lovingly licked its long limbs, contorting itself into impossible and revealing positions, before sitting primly upright and gazing with wide blue-eyed innocence at the assembled lustful males. Goaded into a frenzy of thwarted desire, the cats took out their frustration on each other. But for all their flexing of muscles and sharpening of claws, it did none of them any good. The Siamese cat remained impregnable.

Kate had never taken any interest in animals until Hemingway had moved in. Now, even though she still did not like to think of herself as a cat owner, she found that she noticed other people's cats, comparing them with Hemingway. She had been told it was the same with babies.

She banged on the side of Hemingway's bowl again. She could have counted up to a hundred by now. He was probably sulking, trying to teach her a lesson and would stay away until he thought she was worried enough to give him an extra large helping of salmon rather than a scolding when he returned. It was an old trick. Well, two could play at that game. Kate closed the window and locked it.

Still fired with a need for further self-improvement if not self-mortification, she made for the bathroom where she turned the shower to cold and stepped under it. The freezing jets of water stung her body and took away her breath. Testing her self-control to the maximum, Kate stood, teeth chattering, trying to convince herself that a cold shower was not only good for her circulation but also for toning up her muscles, particularly her pectorals. But the only things standing up proud and erect were the goose-pimples which covered her body like a rash.

Unable to bear it a moment longer she stepped out and hurriedly towelled herself dry, trying to rub some feeling back into her frozen limbs. Teeth still chattering, she pulled on jeans and a T-shirt, and made some coffee. She stood, cradling her hot mug between hands, still cold, waiting for some semblance of feeling to return. Unfortunately, as it did, so did the dull pulse of a headache.

Kate snapped two paracetamol out of their white plastic casing and tossed them into her mouth, cautiously sipping some hot coffee. One of the tablets caught at the back of her throat and for a moment its bitter soapy taste almost made her gag. She quickly swallowed some more coffee and the shock of a mouthful of scalding liquid supplanted the nausea, causing her to have a coughing fit.

The telephone rang and Kate reached for the receiver but was overcome by a fresh bout of coughing, so she let the answering machine come on. Much to her surprise, it was Paul Hegley. Kate's hand reached for the receiver again, but then she decided she was still feeling too raw to discuss the night before.

'Kate. This is Paul Hegley. I've left it late to call because I thought you might not be feeling too good this morning. I'm hoping we might make a fresh start over dinner. I'm out of town on business for a few days, but wondered whether you might be free on Saturday night. Do leave a message on my machine. Oh, and my remedy for a bad head is freshly squeezed orange juice sweetened with honey and topped up with soda water. Don't touch caffeine or drugs, they won't do you any good.'

Kate pressed the delete button on her machine and wiped the message. Why did healthy people always feel they had to proselytise to the non-converted? Whatever residual attraction she felt for Paul Hegley was evaporating fast. Why bother spending time squeezing oranges? It was much easier to buy juice in a convenient carton from a supermarket. She drained her mug of strong black coffee and refilled it. The caffeine was beginning to have its desired effect and she felt fully awake.

Kate considered ringing Jessica to apologise. She always found that apologies were easier if made sooner rather than later. Left, they had a way of either not being made, or of reminding people of the wrong committed against them when they had already forgotten it and thereby risking causing more harm in the process. But before she could pick up the telephone it began to ring again. Once again she waited for the answering machine to cut in. This time the caller was Max.

'If you wanted to make me jealous last night you succeeded. I wanted to kill that man. Kate, my darling, sexy Kate, if I've made you angry let me make it up to you. I'll do anything you want, anything. Just call me . . . *please.*'

His voice had started off rough, even angry, but it then became pleading. Kate clenched her hands, determined not to pick up the receiver, wanting to hate him. But when he had finished speaking she replayed the message. Max had called her his darling Kate.

Eleven

• • •

Kate vowed that if she heard another person saying 'looks like we've had our summer then' she would strangle them with her bare hands and cheerfully serve any sentence the courts imposed.

The promise of the warm sunny days of early April had proved false and now seemed as if they belonged to another time. They had been followed by day after relentless day of grey, cold, penetrating rain, which threatened to continue until the end of May. The television news bulletins couldn't make up their minds as to whether they should lead on the good news – that as the rainfall had been higher than average, householders might be spared the dire warnings of drought, which now seemed to accompany every British summer – or on the bad – that the unseasonable cold, combined with the rain coming at the wrong time, was causing problems for farmers, so there would be crop shortages and higher prices in the supermarkets later that year.

The panoramic view of the Thames from Somerset House and Waterloo Bridge upriver to Charing Cross Station that normally greeted Kate from her ninth-floor office was obscured by a veil of driving rain, as it had been for days if not weeks now. She sipped her espresso, her mood as grey and depressed as the weather.

It was nearly six weeks since Jessica's party and she had not seen or spoken to Max. He had left several messages wanting to see her and she had called back at times when she had known he would not be in his office to say she was too busy. It had been cowardly, but then again, she had reasoned, it would be cowardly to end the affair by leaving a message on his answering machine. It was over, of that she was certain, but she wanted to end it when she was ready.

She had not replied to Paul Hegley's phone messages either. She had felt both guilty and flattered by his persistence, and considered she at least owed him an explanation for her behaviour after Jessica's party. But at the same time she did not want to be reminded of that night. Her feelings were still too raw.

She had been avoiding Jessica, too. Partly because Paul had recruited her to try and get Kate to go out with him and Kate had no intention of explaining why she did not, and partly because her guilt at speaking so sharply to Jessica had been replaced by anger when Jessica had allowed Hugo to buy his pardon with a pair of emerald and diamond ear-rings.

By accepting them, Jessica had tacitly condoned Hugo's behaviour and she had wanted Kate to do the same. But if Jessica could not remain angry with Hugo, Kate intended to do so on her behalf. However, Kate could not escape the feeling that she was behaving more than a little like Jessica towards Max and she did not like herself very much for it.

Usually, if things were wrong in her personal life, Kate had always been able to plunge herself into her work. It was what gave her the greatest sense of satisfaction, but since Jordan had taken over, six weeks ago, all sense of satisfaction and pleasure had disappeared.

Jordan had wasted no time in beginning what he euphemistically called a 'restructuring exercise'. Entire departments had disappeared, only to reappear under a new name, while others had simply vanished, and departments which hadn't disappeared like Atlantis, had found themselves with new bosses, or with old bosses with new titles.

To answer critics inside and outside the building – of whom there were many – he had launched a public relations offensive, giving endless newspaper and television interviews. So ubiquitous was his presence on other television channels that the current joke in the bar was that the man sitting behind the desk on the twenty-second floor was just one of many clones. The real Jordan, if real could be applied to someone like him, was probably sailing somewhere in the South Pacific on his newly acquired yacht, of which the gossip columnists had made much, featuring photographs of Jordan and his family posing proudly on the deck, all kitted out in blue and white with matching peaked sailing caps.

Kate had found herself forced to spend a lot of her time attending meetings with grey-suited management consultants. They seemed to have taken over the building since Jordan arrived, smoothly colonising the offices of the departing production staff like some kind of occupying force, although their demeanour was more like that of a sinister religious cult. Male or female, they all had similar short, glossy haircuts and gleaming, well-groomed, twenty-something faces. They were never seen alone, always in a group, as though for protection – or was it fear of contamination? – from the alien elements around them.

The contrast between them and the old television hands was never so marked as it was in the bar. They sat over their single glasses of mineral water while the tables of the Channel's rapidly diminishing production staff were crammed with empty beer, spirit and wineglasses until they could not hold any more. And, as glasses were drained, the ashtrays in the one place in the building where smoking was allowed over-flowed.

Something akin to inertia had settled over pro-gramme-making departments like Kate's. Nothing could be done without a focus group being formed to discuss it, whether it was an idea for a documentary series or the installation of a new coffee machine.

For the first time in her life, Kate no longer looked forward to coming to work. The challenge it presented had always got the adrenalin surging through her veins even before she got up in the morning, no matter how late she had stayed up the night before. At least she still had the weekly current affairs series to concentrate on, but even that was coming rapidly to an end. It normally ran until the last days of June but Jordan had cut its run by four programmes.

When she tried to give her production team pep talks they stared at her with the eyes of condemned men and women, even the relentlessly cheerful Jenny. In truth, there was little she could say to reassure them. The announcement of redundancies continued almost every day, and a sense of fear and insecurity now pervaded the Channel – someone had nicknamed it the Gulag. She had given up trying to find new and original things to write on farewell cards, limiting herself to 'good luck' after the first ten or so that Ruby had placed on her desk for signature. What else was there to say?

Kate swung her chair round from the window and looked at the television that was permanently on in the corner of her office, its screen divided up into many smaller ones so that she could monitor what other stations were transmitting. Up in the right-hand corner she could see the figure of a tiny weatherman. She pointed the remote control at the set and he jumped in size, his incongruously bright striped sweater filling the screen as he gesticulated at a map covered in fluffy cloud symbols, all indicating heavy rain. Kate reduced him to thumb size again and turned back to her desk. Lying on it unopened was a letter marked personal and highly confidential. Ruby had placed it there some ten minutes ago. Kate picked it up and began to rip open the envelope, although she already had an idea of its contents. Similar missives had appeared on other people's desks. It was from Jordan. She began to read.

It had taken him – or more likely someone in the personnel department – three pages of closely worded excuses backed up by screeds of legal self-justification to say that her department was being reorganised and that, as a result, her present job no longer existed. She had a choice: either to accept redundancy or to be interviewed, along with other candidates, for what appeared to be her own job but under another title. As if that weren't enough, she would only be offered a short-term contract. All staff jobs and contracts over three years were being 'phased out'.

That was a useful phrase, mused Kate – 'phased out'. It was a bit like using the term 'to terminate' rather than 'to kill'. It allowed those who gave the orders to distance themselves from the human consequences of their actions, as though it was only some vague concept like a job that was being 'phased out' rather than a person being sacked and deprived of their livelihood – or was she being overly dramatic? She swung round to face the window. Either way, she was being faced with the choice of being 'phased out' or of dealing with the humiliation of being interviewed for what was her own job.

There was a cautious tap at the door and Ruby poked her head round. Kate swung back, gave her a wan smile and beckoned her in. Ruby carefully closed the door behind her, cutting out the rest of the office. 'Bad news?'

Kate nodded.

'Word on the grape-vine is that envelopes like that have been landing on desks throughout the building. It's about your job, isn't it?' asked Ruby.

'A job that no longer exists according to this.' Kate picked up the letter between her thumb and forefinger as though it were contaminated. She let it drift down into the waste-paper basket.

Ruby nodded sympathetically. 'What are you going to do? Interview for your own job?' She obviously knew the contents of the letter. Nothing remained confidential for long with Ruby, she had moles in every department.

'I don't know,' said Kate bitterly. And she didn't. The choice she had been offered was hardly a choice. The only thing she knew was that right at that moment she had to get out of the building and as far away as possible from the Channel as she could.

She stood up and began pushing the papers on her desk into a haphazard pile. 'I'm going home.'

Ruby waved her away and took over, sorting the piles out systematically. 'You've got another focus group presentation at five thirty. Shall I tell them you've been unavoidably detained?'

'Tell them whatever you want,' said Kate shortly as she pulled on her coat and walked towards the door, but then she stopped and turned back. 'I'm sorry, Ruby, I shouldn't take my bad mood out on you.' She gave Ruby a kiss on the cheek. 'Thank you. I'm not sure what I would do without you.'

'Yes, you are,' said Ruby, looking suspiciously as if she was blushing under her dark skin, 'and whatever you decide, I'm there for you, stay or go.'

Thirty minutes later Kate emerged from the shelter of Angel station just as yet another downpour began. She stepped back inside, intending to open her umbrella, only to realise she had left it on the train. It was the

147

third one she had lost in a month. Cursing herself and the rain under her breath, she buttoned up her raincoat and turned up the collar. She could wait until the rain stopped, but that might be next week.

She stepped out, knowing she would be soaked through before she got home. As she had already discovered to her cost, her raincoat was shower-proof, not rain-proof. This subtle but important distinction had not been made clear to her when she had purchased it. She had assumed that anything sold under the generic term 'raincoat' would be just that – a coat for protection against the rain – but her so-called raincoat was only suitable for the briefest, lightest showers of the sort which hardly required a coat in the first place.

By the time she turned into the end of her road Kate was soaked through. Rain coursed down her face onto her neck and from there onto her clothes, which were already wet from the rain seeping through her coat. To complete her misery the puddles on the uneven pavement had merged into one vast muddy lake and, with every step she took, water splashed up her legs. There was no point in keeping her head down, as everyone else who was unfortunate enough to be caught in the rain seemed to be doing, since it provided no protection. The rain lashed her face either way. So she walked head up, looking into the lighted windows of the people who had the foresight to be warm and dry at home, promising herself that in another two hundred yards she would be the one inside looking out, wrapped in warm towels and with a large malt whisky in her hand.

She could almost taste the whisky when the sight of a cat sitting in a window framed by velvet swag curtains brought her to a sudden stop. Through the glass she could see a spacious sitting-room with a baby grand piano in one corner and an open fireplace in which a log fire was burning. It was a welcoming sight and the cat was clearly at home. As Kate stood watching in the rain, a girl of about eight came over to the window. She perched next to the cat who rubbed the side of his head against her. She gathered him into her arms and buried her face in his fur. He responded by licking her face with his little pink tongue. The girl produced a large red ribbon, which she proceeded to tie around his neck. The cat made no objection to having a ridiculous bow hanging under his chin. In fact, he looked as though he was used to being a child's plaything and sat perfectly still until she had finished. Then he preened himself for her admiration.

Kate watched, trying to convince herself it was a cat who merely resembled Hemingway. There had to be plenty of other large grey cats around the neighbourhood. It could even be from the same litter as Hemingway. But then the little girl, whose mass of angelically curling blonde hair was beginning to irritate Kate, reminding her of Violet Bott in the *Just William* books, held up a ball of wool and the cat reached up a paw. It was his right front paw and it was tipped with white.

Kate advanced further up the front path. Her hair was now plastered to her forehead and the rain kept running into her eyes, almost blinding her, but she needed a closer look. The cat was fatter than Hemingway and fluffier, but then Kate spotted the large triangular-shaped piece missing from his ear.

It was him.

A man appeared at the door of the room and Kate shrank back from the light. She was standing right beside the window and a casual observer might well have mistaken her motives. The man said something and in response, the little girl picked Hemingway up and carried him out of the room, her arms linked under his front legs so his back legs dangled ridiculously around her knees, the lopsided red bow unravelling as

149

she walked. When they had gone, the man turned off the lights and Kate was left in darkness.

The downpour had stopped, but she hadn't noticed. She was standing under the branches of a sweet-chestnut tree which dripped steadily on her like rain. The tree had been covered with blossom, but it had been beaten to the ground and now looked like fallen snow – mushy and brown. Kate turned away and slowly began to walk towards her flat.

Hemingway had never returned after the night of Jessica's party when she had so disastrously invited Paul Hegley to her flat. At first she had told herself she didn't care and that, like a bad penny, he would be bound to turn up. But as the days and weeks passed, she had begun to fear the worst. On at least two occasions she had seen what she thought to be a small dead furry body lying in the road and had rushed across, heedless of traffic, her heart in her mouth, thinking it was Hemingway. On both occasions the fur had turned out to be a bundle of rags but she had still been badly shaken.

How could she feel upset because she had been betrayed by an ugly, bad-tempered tomcat? She should be glad he was gone. She had tried hard enough to get rid of him when he had first moved in. Anyway, he had never been hers in the first place. Her flat had merely been a convenient warm place to stay, its owner someone stupid enough to buy him the expensive salmon he liked. For all she knew he could have been a bigamist, living in two homes all the time. He had looked so at ease in the house where she had seen him that he might have lived there all his life. Kate roughly wiped her cheeks with the back of her hand. They were still wet even though it had stopped raining some time ago. How could she have allowed herself to get so stupidly attached to a cat?

As she put the key in her door she heard her

telephone start to ring. She was tempted to leave it to the machine to answer, but there was something about the urgency of a telephone ringing when she came through a door that always made her pick it up.

'Yes.' Kate did not feel like encouraging conversation.

'Dear heart? Is that you?' Robert's voice echoed down the line from far-away Majorca.

'*Robert*!' Relief flooded through Kate's body and it sounded in her voice.

'Dear heart, is something wrong?'

'Everything,' said Kate shortly, 'but it's much too complicated to go into now. How are you and how is Oliver?'

'We're blossoming like two young lovers discovering love for the first time. We're like every sentimental love-song you've ever heard only better. At night we dance cheek to cheek on the terrace like Ginger Rogers and Fred Astaire. I'm Ginger, of course, as I've always looked better in backless satin than Oliver. And I do declare the stars have never looked lovelier.'

'Oh, Robert, I'm so happy for you both. It cheers me up to know that love is still alive and well, even in Majorca.'

'Do I detect a note of cynicism in your voice, darling child? Does this mean *that* man is still sniffing around?'

'No. I've finished with him.' It wasn't exactly a lie. The affair was over. It was just that she hadn't told him so directly.

'There really is only one remedy for a broken heart: drop everything and get your sweet little ass over here right this minute.'

'But I can't . . .' Kate stopped.

Why not? She was owed weeks of leave and the series was virtually wrapped up. The final, and probably last, programme would be transmitted in two

151

days' time and she no longer had the summer specials to think about. She didn't even have to worry about who would look after Hemingway any more. A short break would give her the chance to consider what she should do. It wasn't a time to be spending money on a holiday as she soon might not have a job. But what were credit cards for if not for emergencies like this?

'Are you *sure* it would be all right? What about Oliver?'

'I'd be absolutely delighted.' Oliver's public-school accent cut in. He had been listening on an extension. 'I've given Robert orders to bring you here on numerous occasions without success. We'd both love you to stay as long as you want. When can you come? We'll meet you at the airport.'

'Well, I'm not sure . . .' Kate hesitated – everything was happening too fast.

'No buts.' It was Robert. 'There are flights every day from Heathrow and Gatwick. Just stick a spare pair of knickers in your handbag and we'll provide all the rest. On second thoughts, don't even bother with the knickers. Oliver and I go without ours when we're here and nobody notices, or at least they haven't said anything to our faces yet.'

Kate laughed.

'That's better. So when can we expect you?' demanded Robert.

'Well, our last programme is going to be recorded on Friday. It will be an interview with the Prime Minister. I wanted to go out with a bang, although I think it's unlikely. He's not going to say anything that hasn't been scripted by one of the spin doctors he surrounds himself with, *and* it appears he and Jordan have become good sailing buddies. So all in all, I'm not holding my breath for any great revelations and we should be wrapped and edited by the end of the day. So how about Saturday?'

'Done,' chorused Robert and Oliver together.

Kate replaced the receiver and turned on the lights. There was a circle of drips on the floor where she had been standing. She caught sight of herself in the mirror above the fireplace. She looked drenched. Her hair hung in sodden ringlets around her face, which was chalky white apart from her eyes. They were dark and tired, and her mascara – smudge-proof not water-proof – had obligingly smeared an uneven black line below her lashes.

Kate kicked off her shoes, threw her shower-proof raincoat over the breakfast bar and poured herself a large whisky. Then she opened the window, took in Hemingway's bowls and threw them into the rubbish bin. *She* was going on holiday.

Twelve
• • •

Robert stood like a beacon of light in Palma airport. Around him swirled a mass of tourists, clutching suitcases and bags and packages and precious holiday souvenirs, bought under the influence of too much sun and *sangría*, which would soon be thrown into some dusty corner and forgotten. While everyone else was dressed in multicoloured holiday clothes, Robert was pristine in white; white shirt, white linen trousers, white espadrilles and a white cotton sweater slung about his shoulders.

Kate fought her way through the crowd, struggling under the double weight of her flight bag and her suitcase. She had lost out in the battle for the one remaining trolley to an extremely large woman wearing an inadvisably short pair of shorts and T-shirt proclaiming 'Housewives do it with rubber gloves on'.

As Kate approached Robert he put his hands on his hips. '*Well*!' he declared in a voice that could be heard clearer and louder than the flight announcements on the tannoy, 'and what did I say about bringing only *one* pair of knickers?'

Tourists turned and stared, some open-mouthed, others sharp-eyed with curiosity, hopeful that they were to be provided with a diversion from the boredom of shuffling forward in yet another queue. Kate ignored them. She dropped both her bags and surrendered herself to Robert's hug.

'Where's Oliver?' she asked after they had said their hellos and were making their way to the exit, Robert now gratifyingly carrying her suitcase.

'One of us had to stay at home and prepare the fatted calf for our prodigal daughter, or at least keep a careful watch on it. My Spanish is not yet quite up to dealing with our little treasure Francesca who likes to burn all meat to a crisp if she's not watched, so the chore fell to Oliver. Hired help is not what it used to be. I remember the days when you could take them out and hang them from the nearest tree and flog them for burning the toast. When I was little, I thought my ole mammy was a bat, she seemed to spend so much time hanging from trees.'

'Robert!' Kate was smiling, but sometimes she was not sure whether to laugh or cry at his jokes.

'Here's the winged chariot,' Robert announced as they reached a tiny, bright-yellow Seat parked in what was clearly a place reserved for the many coaches which were lining up to collect the package tourists. There was a perspiring policeman standing beside it.

'*Sí, sí*, I go now,' said Robert loudly as he loaded Kate's bags into the boot.

Oliver spoke Spanish fluently, but Robert's vocabulary was limited to '*sí*' and '*gracias*'.

The policeman began to talk very fast, gesticulating at the car and producing a notebook.

'I know, I know, I've been a very bad boy,' said Robert soothingly as he got in. He revved it up and drove off very fast, causing the policeman to leap hastily back onto the pavement, dropping his pad.

Kate grabbed the strap that hung from the roof above the door with one hand and reached for her seat-belt with the other as they swung out into the busy traffic. Although he had not mastered the language, Robert

155

appeared to be expert at the Spanish way of driving, which was to keep one foot hard down on the accelerator at all times, while one hand rested on the horn and the other hung out of the window in order to gesticulate at fellow road users, particularly those who dared to get in the way. To be seen steering the wheel, obeying road signs or signalling your intent was to lose face.

When she was safely strapped in, Kate reached into her handbag and found the sun-glasses she had bought in Duty Free. Once she had got through the luggage check-in and security control, she had suddenly realised that she really was going away, and she was filled with a sense of freedom and the need to celebrate. So she had made rather more use of her credit card than she should have in the Duty Free shops.

Ignoring the traffic speeding on all sides, Robert turned and took a long considered look. Just when Kate was ready to scream to look out, he swivelled back and took avoiding action, overtaking a slow-moving truck on the inside, his hand jammed on the horn.

'Very stylish, dear heart,' he said when they were safely past. 'I'm so glad you didn't buy Ray-Bans, they're absolutely *de trop* now you know, simply *everyone* wears them.'

'Snob,' retorted Kate, but she was pleased he liked them. Robert had a wonderful sense of style and she hated to disappoint him.

They were now out into a countryside that Kate had not expected to see. Her impressions of Majorca were only of cheap package tourism, high-rise concrete-block hotels, and mock-English pubs offering warm beer and fish and chips. But this was a traditional Spain, seemingly unaffected by the foreign invasion of its southern coastline. The landscape was flat and cultivated, punctuated by the occasional windmill, picturesquely turning slowly in the breeze, and white-washed farmhouses, with single sentinel palm trees standing guard at their entrances, witness to their Moorish past. Elsewhere there were orange, lemon and olive groves, and almond trees still frosted with blossom. The occasional sad-eyed donkey plodded along the roadside, stoically bearing its heavy load, its owner with the age-old face of the rural peasant sitting side-saddle, prodding the beast occasionally with a stick. Although to what effect, Kate could not see. The donkey's pace never varied from very slow.

As he drove, Robert recounted the numerous joys of being in Majorca. The meals he and Oliver had eaten, the local wines they had discovered – some wonderful and others execrable – and the progress he was making on his book. Kate occasionally felt him looking side-ways at her, but he tactfully did not press her to talk. She just wanted to take in her surroundings and adjust her eyes to the Mediterranean light. After the chill damp of London, the warm breeze felt wonderful on her skin. Robert had apologised for the air-condition-ing not working, but Kate did not mind. Although she knew her hair would be thick with dust by the time they arrived, she wanted the windows open.

About twenty-two kilometres to the west of Palma, the road began to climb up into the Sierra de Alfabia, its rocky mountainsides clad with pine and carob trees, holly oaks, and pencil-slim cypresses. The road now twisted and turned alarmingly, but Robert did not seem to think it necessary to let the needle of the speedo-meter drop by more than a few kilometres per hour, although at least he talked less. Passing large, slow-moving vehicles on the winding road seemed to provide him with a challenge he relished, greeting each hair-raising success with a blast on his horn and a merry wave of his hand out of the window at the driver behind.

They had been inland for quite some time when suddenly Robert slowed down. 'Close your eyes,' he commanded.

'I'm not sure I want to,' retorted Kate. 'If I'm going to die because of your Michael Schumacher fixation, I intend to do it with my eyes wide open.'

'Tut, tut. And here was me thinking that you liked men who were fast with their gear-stick. Now do as your Auntie Robert says and *close* your eyes.'

Kate obeyed.

The car drove a little further and then stopped.

'Now open them,' commanded Robert.

'Oh!' The exclamation was wrenched from Kate by the beauty of the view that lay before her.

They were three hundred feet above a sheer drop to the sea, but pine trees still managed to cling to the hillside among the tumbled boulders. Far below, a cerulean-blue Mediterranean fringed the scalloped coastline, lace-edged with tiny white beaches.

Robert looked satisfied at the effect. 'Now you understand why poets and painters and old reprobates like Oliver and myself have always come to this part of Majorca.'

Kate nodded. 'It's breath-taking.'

Robert started the car and began to drive more slowly this time, not just because of the sheer drop to the sea, but to allow himself time to look as each turn in the road brought yet another exquisite panorama of the coastline.

'Robert Graves used to live in the next village to ours. He's buried in the churchyard there. But Deya is no longer as it used to be when he first came. It's too full of would-be poets and loud American students writing dissertations on Graves, and you know just how frightfully *loud* Americans can be.' He gave Kate a sideways grin. 'Anyway, when Oliver first saw the house where we now live, it was a case of a *coup de foudre*. He knew he couldn't live anywhere else. However, that's not to say we haven't had problems renovating the place. When I say he fell blindly in love, I mean just that. Like all lovers, he was blind to the lack of mains electricity, telephone *and* any form of hot water. That's not forgetting the feral cats which had made one of the rooms their own and the pine martins that had undermined part of the foundations. Over the years we have slowly managed to get all those things sorted out but then a storm this winter partially destroyed the roof. I can't *tell* you the difficulty of explaining to our Spanish builder, Miguel, that no, we *don't* want a new roof with bright new tiles, we want the roof to look as it should – beautifully aged. Miguel is a sweetie, and he's divine in that dark, satanic, Spanish-looking way, but he just couldn't appear to understand why anyone should want to pay for something that looked old. The logic here is that if you have money, you buy something shiny and new-looking so that everyone can see you are wealthy. In the end, Oliver and I took to driving around the countryside with a selection of broken tiles from our roof looking for ruined buildings and trying to match ours to any that were in a good condition. We had to deal with some extremely puzzled and sometimes downright angry owners. But in the end we got what we wanted and, much against his will, Miguel has done a wonderful job, as you'll see in just a few more minutes.'

They turned off the main coastal road and headed up a steep track, which appeared to be designed for donkeys or goats, not cars. Kate found herself clinging onto the strap again as the car jolted and bumped over deep ruts and stones. Robert insisted she close her eyes once more as they approached the house and she dutifully obeyed. When he said she could open them she gasped again.

She had seen photographs of the old house Oliver and Robert had restored together, but they had not done it justice. It was built into the side of the hill and its roof, just as Robert had described, was of many-hued terracotta tiles. Its walls were of weathered grey-gold stone, set with shutters painted peacock blue. A lemon tree, covered with pale lemon fruit, stood beside the front door. Brightly coloured ceramic Majolica ware pots of every shape and size, filled to overflowing with red and pink geraniums, crowded window-sills and the wide stone steps leading to the front door. More ceramic and terracotta pots, some of them four or five feet high, containing graceful palms that would have gladdened the heart of a keeper at Kew Gardens, had been placed on the wide terrace that jutted out over the hillside on the far side of the house. The terrace was protected from the sun by a ceiling of trailing scarlet bougainvillaea.

'It's absolutely gorgeous,' declared Kate, giving Robert a hug.

'I knew you'd like it, dear heart. We do. It's our Shangri-la.' He lifted Kate's luggage out of the boot and then looked anxiously at the front door. 'I thought Oliver would have heard us arriving and been here to meet you. Never mind, let's surprise him.'

He led the way – not to the front door, but to the terrace. As they reached it, Kate could see that the entire wall stretching along it had been removed and replaced with glass sliding doors, which were open. From within came the swelling sound of Maria Callas singing Mimi's farewell aria from *La Bohème*. Robert dropped the cases and taking Kate's arm, walked her to the edge of the terrace so she could see the view of the sea far below at the foot of the mountain.

He took a deep breath. 'Only the divine Miss C could do justice to such a view, don't you think? Listen.'

Callas uttered the last dying words of the ill-fated

Mimi and when Kate looked at Robert he had tears in his eyes and so did she. They stood there together as the chords faded away.

'I always thought it was the divine Miss M with you,' she said in the sudden silence.

'When Oliver and I met, it was a fortuitous meeting – not only of two people, but of two cultures. I introduced him to the divine Miss Bette Midler and he introduced me to the divine Miss Maria Callas. It was a marriage made in heaven.'

And marriages did not come much stronger than the twenty-year relationship between Robert and Oliver. Oliver was at least ten years older than Robert. Kate guessed him to be about sixty-seven or sixty-eight. They had met in London in the mid-Seventies when Robert was one of the leading lights of the burgeoning gay scene which was flexing its well-toned muscles after the emergence of the Gay Pride movement. Oliver was married, although he and his wife had lived in separate homes for ten years. They had agreed to keep up the fiction of their marriage for the sake of his family and hers, as well as his career in the Civil Service. Oliver had never been openly gay, or even admitted it to his wife. They had just agreed that the marriage was unsatisfactory.

Because of his wife and his position, Oliver felt he could not openly seek a gay relationship, so his sex life had been confined to occasional risky meetings with strangers. He had met Robert in a drag club in Soho where Robert had been performing as his *alter ego* Greta.

Robert had often told Kate that they had probably saved each other from despair as well as from AIDS. Both had been at risk: Robert from his wildly promiscuous life-style before he met Oliver and Oliver from strangers in public toilets. It had been love at first sight for both of them and they had been faithful to each other ever since. Robert joked about his little conquests, but these were just flirtations. He would never have betrayed Oliver, even though their relationship had to remain secret because Oliver held an important, and delicate, position in the Civil Service. However, once he had retired and been awarded a CBE for his services, Oliver had quietly divorced his wife.

'Kate, how wonderful to see you at last.' It was Oliver, standing in the terrace door. 'I'm so sorry I wasn't at the front door to meet you.'

Kate went over to him and hugged him, kissing him warmly. 'Oliver, how are you?'

'I've never been happier. Whatever anyone tells you, life really can begin at forty. It did for me.'

He did look happy. His hair was now completely white and he had let it grow over his collar, complementing his healthily tanned face. He was a lot shorter than Robert, not much taller than Kate's five foot eight, and quite solidly built. He was dressed in a faded denim shirt and baggy, dark-blue trousers of the sort favoured by Frenchmen, and on his feet he wore red espadrilles. He did not look like the Oliver she had known in London, with his closely clipped hair and three-piece, pin-striped suits, tailored in Jermyn Street.

He took her arm and led her inside. 'There, what do you think of our hideaway?' He waved his hand at the spacious room.

Together they had redesigned the interior of what had probably been a simple farmhouse so that it now resembled something from a film set. The room stretched back about forty feet into the rock face of the mountain itself. The stone floor, which was on two levels, echoed the rock of the mountain, although softened by cream goat-skin and Zebra-patterned rugs. On the lower level a wide semicircle of soft blond leather seating looked out over the terrace, guarded at each end by massive wrought-iron candelabra, over six feet high, each holding ten large church candles, their wax creating twisted sculptures of parchment yellow where it met the iron. A stone table, seemingly hewn out of a single boulder, its top polished like glass, stood in front of the seating. In the centre stood a bowl carved from olive wood, overflowing with fruit. Although Oliver had claimed this was their hideaway, Kate noticed that there were yesterday's editions of the *Daily Telegraph*, *The Times* and the *Financial Times* on the table, as well as piles of the current month's glossy magazines not only from Britain, but also from France and America. She guessed the former to be Oliver's reading matter while the latter were for Robert.

Two sets of three wide stone steps on either side of the sitting area led up to the next level. In the centre of this stood a long, ornately carved table, with twelve matching high-backed chairs around it. Another candelabrum stood on its richly polished dark surface and two more stood at the elbows of the chairs at each end.

'What do you want me to say?' she asked, looking from Oliver to Robert who were now standing on either side of her. 'I've run out of superlatives. I only wish I'd brought my tap-dancing shoes and my feather boa; I'd join you both in "Putting on the Ritz". The setting could not be more perfect.'

As she was talking, Oliver had slipped an arm round her waist, now Robert added his and they began to lead her up the stairs.

'Dear heart, you need never worry about being short of feather boas when you stay with us. Come, let us show you the rest of our love nest, including a collection of feather boas that is beyond your wildest dreams!'

Thirteen

• • •

Kate knelt on the low carved bench and opened her bedroom windows wide, breathing in the warm breeze, laced with the scent of flowers and citrus fruit. Resting her elbows on the window-ledge she gazed out, entranced. It was impossible to tire of the view of the pine-clad mountainside tumbling down to the jewel-like sea.

She had slept late. Robert and Oliver had been determined to make her first night in Majorca a memorable occasion and they had succeeded. When she came down to dinner the house was ablaze with candles and filled with the anguished voice of Maria Callas singing Tosca. The fatted calf Robert had mentioned in the car turned out to be the most succulent lamb Kate had ever tasted. She had gone into the kitchen to congratulate Francesca, who had turned out to be a pretty young woman who blushed at her praises when they were translated by Oliver. Ruby-red wine glowing in crystal decanters had flowed until after one o'clock, when they had retired to the terrace for coffee and some wonderful cognac. By that time there was no need for music or conversation. They just sat in companionable silence, looking at the stars, which were diamond bright in the vast blackness of the night.

Robert always referred to himself as her auntie, but

Kate had felt as though she was between two indulgent uncles, each trying to outdo the other in their solicitude for her. Over dinner, at their prompting, she told them about her problems at work, and with Max and Hemingway and, although she had not intended to, she also told them about what had happened with Paul Hegley.

Oliver had listened quietly and sympathetically, unlike Robert who interrupted constantly, snorting derisively at any mention of Max until Oliver chided him to stop. When Kate had finished, Oliver's advice had been measured and thoughtful. By contrast, Robert's was simple and direct: forget both Max and Hegley.

'Trust me,' he finished. 'I have infallible instincts about men and all of them tell me that Hegley is as wrong for Kate as Max. I can feel it in my water.'

'Infallible!' snorted Oliver. He had thought that Paul had sounded suitable but had counselled caution. 'My dearest Robert, I will bow to your taste in clothes, colours, fabrics, food and even wine, but in men? *Never*!' He turned to Kate. 'If you had seen some of the men in his life before he met me, well . . .!'

Robert bridled. '*You* should try being a beautiful young black man on the scene. Every user, abuser and closet racist in the land homed in on me like flies to honey, which is precisely *why* I learnt to be such a good judge of men. It was either that or die.'

This had provoked a long and good-natured argument on the vices and virtues of men, which at times had Kate convulsed with laughter, particularly when Robert brought the conversation back to Max.

'I'd put money on it that *that* man is a shouter.'

'A shouter?' Kate stopped laughing.

'You know. He shouts his head off when he's climaxing, as though he's announcing the Second Coming.'

Kate was laughing so much she could only nod.

'*And* I'd put even more money on it he's the sort of man who likes to talk dirty?'

'You're making the girl blush,' reproved Oliver, which he was.

'Case proven,' declared Robert triumphantly. 'The man's an utter prick. He's both repressed *and* suffering from an inferiority complex.' He wagged his finger at Kate and spoke in an exaggerated southern drawl. 'The trouble with you, girl, is that you won't listen to your ole black mammie and keep your sweet ass away from these northern men. They have granite in their souls.'

'As a Yorkshireman I must protest at this slur on the north,' said Oliver, feigning injury.

'Well, we all make mistakes,' riposted Robert and raised his glass, 'and here's to the biggest and the best *I* ever made when I fell in love with you.'

Robert had then looked thoughtful. 'Has it ever crossed your mind that *you're* the one who's avoiding commitment, Kate?' he asked.

She had laughed it off. '*Me*? Frightened of commitment?' She held up her hand and started to count on her fingers. 'When I find a man who is tall, dark and handsome, preferably a cross between Sean Connery and Daniel Day-Lewis. Who has the heart of a poet, the body of a builder and a head for money. Who is great in bed and not afraid of emotional commitment. Intelligent and ambitious, but not a workaholic. Has a sense of humour and a butt like Brad Pitt's. Oh, and he must be able to cook like Marco Pierre White. Maybe *then* I'll commit.' She opened her eyes innocently wide. 'Do you think I'm being too demanding?'

Robert had laughed. 'Dear heart, if there were such a man, believe me, you'd have to fight me to the death for him.'

Although she had made a joke of it, Robert's comment had made her think. Was she afraid of commitment or was she just the sort of person who did not need it? Everyone assumed it was a good thing, but maybe it wasn't necessary for everyone, at least when it came to relationships. She was committed to her work. It had always given her the kind of fulfilment that perhaps other people got from relationships and you had control over work, unlike relationships. Or at least she had thought she had until now.

The worst thing about her present situation, she had admitted to Robert and Oliver, was that she no longer felt in control. Even coming to Majorca felt like an admission of defeat. It was as though she was running away and she had never run away from anything or anyone in her life before.

Robert's comment had almost taken her breath away: 'Yes, you have, Kate, from yourself.'

Seeing her evident distress, Oliver had accused Robert of being harsh. But he had refused to back down, insisting that she should think about it. And she would, thought Kate, stretching out her arms and yawning, but right now she felt ridiculously hungry considering the amount she had eaten at dinner.

She could hear voices below and, leaning out of the window, she could just see Robert and Oliver on the terrace. She quickly pulled on a black T-shirt and a pair of white stretch Capri pants, brushed her hair leaving it loose on her shoulders, then with a last quick glance in the mirror, she added her sun-glasses and went downstairs.

'Jackie Onassis if ever I saw her,' announced Robert as she walked onto the terrace. He got up from the small table which had been put outside for breakfast and kissed her. 'Morning, dear heart, did you sleep well?'

Kate kissed Oliver on his proffered cheek and sat down. 'Wonderfully.'

Francesca had heard her coming and came out from

the kitchen with a pot of coffee in one hand and a basket containing some rolls still warm from the oven in the other. A large jug of freshly squeezed orange juice sat on the table and a bowl of charantais and honeydew melon slices sprinkled with ginger stood beside Kate's place.

'We didn't think you'd want anything too demanding after last night, so I told Francesca to prepare just a light repast, I hope that's all right. She'd be happy to cook something for you. In fact, I think she'd do anything for you after what you said about the lamb last night.' Oliver laughed.

'No, this is absolutely perfect,' said Kate breaking open one of the rolls. 'Everything's perfect.'

There were bowls containing butter and honey, and jars of Gale's lemon curd and Cooper's Oxford marmalade in two flavours.

Robert nodded at them. 'Oliver has them delivered by courier every month. *Never* get involved with a nursery-raised man. I've had men wanting me to drink champagne from their shoe – a stiletto of course. Eat whipped cream from their navel and even honey from their c . . .' He stopped as he caught a 'not at breakfast look' from Oliver. He poked out his tongue. 'But this man is turned on by tapioca, and when I dip bread and butter soldiers into his boiled egg, *well*, it's the nearest a man can come to multiple orgasm.'

It was Oliver's turn to blush.

Breakfast took another gentle hour. When they reluctantly decided they could not eat another roll or drink another cup of coffee, Robert and Oliver looked at each other like conspirators.

'Time for the hanging gardens of Babylon, don't you think?' asked Robert.

Oliver smiled happily.

'The hanging gardens of Babylon?' repeated Kate.

'Oliver's life's work,' said Robert. 'He's creating a garden on the mountainside below here.'

'Everyone said it was impossible, which is why the owner agreed to sell me the land. He thought it was a useless bit of ground, so why not make a profit out of a mad Englishman? But I'm working *with* the mountain, not against it. Terracing is a thousand-year-old art in countryside like this. It's hard and it's slow, but when I'm finished . . .' Oliver's eyes glowed with enthusiasm. 'Why don't you two go ahead. I need to get my hat.'

Kate watched Robert's eyes following Oliver as he went into the house. Sometimes it was almost painful to see how much they loved each other.

'We won't get too far ahead,' said Robert, leading the way down the side of the house. 'This is Oliver's baby and he should be the one to show it to you. He should really have been one of those gentlemen landscape gardeners who created parks in country houses for the leisured classes, not a civil servant. But Oliver has spent his life pleasing others, particularly his family. He was brought up to serve his country as generations of the family have before him, usually in the army or politics. *Noblesse oblige* I think he calls it. But Oliver couldn't face either, so he opted for the Civil Service as the next best thing, not that his family saw it that way. He married for their sake, too, but they have never given him credit for the sacrifices he's made for them. They don't give a damn that he spent forty years doing a job he hated, or that he has been forced to live a lie about his sexuality. But they won't forgive him for not getting a knighthood and not producing a son and heir.' Robert's voice was bitter. 'And that wasn't even his problem, it was his wife's. *She's* the one who couldn't have children. Oliver would have had them for her sake as well as his family's, but he's the one who gets the blame because it's *his* family name again.'

They had now reached the top of a flight of steep stone stairs cut into the side of the mountain. Robert turned. 'You'd have thought being born into a dirt-poor family of black sharecroppers in Alabama would be difficult, but when Oliver tells me stories of his family life and that sadistic school he was sent to when he was only six years old I sometimes think I had it easy. At least we *knew* who our enemies were and they weren't in our family.'

They heard Oliver behind them and Robert stopped talking. Oliver had donned a jaunty panama and was carrying a walking stick. He had also tied a red spotted scarf around his neck, which made him look distinctly raffish.

'Oliver's gardening outfit,' Robert whispered to Kate although loudly enough for Oliver to hear and shake his walking stick playfully at him.

They stood back so that Oliver could lead the way and Kate soon began to see what Robert had meant by the hanging gardens of Babylon. Oliver had followed the natural contours of the mountainside when designating the terraces, and if a tree or a boulder stood in the way of the path, the path meandered around it, so that it became part of the garden design. He had planted palms and shrubs along the terraces which offered shade, so that sometimes the trailing plants from above created green, fragrantly scented tunnels over the terrace below. Every so often, where the land naturally flattened out, he had created lush gardens of sun-loving flowering plants, so there was a constant change from shade to light and from green to bright colour. The warm air was heady with the scent of lavender, rosemary, jasmine and roses. Kate had always thought of them as being quintessentially English cottage garden flowers, but they seemed to thrive in the hot Mediterranean climate, their colours brighter, their perfume stronger and their growth more exuberant, as though they had thrown off their natural inhibitions under the heat of the sun, like the English abroad.

A little stream, which started higher up the mountain, had been diverted to provide occasional small, still pools of water surrounded by lilies and other water-loving plants. In one place a tunnel of tumbling bougainvillaea ended in a waterfall of crystal-clear water sparkling over white rocks.

As they walked, Oliver used his stick to point out plants, giving them their Latin names as well as the ones more familiar to Kate. He also constantly drew attention to things that were not quite right and that he intended to change, although Kate kept telling him she thought it was beautiful the way it was, which she did.

Every so often there were resting places, some in the sun, others in the shade. Some were simple wooden benches, others were carved into the rock of the mountain itself. They sat on one of these just below the waterfall, where the land started to become wild and unmanaged, and there were signs of recent work. Oliver produced some plans from his pocket and began to study them, while Robert and Kate leant back and closed their eyes.

The warmth of the sun, combined with the noise of the birds and the constant hum of the bees, made Kate feel drowsy and she could happily have fallen asleep, but the sound of cheerful singing made her open her eyes. Whoever it was, was heading in their direction from further down the mountain.

Robert had opened his eyes too. 'The gardener,' he announced.

A man carrying several large rocks piled into a triangular-shaped container on his shoulders, of the sort Kate had seen farm labourers in the fields using, came in sight. He heaved the rocks onto a pile on the ground and stood up.

'*Buenos días*,' he announced, seeing them sitting there watching him.

He was stripped to the waist, having folded his T-shirt and placed it under the hod carrier to prevent it rubbing his shoulders. His faded jeans were torn so that much of his legs were visible. He had a thin, tanned face, topped by a tangle of dark hair. He was about five foot ten and slimly built although, as Kate could not help noticing, he was also muscular.

He walked towards them, rubbing the shoulder on which he had been carrying the rocks. His hand left a streak of dust on his perspiring chest. He looked enquiringly at Kate.

'This is our friend, Kate, the one we told you about,' said Robert.

He wiped his hand on his jeans and held it out. Kate took it. He had very long, slim fingers she noticed, not the hands of a workman, although she could feel calluses on the palms.

'Hello, pleased to meet you,' she said slowly, wishing she spoke Spanish.

'And I'm delighted to meet you,' he replied in perfect English. 'Oliver and Robert have told me a lot about you.' He grinned.

Kate turned and looked accusingly at Robert and Oliver who were enjoying their little deception. 'Well, they didn't tell me *anything* about you, I'm afraid.'

'Don't look at me,' pleaded Oliver. 'Keeping Liam a secret was Robert's idea.'

'I just wanted to see if Kate would do her "lady of the manor greeting the local peasant" act.' Robert laughed. 'And she did.'

'You *should* have met Liam last night at dinner,' Oliver said by way of apology. 'He lives in the annexe at the back. But he had to go to Puerto de Soller to

172

collect some plants I've been searching months for and the pick-up broke down, so he couldn't get back until this morning.'

'Still, it gave me a chance to catch up with some friends over there and what a night we made of it,' said Liam, running his hand through his hair, liberally distributing dirt as he did. 'The locally brewed gin is a real killer. But I'm sorry I missed the party for your arrival,' he added quickly to Kate.

If he had drunk a lot the night before he didn't look like it, she observed. The mirror now told her in the morning when she had drunk too much. Her skin did not have the power of instant rejuvenation it used to have in her twenties, which was where she would put Liam.

'But you did bring the plants?' asked Oliver anxiously.

'I carried them as gently as I would a new-born babe,' replied Liam, 'but it's bad news about the pick-up. Although the garage managed to patch it up, it needs some seriously expensive work. Should I tell them to order the parts?'

Oliver got to his feet. 'Do whatever is necessary. But show me the plants first.'

'What about lunch?' called Robert as Oliver and Liam set off, heads together already discussing the new plants.

'In about an hour,' replied Oliver over his shoulder.

'Liam?' called Robert.

'I could eat a horse' was the reply that floated back as Liam and Oliver disappeared from view.

'An hour. More like two when those two get together,' declared Robert, stretching. 'Mind you, it will give me time for a quick shut-eye. How about you?'

'I think I'd like to sit here for a little while longer and then maybe wander through the garden,' replied Kate.

'I need some exercise before I can eat another mouthful. I'll be like the side of a house if I stay here too long.'

'You know what kind of exercise doctor *lurve* prescribes: good, healthy sex and plenty of it,' said Robert.

Kate yawned. 'I've decided to become celibate. It makes life so much simpler.'

'Celibate,' snorted Robert. 'That's the same as dead.'

'Sex isn't everything,' said Kate primly.

'And *there* speaks a woman who for the last three years has been going out with a prick because she says he's great at sex!'

'All right. But a woman can change.'

Robert raised an eyebrow. 'Like a leopard . . .'

'Oh, go to bed,' snapped Kate.

Robert pretended to flounce off, then turned. 'Oh, by the way, what do you think of our Liam. Attractive, isn't he?'

'If you like that sort of thing,' replied Kate, closing her eyes and stretching out along the seat. 'Anyway, I've told you. No more men, *ever*.'

Fourteen
• • •

And she had meant it, thought Kate, finding her eyes
drawn to Liam over lunch and then again over dinner.
The last thing she needed in her life right now was a
man. What she required was time to think. She'd
always had a set of rules when it came to men, but
she'd allowed herself to break all of them with Max,
something she didn't intend to do again. Not that there
could be any risk of her doing that with Liam.
Attractive though he was, in a boyish sort of way, he
was obviously gay.

His comfortable, flirtatious rapport with Robert and
Oliver over the dinner-table left little room for doubt
and she knew from past experience that Robert and
Oliver had a habit of collecting beautiful young gay
men like Liam. There was nothing sexual about it – not
actively – they just liked to surround themselves with
beautiful things.

Robert followed her gaze. 'Liam is a writer,' he said,
offering her some more wine, which she waved away.
'Oliver discovered him scribbling away in a bar in
Deya and starving to death, like all great artists.'

'It wasn't *quite* like that,' interjected Oliver. 'Robert
has a habit of letting his romantic imagination run
away with him. Liam is the son of an old friend of mine
in London who wrote and asked me to keep an eye on

him while he was here. Once I had discovered that he liked gardening, the solution was obvious.'

Liam looked at Kate. 'They've both been absolutely wonderful. They've given me free bed and board in return for help in the garden, which allows me to write in the afternoon.'

Kate felt resentful. She hadn't realised that Liam was actually living with Robert and Oliver. She had assumed she would have them and the farmhouse all to herself. 'And have you had anything published that I should know about?' she asked coolly.

'Not yet. But I live in hope.' Liam smiled ruefully at her.

'Liam is working on a collection of short stories,' said Oliver.

'Short stories?' Kate raised an eyebrow. 'Oh, you mean you're a *real* writer.'

Liam looked perplexed.

'Don't mind our little Miss Acid Tongue, Liam, dear,' said Robert waspishly. 'She's just recovering from a bad case of thinking herself in love with a writer who is also a first-class prick. Unfortunately, she couldn't see past his prick.' He put up his hand as though to whisper and leant across to Liam. 'She *claims* it was a particularly big one, but that's what they all say, isn't it? Anyway,' he continued, bringing down his hand, 'as a result she thinks *all* writers are infected with the same syndrome, so we must try to be charitable until she is back to her old self.'

'I'm sorry,' Kate relented. '*Mea culpa*; Robert's right.'

Liam looked sympathetic. 'Hey, no offence taken. I got the feeling you were preoccupied. I'm sorry about the man. He must have been a real bastard as well as a right idiot to let a woman like you go.'

'That's *exactly* what we've been telling her, Liam, thank you. Perhaps she'll believe you,' said Oliver.

'If it will help any, I'm happy to keep saying it,' said Liam.

'Enough, enough.' Kate held up her hands in mock surrender. 'All this "be nice to Kate" stuff is too much. I think I shall retire early and leave you gentlemen to pass the port.'

She got to her feet and walked round the table, kissing Oliver and Robert good-night. When she reached Liam she hesitated, then held out her hand. 'Good-night.'

Instead of shaking it he held it for a moment, then gently brushed it with his lips. 'Good-night.'

Kate looked across the table and caught Robert's eye. He was grinning at her. She scowled at him.

As she went up the stairs, Robert's voice floated after her: 'Sweet dreams.'

But if she had any, Kate could not recall them. The last thing she remembered as she lay down, having opened the shutters which Francesca had tightly locked and barred, was seeing a distant star and thinking that it was actually twinkling. The next moment she woke up to a cloudless blue sky. It was not even eight o'clock, but she could hear someone whistling 'Oh What a Beautiful Morning'. She got up and looked out of the window. Down below Liam, dressed in a shorts and a check shirt, was loading plants into a wheelbarrow.

She leant out of the window. 'Good-morning.'

He looked up at the sound of her voice. 'Good-morning. And how is the broken heart feeling this morning?'

'Better. How could anyone feel anything else in a place like this.' She waved her hand at the view.

'It's mended my heart a few times, too.' He indicated the plants in the barrow. 'These are Oliver's new babies. They're a bit tender so I want to get them

177

bedded down early, before the sun gets too hot. Care to join me?'

Kate hesitated. She did not want Liam to think she needed company like some kind of love-sick adolescent. It was the last thing she was after. But it was such a beautiful morning, it seemed a shame to stay inside. She nodded and, quickly pulling on a pair of jeans and a T-shirt, went downstairs. Oliver's and Robert's bedroom door was still shut, but she could hear Francesca working in the kitchen. The smell of baking bread made her mouth water. Outside Liam was waiting. He picked up the barrow as she appeared and she fell into step beside him.

'This man of yours, what kind of things does he write?' he asked curiously as they made their way down the winding path.

'Film scripts, although nothing recently.'

'Any that I would know?'

Kate named two of Max's early films and Liam looked impressed.

'But he hasn't had much success lately,' Kate continued. 'His wife –' Liam gave her a sharp look at this – 'is now the successful one. She writes cookery books.'

'Ah, the new pornography of the middle classes,' said Liam.

Kate could not help smiling.

'That's better. To use a cliché that should be avoided by all writers, you look beautiful when you smile. You should do it more often. Tell me, is this writer of yours guilty of another cliché – he has affairs because he can't cope with his wife being more successful than him?'

Kate was irritated. What right did he have to pass judgement on a situation he knew nothing about? 'Let's drop the subject of my love affairs, shall we,' she said shortly. 'Tell me about you and Oliver and Robert.'

She sensed that he was about to say something and

then decided against it. Instead, he was silent as he manoeuvred the wheelbarrow around a large boulder, which gave little room for passing on the narrow path. Eventually, he said, 'Oliver and Robert have been marvellous. They really saved my life. Don't listen to Oliver.'

'You mean you actually were starving?' asked Kate.

'I was, but that didn't matter. No, I'd decided to get out of London because I was doing my head in with too many illegal substances, so I thought I'd come here and clean myself up. Swim, walk, catch the sun and write my *magnum opus*. But instead, I discovered how cheap the local booze was and, with the help of a load of other so-called writers in Deya, I was consuming larger amounts of it than were good for my health, let alone my writing. There's a myth and, believe me, it *is* a myth, that great writers drink a lot. Maybe some can, but that's nothing to do with whether they are great or not. A writer needs discipline and I fail miserably in that department. Robert and Oliver took me in, gave me a room and an old computer, said there was food on the table when I wanted it and promised they wouldn't ask about my work or come to my room unless invited, and they have been as good as their word. And they haven't asked for anything in return.'

'What about the gardening?' asked Kate.

'That was my idea. They have an old gardener, José, who still comes several days a week, but he can't do the really hard, back-breaking work and neither can Oliver. Doing heavy physical work in the garden in the morning clears my mind to write in the afternoon, and my day now has a sense of order and discipline.' He stopped and let the wheelbarrow down. 'This is where Oliver wants his new babies.'

They had passed the waterfall and were one terrace lower down where there was a naturally formed grotto carved by the stream, which had at some time flowed much faster and more vigorously than it did now. It was partially open to the sun, but shaded by overhanging trees and vegetation. It was moist and green-smelling.

Kate looked around in wonder and ran her hand along the rock wall, which time and water had moulded into fantastic and sometimes grotesque shapes. 'I keep on getting the feeling that I've stepped through some kind of invisible barrier into another world. I would never have believed that a place like this existed in Majorca.'

'You shouldn't make judgements based on too little information. What you *think* you see may not always be what you get,' said Liam, his back to her as he began to unload the wheelbarrow.

'So is passing judgement on relationships which you know little about,' retorted Kate.

Liam straightened up and turned to face her. He ran a grimy hand through his hair. 'Look, if I've trespassed into your private life with my hobnail boots I'm really sorry. It's just that around Robert and Oliver no subjects are taboo. It's one of the reasons I love being here. I grew up in a family where too many things were never discussed. See this?' He reached into a cleft in a rock and pulled out a long, spindly, pale-green plant. 'It was never meant to be here, but it took root nevertheless. Look how it's grown in the dark: deformed and contorted as it strains to reach the sunlight. That's how I felt when I was in England.'

Kate took the plant from his hand. 'Once again it's me who should apologise,' she said, looking down. 'It's not just Max. Work has not been too great lately, either and I'm afraid it's made me over-sensitive.'

'Never apologise for sensitivity. More people should have it. The world would be a much nicer place.'

'Will this grow outside in the sun if I replant it?' Kate

suddenly felt the need to give the tiny plant a second chance.

Liam shook his head. 'I think that one has already used up all its strength trying to get out of here. But you can help plant these if you like. They thrive in dim light and dampness. This is going to be Oliver's fern garden. Robert wanted to hang gargoyles and chandeliers from the walls and have orgies in here, but Oliver has ruled out that plan.' He grinned. 'Robert's totally outrageous, isn't he?'

Kate smiled. 'That's what I love about him.'

They were still hard at work when Robert's voice drifted down to them. 'Yoo-hoo, where are you? Breakfast is ready.'

Ten minutes later they emerged, laughing, onto the terrace, both of them with earth-stained clothes and dirt under their finger-nails.

Robert greeted them with glee. 'Ah, the children. Isn't it nice to see them playing together without arguing, Oliver, dear?'

'Take absolutely no notice of him,' said Oliver as Kate kissed him good-morning. 'How are my ferns looking?' he asked Liam.

'Well, it will be a little while before we know whether they have settled in okay, but for now, with Kate's help, they're looking good,' replied Liam, pouring Kate and himself some coffee. 'I started extra early this morning because I began working on a new story after dinner last night. Would you mind if I don't join you for breakfast and got back to it?'

'Of course not,' replied Oliver. 'I'm just delighted to hear you're working well. Off with you, now.'

Liam grabbed two apples, distributed some rolls into his various pockets, then, carrying his coffee, he left.

'I'll tell Francesca to leave another pot of coffee outside his door,' said Oliver, getting up.

When he had gone, Robert looked slyly at Kate. 'So

you and Liam went gardening together early this morning. What do you think of him?'

'He's a nice enough boy,' said Kate.

'Believe me, that boy is most definitely a man,' said Robert, rolling his eyes. 'Both Oliver and I can vouch for that.'

'As Oliver would say – please, not at breakfast, Robert. Anyway, why should I care?' Kate loaded butter onto a warm roll and added a large spoonful of honey, licking her fingers as melting butter and honey trickled over the sides of the roll. The honey tasted of oranges.

'Because methinks he fancies you.'

Kate's mouth was open to receive the roll. She put it back untouched on her plate. 'You mean he's bisexual?'

'No. I mean he's straight.'

'Straight?'

'As in straight as a die. H-E-T-E-R-O-S-E-X-U-A-L.'

'I do know how to spell it, thank you,' said Kate tartly.

'Ah, but do you know how to play it? There's the rub, dearest Kate.'

'I do. But I certainly wouldn't want to play it with Liam.'

'And, pray, why not?' Robert sounded hurt.

'I came here because I need to sort out my life, not complicate it. Anyway, even if I did find him attractive, which I do not, he's much too young. I know you mean well, Robert, but he's just not my type.'

'He's twenty-nine.'

'Not even thirty,' said Kate, exasperated. 'See what I mean?'

'Kate Daniels. You are the last woman I expected to be prejudiced against younger men. And as to not being your type? Honey, don't bullshit a bullshitter.

There *is* only one kind of man and he's got two legs, two arms and a p . . .'

'Can't I leave the table for just one minute without the conversation taking a turn for the worse?' enquired Oliver, putting his hand on Robert's shoulder and brushing his cheek lightly with a kiss.

Robert caught his hand and held it there. 'I was just telling Kate about Liam. She hadn't guessed.'

'I'm hurt, Oliver,' said Kate. 'I've discovered that you and Robert have been scheming to set me up.'

'Oh, dear, and we thought you would like him. He's *such* a nice boy. The coincidence of him being here and you coming, suffering from a broken heart – it seemed so perfect. Will you forgive us?' Oliver sat down.

'You know I'd forgive you and Robert anything,' said Kate, 'but *please*, don't try to set up my sex life. It's embarrassing. Is Liam a party to this?'

'Good heavens *no!*' Oliver looked horrified. 'We thought you'd be good for him too. His choice in women has not, up to now, shown the same sensitivity as his writing.'

'He means he's been screwing around,' added Robert.

'That much I'd got right,' said Kate, 'only I thought it was with men. He's almost too good-looking to be straight.'

'Aha! Do I detect a wistful note of longing in your voice?' demanded Robert.

'No, all *you* detect is orange blossom honey and crumbs of freshly baked bread,' retorted Kate.

'I think this is one match we mere mortals must leave to the gods, Robert,' said Oliver. 'Sometimes they move in mysterious ways, as I have learnt since coming here to live among them. We meddle in their business at our peril.'

'As an agnostic, I'll say amen to that,' said Kate, popping some more warm roll into her mouth.

Fifteen

• • •

After the first day or two Kate's life settled into a slow, comfortable rhythm. She took an early morning walk in the surrounding hills before the sun reached its zenith, followed by a late and long breakfast, which often meandered gently into lunch-time. In the heat of mid-afternoon, while Robert and Oliver retired to their bedroom for a siesta, she lounged in the shade of the terrace, half-heartedly reading a book or a magazine. Then she scrambled down the narrow goat track, which led to a small rocky bay below the house, to swim and laze in the sun for a couple of hours. Neither Oliver nor Robert accompanied her to the bay, so she had its one small patch of white sand to herself.

She had been in Majorca a week and all her resolutions to make decisions about her life seemed to have evaporated in the heat of the long, lazy days. She could almost view her life in London as though it had happened to another Kate Daniels, one who had nothing to do with the sybaritic creature she had become. She could not remember the last time she had taken a holiday when she had simply lain in the sun, listening to the sound of the waves lapping the beach and the occasional hoarse cry of a seagull circling overhead, or the thin, plaintive cry of some inland bird, and she had forgotten what pleasure it could give.

She knew she had allowed herself to be seduced by

the magic of the place. But after the first couple of days she had decided to lie back and enjoy it. There was still time to make the serious decisions that had to be made, but not then and there.

Her initial fears that Liam would in some way intrude on her had not been realised. Apart from occasional meals and when she came upon him working in the garden, she had not seen much of him since the first day. He had been working hard on a new story and eating alone in the kitchen at odd times. Francesca was always careful to make sure there were plenty of cold meats and cheeses as well as fruit and bread, whenever he wanted them.

But that afternoon, when she came downstairs dressed in shorts and a swimming costume, and carrying her towel and some suntan lotion, and with *One Hundred Years of Solitude* by Gabriel García Marquez tucked under her arm – a book she had always intended to read, which she had found in Oliver's extensive library – he had been waiting for her.

'If you don't want me to come you just have to say,' he had urged her. 'I hate people invading my space when I want to be alone. But I've just finished the first draft of my story and I need a break and some convivial company.'

Kate had said she didn't mind him joining her and would be glad of the company, even though it wasn't quite true. She enjoyed having the small bay to herself and had even begun to think of it as her exclusive property. They scrambled down the hillside in an awkward silence, Kate ignoring Liam's helping hand over particularly rocky patches. When they reached the bottom Liam announced that he didn't normally bother with swimming trunks when he swam in the bay as there were only goats to see him, but in her honour he had borrowed a pair from Robert. However, when he took off his shorts and revealed the tiny, peacock-blue trunks Robert had loaned him they were barely more than a posing pouch.

He saw Kate looking and shrugged his shoulders deprecatingly. 'A bit brief, I'm afraid, but they were all Robert had and Oliver's were too large.'

Kate turned away, aware that she was blushing under her tan. She could not help thinking that he would have looked far less provocative if he were naked.

'Are you coming for a dip?' he asked, setting off down the beach.

'In a minute.' Kate wanted to put some distance between her and Liam, if only for a short while.

As he swam out to sea with long powerful strokes, she rubbed suntan lotion over her body, glad that she was wearing a fairly businesslike one-piece black swimming costume. After the first couple of days and the realisation, like Liam, that her only audience was the occasional goat, Kate had taken to rolling her costume down to her hips although she did not plan to do that today. She tanned easily and had turned deep golden brown quickly, but she still wanted to protect her skin. In order to get the lotion between her shoulder-blades, however, she was forced into bodily contortions which she did not want Liam to see. Somehow or other, Liam seemed to have a way of catching her embarrassingly off guard.

She had been telling the truth when she told Robert that he was not her type of man, although exactly what that was Kate was no longer sure. She had been convinced that Max was her type. At the thought of him, her first for some time, Kate suddenly saw his face and for a brief moment she felt she could almost touch him.

With some difficulty she put the top back on her suntan lotion bottle, her fingers slippery with cream.

Then she scrambled to her feet and ran down the beach, plunging head first into the sea. It was still only early June and the water was so cold it took her breath away. The sea became quite deep within a few yards of the shore line. Kate forced her way back up to the surface, gasping for breath. She shook her head to clear the water out of her ears, pushed her hair out of her eyes and began to swim. As she got into a regular stroke, the water felt good and clean on her skin, as though she were washing the past, or at least Max, away.

Liam, who was lazily floating on his back about fifty yards from the shore, turned over and began to tread water when he saw Kate swimming towards him.

He had not been able to work Kate out. She was beautiful, of that he was sure – he loved all that wild hair of hers. He also liked the way she was comfortable with her full body in a way that so many women weren't. Without being obvious, it hinted at a sexuality that seemed at odds with her successful career woman persona. When Robert had told him about her before she came he had been predisposed to dislike her. He had met executive women before and it seemed to him that they were either so neurotic that they threatened to fall apart at every moment, or like steel – shiny, hard and unbending.

He had a feeling that Robert and Oliver had hoped that he and Kate would get together. But although there were moments when he sensed that she was attracted to him he could not be sure. One thing he was sure of, though, was that she was giving off the signals of a woman who did not want to be involved.

In a way he was glad. He had had enough roll-on, roll-off relationships to last him a lifetime. Sex wasn't everything, although it had taken him long enough to discover that, and Kate, although sexually attractive, was far too interesting for just a brief fling.

Kate swam a few yards past him, turned and came back. She began to tread water too, shaking her hair like a dog.

'It's cold but glorious,' she gasped, a little out of breath.

'I sometimes swim first thing in the morning. Then it's *really* cold,' said Liam.

Kate shivered at the thought.

Liam looked concerned. 'I think you should get warm. Race you back to the beach?'

Kate nodded and immediately set off.

'Hey, that's cheating. I haven't said go yet,' Liam yelled after her. But within a few strokes he had overtaken her and reached the beach some ten yards in front of her. He stood there grinning, droplets of sparkling water coursing down his tanned body. 'That's what you get for cheating,' he said. 'Winner takes all.'

Kate collapsed, panting, onto her towel. 'Okay. I concede defeat,' she said.

Liam snapped the sides of his swimming trunks. 'Now, as I feel exceedingly ridiculous in these, would you mind keeping your back to me while I slip modestly back into my shorts?' He grinned. It was infectious.

With her back to Liam, Kate began to re-apply her suntan lotion.

'There's a spot just between your shoulder-blades you aren't reaching,' said Liam, now dressed in his shorts.

'I know,' said Kate tartly.

Liam held out his hand for the bottle and, not for the first time, Kate noticed what beautiful hands he had. 'If you will allow me, I can administer lotion to the right place.'

What harm could it do, thought Kate, as she held up

the bottle. 'You have my permission to touch the designated spot only.'

He tugged his forelock. 'Yessir, milady.'

Kate squinted up at him. The sun was in her eyes, but it looked as if he was laughing at her. She rolled over onto her stomach and stretched out on her towel, resting her head on her arms.

Liam took the bottle and knelt down beside her, pouring some lotion onto his hands before applying it to her back like a practised masseur. He started between her shoulder-blades but then began to work outwards and Kate did not stop him. His hands felt wonderful, the pressure firm and relaxing.

'I see you're reading one of my favourite books,' he said.

'Trying to. I'm afraid I don't have much time for reading fiction.'

'I couldn't live without books. I guess that's why I decided to be a writer, although sometimes I think it's the stupidest decision I've ever made and believe me, when it comes to making stupid decisions I'm in a class of my own.'

'I don't think it's stupid, not if it's what you really want to do,' said Kate drowsily.

'It's stupid, or maybe crazy is more apt, to sit down every day knowing even before you have started that you will never produce something like *One Hundred Years of Solitude*.'

'You're asking too much of yourself . . .' began Kate.

'No, I'm not,' interrupted Liam harshly and sat back on his heels.

Kate raised her head.

'There's no point if something can't be perfect. I haven't kept anything I've written. The moment I see even the tiniest mistake, like a spelling, I tear it up. I shall probably destroy the story I finished today.' He looked at Kate with anguished eyes. 'Is it so very wrong to want perfection?'

'No, not wrong,' said Kate slowly. 'But perhaps you have to learn to be a little kinder to yourself. Maybe there isn't just one kind of perfection in writing as well as in relationships.'

They looked at each other for a moment longer, then Kate turned away and sank back down onto her towel. This was all wrong. Something was happening and she didn't know quite what it was except for the fact that she didn't want it to happen. She flinched as Liam put his hand back on her shoulders.

'Relax. You're very tense. I can feel it in your muscles.' Liam began to work across her shoulders and around the nape of her neck.

Kate knew why she was tense and she suspected he knew too. 'Perhaps I should go for another swim; that's good for tension.' She started to move.

But his hands held her down. 'Not until I've finished. I learnt my trade from this beach girl in Bali. She was the best. Only I won't walk up and down on your body, at least not this time.'

Kate was tempted to ask him what else he had learnt from the beach girl, but instead she kept silent. Liam's touch was relaxing. He began to work on her lower back, his fingers reaching just inside her swimming costume. She tensed again.

'Relax,' he commanded.

When he finally stopped she was almost resentful.

He sat back on his heels again. 'I could do the rest of you, but I think we had better leave that until we have been longer acquainted.'

Kate rolled over and sat up. 'Thank you. I enjoyed that.' She sounded prim, but she did not want Liam to get any ideas.

'So did I. You have beautiful musculature.'

Despite herself Kate smiled. 'Nobody has ever put it quite that way before.'

'Maybe they haven't touched you properly before. The English have yet to learn the pleasures of the flesh and I mean that in the true sense. They have at least begun to understand about the sensuality of food, although they've become a nation of obsessive foodies as a consequence, but when it comes to sex too many people still have the "meat and two veg" attitude and ignore the erotic pleasures of just touching. May I?'

Before Kate could give her assent, he took her hand in his and began to massage it. First her palm and then, one by one, her fingers. It was far more intimate than when he had been massaging her back. She had never thought too much about hands before, but watching Liam's long slim fingers working on her she tried to remember what Max's were like. As far as she could recall they were quite small for a man of his size and his nails had been bitten to the quick, like those of a little boy.

When Liam came to her thumb he looked up. 'In some people the Mount of Venus is a highly-developed erogenous zone, yet when is it ever touched?' With his forefinger he traced the swelling flesh at the base of Kate's thumb, then he suddenly bent over and brushed his lips against it.

Kate pulled her hand away as though scalded. She scrambled to her feet and began to pull on her shorts.

Liam stayed where he was, on his knees in the sand. 'Look, I'm really sorry. That was a crass thing to do. The last thing I want is for you to think I'm hitting on you. I like you, I really do. Please,' he begged her, 'can't we forget it ever happened.'

Her shorts zipped up, Kate stopped. Liam looked genuinely sorry. Was she being too sensitive? It had only been the briefest of kisses. But it was how it had made her feel rather than the kiss itself which had

192

caused her to get up. She looked at Liam who was still comically on his knees in the sand.

'Please. I promise. Nothing like that will ever happen again.' He held up his hands as though to plead.

'I'm not interested in a quickie holiday romance.'

'Whoever said I was?'

'How old are you, Liam?'

'I don't know what that has to do with it, but I'm twenty-nine.'

'And I'm thirty-nine.'

He shrugged. 'If you want me to say you don't look it and I could never have guessed I'm not going to. As a matter of fact I've known how old you were since you arrived. I asked Robert. But I'm not interested in your age, it makes no difference to me.'

'Well, it does to me,' said Kate. 'Not me being thirty-nine, I'm happy with that. But you being more than ten years younger does make a difference. As far as I'm concerned it precludes anything but a quick sexual fling and I'm just not up for that at the moment.'

He stood up and put his hands in his pockets. 'I've really made a cock-up, haven't I?'

He looked so miserable that Kate went over to him. 'Liam, I'm sorry. It's not that I don't want to . . . it's just that frankly I seem to be making a mess of most things right at the moment and I don't want to add yet another thing to the list.'

His eyes glinted. 'Another perfectionist?'

Kate could not help smiling as she turned away to begin picking up her beach things. As she pushed her book and her towel into her beach bag she was almost preternaturally conscious of Liam watching her. Slipping her feet into her sandals and settling her bag over her shoulders, she made for the beginning of the goat path back up the hill.

'What was it you said about learning to be a bit

193

kinder to yourself?' Liam called after her. 'How about we both start now?'

Sixteen

• • •

Liam had taken his time, slowly and unhurriedly exploring her as though he were discovering a woman's body for the first time. Once he had reached her toes and started to work his way up again, Kate had been ready to do anything he wanted.

Now she lay, cradling him in her arms as he slept in the simple whitewashed room which had been turned into his bedroom and study, above what had been the stables. The walls were rough stone, the floor wooden and a long, low window looked out into the depths of the pine forest at the back. Unlike the rest of the house it was simply and sparsely furnished: a chair and a table, bare except for an elderly Amstrad computer and some paper and pencils. Against one wall three shirts and a jacket hung from a metal rail. On the floor a pair of well-worn Timberland boots lay where they had been kicked off and on the window-sill there was a pair of faded blue espadrilles, their rope soles frayed almost beyond use and their toes curled up from having been in water and left to dry out. There was also a large, old-fashioned iron bedstead, which creaked and strained with every movement and they had made a lot of those.

As the shadows lengthened and the cool green of the pine forest seeped into the room, Kate felt Liam's body relax and the rhythm of his breathing change as he fell into a deeper sleep. She knew that Robert and Oliver would be waking from their afternoon siesta. Robert usually went down to the kitchen and made some Earl Grey tea at about half past six – an art Francesca still hadn't mastered to Oliver's satisfaction – and they drank it in bed before getting up to shower and dress for dinner.

Kate didn't want them to know what had happened, at least not yet. It could be there was nothing to know. Just one afternoon spent in a white room. Liam did not stir as she eased her way gently off the bed and stepped into her swimming costume, which she had discarded in a heap on the floor. She flinched as it touched her skin. It was still damp, and rough with sand and salt. Pulling on her shorts and holding her sandals, she crept quietly down the stairs. Across the courtyard she could see Francesca preparing dinner in the kitchen. Deciding she was less likely to meet anyone by using the main door, Kate slipped round the side of the house. Just as she stepped into the hallway she heard Robert cheerfully greeting Francesca in the kitchen and, seizing her opportunity, she ran quickly up the stairs to her room.

Tearing off her swimming costume almost before she had closed the door, Kate turned the taps on full in her large marble bath and poured a copious amount of fragrant bath oil from the Penhaligon selection that Robert had so thoughtfully provided into the steaming water, then she soaked for a long while.

Why had she turned back when Liam spoke? If she had carried on up the hill nothing would have happened. Not today or any day. She closed her eyes and the memory of the way Liam's beautiful hands had touched her body came back and she groaned aloud. It was all too much, too soon. She would just have to take him aside quietly and tell him that although it had been wonderful it could go no further.

It was only when she went downstairs to the terrace

for their usual pre-dinner cocktails, and saw to her surprise that Liam was already there, that Kate wondered whether she should have woken him before she left, or at least written a message. When she saw the reproachful look in his eyes she knew that she should.

'Isn't it nice to have Liam with us again for dinner,' said Oliver, handing Kate a gin and tonic. 'He says that his story needs to rest a while before he revises it. I was just telling him how much we've missed him this week. I do so enjoy it when we all get together in the evenings. It's not like just having friends, but more of a family.'

'I missed you too,' said Liam, looking pointedly at Kate before turning back to Oliver. 'But I think you'll like the story. When I've revised it I'd like you to read it.'

'It would give me the greatest of pleasure. The launch party for your first published volume is the only thing that will tempt me back to London. Robert is already planning his outfit for the occasion.'

'Well, you know me,' added Robert. 'I never have a thing to wear.'

They all laughed. Robert had large walk-in wardrobes in both London and Majorca that were perfectly colour co-ordinated and there was not a single item of clothing in either about which he could not remember exactly where and when it had been bought, and when and where he had last worn it.

'I think it's time for some Callas, don't you?' asked Oliver.

Robert rolled his eyes heavenwards. 'As much as I *adore* her golden tonsils, might we have something a little lighter tonight? We haven't heard Bette Midler strutting her stuff for weeks.'

The two of them went inside and began to bicker good-naturedly over the choice of music.

Liam came and stood beside Kate who was contemplating the last dying embers of the sunset from the edge of the terrace. 'Are you embarrassed by what happened this afternoon?' he demanded in a fierce whisper.

'No!' Kate was taken aback by his vehemence. 'Of course not. What on earth gave you that idea?'

'I woke up to an empty bed. It was as though you had never been there.'

'Liam, I had the most wonderful afternoon. No, it was better than that. But sometimes, in the aftermath, people have second thoughts. I thought it best to get away and give us both time to think.'

'And did you?'

'Well, yes.'

'So?' demanded Liam.

This was not how Kate had planned to tell him that there would be no other afternoons. But it seemed she had no choice. 'I just don't want to get involved in something we may both regret,' she said gently.

'You mean you're having second thoughts?'

Kate checked that Robert and Oliver were still occupied with their choice of music. 'No. Not second thoughts. I was the one who talked about not wanting to get involved beforehand.'

'This is not just a casual holiday fuck for me,' said Liam rather too loudly for Kate. She saw Robert look in their direction.

'I know. I'm sorry. It's just that I'm still feeling a bit raw emotionally.'

He reached out and gently touched the side of her face. 'Kate, my beautiful Kate. I don't want to hurt you, I just want to love you.'

The velvet voice of Julie London singing 'Cry Me a River' welled out of hidden speakers, and Robert and Oliver came out onto the terrace, their arms wrapped around each other.

'Compromise can be a beautiful thing in love,' said Robert as they danced slowly round.

Liam held out his hand to Kate and grinned, suddenly boyish again. 'A wise old man, or more likely a wise old woman, once said: those who cannot be beaten should be joined. Shall we dance?'

As their bodies moved to the music, Kate was once again aware of the scent of Liam's skin, which was fresh and green like the pine forest that surrounded the house. She opened her eyes and found that Robert was watching her over the top of Oliver's head, a knowing smile on his face. She stuck out her tongue.

Francesca was trying to signal them from the doorway, anxious not to disturb them, but equally keen that dinner should not spoil. If she found it strange to see two couples, one of them men, dancing, she gave no sign of it. Eventually she caught Oliver's eye and he broke regretfully away from Robert's embrace. At his bidding they went in to dinner, but Robert managed to catch Kate's arm and hold her back from the other two.

'Well?' he hissed.

'Well, what?' replied Kate.

'Dear heart, Francesca has sharper eyes than you think and she confides *everything* to me. Anyway, it's quite obvious that Liam is smitten, so tell your Auntie Robert, was it marvellous?'

Kate's cheeks burnt and she looked down.

'I *knew* it!' Robert was triumphant. He linked his arm through hers and led her to the table. 'Darlings one and all, I think we should have champagne tonight,' he announced.

'And what is the occasion that prompts this decision?' asked Oliver, looking around.

Robert held up his arms, executed a perfect pirouette and started to sing a song from *West Side Story*: 'I feel pretty, oh, so pretty, I feel pretty and witty and gay.' He did another pirouette. 'Does there have to be a reason to drink champagne?' He launched into a high-kicking cancan, this time borrowing the words from *Gigi*: 'The night they invented champagne . . .'

Oliver held up his hands in protest. 'All right, all right. Champagne it is. Anything rather than having to listen to Robert's complete repertoire of greatest hits from the musicals.'

Kate had been laughing so much that she had not looked at Liam, but as Robert hurried out of the room to get the champagne she caught his questioning eye. She held up her hands and shrugged.

Oliver saw the gesture. 'Am I the *only* one in the room who doesn't know what is going on?' he demanded.

Liam looked at him. 'I'm sorry, Oliver, it isn't really meant to be a secret.' He reached across the table and took Kate's hand. 'But I . . . well, I'm in love with Kate.'

Seventeen

• • •

Two pairs of eyes stared accusingly at Kate across the breakfast table. She felt as though she had the words 'fraud' and 'impostor' branded across her forehead in large red letters.

She bent her head and sipped her orange juice. It tasted sour. She wanted to say that it wasn't her fault, that she hadn't set out to deceive them, that they had got it wrong from the beginning. But instead she sipped her juice, unable to meet their hurt gaze.

Robert and Oliver had been acting like two mother hens who had hatched not a fluffy little chick but love. They had strutted and clucked, their eyes alert for any choice morsel which would feed love and make it grow rounder and fluffier. Only Kate seemed to notice that they had hatched a cuckoo.

It had certainly looked like love. It had even behaved like love. Everyone – even Kate – had *wanted* it to be love. But who would dare tell proud parents that their adored new-born is not the most beautiful baby in the world? It would be a brave person to do that and Kate had been neither daring nor brave enough.

Perhaps if she had said something at the beginning she might have been able to lessen the blow. But she hadn't and now, a week after love was seemingly made flesh, it was too late. The damage had been done.

It had taken just one tiny moment of weakness on

her part to cause the damage. Not the moment she yielded to the lure of Liam's tempting body. But the moment of weakness when he first said that word 'love' out loud.

She should have stopped him right then. Told him it was nothing of the sort – merely sex. Well, not merely sex – great sex – but sex none the less. But she had found herself wishing why not? It *might* be love. It was easy to mistake lust for love, something she had done herself. So why couldn't it happen the other way round?

In other circumstances she might have loved Liam. He was sensitive and intelligent, and he was a wonderful lover. Something he had demonstrated time and time again that week.

Her body had not been fraudulent in its response to his. She had wanted him and had gone more than willingly to lie in the bed in his cool, white, pine-scented room, in the heat of the afternoons. But she had not asked him to her room, nor had she spent a night with him. If Liam or anyone else had noticed this, or thought anything of it, they said nothing, but Kate clung to it. It was a clear sign that she had not acquiesced. Not completely. How could they say they hadn't noticed?

There had seemed to be only one way out and she had been a coward and taken it. The evidence now lay on the table beside her plate, glowing, or so it seemed to Kate at that moment, like some malevolent radioactive object which threatened to contaminate the world: her plane ticket back to England.

Robert and Oliver had said she could stay for as long as she wanted, but she had never promised to stay for more than one week – two at the most – and two weeks were now up. Anyway, she thought, reducing one of Francesca's beautifully shaped bread rolls into a pile of crumbs on her plate, she simply *had* to go back. She had a career to think about, not that she had thought about it at all since she had arrived, but that, too, was part of the trouble. If you let them, emotions got in the way of real life.

Kate sneaked a look at Robert and Oliver. They were still staring at her, waiting for her to explain herself, their half-eaten breakfasts abandoned. She didn't see that there was anything *to* explain. Maybe it was slightly short notice to announce at breakfast that she was catching the six o'clock flight to Heathrow that evening, but surely they understood that today was Saturday and she needed to be back at work on Monday morning? She had been lucky to get a seat at all. It was the last on the flight and only free because of a cancellation, according to the girl at the airline office – she had made the call after creeping down the stairs to the telephone before anyone else was up.

She had not meant to deceive them. What was the point of needlessly upsetting them until she was sure she could get a flight? And that was another reason she had taken the seat tonight. She had known they would react like this but now they had only a few hours to feel upset before she left and they wouldn't have time to talk her out of it, although just the look in both their eyes was enough to make her resolve falter, if not crumble altogether.

'Have you told Liam?' asked Robert finally.

'Told Liam what?' asked Liam cheerfully as he walked into the room, sweeping some rolls onto his plate and sitting down all in one easy movement.

In the silence, Robert and Oliver looked at Kate again, and Liam's eyes followed theirs. 'Am I missing something important here?' he asked, a bread roll half-way to his mouth.

To her horror, Kate found her cheeks growing hot under the gaze of three pairs of eyes. Why did she suddenly feel so guilty? She looked beseechingly at

203

Robert, wanting him to rescue her, but the expression in his eyes told her that she would find no lifeline there. She poured herself some coffee and then, holding her cup between her hands as though for protection, she forced herself to look at Liam. 'I'm going back to London this evening.'

The bread roll remained suspended in his hand, half-way between his mouth and the plate, as he stared at her, hurt and bewilderment merging into one. Then he slowly turned to look at Robert and Oliver, as though hoping they would tell him it wasn't true. But Oliver nodded.

Liam turned back to Kate. 'There's something wrong in London? You're going but then you're coming back?'

She shook her head. 'I'm going home. I have to get back to work.'

He dropped the roll onto his plate and leant back in his chair as though he needed space to breathe. 'But you said you hated work, that you were thinking of taking the redundancy money and having some time off, maybe even writing a book in a place like this.'

She had said *something* like that, thought Kate, as she felt Robert and Oliver looking questioningly at her. But, in her defence, it had been said in the afterglow of making love on the beach in what Liam and she now considered their private cove, the waves lapping gently at their feet, the scent of wild herbs in their nostrils. People said things they did not really mean at such moments, dreamt dreams that could never be reality. That lay back in London and she had to return to it.

She looked at Robert and Oliver – they would understand that she had been only dreaming – but she received no understanding in return. She turned to Liam. 'I merely said it was a nice idea. I never said it was a serious option.' She tried to smile at him. Surely he could see how foolish a notion it had been?

But Liam did not smile back and when he spoke his

voice was rough with emotion. 'You can't leave. I love you. We *belong* together.'

Oliver stood up and pulled Robert to his feet. Robert started to speak but Oliver shook his head and, taking him by the arm, led him back inside the house, leaving Kate and Liam together.

'Nobody belongs to anybody, Liam,' Kate said rather too sharply. 'Look, we've had a wonderful time, can't we just leave it at that? If we end it now, while things are still good, perhaps we can stay friends.'

'So you not only want to stick a knife in me, but you also want to twist it round? For friend substitute eunuch, because that is what I would feel like if I had to be a *friend* to you.'

'Don't be so dramatic, Liam. This relationship was always going nowhere from the beginning. I said right from the start that it was impractical because of the differences between us.'

He took a deep breath. 'Okay, so let me try to be rational, like you. Far be it for me, a mere man, to point out, but would the difference in our age make any difference if *you* were a man and I a woman?'

'That's not the point and you know it. It's how *I* feel about it. And it's not just the age gap, there are other problems too. What if you wanted children?'

'And if I did?'

'I'm nearly forty.'

'You're still nearly a year off your fortieth birthday, but I won't quibble about that. The question is, do you *want* children?'

'I'm not really sure. It's not a question I have had occasion to address much.' Kate knew she sounded both pompous and defensive, although she had not meant to.

Liam's mouth twisted wryly. 'Really? Most women I know have *addressed* the question of children thoroughly.'

'Contrary to your no doubt scientific survey of women, not all women think about children all the time.' Liam almost seemed to wince at her angry words and Kate felt a sense of despair. She had not wanted to hurt him.

Liam was silent for a few moments and when he next spoke his voice was quiet, pleading. 'My mother didn't get around to producing me until she was forty-six. She said she did not see the point in it until then. So you see, you still have plenty of time and, when the right moment comes, surely we could make the decision together. Isn't that what love and relationships are all about?'

'I've never mentioned the word love,' replied Kate gently. 'You were the one who used it, not me.'

Liam took her hand in his and began to trace the lines on her palm with the forefinger of his other hand as though he was trying to memorise them. 'Do you mean that what happened between us means nothing to you?'

Kate tried to pull it away, but Liam wouldn't let go. 'No, of course not. It was very . . . nice.'

'*Nice*!' He laughed shortly and released her hand. 'Is that what you call it? Nice. A word that should be expunged from the English language: so vague, so indeterminate. A word used to avoid feeling. Nothing *nice* could feel anything.'

'I didn't mean it like that and don't turn the writer on me,' said Kate, angry again. 'I've had enough of writers to last me a lifetime. This is real life, not some fictional fantasy. *Yes*! If your male ego must be satisfied, the sex was great, but that's all it was, *sex*.'

He caught her hands in his and forced her to look into his eyes. 'It may have been just sex for you but I was making love and, while my male ego might want to believe I'm a sexual superman, I don't, *can't*, make love like that to just any woman. If it was great it was because of you, or perhaps *you're* like that with every man you sleep with,' he ended harshly.

Kate tugged free of his grip. 'When I use the word love I mean it. I don't scatter it around like some character in a romantic novel.'

It was a cheap jibe and she knew it, but it had the effect she wanted. She had driven him away. He had left the table and she had not seen him again after that. He had not joined them for lunch – which had been a sad, silent affair, Francesca serving them with a stifled sob every time she looked at Kate – or come to say goodbye when she left for the airport.

Even Robert's driving seemed to reflect the change in mood which had come over everybody. He slowed down approaching corners and signalled his intention to overtake on several occasions, rather than just pulling sharply out and putting his hand on the horn. Kate kept quiet as they drove, looking out of the window at the dramatic coastline scenery, trying to imprint it on her mind. Although she had promised Oliver and Francesca that she would be back soon, she knew she would not have the heart to return, not for a very long time. She was aware of Robert's searching glances in her direction, but she steadfastly ignored him. There was nothing more to say. She had made up her mind and he could not change it.

They had left the coast road and were heading south through the centre of the island when Robert eventually spoke: 'I think you're doing the right thing.'

Startled, Kate turned in her seat and stared at him. 'The right thing?'

Robert nodded, his eyes on the road. 'If you don't love Liam you're doing the right thing. He's worth more than just a holiday fling.'

Kate looked back at the road. 'Well, I don't love him.' She sounded full of self-justification and she knew it.

She turned and looked at Robert again. 'But I did *try* to love him, for your and Oliver's sakes.'

'I know. We love you both and thought that because we loved you, you would love each other. It was a mistake. But you should never try to love anyone for their sake or anyone else's, including yours. You either love someone or you don't. It's as simple as that.'

'I know,' said Kate, 'and no one is more sorry than me that things didn't work out with Liam, but happiness is hard to find.'

'You don't have to tell *me* that, dear heart, but I do sometimes wonder whether you are looking for it in the right places.' He glanced sideways at her. 'At the risk of you getting all shirty again, can I offer you a little bit of advice which may sound strange coming from someone with a past record like mine? I think you use sex as a way to avoid love.' He held up his hand as Kate started to protest. 'Hear me out. What I mean is that you have an enormous capacity for love yet you seem to fear it, so you settle for sex which is so much less demanding. You can take off your inhibitions at the bedroom door and put them back on again when you leave, and the meeting of two bodies gives the illusion of shared emotion. But all it brings is momentary physical satisfaction, no more than that and, believe me, there isn't a form of sex I haven't tried. Looking for love in sex is a fruitless quest.'

Kate was silent. Maybe Robert was right. But when she looked around, being in love seemed to be an excuse to abdicate responsibility for your life. She had only to think of Jessica. No matter how many times Hugo humiliated her she forgave him and for what? For love?

And Harriet – what must it be like to be married to Max? Was love her excuse too? Even her father had virtually given up sex for love of her mother, not that

that was quite the same thing, Kate knew, but why did one person always have to lose when it came to love?

Only Robert and Oliver had proved the exception, which was why she clung so tightly to them. She could believe in love when she saw them together. They were so different in everything, yet neither of them had given up his differences in order to love the other. Each had remained himself and the relationship – as well as they themselves – had been stronger because of it. Most people seemed to be diminished by love, or at least by what they described as love.

Liam appeared to think that loving someone was enough and that love would automatically be returned in kind. He had sworn that he would go anywhere, do anything, as long as he could be with her. But that wasn't love, that was self-abasement.

Kate turned and looked out of the window at the passing countryside, not that she saw any of it. What was so painful about Liam was that he reminded her of herself. There had been a time when she had been prepared to do anything for love – for Max. The affair they'd had at university might have been little more than a drunken one-night stand, but for her it had lasted much longer. She had tried to bury the memory of her as the young student, hanging around in the bar, wanting desperately to see him, to know why he had not called her, only to watch him walk in with another girl on his arm, studiously ignoring her pleading eyes. Humiliating her.

She had thought that the summer vacation would make her forget, but on the first day she had returned for her final year she had walked into the bar to hear the news of his wedding being laughed at by all the other students. The pain was as real as being kicked and she had had to run out, clutching her stomach. It was the first time she had learnt that emotional pain could be as exquisite and as real as anything physical, and she had let him do it to her twice: first all those years ago, then in the restaurant when Jessica had told her about the child.

Kate suddenly realised that the reason she could not see anything was that her eyes were misted with tears. Keeping her face turned away from Robert, she hastily dug in her bag for a tissue and loudly blew her nose.

'Who says I'm looking for love?' she demanded when it was safe to look at Robert again. 'It's not part of the UN Declaration of Human Rights that everyone should fall in love. If we spent less time looking for love and more getting on with our lives the world would be a much happier place.'

Robert turned and looked at her for a lot longer than was safe for other road users. Kate was about ready to scream at him to take notice of a heavily laden lorry that was lumbering towards them on the wrong side of the road when he looked back, executed a dangerous avoidance manoeuvre on the verge of the road while gesticulating rudely at the lorry driver, then righted the car onto the road again. He turned abruptly right in front of the oncoming traffic onto the road leading to the airport and did not speak again until after he had parked.

Then he swung round in his seat. 'If I didn't know you better, Kate Daniels, I'd say you were scared of love. Well, let me tell you something, scared or not, there's nothing you can do to avoid it. If it's going to get you it will, full-frontal or stealthily from behind. Either way, there won't be a thing you can do about it once it gets you and I intend to be there when it does to wave goodbye to your "I'm in control" rational self as it flies out of the window.'

As the plane began to taxi onto the runway, Kate permitted herself a small smile. Robert was such an old-fashioned romantic. It was why she treasured him so much: he was a dying breed.

She looked down at the day-old English newspapers in her lap, which she had seized on hungrily. But they offered little to divert her with their tales of economic ills and 'love rat' soap stars. As the engines thrust the plane into the air and Majorca slipped off below her, she settled back in her seat, waving away the stewardess's offer of earphones to watch the in-flight movie – it was a sentimental love story – and began to anticipate the pleasures of being back in her flat, surrounded by her books and music, and the familiar sounds of her neighbourhood.

Her anticipation grew as the taxi from Heathrow sat in an endless queue of vehicles edging their way through the contra-flows along the M4 and reached its peak as she turned the keys in her lock. But her homecoming did not live up to what she had expected. Rather than being welcoming, her flat was not only musty with the stale air that had been trapped in it, but it also felt empty, as though it had lost the imprint of a human presence.

The chill, wet spring had changed into warm summer while she had been away. Kate walked from room to room, opening all the windows, causing the dust motes which had been lying low to swirl up and dance in the bright sunlight, making the place feel even more uninhabited. She put a CD on in an attempt to fill the emptiness, but it sounded hollow and desperate, so she switched it off. Searching her cupboards, she found a packet of coffee. It had been opened before she went away so the beans were stale and it tasted brackish, but at least its faint aroma fragranced the flat and made it feel a little more like home.

Her mailbox was stuffed full, but the post took no more than a couple of minutes to open. Kate could tell at a glance that it was mainly bills, credit card statements, glossy circulars and the usual consignment of junk mail promising that she could win large sums of money if she would only put a cross in the square and agree to accept – on a trial basis only – this publication or that catalogue. She screwed them all up and threw them onto the floor. Then she poured herself another cup of coffee and, grimacing at the lukewarm liquid which succeeded in tasting both weak and bitter at the same time, went over to her answer phone.

The message counter had been soundlessly demanding her attention from the moment she had walked in the door, but she had been trying to ignore it. She could have checked her messages while she was in Majorca, but had decided not to. She had wanted to be free of England and all its problems, but she had merely been putting them off until now, she thought wearily.

Her finger wavered over the play-back button. Ten messages registered on the counter. After another sip of coffee and a further grimace, Kate pressed the play button.

The first voice was instantly recognisable. It was Max.

'Babe, I'm calling from LA. It's great. But whatever the old Beach Boys song says, those Californian girls don't have a thing on you. Sorry I didn't call you before I went, but when the summons comes from Hollywood you just gotta get on the first plane. I'm working on a rewrite of my treatment for Chuck so I'm going to be here for at least another week or so and I'll call you again soon. Sitting in this hotel room all alone with its king-sized bed and choice of six porn channels on cable TV is making me ravenous for your sweet c . . .' Kate stabbed the delete button.

'Hello. This is Paul Hegley. Jessica tells me that you are away on holiday. I'm hoping that's why you did not return my other messages. If it is, let me know when you get back. I would still very much like to buy you dinner.'

He was persistent, she had to give him that, thought Kate as she pushed the delete button.

The next two messages were from Claire, asking her to phone home.

Then there was another message from Max. This time he sounded a little drunk. 'Hey, ba*by*. Where are you? I've tried to call you several times and only the disembodied sound of your voice comes back across the transatlantic air waves. I'm still here. Chuck keeps asking for rewrites. I'm beginning to feel like the writer in that film who is holed up in a cheap motel writing a script with a load of madmen for neighbours. This place is crazy. Wish you were here.'

It was followed by another message from Claire, sounding impatient. Kate deleted it without even listening to it.

The next message was from Jessica. She sounded bubbly and delighted. 'Kate, darling, I do believe that Paul Hegley has really got the hots for you. I think it's very naughty of you to go away without calling him, but I've smoothed things over and he's waiting impatiently for your return. Aren't I a good friend? Oh, and Hugo took me away for the most gloriously romantic weekend while you were in Spain. Champagne, four-poster bed, the whole works. I really think he means to be a good boy from now on. Love and kisses.'

What was Hugo trying to hide? Kate thought as she pressed the delete button. A weekend away, a four-poster bed and champagne, and all that *after* he had already given Jessica roses and emerald and diamond ear-rings. He must have done something really wrong to be trying so hard to be the model husband. Hugo never did anything without a reason.

'What's going on? I called your office, they said you are away on holiday in Spain or something.' It was Max again. This time he sounded aggrieved. 'This isn't anything to do with that man at the party, is it?'

The next message was Claire again. The moment Kate heard her voice she irritably punched the delete button – what was the point of listening? Claire's litany was always the same: Kate didn't call home enough and was neglecting their parents. She played the last message, it was Max again. Kate's finger hovered over the delete button, but something about his voice made her listen.

'Kate. I'm sorry. I miss you. I *need* you. Chuck says if I can turn this treatment around we'll have a hot property, but I'm on the fiftieth rewrite already. Looks like I'm going to be here for another week or so yet. Please call me.' He then gave his hotel and room number.

Kate sipped her coffee, the horrible taste forgotten. Max had never said he needed her before, not in that way. She put down her mug and replayed his message, this time scribbling down his number. She dialled it immediately. Allowing for the time difference it would be early morning in California. A bright American voice, anxious to please, answered after only two rings and put her through to Max's room.

This time she had to wait a while for the receiver to be picked up and when it was, a sleepy woman's voice answered: 'Yeah?'

Eighteen

· · ·

'We'll bear you in mind for anything that comes up as we'd simply love to have you working with us. But the only opening we have right at the moment is for a humble producer, nothing for someone of your talents and experience. You do understand.'

Kate forced herself to smile even though the speaker on the other end of the telephone could not see her. She knew it would be reflected in her voice and she did not want to sound desperate even though that was how she was beginning to feel. 'Of course. I'm not even sure whether I want to leave the Channel right now as there are so many exciting things happening here, but it's always worthwhile knowing what possibilities there are outside for a future date. One can never be too sure.'

'Absolutely ... well, let's have lunch some time, shall we?'

The conversation was over.

Kate put down the receiver. There would be no lunch. Unless a time and date were specified and agreed it was merely yet another way of giving someone the brush-off. He had been lying and she knew it, but then she had been lying and he knew it. It was simply a question of understanding the code. Nobody took you out to lunch unless they wanted something from you and right at that moment nobody wanted anything from Kate because they knew that not only was she no longer in a position at the Channel to give them anything, but the chances were she would probably soon have no position there at all. Nothing remained secret for long in the television industry, especially bad news.

It was a lesson she had learnt when she was a young journalist. She had asked naïvely why they did not report more good news and was told that good news made people feel bad. No matter who they were, everyone had some sort of problem and if they thought other people didn't it depressed them. However, bad news made people feel good because whatever their difficulties, they could point and say: 'Well at least I don't have *their* problems.'

Kate closed her filofax. There was no point in calling anyone else. Since she had got to the office that morning she had made four phone calls. They were to people whom she had considered, if not quite friends, at least extremely convivial acquaintances. At different times, all of them had taken her out to extremely expensive lunches and offered her good positions in their companies. Out of loyalty to the Channel and to Leo she had turned them down, even when they had promised her more money than she was then earning.

The lunches had invariably ended with them urging her to give them a call if she should change her mind and since she had, she had called them. She had not plunged in straight away and asked them directly for a job. That wouldn't be playing the game. Instead, she had casually brought up the subject almost as though in passing, so as not to embarrass either them or her if the answer was no, which it had been, although no one had actually used the word 'no' or any other like it. The television industry was a small world and it was the nature of the business that someone who appeared to be on the way down one day could suddenly

216

become your boss tomorrow. So it was important not to make enemies.

A buzz on her intercom interrupted Kate's thoughts. It was Ruby: 'That witch up in Jordan's office wants to know if you'll be free on Thursday at ten fifteen for an interview board for your job. I've been using delaying tactics for the last week while you were away, but now she says it's last orders. Either you board or no job.'

Kate knew Dorothy Mackay would not have phrased it quite like that, but she was thankful that Ruby did not quibble with words. She'd had more than enough of that today. 'Tell her I'll board,' she said wearily.

What choice did she have? The day after tomorrow was sooner than she had expected. She had assumed it would take them at least a month to advertise the job and then to whittle down the candidates to the few they intended to short-list for the board. The haste with which it was happening suggested that Jordan had someone in mind and she was pretty certain it wasn't her.

Kate looked out of the window at the concrete and glass towers that dominated the London skyline. She should have stayed in Majorca. Could it have only been two short days ago that she was in the glittering Mediterranean sunshine?

Kate closed her eyes. She could be lying in the small cove right now, the salt from the sea drying on her skin, the warm golden sand beneath her body, Liam stretched out beside her, but the figure of Max, large and naked in some LA hotel room, a perfectly sculpted Californian blonde with mountainous silicone breasts lying beside him, intruded on her day-dream. She opened her eyes to wipe out the image. '*Damn* you, Max,' she whispered fiercely. 'You're a bastard.'

She swung round in her chair and gazed bleakly out of the window. Why had it taken so long for her to admit she was in love with him, only to find that she

217

now hated him? She had let him mess up her life twice, but it was finally over. There could be no going back.

Nor could there be any going back to Liam. It was so tempting, but he was too gentle, too loving. She would end up hurting him again. Anyway, he was in love with the Kate he had met in Majorca, not with the real one here in London.

The trill of her private outside line made her jump and she turned back and grabbed the receiver. '*Yes!*'

'You're a hard woman to track down, or should I be getting the message that you don't want to see me?'

Kate did not recognise the voice. 'I'm sorry, who . . .?' she demanded irritably.

'Paul, Paul Hegley. Remember me? I'm the man who keeps leaving messages on your answer phone. Since my phone has stubbornly refused to ring in return, I decided to take lateral action and I twisted Jessica's arm in order to get your private number as your secretary is very protective.'

She would have to have a word with Jessica about giving out her telephone number, thought Kate grimly. She kept her voice distant and businesslike: 'I'm sorry. I've been very busy lately.' Which she had, not that it had been the real reason she had not returned Paul's calls. 'Anyway, according to your messages, you've been busy too,' she accused.

'True. So does this mean that you might consider having dinner with me? I feel our relationship rather got off on the wrong foot and neither of us gave a good account of ourselves. I thought we could try rectifying that over a bottle of good wine and some food.'

She had to give Paul Hegley credit for trying, thought Kate. Most men would have vanished, never to be seen again after her drunken display, and if that hadn't put them off, they would not have called after the first two messages went unanswered. Part of her was annoyed, but the other part was intrigued. 'I think if anyone should apologise it should be me. I'm afraid I was not exactly at my best,' she said, allowing some warmth to creep into her voice. 'I hope your hand has recovered.'

'My hand?'

'Don't you remember? My cat took a swing at you.'

'Oh, that. Bit of a tiger, isn't he, but I think he met his match.'

Kate didn't reply. It wasn't the way she recalled it. Hemingway had been the one to draw blood.

'Anyway,' continued Paul, 'let's agree to say no more about that evening and begin again as though it never happened. Starting with dinner tonight, if that's possible.'

'Tonight . . .?' Kate was startled. This was a change in his tactics.

'I know it's very short notice and you probably have at least a dozen parties to go to, knowing you media types,' he ploughed on. 'But I'm away again tomorrow on business for a few days and I have a feeling that if I try and make a date with you for when I return you will find plenty of excuses to cancel it. Am I right?'

Kate hesitated. 'Well, I do have something on . . .'

'But you could put if off . . .?'

'I suppose it would be possible . . .'

'Then I'll meet you at the Savoy at eight,' said Paul triumphantly and put down the telephone before Kate could utter anything else, leaving her with her objections unsaid on her lips.

Ruby put her head round the door as though she had been waiting for Kate to finish her conversation. She had changed the colour of her hair from white to a startling orange-gold while Kate was away on holiday. 'Do you mind if I go early tonight? I've got something on and I want to wear something *really* special.'

Kate wondered what on earth could be more special

than what Ruby was already wearing. Her stretchy violet-blue lace see-through top revealed plump, firm breasts and her skin-tight red biker shorts showed off her dark-brown, velvet-sheened legs to startling perfection.

She smiled. 'No, of course not. I'm going to try and get away at a civilised hour myself tonight. I've got a date too and I need to get changed . . .' She stopped. She couldn't believe that she'd just announced she was going on a date. She sounded like a fourteen-year-old.

Ruby came into the room, her mobile face alight with curiosity. 'About time, too. Who is he? Anyone I know?' she demanded.

'He doesn't work in the media, thank goodness. He's just a friend, no one special,' replied Kate lamely.

Ruby wagged a long, vermilion-painted false nail at her. 'Now don't go telling me that, girl. You need to find yourself someone special. You spend too much time at that desk and don't try to kid me that heap of mahogany-veneered junk is going to keep you warm at night. This place will suck the sweet juices out of you and leave you high and *dry* if you let it. So you get outta here and put something on that will make this nothing special man sit up and see that you're an extra special woman. You gotta keep those men on their toes or else they'll use those feet for walking into some other sister's bedroom, *believe* me.'

Kate found herself smiling again at Ruby's words as she searched desperately through her clothes for something to wear. She had been later getting home than she had intended. After Paul's call she had begun to make some notes on what she wanted to say at her board on Wednesday and had not kept track of the time. She had not left the office until nearly quarter to seven and, as always when she was running late, there had been a delay on the Underground. She had been stuck for nearly fifteen frustrating and hot minutes in a train just outside her station. When it had eventually inched forward and disgorged its angry and miserable travellers, Kate had rushed home and taken a long shower to cool herself down.

It would do no harm to make Paul Hegley wait, she thought, as she held up a blue silk blouse to see whether she could wear it without having to iron it, which unfortunately she couldn't. He had been rather too sure of himself. And the Savoy! If he was trying to impress, this could turn out to be the shortest relationship on record.

Still naked from the shower, Kate strode into the kitchen where she poured herself a large whisky. She returned to her bedroom and, with her whisky in one hand, she rummaged with the other through the large bag where she kept her underwear, throwing bras and knickers and tights onto the floor. She found what she was looking for near the bottom: a bra that thrust her breasts up to near her chin, which she had worn once and sworn she would never wear again as she had spent the evening with men leering down her cleavage. She found some flimsy lace knickers, put on both garments and studied the effect in the mirror. There was no mistaking their message.

Mindful that her breasts were in danger of toppling out of the absurd shelf-like concoction of wire and material she was wearing, Kate got down onto her hands and knees and peered under the bed. Somewhere there among the drifts of grey fluff were a pair of ridiculously high strappy Manolo Blahnik sandals. She had bought them after a rather long lunch and, once she had sobered up, had decided they were far too high to wear safely. Spotting the box, she pulled it out. Tonight they would get their first outing.

The sandals were a translucent, pearly blue. As impractical a colour as they were too high. But they reminded Kate that she had the perfect dress to wear with them. It would be exactly right for cocktails at the Savoy. It was a deceptively simple tube of lavender silk patterned with the faintest tracery of cream. It was sleeveless and held up by the thinnest of shoelace shoulder straps, and cut low and draped across the front so that the full effect of her breasts would be revealed. Although it was demurely calf-length, it was split to the thigh on one side. If she was going to make a statement about her intent, she might as well underline it.

After slithering into the dress, Kate quickly piled her still damp hair on top of her head, pinning it into place and teasing soft tendrils down onto the nape of her neck. She applied some deep plum-coloured lipstick and a generous splash of Chanel No 5 to her wrists and neck, adding a further touch between her breasts for good measure. She gulped down the rest of her whisky, then stood in front of the mirror again. The statuesque woman looking back at her was a stranger, but she was ready. Although quite what for, Kate was not too sure.

Ready to catch a man perhaps, she thought, checking her make-up in her handbag mirror as her taxi turned off the Strand and into the entrance of the Savoy. That would be one in the eye for Max. And why shouldn't she? That's what everyone kept telling her she ought to do – catch a man before it was too late – and Paul Hegley would be as good as any. He was attractive, solvent and single. Wasn't that all that mattered?

Kate tossed her wrap over her shoulder and strode past the liveried doorman into the Savoy with as purposeful a stride as her high heels and tight dress allowed, which was not very purposeful. Paul was sitting in an armchair, a *Financial Times* on the table in front of him. As Kate walked in he was looking at his watch, a frown furrowing his good-looking face. He

222

gave the impression that it was not the first time he had checked the time and did not like to be kept waiting. But his frown turned to a stare of frank admiration when he looked up and saw her. He got swiftly to his feet and strode over, grasping her hand in his. 'Kate. You look wonderful.'

It was on the tip of Kate's tongue to apologise for her lateness, but she decided against it. Apologies did not go with her shoes.

She smiled. 'Thank you.'

He put his hand on her elbow and steered her towards the bar. 'I thought we could start with champagne cocktails here, then I have a table booked for nine at this little French restaurant I know.'

It was against her better nature, but Kate allowed herself to be guided. If she was going to do this relationship thing as it was expected of her she might as well do it properly. She bestowed another gracious smile on the man at her side. Her mother would be proud of her.

Nineteen

• • •

Kate struggled angrily out of the bath and pulled on her wrap. She had promised herself the luxury of a long, relaxing soak, but the person with his finger on her doorbell was not going to go away until she answered. She left a trail of wet footprints across the floor.

'Yes?' she demanded into the intercom.

'Er . . . a delivery for Daniel.'

'*Miss* Daniels and I'm not expecting a delivery.'

'You'll want this one,' a cheery voice assured her.

'I'd better,' Kate murmured under her breath as she pressed the buzzer.

Pulling her bathrobe around her, she opened her front door a few inches and peered down the hall. A large bouquet of red roses on two legs was walking towards her. As it reached the door, the flowers were lowered to reveal a skinny, shaven-haired youth of about seventeen or eighteen. He held up a scrap of paper and studied it for a moment, his lips moving as he silently read what was written on it.

'It says Daniel on here. I thought it a bit odd sending red roses to a bloke but you can never tell these days. Some of the orders I've delivered would make your hair stand on end . . .'

'Thank you,' said Kate, cutting him short and holding out her hand to receive the bouquet while keeping the door closed enough to conceal her state of undress, but the youth appeared to have X-ray eyes. He stepped back, taking it out of her reach.

'It has to be signed for. Can't hand it over without the old moniker saying you got it. Orders.' He waited.

It was a tussle of wills in which Kate's desire to know who had sent her the roses eventually lost her the battle. She opened the door, rewarding him with a glimpse of her damp breasts as his prize.

He advanced into the room bearing the roses like a trophy before she could stop him. 'Where shall I put these?' he asked, making for the kitchen.

'*I'll* take them,' said Kate, stopping him in his tracks. 'Where do I have to sign?'

He reluctantly turned back and handed her the scrap of paper. Kate scrawled her name on it and then, taking the roses, ushered him swiftly out of the door. There was a small envelope tucked in the heart of the bouquet. She tore it open. If this was some kind of peace offering from Max . . .

The card inside read: 'Thank you for Monday evening. I look forward to seeing you tonight at eight. Regards, Paul.'

A dozen red roses to remind her to be on time? Regards? After they had spent a night of passion – well, not quite passion, but certainly passable sex – on Monday? Paul might be given to romantic gestures like sending flowers, but he certainly didn't have a romantic turn of phrase. For a moment Kate could not help remembering the small posy Liam had gathered for her from Oliver's garden in Majorca. He had brought them up to her bedroom still fresh with the morning dew, together with freshly squeezed orange juice and some of Francesca's newly baked rolls. He had perched on the end of her bed and, demanding that she not look at him, he had read her his story. It had been a delicate but bitter-sweet love story set in a Majorcan village, written with a poet's feel for words.

Kate dropped the roses on the kitchen counter. They had somehow taken the excitement out of the evening. She had been looking forward to her second date with Paul, particularly since she had been summoned to Jordan's office just as she was about to leave the Channel that afternoon and told that she had been appointed head of Popular Series and Special Features – the unwieldy new name her old department now went under. It had taken her by surprise as she had thought that her board that morning had not gone well. Now the news had sunk in she wanted to celebrate. However, Paul's message, as well as the flowers, were so formal and correct that she suddenly felt curiously flat.

Kate considered the roses again. Each bloom was as exquisitely beautiful as the next. Maybe she was being a bit unfair to Paul. Beautiful words came easy to Liam, that's why he was a writer, and it was difficult to think of something to say on those little cards when you were usually in a hurry and being watched by the florist.

Due to her, their relationship had not had the most auspicious of beginnings and he was trying so hard. Paul might be a little staid, but why was that such a bad thing? It would be rather nice to have a reliable man in her life, someone she could depend on for once.

Kate glanced at her watch. It was only twenty-five to eight; she still had plenty of time. She dropped her robe on the floor and stepped back into the bath, but had only just lain back and closed her eyes when the telephone rang. She started to get out again and then decided to ignore it. Whoever was calling could speak to the answer machine.

The bathroom door was open so she could hear her tinny voice asking the caller to leave a message, followed by the loud bleep. There was a moment's silence then she heard her sister's voice: 'Kate, this is

226

Claire, are you there? Please answer the phone if you are. It's important.'

It was always important with Claire, thought Kate. Why couldn't she ever ring up just to say hello and have a chat?

'I've been trying to reach you for nearly two weeks, why haven't you replied to any of my messages? Have you been away or something? You are most inconsiderate. I really do need to speak to you. If you don't call I'll . . . well, I'll be very angry. You can be so selfish at times.'

The phone went dead. Kate could imagine Claire slamming the receiver down in frustration and then calling their mother to complain about her. Well, they could have a good moan together. She didn't care. She closed her eyes and tried to relax, but the water was nearly cold. She stretched forward to turn on the hot tap but before she could reach it the front doorbell went again.

Kate rose dripping out of the bath and pulled on her damp bathrobe. There was no point staying in the bath any longer, the pleasure had gone out of it. Anyway, it was probably Paul arriving early. She checked in the mirror as she passed to make sure she didn't look too awful and went to the door.

She picked up the intercom. 'Paul?'

'Aunt Kate?' The voice was young and very uncertain.

'Who is this?'

'It's . . . I'm . . . it's Jonathan.'

Kate buzzed the door open and waited in the hallway. A tentative-looking Jonathan stood there, a haversack on one shoulder. Kate had not noticed, but since she had got back into the bath it had begun to rain heavily and he was soaked through, his hair plastered onto his face. He stood, looking around uncertainly, dripping onto the hall carpet.

'Aunt Kate?'

'Down here,' Kate called, switching on the hall light. The rain had made it very gloomy.

He made his way towards her.

'What on earth are you doing here?' she demanded.

He hung his head. 'I've decided to leave home. I didn't know where else to go.'

It was quarter to eight, Paul would arrive in fifteen minutes and she was not even dressed but Jonathan looked awful – he was shivering and his feet were muddy and wet.

She stepped back to let him pass. 'You'd better come in and explain, but first you have to get out of those wet clothes,' she said crisply.

Coaxing Jonathan into discarding his damp gear was harder than Kate had anticipated – she had forgotten the prudery of adolescence. Eventually he reluctantly undressed, passing item by to him embarrassing item from behind the bathroom door. Once she had determined that she had them all, including his underwear, she ordered him into a hot bath. She was busily stuffing his clothes into the washing machine when the doorbell rang again.

Kate rushed to the mirror. This time it *would* be Paul and she looked a sight. Her brush and comb were in the bathroom, together with her make-up bag, so there was nothing she could do to repair the damage even if she'd had time. She ran both hands through her hair but, if anything, it looked worse: a wild, uncombed mess. The bell went again, this time more insistently. Kate shrugged her shoulders; she would just have to do.

The smile on Paul's face changed to a look of puzzlement and then evaporated altogether as he saw her old torn jeans and faded sweat-shirt.

'I thought we had arranged to go out this evening. Didn't you get my flowers?'

'Yes, they were beautiful. Thank you,' said Kate,

guiltily aware that she hadn't even put them in water. 'But I'm afraid something's come up and I can't make it. I'm sorry.'

'But I've got a table booked for eight thirty. You normally have to wait months to get one at this place but I managed to pull a few strings. If we don't turn up my name will be mud with the *maître d'*.'

'I'm sorry, Paul, I really am. I would have let you know earlier but it's an emergency.'

'Well. Can I at least come in so we can discuss this like civilised people?'

Kate hadn't realised she was holding the door, not allowing him inside. 'There's not much point. It's a family matter, I . . .'

She stopped, watching Paul's body stiffen and his eyes narrow as he saw something over her shoulder. She turned, following his gaze. Jonathan had emerged from the bathroom, naked except for a towel wrapped around his waist. He was rubbing his hair dry with another, revealing his broad shoulders and slim but already well-muscled body.

She had a very handsome nephew, thought Kate, looking at him, but nature had been a little unfair in giving him a man's body when there was still only a young boy inside to inhabit it.

Jonathan stopped in his tracks as he saw Kate and Paul looking at him, then turned on his heel and disappeared back into the bedroom.

When Kate turned back to Paul, his face was rigid with anger. For a moment she didn't understand, then it dawned on her. 'You didn't think . . .?' She began to laugh, but caught sight of Paul's face again and stopped. 'It's not what you think, it really isn't. Jonathan is my . . .'

But Paul cut her short. 'Don't tell me. He's just a *friend*?'

'No. He's my nephew,' replied Kate, irritated. 'I wasn't expecting him. He's run away from home.'

'He looks more than big enough to look after himself, nephew or no nephew.' Paul's voice was heavy with sarcasm.

'He's only a boy and right at this moment he's in need of someone to talk to, so I'm afraid dinner must wait,' snapped Kate. 'I've said I'm sorry. What more can I do?'

Paul held up his hands as though in surrender. 'Okay, okay. I'm sorry too. I think of nephews as snotty-nosed little schoolkids, but I really wanted to see you tonight. Monday night was wonderful and I was looking forward to a repeat episode.' He gave her one of his crinkly smiles.

Kate softened. She was being unreasonable. Paul had every right to be angry. 'I have good memories of Monday too. Can I give you a call tomorrow when I know what's happening?'

He bent forward and kissed her lightly on the lips. 'I'll be waiting.'

Kate put her arms around his neck and pulled him back down. She kissed him long and passionately. 'I promise I won't keep you waiting long.'

After he had gone, she went to the bedroom door and knocked. 'Jonathan? You can come out now. He's gone.'

The door opened cautiously. 'I'm sorry, I didn't know you had company. I've messed up your evening, haven't I? He looked awfully angry.'

Kate shook her head. 'It doesn't matter. He'll survive. You gave him a bit of shock. He thought he'd caught me with my younger lover.' She smiled.

But Jonathan blushed furiously. 'I'm sorry, I really am . . .' he stammered.

'Are you hungry?' asked Kate. He nodded. 'I haven't

got much in, but if you can wait a few minutes I'll pop to the corner shop.'

'I don't want to put you to any trouble . . .' Jonathan began, but Kate had already put on her raincoat and seized an umbrella.

It did not take her long to load a shopping basket with milk, bread, eggs, bacon, sausages, tomatoes and a packet of chocolate digestive biscuits. Items chosen on the premise that seventeen-year-old boys raised in Surrey probably favoured basic food groups, which was soon proved correct. Jonathan wordlessly devoured the enormous fry-up she concocted as though he hadn't eaten for a week, hungrily mopping the plate clean with his fourth slice of bread and butter. When he had finally declared himself unable to eat anything more, Kate made him some tea, which she laced heavily with sugar. Jonathan wasn't suffering from shock – if either of them was finding it difficult to deal with the situation it was her – but it somehow seemed the right thing to do and it appeared to loosen his tongue.

'I don't want to do A levels and go to university like Mum and Dad want me to. No one's asked me what *I* want to do and I don't see the point of it. What's the point of anything these days? We're all going to die anyway.' Jonathan sounded despairing and the dark eyes that stared at Kate over the rim of his mug of tea looked in danger of filling with tears.

This time it was Kate who was left at a loss for words. To give herself time to think she got up and switched the washing machine over to spin mode, then checked on his trainers, which were gently steaming away on top of the radiator. She returned to the stool opposite Jonathan who was dunking a chocolate biscuit into his tea.

'Does your mother know where you are?'

Jonathan looked down for a moment or two. The

231

biscuit in his hand was fast disintegrating into his tea. Then he looked up, defiantly sticking out his chin. 'They won't miss me. No one will miss me. All Mum can think about is Matthew, and Dad and Philip are in a world of their own. The only thing they care about is computers.'

'I'm sure that's not true.' But Kate sounded as unconvincing to herself as she imagined she did to Jonathan. She tried to be a little more commanding. 'Anyway, you must call your mother right now. She'll be frantic.'

'But I don't want to go home.'

'Where would you go? What would you do if you left home now?' demanded Kate.

Jonathan looked hurt. 'I thought I could stay with you, but if you don't want me either . . .'

'I never said that . . .'

'But it's what you meant,' interrupted Jonathan with the acuity of adolescence.

'I would like you to come and stay, but not like this. You need to finish school even if you decide not to go to university. Perhaps if there's something else you'd like to do, something you can train for, your parents might listen. I'll even talk to them if you think it would help, but you have to be sure of what you want first. University can be fun and it will also be the last opportunity you'll have for the luxury of time to consider who you are and what you want to do before you join the rat race like the rest of us.' Kate was talking fast and thinking even faster, remembering how desperate she had been to get away from home and from Surrey at Jonathan's age. She had felt as though she were suffocating.

'But I don't *want* to join the rat race.'

'I didn't mean it quite like that,' Kate backtracked. 'Not all jobs force you to grow whiskers and a tail.' She smiled encouragingly at Jonathan but her attempt at humour fell flat.

'I want to do what you do.'

'In that case getting a degree would be advisable.'

'Why?'

'Well, because . . .' Kate struggled to find an answer. 'Because television may seem exciting and glamorous from the outside, but it's very hard work. Three years at university will give you time to explore other options too.'

'But Mum says you always wanted to be a journalist and *you* never changed your mind.'

'But I was . . .' Kate stopped herself. She had just been going to say that she had been different. No, she hadn't.

She felt a sudden unwelcome weight of responsibility towards Jonathan. He looked up to her, wanted to follow in her footsteps. How could she disappoint him? Yet, at the same time, how could she encourage him when she was beginning to think that maybe she had got it wrong? She felt his eyes watching her and willing her to tell him he was right.

'I wanted to be a journalist then because there were so many things I wished to understand and to explain, and I wanted to explain them to other people too, and make them sit up and think, but now I'm not so sure. Things have changed. Journalism, television, everything has changed . . .' Any triumph she had felt earlier at being offered her job back had now completely gone. By accepting Jordan's offer she had also accepted that she would have to produce the kind of programmes he wanted, not the ones the idealistic young student of twenty years ago had dreamt of making. She had allowed herself to be bought for the price of her mortgage.

For once she was grateful for the shrill tone of the telephone interrupting her.

'Kate, it's Claire. Thank goodness you're there at last. I've been trying to reach you all day. Has Jonathan called you? He didn't go to school today and no one knows where he is.'

'Claire . . .' Kate could see Jonathan shaking his head and mouthing 'no'. She hesitated, but the fear in her sister's voice overcame her misgivings. 'He's here with me.'

There was a hoarse sob of relief on the other end of the line.

'He's absolutely fine. Don't worry. I'll keep him here tonight and give him the fare home tomorrow,' said Kate. 'He spent all his money getting to my flat.'

Jonathan advanced towards her, his hand holding the towel in place at his waist. 'I don't want to go home,' he declared loudly.

'Was that Jonathan?' demanded Claire. 'Let me speak to him.'

Kate held out the telephone but Jonathan backed away, waving his hand. 'I don't want to speak to her.'

Kate put the phone back to her ear. 'We seem to have a problem. Jonathan doesn't want to speak to you and neither does he want to come home. Why can't he stay over until the weekend and I'll bring him home on Sunday evening.'

'And reward the little bugger for giving me a heart attack by allowing him another day off school?' Claire's relief had turned to anger. 'I can be with you in an hour and then he's coming back with me if I have to tie him to the roof of the car.'

'I think that would only make things worse. Let me talk to him. I'll bring him home afterwards if you insist,' said Kate.

'Why do you think he'll listen to you?' demanded Claire. '*I'm* his mother.'

'That may be why,' replied Kate shortly.

There was silence on the other end of the line. Then:

'If you're not here within an hour I'm coming to get him.'

'Make that two hours,' said Kate.

There was a click as Claire put down the phone.

Kate turned to Jonathan. 'I think your mother is angry.'

'She's always angry these days.'

'Maybe because she cares about you and is anxious that you do well. Being a parent can be a very frightening thing.'

Jonathan looked at her with disbelief. 'Being a parent, *frightening*?' He snorted with disgust. 'Anyway, is she going to let me stay?'

Kate shook her head. 'I've agreed to take you home tonight.'

'I'm not going back. I'm sure I can find somewhere to crash. I'll sleep on the streets if I have to.' He started towards the bedroom.

'Jonathan!' With a sense of shock, Kate realised she had sounded just like her mother. 'You are not going anywhere. You will get dressed and then I'll take you home.' She held up a hand as he started to protest. 'However, if you promise me there will be no more running away I'll talk to your mother and try to make her understand your feelings about university, and suggest that you should jointly discuss other options.'

Jonathan looked hopeful. 'You promise?'

'I promise I'll talk to your mother. I can't swear she'll listen. However, if you're really serious about television, perhaps I can organise a little work experience for you during the holidays.'

Jonathan's face lit up.

'But it will be dependent on you working hard at school. Television is no easy option,' said Kate firmly. 'Now go and get dressed and no trying to make a run for it out of the window.'

Jonathan gave her a broad grin and disappeared into the bedroom.

Kate began to clear up the kitchen. As long as her car behaved – which it ought to after nearly a week in the garage and six hundred pounds' worth of repairs – she reckoned that at this time in the evening it would take about an hour and a half to drive to Claire's house.

She stacked the dirty dishes in the sink and left them there, then searched for a vase for the roses. It had been thoughtful of Paul to send them and she had been ungrateful earlier. The least she could do was arrange them properly. But her cupboards yielded nothing that resembled a vase. She abandoned her search and found a bucket under the sink, which she filled with water. At least that way they would stay alive until tomorrow when she would buy herself a proper vase.

Just then Jonathan came out of the bedroom dressed in a pair of slightly too small yellow jeans and an old sloppy jumper that Kate had lent him, her investigation of the contents of his rucksack having revealed that his idea of useful things to pack when intending never to return home was woefully lacking in essentials.

He grinned ruefully and ran his hand through his still damp hair. 'Can I help with the washing-up, Aunt Kate?'

Kate shook her head. 'It can wait and if we're going to be friends, which I hope we are, no more Aunt Kate, *please*. Just plain Kate from now on. Okay?'

He grinned again.

Twenty

• • •

Half an hour later, all Kate's good intentions had evaporated as she leant forward in her seat, straining her eyes to see the road ahead, which was obscured by a veil of driving rain. The windscreen wipers only wiped the rain clear every second wipe and, to add to her discomfort, the right side of her face and body was damp and getting wetter by the second, as the only way to prevent the inside of the windscreen misting up was to keep her window open. Not for the first time since she had got into the car to drive Jonathan home, Kate cursed herself for her stupidity: for suggesting she do it rather than letting Claire come to her flat and argue it out with Jonathan; for promising that she would intercede between him and his parents, which would mean that she would inevitably be the one who would end up arguing with Claire and probably even be accused of causing Jonathan's problems in the first place; at choosing to drive to Surrey on a wet, cold and thoroughly miserable evening when she could have been sitting in a warm and no doubt expensive restaurant, sipping wine and eating some pretentiously named but delicious morsel instead of listening to her stomach rumble with hunger.

She glanced sideways at Jonathan. He had not spoken since they got into the car, but then neither had she. She had suddenly found herself curious about his

237

life – not as Jonathan, her nephew and godson, whose litany of exam results and personal hygiene failures she was familiar with from Claire's phone calls, but as a person.

'Paul – that's the man who came round earlier – and I have only just started going out. Do you have a girl-friend at the moment?'

Kate cursed silently; what an inept way to open the subject. Beside her she felt Jonathan's body become tense. What right had she to ask him about his personal life? As Claire was so fond of pointing out, it wasn't as though she had taken much interest in him as either his aunt or his godmother.

'I'm sorry, Jonathan, I shouldn't have asked you that. It's none of my business. I don't want to sound like your mother.'

Jonathan's body relaxed. 'You could *never* do that. It's just that girls . . . well, you know, they're difficult.'

Kate nodded, concentrating on the road ahead. 'I know.'

'They expect things . . .' Jonathan turned his head away and looked out of his window. 'They seem to know so much, yet they expect you . . . men . . . to be more experienced, to do things . . .'

Kate waited for a moment or two. 'You mean physically?' she prompted gently.

Jonathan nodded. 'But I haven't, well . . . I haven't gone very far.'

'But you're only sixteen. There's no reason why you should have had sex yet.'

'Seventeen. But everybody else has.'

'Or so they claim,' said Kate. 'But do you want to have sex yet? It's a big step, or at least it should be.'

But she hadn't treated it like that, had she? She had seen her virginity as a millstone hanging around her neck – almost as an embarrassment. Within a week of going to university she had made sure she was no longer a virgin. During the round of freshers' week parties she had picked another student after making sure that he was going to a different college so that she would not have to meet him again and, without much preamble, had invited him back to her room. It had not taken long and half an hour later they had returned to the student union bar. Kate had never seen him again and could not remember his name – she wasn't even sure if she had known it in the first place. There had been no romance involved and little physical effort on her part. She had just wanted it over and done with so that she could feel she had left Surrey, and her mother, behind her.

'I would like to, but only with someone I love.' Jonathan's shy voice brought Kate back to the present. 'I think there should be some commitment, but the girls I meet just seem to want to go out and have a good time.'

'There will be plenty of girls who want otherwise, I'm sure of that,' said Kate. 'Take your time and don't rush into anything, especially like running away from home.' She glanced at Jonathan and was rewarded by a rueful smile. 'Only do things because you want to, not because other people say you ought to, or because everyone else is doing them. Now, tell me why you think you want to work in television.'

It was only as Kate turned the car off the road and up the short drive to her sister's house that Jonathan stopped talking and once again assumed the sullen demeanour of misunderstood adolescence, just in time to greet his mother who was waiting at the front door with her arms crossed. Kate gave his arm a reassuring squeeze. At least it had stopped raining.

Jonathan hung back as they got out, clutching his rucksack to his chest. Claire advanced purposefully towards him but Kate stepped between them.

'Don't be *too* angry with Jonathan. He knows he's

done wrong. You're both tired so why don't you leave any discussion of what has happened until tomorrow?'

'Have you *any* idea of what that boy has put me through today?' asked Claire, her voice trembling with emotion. 'Anything could have happened to him, *anything.*'

Kate put a hand on her sister's arm and guided her back towards the house. 'But it didn't, did it?' she said soothingly. 'Let's have a drink. I think we both need one. Where's Roger?' she asked as they stepped into the hall.

'He's away. Some conference up north. He won't be back until tomorrow. I haven't told him. I didn't know what to say. Only Mother knows. She came over earlier but I sent her home when I knew he was with you.' Claire twisted round trying to speak to Jonathan, but Kate kept a firm hold on her arm.

'Jonathan is tired and he's going to his room, aren't you, Jonathan?' said Kate.

There was a grunt of assent and then a muffled 'sorry, Mum', before Jonathan leapt up the stairs, two at a time and disappeared.

'I think some whisky is called for, don't you?' asked Kate guiding Claire into the kitchen.

Claire nodded and mutely pointed at a cupboard. Opening it, Kate found enough bottles of whisky, gin, brandy and other spirits to stock an off-licence. She selected a single malt from among the half-dozen or so bottles of whisky, and poured a large measure for Claire and a smaller one for herself. After adding a dash of water, she took them to the table. Claire gulped at hers without thinking and began to cough. It at least brought the colour back to her face. Kate had not noticed before, but there were lines deeply etched around Claire's eyes and at the corners of her mouth.

'Jonathan's fine, he really is,' she said reassuringly.

'He's just being seventeen and asserting his independence.'

'What would you know about children?' demanded Claire. 'How can you possibly understand what it's like when you discover that your child is not where you expect him to be? The panic that begins to set in when every place you call yields the answer that he's not there and that nobody has seen him? You tell yourself that he's sensible, that he's almost grown-up, that he's not a child any more and he's too old to run across the street after a ball, or take sweets from strangers and get into cars with them, but nothing helps as the seconds, then the minutes, then the hours tick by.' She pushed her hands through her hair, making it stand up on end. 'All you can see is the tiny, helpless baby you held in your arms, his skin so soft and so sweet-smelling, his ten, perfect, pink little toes and his ten, perfect, pink little fingers curling round yours, so vulnerable, so helpless . . .' She began to sob, her shoulders heaving.

Kate sat, feeling clumsy and useless in the face of Claire's explosion of pent-up anxiety. They had never been close. A kiss on the cheek was the most physical affection they had ever shown each other and they had never discussed their feelings except to yell their dislike of each other during arguments. She hesitated, then got up and walked round to where Claire sat. Feeling awkward, she bent down and held her. Claire tried to pull away, but then turned and clutched at her, burying her face in Kate's midriff, screwing her sweatshirt up in her hand like a child holding a security blanket.

After a while her sobs began to subside and for a moment Claire was still. Then she pushed Kate roughly away. 'Don't think you can come home now and make everything all right. Where have you been for the last two weeks and why haven't you returned my calls?' She fumbled for a tissue in her pocket and angrily blew her nose. 'Jonathan running away was the last straw after all the problems with Daddy.'

'What problems? Has something happened?' demanded Kate, alarmed.

'Of course. You wouldn't know, would you? How could you when you never get in touch? He had a heart attack last week.'

Kate sat down heavily. 'A heart attack? Father?' she repeated faintly. 'Is he all right? Why didn't anyone tell me . . .' She stopped.

Claire's tear-streaked face looked triumphant. 'I *would* have told you if you had returned my calls. But as it was, it turned out to be a false alarm. Mummy didn't take any chances and called an ambulance, but although they kept Daddy in overnight just to be sure, they let him out the next day. He's under doctor's orders to be careful and has to go for regular tests from now on. As you can imagine, Mummy has been distraught, but Jonty has taken it the worst of all. He's very fond of his grandfather.'

Kate was silent. So the great investigative journalist had failed to get to the source of Jonathan's unhappiness. She had allowed her own preoccupation to cloud her judgement – something she had so often criticised other people for doing. She felt foolish.

'Jonathan didn't say anything . . .' Kate began.

'Why should he? It's not as though you are ever around for him to talk to. You aren't around for any of us to talk to, you never have been. Your work has always been more important to you than any of us.'

'That's not true,' said Kate, although she knew it was not far from the truth, 'and I would have returned your calls if you had left a message saying that Father was ill,' she added lamely.

'Is that what it takes to make you call home? Daddy nearly on his deathbed?'

'Don't be so melodramatic,' snapped Kate. 'You said

it was a false alarm. Anyway, I was away on holiday and since coming back things have been hectic. I meant to phone you . . .'

But she hadn't, had she? Although she did not want Claire to know, the news about their father had really shaken her. Supposing it had been a heart attack? Supposing he had died? She turned away so that Claire could not see her face.

'That's it. Turn away! Pretend we don't exist. Go back to your glamorous life and high-flying job. Forget about us mere mortals who have to live in the real world and deal with real problems,' said Claire angrily.

'*Real* problems, *real* world. If you think you live in the real world here then you obviously haven't been reading the same newspapers as me. There are people out there who . . .' Kate stopped. Who was she to pass judgement on reality? Claire's fear that something had happened to Jonathan had been only too real. 'I'm sorry,' she finished hopelessly.

They sat in silence, not looking at each other.

Had there ever been a time when they could talk to one another, thought Kate. When they could say more than two sentences without wilfully misunderstanding each other? At what point had they stopped trying to be sisters and become the two strangers sitting at this table?

She looked at Claire. 'My life's not as you imagine, not at all,' she said wearily, 'and I'm sorry about Father. I really am. You're right, I have been selfish. I should have let you know where I was, I should have called. I don't know what I would have done if anything had happened to him and I wasn't here. I could never have forgiven myself . . .' She stopped as her throat constricted.

Claire sniffed and blew her nose again. She gave Kate a watery smile. 'We're a right pair, aren't we?'

Kate nodded.

Claire reached across and plucked at Kate's sleeve, which was still wet from the drive. She suddenly became maternal again. 'You're soaked! Go upstairs and find something to wear in my wardrobe. You can't possibly walk around like that. You'll catch your death of cold.'

'Not before I've called Father.'

'You can do that from the extension in the bedroom. Go on,' Claire urged.

Kate dutifully did as she was bidden and went upstairs where she dialled her parents' number. Luckily her father answered, full of reassurance. According to him, Cissy and Claire had got over-excited about a bout of bad indigestion. It had been uncomfortable but hardly life-threatening and he had only agreed to go in the ambulance because he was sure that Cissy would have had a real heart attack if he didn't.

Kate was smiling as she put down the phone. She could imagine what her mother would have been like although she was relieved that she had overridden her father's objections and got him to the hospital. She stripped off her sweat-shirt but a quick search of her sister's wardrobe revealed that none of Claire's blouses would fit her, so she borrowed one of Roger's shirts.

'That's better,' declared Claire as she returned. 'Look, I'm sorry about before, I must have been bottling it up all day.'

Kate sat down. 'No problem. I *do* understand even if you think I don't. Even we allegedly hard-nosed career women can have bad weeks and mothers don't have a monopoly on feelings you know.'

Claire smiled apologetically. 'I know. I used to hate it when Mummy seemed to think that she was the only person with any feelings and now I'm behaving in the same way. Maybe it's genetic.'

'As long as you don't become all dramatic when the boys misbehave and pretend to faint.' Kate closed her eyes and put her hand to her heart. 'Ah, you do not understand how a *motherr* is made to *sufferr*,' she mimicked her mother's French accent. They both started to giggle.

'She's not all bad, you know,' said Claire when she'd stopped laughing.

'I know,' said Kate. 'But I've always felt that she is criticising me. She doesn't even have to say anything. All she has to do is just look and I can tell by the way she purses her lips or arches her eyebrow that she doesn't approve of the clothes I'm wearing. I shouldn't be worried at my age, but it still rankles.'

'I know she can be difficult at times, but you should try to understand her better.'

'Maybe she should try to understand me better, too,' declared Kate. 'Understand that marriage and children aren't the be all and end all of my life.'

'How can you be so sure?' demanded Claire, pouring some more whisky into both their glasses. 'It's not as though you've tried having either.'

'I've never looked upon marriage or children as things to be tried out,' said Kate drily.

'Maybe not children, but marriage at least. You've never even lived with anyone. I really can't understand why you don't have a man, unless of course you do and he's married, which is why you don't talk about him.' Claire waited, her hawk-like eyes on Kate's face, watching for the tiniest betrayal of movement. 'It is that, isn't it? You haven't mentioned a man's name in ages and since you're no nun, it stands to reason that if there's a man there's something wrong with him.'

Kate drank some whisky before she replied. 'Maybe I haven't mentioned anyone because there's been no one special.'

Claire's eyes had never left her face. 'I may not have a degree or any other qualification that's worth much, but the one thing that raising three children makes you

245

an expert in is knowing when someone is telling the truth and your face says there *is* someone and that you're unhappy. *Is* he married?'

Kate started to shake her head but, to her surprise, Claire suddenly became angry again. 'Don't treat me like a child,' she snapped. 'You come here once in a blue moon and look at this house and my life, and think you know all there is to know about who I am and what I think. You've even decided what moral stance I will take . . .' She paused as though out of breath.

When she next spoke, her voice had a slight tremor in it. 'But married people have affairs, even here in deepest Surrey and, believe me, it's not worth all the pain it causes.'

Kate stared at her sister. '*You* had an *affair*?' she demanded – even accused. 'When?'

'Ten, nearly eleven years ago now,' replied Claire.

'Who with?' Kate found herself thinking about all Claire's and Roger's friends. She knew from her sister that a number of the couples they socialised with had changed partners as the result of affairs over the years, but she hadn't imagined Claire to be the type, or Roger for that matter.

'It wasn't someone from around here. I might be a suburban housewife but I'm not *that* stupid,' said Claire. 'He was French.'

Kate waited impatiently.

Claire sipped her whisky. 'You remember when Mummy got involved in finding accommodation for French students who wanted to spend the summer here improving their English? The people who promised accommodation were always letting her down at the last minute so Roger and I always ended up offering to help out. Well, it was one of those students.'

'But they were barely more than schoolchildren,' protested Kate.

'He was eighteen and he was most certainly not a child,' said Claire tartly. 'Mother is right about the French being much more advanced at certain things than the English and in some things the English probably *never* catch up with them, no matter what age. Anyway,' she went on, 'I was only twenty-five at the time.'

Kate sat back in her chair. She felt stunned. But even as she digested Claire's revelation another thought wormed its way into the front of her consciousness. She looked at Claire. It wasn't possible and she knew Claire would probably not speak to her again for asking, but she had to know.

'This affair, it was nearly eleven years ago?'

Claire nodded.

'But wasn't that when you were pregnant with Matthew?'

Claire slowly lowered her glass to the table. She looked down for a few moments, then directly into Kate's eyes. 'It was when I *got* pregnant with Matthew.'

'So Matthew is not . . .?' Kate began, but hesitated. What she was thinking couldn't be possible. Not Claire.

'Roger's son?' finished Claire. 'No. His father is a Frenchman called Jean-Claude who, incidentally, is a musician and not a footballer before you ask. And also before you ask, no, Roger doesn't know and neither does Mother. Why should my urge to confess cause needless pain? You're the only person I've ever told.'

Kate was puzzled. She and Claire had never shared secrets even when they were younger. 'But why tell me now?'

'Because today it was all I could think about between images of Jonathan under the wheels of a car somewhere, or kidnapped, or worse. Suddenly I knew I wanted, no, *needed* to tell someone, someone I could trust, and you *are* my sister despite appearances to the contrary,' replied Claire.

Kate held up her hands. 'I don't know what to say.'

'I'm not asking you to *say* anything. That's the last thing I want you to do. I want you to try to understand,' said Claire urgently.

'Understand? What makes you think I wouldn't understand?' asked Kate.

'I'm not talking about you understanding the sexual urge that led to Matthew's conception – although it was an accident by the way – that part is easy.' She shrugged. 'Roger was working all hours to build up the business. I was either alone or with two young children, and I felt unattractive and neglected. Along came a young, handsome Frenchman, who played love-songs on his guitar and wanted me to help him read English romantic poetry. I introduced him to Elizabeth Barrett Browning and to Christina Rossetti. If you remember, the only time I ever got decent marks at school was in English Lit. And he introduced me to . . .'

For the first time in a long while Kate saw her sister smile. Not the smile which was merely lips being stretched to indicate recognition of yet another request or to soothe an irritated child or husband, but one that lit her up from within. It made her look different: softer and younger; still full of hope.

'Well, let's just say he introduced me to some things I hadn't experienced before, but it's not that I'm talking about,' she said, suddenly back to her old self. 'It's about you and me. I've always had the feeling that you're judging me. You were the clever one at school and I was the dunce. But what made it worse was that when I went out and had fun, you would refuse to come along. Instead you stayed at home and studied, as though you wanted to show me up. Then, when I wanted to get married, you came home from university and lectured me on how wrong I was. You never said good luck or wished me happiness. As ever, I was wrong and you were right, and you were at university, so that proved it.' Claire held up her hand as Kate tried to interrupt. 'And since then, on the occasions that you *do* deign to come home, you treat me like an idiot, as though I have no brains. I'm just an automaton who services Roger and cleans up after the boys, not worthy of proper conversation. You treat me just like men treat women.'

They stared at each other for a few moments.

Kate looked away first. She did not like the image of herself that she saw in her sister's eyes. 'I never said you were a dunce at school,' she said accusingly, 'and the reason I didn't go out much was that I was never very good at parties. I'm still not. But you and Mother made me feel like *I* was the one who was some sort of freak because I wasn't interested in endless shopping expeditions and didn't have all the boys in the neighbourhood queuing up to take me out as you did.'

'That's because they were in awe of you. So was I. I probably still am. Look how much whisky I've had to drink in order to say this, but then as well as now, you were so distant and glamorous. I really envied you.'

'Glamorous? Me? *You* were the pretty one, everyone said so,' protested Kate.

'I was pretty in a conventional sort of way, but you were different. You had this aura of . . . of *sophistication* about you. Everybody said it was because you were half French but nobody thought that I was. I hated you. Anyway, I might have been Mummy's favourite but you were definitely Daddy's. You couldn't do anything wrong in his eyes. He simply dotes on you and always has.'

'I might get on better with Father, but at least you don't have to put up with Mother constantly pointing out what a failure you are because you haven't given her cause to buy a new hat and erect a marquee in the garden with a cold buffet for two hundred people. As

249

far as she's concerned, I've failed in my duty as a woman *and* a daughter by not getting married,' said Kate indignantly.

'And in *your* eyes I've failed in my duty as a woman precisely because I *am* a housewife, or so you said when you came home from university all fired up with women's lib. You managed to make me feel like I was going to commit some sort of heinous crime against humanity, not just get married,' countered Claire, equally indignant.

Kate turned down the corners of her mouth. 'Oh, dear, was I that bad?'

'That bad! You told me I was selling myself into bondage and that marriage was just a form of legalised prostitution for women. I cried myself to sleep the night before my wedding and woke up with eyes that looked like I'd gone ten rounds with Muhammad Ali. I've never seen Mummy so furious. Then you and she had another awful row, shouting at each other behind my head as the hairdresser was trying to put my hair up. One minute you were yelling at each other, the next you both turned on the poor hairdresser, Mummy telling her that she was putting the tiara on all wrong and you saying that I was being done up like a sacrificial lamb for the slaughter.' Claire started to laugh. 'So much for the happiest day of my life.'

Despite herself, Kate began to laugh too. 'I'm sorry. I behaved really badly. I must have looked a sight walking down the aisle in that awful concoction of a bridesmaid's dress with my great clod-hopping Doc Martens underneath.'

They laughed together and, for a little while, were incapable of speech.

Eventually Claire caught her breath. 'I don't think Mummy has ever forgiven you for the boots.'

Kate was suddenly serious. 'Have you?'

Claire was silent for a moment or two. 'I think I have. Now.'

'So can we call it about even on old scores?' asked Kate.

Claire nodded. 'I'd like that. In fact, why don't we drink to it?' She poured two more generous measures of whisky into their glasses.

Kate held up her hand in protest. 'Whoa! I'm driving.'

'You can always stay the night. We can have a girls' session. We never had any when we were younger. It's about time we caught up,' declared Claire. 'And while we're into confessions, you can tell me about this married man of yours.'

Kate looked at her. 'As long as this is strictly between us? I know how you and Mother talk.'

Claire handed her another glass of whisky. 'Everything said at this table is protected by the laws of the confessional box.' She held up her own. 'Shall we drink to secrets between sisters?' They clinked glasses.

Kate found it easier to talk about Max than she had expected. It was almost a relief.

'Well, he sounds like he was a right bastard to me,' said Claire when she had finished. 'But all the most attractive men usually are, aren't they?' She waved her glass tipsily. 'Tell me, which do you think comes first: does being attractive make men bastards or does being a bastard make them attractive?'

Kate drank some more whisky as she considered this. 'I think being a bastard comes first. Not all good-looking men are bastards, which is probably why I'm not attracted to good-looking men, if that makes any sense. Nobody would describe Max as handsome, but *God*,' she groaned, 'I found him attractive. Probably still would if I saw him again and that's the trouble. *Not* that I have any intention of doing so, I hasten to add.'

'And the sex was great?' said Claire pouring some more whisky into her glass.

'Better than great. We just had to look at each other and we wanted to tear each other's clothes off and have sex on the spot. I can't explain it. It was like a physical compulsion that overrode my brain and all the warning signals it gave off that I shouldn't be doing this.'

Claire drained her glass. 'I wish Roger would tear my clothes off, just once. It's not that we don't have nice sex, we do, but it's exactly that – nice. He's so respectful. He treats me as though I were made of glass, constantly asking me if I'm sure I'm all right, is he hurting me, have I had enough – which usually means he has. I rarely have, but if I said I hadn't he would get upset that he wasn't satisfying me.'

'But he isn't,' Kate pointed out.

'Well, he is, sort of. You know, in that being together as a couple sort of way – comfortable.'

'I'm not sure I do know,' said Kate. 'I've never really thought of sex as being comfortable. Exhilarating, wild, funny, dangerous and even, on occasion, boring, but not comfortable.'

'That's probably because you haven't been married. It quickly settles into being comfortable, that is when neither of you is too tired to have it in the first place, and when the children have grown up enough not to interrupt you at a vital moment.'

'Why don't you try to liven it up a bit? Have sex somewhere else in the house other than the bedroom and if you can't get privacy, drive to the local lovers' lane and do it in the back of the car. That always forces men out of a rut and into trying new positions. You can't do much else in the back of a car. Failing that, indulge in some oral sex when he's least expecting it. That tends to jump-start most men.'

Claire blushed and giggled at the same time. 'If I performed oral sex on Roger it would not so much

252

jump-start him as give him a heart attack. He's like Hugh Grant: he thinks oral sex is only done by prostitutes.'

'You mean you don't . . .?' asked Kate incredulously. Claire shook her head.

'*Never*?'

'Never.'

'Well! Now I really *am* shocked,' said Kate.

'This *is* Surrey remember.' Claire giggled. 'Anyway, I'm not even sure I know what to do.'

'There's no great mystery. Think of your favourite flavour of ice-cream and go from there. Believe me, your instincts will tell you what to do.'

'Talking about ice-cream, would you like some? I have chocolate-chip-cookie, pistachio or double Devon vanilla cream.'

'How about a scoop of each?' suggested Kate.

Claire got up and fetched a large bowl. She put several scoops of each flavour into it and added two spoons. She placed it in the centre of the table and refilled both their glasses.

'But there must have been someone who at least made you *think* about getting married. Doesn't the idea of being alone ever frighten you? It terrifies me. I don't think I could cope. The thought of Roger ever leaving me makes me feel physically ill. I'm just not one of those women who can live alone. I *need* a man.'

'How do you know? You've never tried being by yourself. You went straight from home into marriage.' Kate spooned a mouthful of chocolate-chip-cookie ice-cream into her mouth. 'I'm not saying being single is easy, or that I wouldn't choose to be with someone if I could. But how do you *know* if you've met the right someone? You seemed so sure about Roger right from the start and you were right, despite everything else that's happened, he was the one. *I* want to be that certain before I take the plunge.' She dug into the ice-cream, trying to get a bit each of chocolate, pistachio and vanilla onto her spoon at the same time. 'I've met someone recently. Our relationship has got off to a bit of a shaky start, but it hasn't frightened him off, so he has already earned a lot of brownie points. More than that, he appears to be most of the things you would want in a man, but how can I be sure?'

'Sometimes you can't be. All you can do is take a chance and hope that you will be proved right. With Roger, I was sure with the pig-headedness of youth. I know now that there are probably hundreds of other Rogers out there whom I could have married. He just happened to be the one who was around when I decided that, because you were the brainy one and had gone to university, I would prove to everyone that I could be independent too by getting married.' Claire pointed her spoon at Kate. 'Don't get me wrong, I love Roger, I really do, but there was no magic in it. Or if there was, I stopped believing in it the day I got married. Funny thing is, although Roger is a deeply logical man with his computers and all that, in an odd sort of way I think *he* is the one who still believes in magic. I think most men do.'

The ice-cream on her spoon began to drip onto the table, but Claire did not notice. 'Perhaps it's because whatever they think, men never really have to engage with the basics of life in the way we women are forced to because of our bodies. We have to cope with menstruation and childbirth, and after that our intimacy with our children's bodies never lets us get far from the basic facts of life. Like what goes in, must come out and usually very messily. Men try to help, but they're not really connected in the same way, so they are able to keep a sense of wonder, which women are denied. Maybe that's why they remain perpetual little boys. Women can never really escape the physical consequences of their actions in the same way men can.' At last she put the spoon of melting ice-cream into her mouth, some of it dripping unheeded onto her blouse.

'They can if they remain single,' said Kate quickly. 'Anyway, you've just proved my point about marriage being bad for sex. It destroys lust and I'm a great believer in lust. Max isn't the only married man I've had an affair with, as you've probably guessed.'

Claire nodded. 'I thought as much. I remember a time when you used to talk about your boy-friends, or at least mention their names, but you haven't in years. I put two and two together.'

Kate drank some more whisky. 'Married men have a lot going for them. For a start they're usually so much more grateful than single men and one hell of a lot more anxious to prove themselves in bed. They also have the advantage of going home to their wives and, believe me, I *do* encourage them to go home. I have this theory that marriage means that the intimacy of sex is replaced by the intimacy of unpleasant bodily functions and I for one do not want to share a bed with someone who snores, grinds his teeth or is flatulent.'

'But sex isn't everything. What about children?' asked Claire. 'My three may drive me crazy, but I wanted them all, desperately – Matthew, perhaps, most of all. Although I love them equally, he's the one who is truly mine in a way I can't explain and which makes me feel guilty. But the one *real* sense of achievement I have had in life is watching them grow up.'

Kate dug her spoon into the pistachio ice-cream. 'Until recently I never thought consciously about either having or not having children. I just assumed that when I met the right man I would have them. But suddenly no one will let me forget that I am that aberration of nature – a childless woman. It's as if I'm walking around with some kind of clock emblazoned in the middle of my forehead indicating one minute to midnight. People thrust their babies at me as though I might somehow catch the urge to have children from them, but if anything, it puts me off the idea of children. And please,' she added quickly, 'don't say it's different when they're yours. If just one more person says that to me I might be tempted to kill them instantly and I'd hate to lose you just when we've discovered it's possible to be friends as well as sisters.'

Claire held up her hands. 'I promise I'll never say it to you, although of course it is . . .'

Kate flicked her spoon at her. A splodge of pale-green ice-cream slipped slowly down the front of Claire's blouse. Claire dug her spoon into the choco-late-chip-cookie ice-cream and retaliated. She missed and it hit the dresser behind Kate's head. Claire started to giggle and soon they were both helpless with laughter. Behind them the door opened and a pyjama-wearing Matthew slid cautiously round the door, poised for flight at the first sign of retribution. His mouth dropped open at the sight of his mother and aunt, giggling uncontrollably and covered with splodges of ice-cream. His expression turned to a mixture of bewilderment and disgust at this unseemly display by his elders and, after a moment or two, he turned on his heel and marched out, scandalised, causing Claire and Kate to laugh even louder.

'Stop, please *stop*,' begged Claire, wiping her eyes. 'I'm not sure I should encourage you to stay in my house if I really want to become an aunt. Any contact with my lot is enough to send anyone rushing out to get sterilised.'

And with that the two of them began to laugh again.

Twenty-One

• • •

'I'm *so* pleased, Kate, I really am. I think Paul's absolutely perfect for you. He's got everything you could possibly want *and* a house in Holland Park,' said Jessica happily.

She was curled up on the opposite end of the sofa from Kate. It was Saturday morning and they were having coffee in her green morning-room, as she liked to call it. The french doors leading to the garden where Kate had first met Paul were open, but no fresh air was coming in. Although it was barely ten o'clock, the air was already thick and oppressively hot as it could be only in July in a big city like London. Jessica looked even more childlike than usual. She had tied her mass of hair up in ribbons in order to be cooler and wore a long, sleeveless pinafore-style printed cotton dress which revealed her thin white arms and bony shoulders.

Through the french windows Kate could see Thomas, Jessica's three-year-old, rushing madly up and down the garden, trying to kick the multicoloured ball that his nanny, Maria, was tossing to him. Maria was even tinier and more childlike than Jessica, if that were possible. But while Jessica's thinness suggested vulnerability, Maria's boylike figure indicated a toughness accentuated by a pair of diminutive red shorts and cut-off T-shirt that displayed her perfectly flat, golden-brown midriff. In contrast, little could be seen of Thomas's pale, stocky little figure as he was dressed in a pair of baggy striped shorts and shirt, topped by a floppy sun-hat.

He had been a big baby and threatened to grow into a large child, expanding outwards as well as upwards. He had inherited Jessica's and Hugo's red-gold colouring, but not their slim builds, although Kate had always suspected that Hugo was the type who could incline to corpulence in later years. His chin was already beginning to show the evidence.

Kate watched as Thomas petulantly sat down on the grass and refused to run after the ball. Not that she would have admitted it to anyone, least of all Jessica, but she did not like Thomas very much and she had the distinct feeling he did not like her either. She knew it was absurd to dislike a three-year-old child, but she found his pale-eyed gaze disconcerting. At times it was almost as though there was a little old and not very nice man hiding inside the body of a child. But more than that, he was a bully and his main victim was Jessica.

Thomas was old enough to know when he was hurting someone and that it was wrong, yet he pulled and twisted Jessica's hair with his chubby little fingers until she had tears in her eyes. Kate had often seen the purple bruises on her arms where Thomas had punched her. It could be accidental – just rough play by a child who did not know its own strength. But Kate had seen the look in Thomas's eyes just before he hurled himself at Jessica and she knew he intended to hurt her and, when he pulled Jessica's hair, the more she begged him to stop, the more he seemed to enjoy himself.

Thomas played rough games with Maria, too, but she encouraged them. Kate had heard them both in peals of laughter as they pinched and punched each other.

Maria was the only person who seemed to be able to make Thomas laugh, or do anything for that matter. He would chatter away happily with her, but when Jessica wanted him to talk he reverted to baby grunts.

'And I know that he *says* that he doesn't want children.' Jessica was still talking about Paul.

Kate made a concentrated effort to listen. She was exhausted. She had worked three weekends in a row at the Channel. She might have been made the head of the department but it had proved a Pyrrhic victory. There was hardly any department to be head of any more and Jordan's cost-cutting was forcing the few remaining staff to do the work of those who had left. She had promised herself a long lie-in that morning to make-up for it, but she had not seen Jessica in weeks and she had sounded so disappointed that Kate could not make lunch the following week either that she had agreed to come over for coffee.

'But men can always be talked round to it.' Jessica was still speaking. 'If he really likes you – which I'm sure he does – then he'll want a child with you. It's a basic instinct with them. They like to think they've put their genetic stamp on the world and together you'd have such *pretty* babies too' – this was almost an appeal.

'His house in Holland Park is not that big. In fact, it's not a house at all; it's only a small mews cottage,' said Kate.

'A mews cottage in Holland Park,' interrupted Jessica enthusiastically. 'That sounds perfect to me.'

'And as for children,' continued Kate, 'don't you think it's a bit too soon to be talking about them? I've only known him a few weeks and between his work and mine, we've not seen much of each other in that time.'

'You've known him since April, that's over three months,' accused Jessica, 'and you don't have to see someone that much to know that they're right for you. It can be love at first sight and you can be happily married for a hundred years.'

'I'm afraid I don't have your romantic view of life, Jessica,' said Kate wearily. 'It's one of the things I admire about you. I believe everything in life has a sell-by date, while you go into everything thinking it will last for ever. I'm just an old cynic compared with you.'

'You're not at all,' protested Jessica. 'You're my dearest and oldest friend. I wouldn't want anything but the best for you. For example, one of the good things about Paul is that although he has been married, it was some time ago and he emerged from it financially intact. However, the fact that he has *been* married, however long ago, means that he has had a little house training. Men who reach their forties without being married or living with anyone are a nightmare. The thing is,' she finished, 'when a man like Paul comes along, which they don't do too often, you can't wait for them to make up their own minds. You have to grab them while they're still dazzled by you.'

'I don't think Paul is exactly dazzled by me,' said Kate. 'I don't believe he's the kind of man to be dazzled by anyone. He is – how shall I put it? – a *cautious* man.'

'Oh, but doesn't that make you feel so *secure*,' said Jessica. 'And he's so old-fashioned and gentlemanly with it, too. He sent me such an *adorable* little note thanking me for my party – and flowers.'

They were the words she, too, would use to describe Paul, thought Kate: old-fashioned. He sent a note and flowers each time they met and, like an old-fashioned gentleman, expected to take the lead. She did not mind doors being opened for her or chairs being held; in fact, she quite liked it. Nor did it bother her much that he took it for granted that he should take the lead in arranging their evenings together, booking restaurants and seats at the opera on the assumption that she would be happy with his choice. She had been too preoccupied with work to wish it otherwise.

But apart from that first disastrous night at her flat, he seemed to expect to take the lead in bed as well. At first she hadn't cared. He was a skilled if somewhat clinical lover and the memory of that initial disaster had still been at the back of her mind. As that receded, however, she had tried to vary the way they made love but to no avail. Whatever she did, Paul always ended up on top. Some nights he had not even wanted sex, and had given her a chaste good-night kiss and left her frustrated on her doorstep.

In other ways, though, he was an amusing companion. He did not talk much about his work. He was some kind of management consultant, which appeared to involve him spending a lot of time flying around the world. He was interested in her job, but refreshingly unimpressed with television. His choice of restaurants was always both excellent and expensive, and one night he had booked a complete box at Covent Garden, together with champagne and smoked salmon and strawberries. But while Kate enjoyed some opera, she found *Don Giovanni* dour and doom-laden and, already exhausted by a long day at work, had fallen asleep, much to Paul's obvious annoyance.

Robert had roared with laughter when she recounted the incident during one of their regular hour-long telephone calls but, unlike Jessica, he remained sceptical about Paul. Particularly after he had demanded, and received, details of their sex life.

He had snorted with disbelief when she had admitted to not having sex at all with Paul on some occasions. 'I think I should come back to England *immediately* and check out that he's not a closet gay. At the very best this man is controlling. *I* think you're sexy and I *am* gay. In fact, according to Oliver, I'm a screaming queen.'

'How is Oliver?'

'He's fine and sends his love, and wants to know when you are coming to visit us again.'

'I will, when work allows, I promise,' said Kate, knowing that her promise was hollow. It had always been difficult to take holidays in the past, but now it was impossible. She was trying to put together ideas for three different series all in keeping with Jordan's demand for life-style programming. Unfortunately, word had got out about her plans and it seemed that there was not a publicist, agent, or publisher in the country who had not sent her a press release, book, video or pile of glossy ten-by-eight photographs – and sometimes all of them together – of the person he or she claimed would be the next cookery, gardening or interior design 'guru'.

'You could always bring this Paul character with you to Majorca, then it would give both Oliver and me a chance to give him a thorough inspection.'

Kate wondered whether that meant Liam had left. Robert had tried to talk about him a number of times after she had first come back to England, but she had refused to discuss him and he had not mentioned him in a long while.

She changed tack. 'Anyway, *you're* the one who's always lecturing me that sex isn't everything and that love is what matters. I enjoy his company. Isn't that enough?'

'You don't sound too sure about him to me, dear heart. Either the spark's there or it's not,' said Robert firmly. 'I'm not saying you have to act on it, but do be sure it's there in the first place. You can't ignite a fire without a spark and while you have been boringly fulsome in praise of his manly virtues, it's his vices that will make him interesting. Is he *sexy*? And by that

I mean does the air tingle between you, like it did between you and Liam?'

'Perhaps I'm done with tingling and getting burnt.'

'Dear heart, we all need at least a little tingle, young or old. It's what makes life worth living.'

Kate knew he was right. Perhaps the fault was hers. She was so exhausted at the moment that she wasn't sure she would know a tingle if it hit her between the eyes. Or perhaps it would happen when she knew Paul better. After sleeping with him three, no, four times, she still didn't feel she *knew* him.

She knew he had been married, and the name of his ex-wife and that of her second husband. She even knew where he bought his clothes – Gieves & Hawkes – as she had peeked inside his wardrobe while he was downstairs. She also knew that unlike her, he was very organised as well as very neat. All his suits were hung in perfect colour co-ordination and his ties alongside them in the same manner. He sent his shirts to a laundry, which returned them crisply folded and wrapped in Cellophane, and these, too, were stored according to colour. The first night they had made love she had been left impatiently sitting up in bed while he had folded and hung all his clothes. He had even picked hers up from the floor where she had dropped them and hung them up as well.

And then there was his house, or rather, his mews cottage. It was difficult to tell much about him from that either. It was tasteful but sterile. Decorated in stark white, grey and black, it was an interior designer's idea of a bachelor residence. There was nothing personal about it at all. Everything, including the pictures on the walls, had been selected and placed in position by the designer for effect. There was nothing to tell her about the man who lived there.

But since when had such things been important? She hadn't decorated her flat since she had moved in, nor

263

bought much furniture, so what did that say about her? She and Paul were two of a kind, which was a good basis for a relationship. She would just have to try harder to make it work the way she wanted. Anyway, what did Robert know about straight men?

'I think Paul's wonderful too,' she said firmly to Jessica. 'I'm seeing him again tonight and we're planning to have a long, lazy Sunday together tomorrow. It will be the first time we've had a chance to be with each other for any length of time. I seem to spend all my time at the Channel these days and he's always on a plane somewhere.'

There was a loud wail from outside and Jessica started up, but Maria, who had surprising strength in her slight frame, had already scooped Thomas up from where he had fallen, perched him on her hip and was comforting him.

Jessica sank back down onto the sofa, her face thoughtful. 'I'm so glad you could come over today, Kate. There's something I've been wanting to talk to you about for ages.' She smiled a little far-away smile and her hand went to her stomach. 'Nobody knows yet, so you must promise to keep it a secret for the time being . . . but I'm pregnant again.'

'Jessica! I'm so pleased for you.' Kate leant across and kissed her on the cheek. 'I know you've wanted another baby for ever.'

'It's only eight weeks. That weekend with Hugo, you remember? The four-poster bed? It seemed so right, to seal our reconciliation.'

'How on earth did you get Hugo to agree?' asked Kate curiously, 'or perhaps I shouldn't ask?'

Jessica flushed a delicate pink. 'He doesn't know.'

'You mean he doesn't know that you're pregnant yet, or he doesn't know that you were trying?'

'Neither.' The word was said almost in a whisper, but then Jessica looked defiant, or at least an imitation of it. 'But I *know* he'll be happy when I tell him. Men are like that. It was just the thought of another baby that he didn't like. Now that it's actually happening, he'll be fine. I *know* he will.'

Kate wished she could be so sure, but Jessica was probably right. Hugo would grumble but go along with it. What else could he do? She gave Jessica an encouraging smile. 'When are you going to tell him?'

'There are just a few more checks I have to have done, to make sure everything is all right ... once you're past a certain age there are things that ...' Jessica's voice trailed off, her eyes clouded with fear.

Kate nodded. 'I know. Wouldn't it be better if Hugo were with you for the tests? You should have someone to hold your hand.'

Jessica shook her head vehemently. 'He *hates* anything like that. He would be even more resentful if I asked him to come along. Once I know everything is perfect I'll tell him.'

'Would you like me to come with you? I don't think you should be alone,' said Kate.

Jessica's face lit up with relief. 'Oh, *would* you? I was so hoping you might offer but I didn't want to ask. I know how busy you are and the amniocentesis test is next Wednesday.'

'Of course I'll come,' said Kate, mentally rearranging her meetings for that day. 'There's no way I'd let you go by yourself. That's what friends are for, isn't it?'

Just at that moment Kate's mobile phone played its falsely merry little tune. She had reluctantly started to carry it everywhere as Jordan insisted that all the people he called his 'main players' were 'on-message' at all times.

With an apologetic grimace at Jessica she answered it: 'Kate Daniels?'

'It's Paul.'

265

She smiled at Jessica. 'Hi, Paul. I'm looking forward to tonight.'

'I hope you haven't got anything too elaborate planned.'

'No. I just thought I'd throw a salad or something together.' It was to be the first time Kate was going to cook dinner for Paul at her flat. She had spent nearly two hours and a fortune in a late-night supermarket on her way home last night and, despite her tiredness, had got up at seven that morning and cleaned her flat for an hour. She had taken three large black plastic bags filled with empty take-away containers, the result of her many late nights at work, as well as the newspapers that she hadn't had time to read, down to the dustbins. Her fridge was now full with salmon waiting to be poached, lamb to be stuffed and roasted, vegetables to be chopped, fruit to be soaked in liqueur and cream to be whipped, all dishes suggested by Claire on the basis that they were adored by men and absolutely foolproof to cook. Even by someone like Kate, whose normal culinary activity was limited to placing ready-prepared meals in the microwave.

'Well, I'm glad to hear that you've not gone to much trouble. I assumed you wouldn't as I never took you as the "slaving over the hot cooker" sort of little woman. I'd much prefer to see you looking beautiful across a restaurant table than wearing an apron.'

'Paul, is there some point to this conversation?' asked Kate.

'I'm afraid so. I have to cancel this evening as I've been called in to trouble-shoot on a project in Malaysia and I have to catch the overnight flight tonight so dinner is off. But I promise I'll make it up to you when I get back.'

Kate took a deep breath. She was not going to get angry. He had as much right to cancel dinner because of work as she had to cancel because of Jonathan. 'I shall miss you, but I do understand and don't worry about dinner. You'd have probably ended up with a take-away pizza.'

Paul laughed. 'I thought so. See you in a week's time, then.'

Kate put down her phone.

'He cancelled?' asked Jessica, looking more upset than Kate felt.

'He has to fly to Malaysia tonight. Some sudden emergency in the Orient.'

'Oh, Kate, I'm so sorry.'

Kate shrugged. 'It will give me a chance to get some work done and have an early night. I could do with one. Anyway, the last thing I want to do is cook. I never thought I would say this, but I'm fed up to the teeth with food. Jordan wants a new series and I've spent the last week reading cookery books and trying to discover the next Delia Smith. Have you any idea how many cookbooks are published each year? Cookery writers put Jeffrey Archer to shame.'

Jessica looked thoughtful. 'Have you thought about Harriet? I know you've never really liked her, but her books are very popular and she's been terribly sweet to me, about wanting a baby and all that. She's one of the few people who understand. Not that you don't, of course, and I wouldn't want you to think that I talk more to Harriet,' she said hurriedly. 'But you know what I mean . . .'

Kate smiled. 'Just because it isn't important to me doesn't mean I can't understand how important it is to someone else.'

'Then you will consider Harriet? For the series, I mean,' urged Jessica. 'I've got copies of all her books. You could borrow them if you want.' She was already getting to her feet.

Kate shrugged. Why not, she thought? She had

nothing to lose by taking a look and she had the rest of the weekend to do it in.

Twenty-Two

• • •

'Max is a bastard, but then, all men are bastards aren't they? It's congenital. They can't help it. The problem is women who think they can and try to change them.' As she finished speaking, Harriet's agent, Sheena, blew a long stream of pungent Gauloise cigarette smoke out of her nostrils. She looked into Kate's eyes. 'But you don't strike me as that kind of woman. I hope I'm right.' She stubbed out her cigarette with a heavy hand. It was at least the sixth she had smoked since they had sat down to lunch.

Lunch had been at Sheena's suggestion rather than Kate's and she had insisted that Kate paid while she chose the restaurant. 'You *do* work for a television channel after all, so the least you can do is buy me lunch on expenses, and I hope you're not going to go all politically correct on me and insist on one of those places where they act like latter-day Hitlers and ban smoking.'

Kate was beginning to understand why Sheena was said to be such a good agent. She had a way of asking for things that was hard to refuse, which was probably why Harriet would not talk to her unless she had first spoken to Sheena.

'I know we're old friends,' she had said when Kate had called her, 'but precisely because of that I think you should discuss this with Sheena first. She's my

269

agent and if she thinks it would be good for my career I'll consider it, although I can't make any promises.'

Harriet's assumption of friendship had irritated Kate, as had her insistence on Kate talking to her agent first. It was not as though they were in Hollywood and she had been tempted not to call Sheena. But although she had initially thought Jessica's suggestion that Harriet present a cookery series ridiculous, having read one of Harriet's books she had changed her mind. She had an instinct that its blend of vegetarian recipes with alternative therapies like herbalism and aromatherapy, as well as anecdotes about the trials of being a mother – all the stuff she hated – was just the sort of thing Jordan wanted and she had been proved right.

When she had casually mentioned Harriet's name to him he had been enthusiastic. 'Perfect! Just perfect! My wife is one of her biggest fans. She's raised the children on Harriet Gordon recipes; won't give them anything else. Do you want me in on the initial meeting?'

'I'm sure I can manage that by myself,' said Kate drily, but then she hadn't been able to resist adding: 'Actually, I do *know* Harriet. We were at university together.'

She had immediately regretted it, but despite Jordan's often reiterated dislike of universities and those who went to them, he had looked impressed. 'Good. That should give you more leverage because I want this woman, Kate. From what my wife tells me she projects just the right image for this Channel. I think she has the potential to out-Delia Delia. Think of the marketing and placement potential. We all know that books based on successful television cookery series walk off book-shop shelves in their thousands, but no TV channel in this country has yet exploited the full potential of a cookery series and all its spin-offs. We could sell Harriet Gordon food, crockery, kitchen utensils, even entire kitchens off the back of a series.' He made an expansive gesture with his hand. 'I can see it now, supermarket shelves stacked high with jars of Harriet Gordon's Special Recipe salad dressing, all with the Channel's logo emblazoned on the label. I think you may have come up with a winner with this one, Kate.'

'I think we should reserve judgement on that until after Harriet has agreed and we've screen-tested her,' cautioned Kate, getting up, anxious to end the meeting before he could come up with any more ideas.

'Everyone has their price in this business, Kate,' said Jordan looking up at her, 'and the reason I pay *you* such good money is that I trust you to deliver what I ask for and if that means making someone look good who doesn't, that's your job. I do hope my trust in you is not misplaced. Remember, Kate, the camera *always* lies.'

So now she was trapped, thought Kate, watching Sheena sip the glass of straight vodka, which had appeared almost the moment she had sat down and had been continually replenished throughout the meal by a waiter who seemed to know her habits. She had not wanted wine, announcing loudly that it gave her a headache in the afternoon and, having ordered the most expensive items on the menu, she had barely tasted them before pushing her plate aside, preferring vodka and her cigarette, which was held in a long ebony holder.

Although the hands that clasped the holder were square-shaped and roughened, the nails bitten to the quick, the rest of Sheena's appearance had a definite style, which Kate could not help but admire for the statement it made. Her hennaed hair was flamboyantly streaked with pink and she wore an emerald-green silk trouser suit with a mauve-and-yellow scarf draped around her neck. Sheena was not a woman who could be ignored easily. But while Kate admired her for that, she did not particularly like her and had a feeling that doing business with her was going to be difficult.

This was increased by the fact that Sheena had made it quite obvious that she was attracted to Kate.

Her eyes now glittered over the top of her vodka glass. 'I like to know what kind of woman I'm doing business with,' she continued. 'It makes things so much easier, don't you think? Now Harriet is the kind who thinks she can change men. All she has to do is be the good little woman and they will relent and become good little husbands, but I've told her she'll never change Max. He's an unreconstructed bastard and always will be. He's led by his prick and it will take him anywhere that's warm and moist, and to say it doesn't discriminate about where it goes is an understatement. I was Max's agent before I was Harriet's so *I* know. I could tell you tales about that man . . .' She paused to light another cigarette. 'Rampant isn't the word for him. I've tried both to warn and protect Harriet but this time I think he's gone too far, even for her. I have my contacts in LA and I know all about what he's up to and with whom. This time Harriet *won't* forgive him. I'm going to make sure of that.'

Kate knew that she was not going to like the answer to her next question and that she shouldn't ask it. But rather like the heroine in a horror movie who the script dictates must go upstairs alone and look in the dark loft, she had to ask. She tried to keep her voice expressionless. 'What has Max been doing in LA?'

'He's been screwing his ex-wife, Marianne. The Hollywood tom-toms say he's hoping she'll produce his next script because she's just been appointed chief executive in charge of development at one of the big studios, but my sources also say that she has no intention of touching his script.' She exhaled another long stream of smoke and smiled. 'I don't know about you, but I rather like the idea of a woman operating the casting couch for her own pleasure, don't you? I've always thought the old adage about never mixing business with pleasure was rubbish. I think sex spices up business and vice versa. It's all to do with power, the ultimate aphrodisiac.'

Kate was glad that Sheena was happy to talk. She was still trying to digest the news about Max, but it was stuck in her throat like a fish bone that threatened to choke her.

'I'd like to think we could do business together, Kate.' Sheena's voice was suddenly softer and Kate realised that this time she was expecting a response from her.

Kate had always avoided flirting with men, however attractive, if their relationship was to be professional. It avoided dangerous complications. Could she operate on the same principle with a woman, especially one who seemed to be hinting heavily that doing business with her was dependent on their personal relationship?

'I'd like to discuss the possibility of Harriet presenting a series based on her cookery books,' she said coolly, 'and I'd prefer to keep her personal life and all personal issues out of the negotiations unless they are strictly relevant to her capacity to front a television series, like the fact that she is pregnant and due at any moment.' She looked Sheena in the eyes.

Sheena held her gaze for a moment or two, then looked down as she stubbed out her cigarette. 'I like you,' she announced. 'No bullshit. Harriet is due in a month and I give you my *personal* assurance I will make sure that nothing – babies, Max – *nothing* will get in the way of her making a successful series after that.' She held out her hand. 'Are we in business?'

Kate nodded and shook her hand. 'Subject to contract and pilot programme approval,' she said warily.

Sheena snapped her fingers and a waiter materialised from nowhere. 'Champagne!' she barked, 'and a bottle of your best. None of that house rubbish, it gives me the gyp, and anyway, Channel 22 is paying for this.' She smiled across at Kate. 'And as for the other business, I'm happy to wait until we have launched Harriet onto the ether. Some things are worth waiting for.'

After several abortive attempts, Kate finally escaped the restaurant, leaving Sheena to drink most of the champagne, which she seemed happy to do. Paying the very large bill, Kate gave thanks that this was one expense Jordan wouldn't question.

Outside in the busy Soho street the realisation of what she had got herself into finally sank in. In a way she had been blocking it out, refusing to see Harriet as Max's wife, merely regarding her as yet another possible TV presenter. Kate had told herself that it was the only professional way to behave. If Harriet was the best person for the job then it didn't matter what else she was.

But now she could no longer avoid the consequences of her actions. She was going to have to work with a woman whose husband she had loved and she had to face the fact that at some point she was bound to see Max again. It was unavoidable.

Kate reached the corner of Old Compton Street and stopped, looking up and down for a taxi. But she was over Max, wasn't she? And, more than that, she now had Paul. Perhaps she should even suggest that they all go out to dinner together in a foursome. Max would love that, she thought grimly. But no. She wasn't going to play any silly games. She would deal with Max if and when she saw him.

Seeing a cab with its light on, Kate raised her arm.

But a dark-suited businessman stepped onto the pavement a few yards in front of her and flagged it down before it could reach her.

Kate sprinted forward and, in one smooth action, ducked under his raised arm, opened the door and stepped inside. 'This one's mine, I think,' she said to the outraged face peering at her through the open window. She gave him a little wave as the taxi drove off down the street.

Twenty-Three

• • •

Two pairs of eyes inspected Kate over the top of a white wicket gate. The girls to whom they belonged were dressed in identical lime-green T-shirts and red and yellow striped dungarees, their feet encased in matching polka dot socks and blue deck shoes. They looked fresh and summery, if a little bright.

Kate, on the other hand, felt extremely hot and dusty. The walk from the railway station was a lot further than the 'just five minutes up the lane' that Harriet had described. Added to that, the train from Liverpool Street station had a malfunction in its heating system according to the short but nasally unapologetic announcement from the guard. It had meant that on an extremely hot August day the heating had been full on throughout the journey.

As if that had not been enough, for most of the time a small but noisy child had raced up and down the carriage with a model of a fighter jet in its hand, loudly simulating the noise of an aircraft involved in aerial combat. Much to Kate's annoyance, instead of restraining it and pointing out that running around was making it thirsty and that the sugar-laden fizzy drinks it kept demanding would not quench its thirst, its parents had given in to its shrill demands.

So she was not feeling well-disposed towards children: either to the two who were now staring at her so

276

rudely, or to kids in general. Nor did she feel well-disposed towards their parents, who in this particular case were Harriet and Max.

That Max was the father of these two was inescapable. They looked disconcertingly like him. It was *his* eyes, although in the faces of two little girls, that looked back at her from under two dark fringes. Not for the first time, Kate wondered why she had agreed to this weekend.

She had wanted a meeting in the more neutral surroundings of a London restaurant, but according to Sheena, Harriet was only agreeable to further discussion of the series if Kate would come to Cambridge. Harriet and the children always spent the school holidays in the country, so that the girls could ride their ponies and take part in the local gymkhanas, and she did not want to interrupt their routine.

'This is also where I experiment with all my new recipes, so if you want to get a full picture of how I work, I'm afraid you'll have to come here,' Harriet had said when Kate had called her in a last-ditch attempt to convince her to come to London. 'And not that I would want to use my condition in any way as an excuse, but I am *very* pregnant and, in the circumstances, a journey to town would be very stressful.'

There was a certain irony in the present situation which, despite her present discomfort, Kate found grimly amusing. Max loathed country life and all that went with it, declaring it to be a load of middle-class shite, so he avoided going to Cambridge whenever he could. In the past it had meant he and Kate could steal more time together. Now, here she was, taking advantage of his absence in LA to sneak in and see his wife.

Perhaps 'sneak' wasn't quite the right word as she had been invited, after all. But it was rather the way she felt. There was going to be a moment when she would have to confront Max, but she did not want it to

277

happen quite yet. She wished to be sure of Harriet first and also of herself.

Paul wasn't helping much. He made assumptions about their relationship that made her appear unreasonable. He had got back from his business trip to Malaysia the day before and had called to confirm their dinner arrangements for tonight. She had forgotten all about them when she had agreed to the weekend with Harriet.

'But you can't. I've just spent fourteen hours on a plane, after a week in a tropical hell, with humidity at one hundred per cent and workers who don't know their arse from their elbow, and all that kept me going was the thought that we would be together this weekend.'

'Spending a weekend with Harriet is not my idea of fun either, but it's a case of the mountain and Muhammad. I have to go to her.' And she did, thought Kate. Jordan had already begun to prepare a marketing and publicity campaign for the series, and she hadn't even found out whether Harriet could read auto cue.

'Surely you told this Harriet woman you had something planned?'

How could she say she had forgotten – that dinner with him had not even crossed her mind? 'I had something planned for last weekend too, if you remember,' countered Kate.

'But that was different,' insisted Paul. 'That was important. I often have to go off on short notice. It's part of my job.'

'It's part of mine too. This is equally important,' she had been stung into retorting.

'I hardly think some silly woman who cooks nut cutlets is in the same league as a major engineering project.'

Kate knew it wasn't, but she didn't want to be reminded of it, particularly by Paul. 'This is *my* job,

Paul, and it's important to *me*, and I'm afraid I and my job go together.'

'Okay, okay. I get the point. What about next weekend? Will there be any putative media stars demanding your presence then?'

Kate had not liked the way he pronounced the word media. Somehow he managed to suggest it was slightly offensive, but he had a right to be angry.

'Next weekend would be lovely and I promise you my job won't get in the way again.'

The wicket gate creaked as the older of the two girls swung it forward, pushing off with her foot and standing on the rungs next to her younger sister.

As the gate came to rest in front of Kate, barring her way, the girl spoke. 'You must be the producer woman. Mummy is expecting you, although she *was* expecting you on the earlier train. *We* are the Gordon children.' She indicated her sister. 'This is Fleur, she's seven and three quarters, and I'm Emma and I'm nine.' She jumped to the ground and swung the gate open. 'You can come in now.' She took her sister's hand as Fleur climbed down less confidently and waited.

'I'm Kate,' said Kate, uncertain, as usual, how to talk to children, but this pair were even more unsettling than normal because of their resemblance to Max.

They fell in step beside her, their feet crunching loudly on the pebbled drive, which was flanked by high, dark-green, shiny-leafed rhododendron bushes.

'Mummy says that we are to make you welcome,' piped up Fleur.

'That's very kind of her,' replied Kate.

'If you like, we can take you on a tour of the house and gardens,' suggested Emma.

'Perhaps we can do that later, because your mother and I have a lot to discuss.'

They walked in silence for another ten yards.

'Our daddy has planted a tadpole inside our mummy so that she can have another baby.'

Nonplussed, Kate stopped and looked down at Emma. 'I'm sure it will be nice for you to have another sister or a brother.'

The two girls exchanged looks which suggested that an addition to the family was not welcome, or was it just the heat which was getting to her, making her see what was not really there? thought Kate. She resettled the strap of her small overnight case which was cutting into her shoulder and started walking again. After about a hundred and fifty yards, the green wall of rhododendrons suddenly ended, revealing a perfect English vista of a lovely old double-fronted Regency manor house, built in soft grey stone with a large lawn sloping down to a lake in front of it.

'What a pretty house,' exclaimed Kate.

'*We* like it,' announced Emma, 'and Fleur and I intend to live here after our parents are dead. Just the *two* of us.' She looked up at Kate, her eyes round and innocent.

'*Kate!*' Harriet was waving from the front door.

With a sense of relief she had not expected to feel when seeing Harriet, Kate hurried forward and kissed the cheek that was offered to her. Harriet looked much better than the last time Kate had seen her. Her face, devoid of her attempts at make-up, had a healthy glow from the sun, while her body appeared to have accepted the heavy weight of pregnancy and her swollen stomach seemed to be held before her more easily.

'You've met the girls,' said Harriet proudly.

Kate knew that usual social niceties demanded some admiring comment on what wonderful, good or beautiful children they were at this point, but she was struggling hard to find one that was apt. 'They're awfully alike, aren't they?' she managed.

'Like the proverbial peas in a pod,' said Harriet, 'and Emma likes to keep it that way. She's the arbiter of style in this family. Fleur always follows her. The dynamics of the relationship between those two are wonderful to watch. Emma is quite the little mother.'

'Yes, so I've noticed,' said Kate drily.

'Lunch *is* ready. We always have more like a brunch on Saturdays when we're in the country. So why don't I run you straight up to your room and you can quickly freshen up before you join us?'

As she followed Harriet's slow progress up the stairs, Kate found herself apologising for her late arrival, although it was only just one thirty. Harriet showed her into a Laura Ashley co-ordinated chintz bedroom and indicated the door opposite hers as being the guest bathroom.

'We'll see you in a minute, then? Just follow the sounds of life when you come downstairs. You'll find us in the kitchen.'

Kate splashed cold water on her face and changed her blouse for a T-shirt. Then she twisted her hair and secured it on top of her head as it was cooler with it off her neck. She opened the window wide and sat down on the edge of her bed for a moment, trying to compose herself before she went down. It was going to be a long twenty-four hours in Harriet's company. What *had* she let herself in for? She took a deep breath and got up. She could not put off the moment any longer.

Finding her way downstairs, Kate was conscious of the coolness of the house. It was the kind often found in old buildings and usually meant that they were freezing, as well as damp, in winter, but today it felt good. The house was even larger than it looked from the outside and bore the signs that it was being renovated to make it look like a genuine country house. But it was an urban dweller's idea of the country, born out of magazines rather than rural living.

281

The sound of quarrelling voices led Kate down a dim corridor beside the stairs to the kitchen at the back. As she walked through the door, the voices stopped and the two girls looked up from where they were seated at a large table set for lunch, and smiled innocently at her as though they had not been fighting. Harriet was ladling soup into bowls.

'We were just going to start without you. I wasn't sure how long you'd be and I try to teach the children that punctuality at meals is *so* important. Do sit down.'

Kate sat in the chair nearest her. Emma and Fleur were on the other side of the table.

Harriet's renovations – for Kate was sure that they were her province rather than Max's – had not got as far as the kitchen. It was a beautiful room with a flagstoned floor and old cupboards in muted greens and greys that bore the imprint of age and use. Even the original black kitchen range was still in place.

'What a wonderful kitchen,' said Kate.

'I suppose it is, in a way,' said Harriet, handing her a bowl of soup. 'But not really practical, of course, and it's very hard to keep it looking spick and span. Those cupboards, ugh!' She shivered theatrically. 'I've got a new kitchen on order. It's being handmade by local craftsmen. We do like to show that we're part of the community here, not just weekenders like so many people who have bought properties in the area since the M11 opened it up.'

'So you spend a lot of time here, then?' asked Kate conversationally.

'Not as much as I'd like to. I think Max would be able to write much better here, but he insists he can only work surrounded by pollution and noise and city streets. He says they keep him sane because they are real and that all this' – she waved her hand – 'isn't reality.'

'And how is Max?' asked Kate casually.

'Max is fine apart from a bad case of jet lag,' answered his voice from behind her.

Kate jumped. Max's voice had sent a charge like an electric shock through her body. She turned. He was leaning against the door frame, his eyes bleary with sleep, one hand rubbing his head in a gesture that was entirely familiar to Kate. He yawned. 'That eleven-hour red-eye from LA always makes me feel like shit warmed up.'

'*Max*!' said Harriet sharply, nodding at the children.

He winked theatrically at the two girls and they stifled giggles behind their hands.

He ambled over and sat down at the head of the table.

'I didn't know you were back.' Kate tried for an even voice. Her hands felt as if they were trembling and she was keeping them out of sight under the table.

He looked at her for a moment, their eyes locking. Then he glanced away. 'I couldn't bear another day in that lonely hotel room. I was missing my two beautiful women.' He held out his arms to Emma and Fleur, and they scrambled off their chairs and rushed round and attempted to scramble onto his lap.

'Not at the table,' said Harriet sharply. 'Now your father has woken up we can eat.'

The two girls reluctantly returned to their seats and Harriet placed bowls of soup in front of them.

Max began to spoon soup quickly into his mouth. Harriet pushed a bowl towards Kate. 'Do help yourself to some yoghurt. It goes beautifully with the soup. It's made from goat's milk as both Emma and Fleur have an allergy to cow's milk.'

Kate forced herself to concentrate on the food. She was here to deal with Harriet, not Max. The soup was chilled and creamy. 'Mm. It's very nice, but I can't quite recognise the taste.' Her voice sounded false to her ears, but Harriet did not seem to notice.

'Sorrel and spinach with a touch of mint – one of my recipes,' she replied. She looked at the children who were sitting silently, their soup untouched. 'Eat up. What's the matter with you two?'

'I thought we agreed we would say grace before meals,' said Emma petulantly.

Harriet put down her spoon. 'Yes, I suppose we did, didn't we, darling.' She looked meaningfully down the table at Max who was still hungrily slurping soup into his mouth. He reluctantly lowered his spoon. 'You see,' she explained to Kate, 'we have a family conference on Saturday mornings at which we all co-ordinate our week. I think it's very important that children learn the value of time and how to organise themselves to make the best of it. So we discuss what each of us has planned, giving school and extra-curricular activities equal importance to whatever Max and I are doing. We also discuss family matters. If anyone's behaviour has been particularly irritating, we talk about it, or if one of us has a problem we air it. It creates a very close family. This week Emma expressed the wish that we say grace with our meals and, although Max wasn't here to discuss it, I felt we should allow it. I was brought up a Catholic and as I know Max hates all religions, particularly Catholicism' – she glanced quickly in his direction when she said this – 'we agreed the children should not be brought up in any religion. But without any influence from me, Emma now says she wants to consider Catholicism and since we feel the children ought to be encouraged to explore new ideas for themselves we mustn't interfere, must we, darling?' She looked at Max again.

His face was thunderous but he said nothing. This picture of Max the family man was not one Kate had seen before. She wondered whether his silence was because she was there or because he really felt that he should give in to the whim of a nine-year-old.

Harriet looked encouragingly at Emma. 'Go ahead, darling.'

Emma and Fleur bowed their hands and clasped their hands together. Kate placed her spoon in her bowl and sat back. Only Max continued to hold his, although he did not use it.

Emma screwed up her eyes tightly. 'We would like to ask the blessing of the Almighty on this our humble repast, and we thank him for all his bounty and for all our family gathered around this table. Amen.' She opened her eyes.

Fleur repeated 'amen' after her and Harriet quickly added an 'amen' too. Emma picked up her spoon and Fleur followed suit. She then dipped it into the soup and Fleur did the same. They began to spoon it into their mouths with almost perfect synchronisation.

'Have you ever been to this part of England before?' asked Harriet, looking at Kate and ignoring Max's still angry expression.

Kate shook her head. 'No, I'm not really familiar with it.'

'I'm a native of these parts,' Harriet continued, 'which is the reason we bought this place. It used to belong to the local squire and when I was a small girl I used to come to the fêtes which were held in the grounds. I always had ambitions to live here, so when it came on the market we grabbed at it, didn't we, darling?'

Max looked at Kate. 'I think the expression for it is poetic justice.' There was a trace of irony in his tone. 'Harriet's father was a farm worker and the family lived in a tied cottage, one of those little ones you passed on your walk from the station, as a matter of fact. They're all roses round the door and pretty pastel colours now, because weekenders from the great smoke have bought them and done them up. But when farm labourers lived in them in the past they were damp and riddled with dry rot, and families slept ten to a room, many of the children dying from deprivation before the age of one. Families were thrown out onto the streets and into the poor house when the father could no longer work, as often as not because he had been injured by some farming implement or grown old and diseased before his time because of the long hours he was forced to put in. It's a side of country life that all the middle-class escapees from London choose to ignore as they buy their weekend cottages, forcing up prices so that real country people can't afford to live in their own villages.'

'My father was the farm manager, not a worker, darling,' said Harriet, pouting. 'He's teasing, Kate, don't listen to a word he says. Things were never as bad as he says. I think he only tells people these stories because he knows it will irritate me.'

'Now would I do a thing like that?' asked Max, pulling a face at Emma and Fleur, causing them to conceal smiles behind their hands again.

Harriet stood up and began to collect the dishes on which she had served salad, crashing them together and smiling with forced gaiety. 'As you can see, Kate, we like our little jokes in this family.'

'That was a very nice lunch, thank you,' said Kate, standing up also and starting to help.

'Yes, it was well up to your usual delicious standard, darling,' added Max soothingly.

Harriet took the salad bowl from Kate's hand and put it back on the table. 'Don't worry about the dishes. I'm putting Emma and Fleur onto punishment washing-up duty. You and Max go through to the living-room. I'll bring some herb tea and then we can discuss the series.'

Max led the way down the passage and ushered Kate through the door ahead of him. The room was large enough to accommodate a baby grand piano in one corner. It was predominantly primrose yellow and pale green, with abundant chintz-covered armchairs dotted about. Two sets of french doors opened onto an expanse of manicured lawn. Max closed the door behind them and Kate turned to speak to him, but before she could say anything he put his arms around her, trapping hers at her sides, and kissed her hard on the mouth, his lips threatening to devour her.

Kate struggled to free herself. 'What are you doing?' she demanded breathlessly when he finally released her. 'Someone could walk in at any moment.'

He grinned. 'It makes it more exciting, don't you think?'

'No. It doesn't,' said Kate, backing away from him.

'But isn't that the idea behind all this?' he demanded, 'so that we can spend more time with each other? When Harriet first told me about your idea for a series I though it was ridiculous. She's hardly the glamorous television presenter sort, is she? But then I realised that it would mean you being around much more, and legitimately, too. So who's going to raise an eyebrow if they see us together – you're my wife's producer.'

'That *isn't* the idea; far from it,' snapped Kate. 'Do you honestly think that I would go to the trouble and expense of setting up a TV series just to see you?' She stared at him bleakly, then turned away. 'I'm seeing someone else, Max. It's over between us.'

Max grabbed her arm and spun her around. 'So that's why you haven't returned my calls. Who is he? Is he someone I know?'

Kate pulled away, rubbing her arm. 'He's got nothing to do with the media. Anyway, what does it matter who he is or what he does?' she demanded, angry at being put on the defensive. She owed nothing to Max, not even an explanation – not after the way he had behaved. She could only assume that Sheena had not

287

as yet told Harriet about Marianne. Perhaps she was waiting until after the baby arrived.

His eyes narrowed. 'Are you trying to make me jealous? Because if you are you're succeeding, and you're succeeding in making me want you even more than I already do.' He came towards her. 'Kate, have you any idea how much . . .'

The door handle rattled and they both stood still.

'Max . . . could someone open the door, please,' asked Harriet's plaintive voice.

Kate side-stepped Max and opened it. Harriet was holding a tray carrying three tall glasses inside silver holders. Kate took it from her. 'Let me help you.'

'Why was the door closed?' asked Harriet, coming in.

'A draught from the windows must have blown it shut. I'll close them,' said Max, making for the french windows.

'Oh, leave them, *please*,' begged Harriet, fanning her face ineffectually with her hand. 'If there's any draught in here I'd welcome it.' She lowered herself awkwardly into a chair. 'I'd forgotten just how hot you can become when you're pregnant. I feel like I'm carrying my own portable heater around with me.' She placed her hand on her stomach. 'I've made chilled mint tea, I hope that's all right. I thought it would be refreshing in this heat and it helps my indigestion. It becomes chronic when I'm pregnant, like wind, as poor Max well knows, don't you?'

Max smiled weakly. Kate handed Harriet a glass of tea, took one for herself and sat down in the chair beside her. She left Max's glass on the tray. He made no move to pick it up.

Harriet sipped her tea. 'I hate to admit it, but I'll be glad when the baby is born. I enjoyed being pregnant the first two times, but this one has been difficult right from the very beginning, hasn't it, darling?' She looked at Max but he had remained standing, his back half towards them, staring out of the window. Harriet turned to Kate. 'When I say from the beginning, I do mean right from the *very* beginning. Both Max and I have had rigorous preconception check-ups, which is when we discovered that Max's sperm count was low. I did a lot of research into it and consulted with my herbalist and Dr Dhondy, my Ayuverda practitioner. Between us we put Max on a rigorous diet, which our conventional doctor pooh-poohed, but it did the job and his sperm are in tiptop condition now.'

'Absolutely tiptop,' murmured Max.

Kate looked at him, but he was resolutely staring out of the windows, his hands dug deep into his pockets. He was still a big man, but here in Harriet's house – for it was her money that had paid for it according to Jessica – he appeared to have shrunk. Outside, he seemed to dominate everything, especially Harriet, but here he was no longer in control. Harriet was. She looked back at Harriet who was talking enthusiastically.

'People just don't seem to understand how important diet is. It can affect everything including fertility. It's one of the things I'd really like to emphasise in this series, Kate, a holistic approach to life.' She reached across and touched Kate's arm for emphasis. 'We must learn to listen to our bodies and work with them, not against them. I know *exactly* the moment when my body is ovulating and when it's at its most fertile stage. During the time we were waiting for Max's sperm count to get up to speed I used to visualise millions and millions of Max's little sperm all wriggling madly around inside his scrotum fighting to get out, and I imagined my egg, all round and voluptuous and fertile, sitting there waiting for them. Then I concentrated on the moment when Max surged inside me and launched all those wriggling sperm up into my vagina, and they raced madly towards my egg, the strongest ones forging ahead like Olympic swimmers, leaving the weak ones behind, until one reached its goal and *bingo* – in he went. Then my egg surrounded and absorbed him.' She sighed. 'It gives me *such* a lovely feeling even now and I'm convinced that visualisation combined with the right diet did it for me. If I'd listened to conventional doctors, who kept on about Max's sperm count and what they called my advanced age, I'd never have got pregnant. I think it's so important to *think* fertile and prepare one's womb, so that one's *whole* body is primed for the right moment.' She sipped her tea and looked ruminative for a few moments.

Kate glanced across at Max – surely he would say something – but he continued to stare out of the window. She turned to Harriet. 'Are you sure you want to consider a series like this right at the moment? It will be very stressful and you have to think about the effect not only on yourself but on your new baby and the girls, too.'

'Coping with several jobs at the same time is what women do well,' said Harriet with surprising forceful-ness. 'I wasn't sure about it at first' – she turned towards Max at this – 'but I am now. The more I think about it the more I think I have to say. In fact, I've got so many ideas for the series I feel that I'm bursting with them, rather like Harry.' She patted her stomach. 'That's the baby's name, by the way, we know it's a boy, which is why I think it's the perfect time to do the series. I feel like I'm going to give birth to two babies rather than one and you're my birthing partner as well as one of my midwives.' She looked at Kate, trust shining in her eyes. 'Don't you think it's going to be exciting to be producing a baby together?'

Twenty-Four

• • •

Kate swung left into the bus lane and put her foot down on the accelerator, overtaking the long line of waiting traffic on the inside. She reached the traffic lights just as they turned green and, indicating right, she cut swiftly in front of a large Mercedes and, ignoring the angry sound of a car horn behind her, sped off. She was late.

It was not her fault. Jordan had called a meeting of department heads just as she was preparing to leave the Channel. The urgency of the summons to his office had suggested it was important. But the faces of the other department heads who had been similarly summoned had betrayed the same sense of disbelief as Kate's when Jordan came round the front of his desk to address them.

'Now, I want to introduce a new weekly exercise where I want you all to feel free to share any problems you have with me and your colleagues. I want to keep positive energy and positive ideas flowing around the building. Negative energy creates blockages and stops the free flow of ideas that are the life blood of communicators like us. I'd like to feel that we can have an open and frank discussion of anything you feel is creating negative energy. It may be something one of the other departments is doing, or you may even think it is something *I* am doing, but either way, I want you to feel you are among friends and that a problem shared is a problem solved.' He looked around. 'Now, who is going to start the ball rolling? Has anyone got a problem they want to throw into the centre for us all to deal with?'

Like his first suggestion, this was greeted with silence.

'Kate, how about you? Is there something you would like to share with us?' he asked.

Kate had been watching the clock on the wall tick away the precious minutes she had hoped to spend getting home and preparing dinner. Now everyone turned to look at her. On some faces she could see a mixture of relief and sympathy that they had not been selected, but most of them had the hungry look of Romans watching Christians in the arena, wanting to see someone put his or her head into the lion's mouth.

Meetings had always been an opportunity to score political points off opponents. But since Jordan had arrived and begun making people redundant, and putting even those who kept their jobs onto short-term contracts, they had turned into gladiatorial contests where the blood-lust was barely concealed. Not just enemies but former friends and allies turned on each other for fear that they would be the next to go if they did not show they had the killer instinct.

For one mad moment Kate considered throwing herself to the lions and saying some of the things she knew they all felt about the way Jordan was running the Channel, but she drew back. 'My only problem is cooking dinner tonight,' she said cheerfully. 'Anyone know a foolproof recipe for an unsinkable soufflé?'

They had all laughed, although Jordan's smile, as he congratulated her on causing positive energy to flow, had seemed a little forced.

Kate jumped a set of traffic lights and flashed her lights impatiently at a taxi driver who had stopped to pick up a fare and had momentarily blocked the road. She had no intention of cooking a soufflé, just a simple casserole, but now she would not have time to prepare even that. Paul was always punctual, almost to the second, and she had intended that everything be ready when he arrived. As things were, she would barely be able to squeeze in a shower.

Knowing she would not have time to cook the meal she had in mind, after leaving the office she had risked leaving the car on a double yellow line while she dashed around the food department of Marks & Spencer. It had made her even later, but at least all she would have to do now was to empty the ready-made food into serving dishes and stick them in the oven. If she hid all traces of the packaging, Paul would probably not know the difference. She thought it unlikely that he had ever bought a pre-cooked meal. He had prepared several excellent meals for her since their relationship had begun and they had all been expertly made in front of her eyes.

She was determined to make this weekend a success after having had to cancel the last one to go to Cambridge. Seeing Max and Harriet together had made her realise just how stupid she had been. In all the time she had been having an affair with Max she had never allowed herself to think of Harriet as a three-dimensional person, made of flesh and blood. She had just been Max's wife. Now, while she could not say that she actually liked Harriet, she had to admire her. As for Max, surrounded by the paraphernalia of children and family life, she had suddenly been unable to understand why she had ever found him so sexy. It had made her determined to work harder at her relationship with Paul. She had never really given it a chance, but tonight she had intended to turn over a new leaf.

Kate made a sharp right turn in front of an oncoming bus into her road, then slowed down to check the line

293

of tightly parked cars for a space. As she drew level with her flat her heart sank. Paul's lean figure was standing outside her front door. He was five minutes early. Spotting a space barely large enough for her car further up the road, she expertly reversed into it, then sat looking down at the carrier bags of food beside her.

She suddenly felt very weary. She never seemed to stop running: from one meeting to the next, around supermarkets, from home to work and back again – even from one relationship to another. But what was the point? She didn't get anywhere any faster. If anything, she got later and later, as she was now. What would happen if, just for once, she stopped running and stayed in one place?

Kate took a deep breath. There was no point in day-dreaming about what might happen. She had to deal with reality – like how to disguise the contents of her shopping bags to preserve the illusion that she was cooking dinner. But would it really matter? Paul had not been attracted to her because she was the kind of woman who darned socks and made gooseberry jam, or so he said. Pushing the more obvious boxes out of sight so their labels could not be seen, she gathered the bags together with her briefcase and got out of the car.

Paul was looking in the opposite direction as she walked towards him. His jaw was set in a fashion which, even at this distance, suggested he was not happy. The sound of a police siren caused him to turn and catch sight of Kate. He came down the steps towards her, reaching for her bags, the expression on his face alternating between pleasure at seeing her and irritation at her lateness. He kissed her on the cheek as he relieved her of the carrier bags.

'Sorry I'm late,' said Kate, fishing for her keys.

'But only five minutes. I count that as being almost punctual by your standards,' Paul answered half-teasingly as he followed her up the steps.

'Well, I'll make sure it doesn't happen again – being punctual, that is,' said Kate, turning and kissing him playfully on the lips.

She opened the door and led the way to the flat. Paul followed her in and placed the shopping bags in the kitchen. Kate watched him look around approvingly. She had got up early and cleaned it before she went to work.

'Why don't you pour us a couple of gin and tonics while I just do a quick change?' She took a bottle of gin and one of tonic water out of a shopping bag and placed them on the work top, then quickly pushed the bags containing the prepared food into a kitchen cupboard. 'I'll put the rest of my shopping away later. It's nothing that won't keep,' she lied as she straightened up.

She watched Paul measuring the gin out into the glasses. She needed to get him out of the kitchen and to keep him out long enough to get the food into the oven and the containers into the rubbish bin. She kissed him lightly on the neck just below his ear, a spot where he was particularly sensitive.

'I need a shower. Why don't you bring the drinks through to the bedroom so you can talk to me while I'm in the bathroom,' she said over her shoulder as she headed for the bedroom, shedding her clothes as she walked.

She was down to her knickers by the time Paul came into the room carrying the gin and tonics. He stood in the doorway looking at her.

'Just how hungry are you?' asked Kate walking over to him and loosening his tie, not giving him a chance to put down the drinks.

'You can be very direct, can't you,' replied Paul.

'Does that bother you?' asked Kate, dropping his tie on the floor and turning her attention to the buttons on his shirt. She followed his eyes down to where his silk tie lay on the floor and saw that he wanted to pick it up. Pulling his shirt open, she pressed her breasts against his chest, one hand now deftly undoing his trouser belt. 'If it does, all you have to do is to tell me to stop.' Her hand reached inside his trousers and his eyes closed, tie forgotten.

Kate kissed him on the mouth and began to work her way down his body, easing his trousers and underpants down over his already stiff erection as she went. She knelt on the floor in front of him and very gently took him into her mouth. His body started to shake almost imperceptibly and an ice-cold shower of gin and tonic sprinkled her naked back but, just at that moment, there was a buzz at the front door.

Kate ignored it and kept going, but there was a second, much longer buzz.

'You have to answer that,' said Paul in a strangled voice.

Kate drew back and looked up at him. 'Why? I'm not expecting anyone.'

'I can't ... not while I know ... you just have to answer it, that's all,' he said through gritted teeth.

Kate got up and reached behind the door for her wrap, then went to the intercom.

'Yes?'

'Kate, thank goodness you're in. It's Jessica.'

Kate buzzed the main front door open and then stood in her doorway.

'Oh, Kate. I've left Hugo. What am I going to do?' The wail of grief preceded Jessica as she rushed down the hall in a flurry of long skirts, tailing off into loud sobs as she threw herself against Kate's breast.

Kate wrapped her arms around her and drew her into her flat, depositing her on the sofa. Keeping one arm around Jessica's heaving shoulders, Kate reached for a box of tissues and pulled out a handful, then began to dab at Jessica's face. The eyes that looked up at her were red-rimmed and swollen.

'Tell me what happened.'

Jessica pushed back her hair and tried to steady her breathing, which was coming out in huge racking gasps. Kate gave her some more tissues and she loudly blew her nose.

'It was awful . . .' Jessica began, but her eyes immediately brimmed with tears and she stopped, gulping as though she could not breathe.

Kate offered her the whole box this time. Jessica put them on her lap and began to pull them out one by one, dabbing her cheeks and dropping them on the sofa beside her.

'Thomas and I had gone to the puppet theatre, you know, the one they set up in the park every summer?'

Kate didn't, but she nodded her head.

'It's very multicultural. It teaches children all about other cultures like Rastafarianism and I do so want Thomas to grow up understanding other people. There's such a sweet little Indian girl in his nursery school. He really likes her. I think her parents are from Hampstead. Anyway, I promised to take him ages ago and he never forgets. He calls them duppets. Isn't that sweet?' Jessica turned tragic eyes up to Kate's face. She nodded again.

'I thought it would be nice, just the two of us because Maria had asked for the afternoon off. She said she had some shopping to do. Thomas wanted her to come with us and he played up a bit, but once I got him into the taxi he was fine and he was really good all the way through the performance too. He loved all the bits where the children had to shout, "Look out, behind you!" You should have heard him . . . but then he was sick. It was awfully embarrassing. He was fine one moment, yelling his head off: "Behind you, behind you" and then he suddenly leant forward and was sick all down the back of the little girl sitting in front of him. He has *such* a delicate stomach and when things upset him he just throws them up without warning. The little girl screamed and screamed until I thought *she* was going to be sick too and they had to stop the performance for a little while. It was unfortunate, really, as she had this lovely waist-length blonde hair. It would probably have been all right if it had been just her dress. Her mother was terribly upset too, as you can imagine, so I offered her some money for cleaning the dress and the taxi fare home. It turned out that they lived in Enfield so I had to give them a cheque. Anyway, I thought I had better get Thomas home, as he had thrown up again, although this time, thank goodness, it was only on the grass. And that was when it happened.'

Tears began to well up in Jessica's eyes and she pulled out another tissue and noisily blew her nose. 'I took Thomas up to the nursery. He heard Maria's voice coming from her room and he was so pleased to hear her that he rushed into her room as he always does, and there they were, on the floor.' Jessica pointed a tremulous finger at Kate's floor.

'Hugo and the nanny?'

Jessica nodded. Tears began to course down her cheeks, this time unheeded.

'Oh, Jessica, I'm so sorry. The man's a shit of the first order. And poor Thomas, too, what a thing for him to see.' As she said it something occurred to Kate that had been nagging at the back of her mind all the time Jessica had been talking. 'By the way, where *is* Thomas?'

Jessica's eyes opened wide and she put a hand to her mouth. 'Oh, my *God*! Hugo's right. I *am* a terrible mother.' She clutched Kate's arm so tightly it hurt. 'I left him in the taxi. What shall I do?'

As though in reply, the door buzzer went again. Kate

disengaged herself from Jessica's fingers and pushed the intercom button.

'I've got a little package here that someone's forgotten,' said a cheerful voice. Kate buzzed the front door open and went into the hallway. There stood the taxi driver and trustingly holding his hand was Thomas.

'I guessed it was some sort of domestic. I've seen a lot of them in my time, so I thought I would keep the little boy amused until it was sorted,' the man said. 'He's a nice little thing, bit like my grandson.'

Jessica rushed into the hall and swooped down on Thomas, gathering him up in both arms and carrying him back into Kate's flat.

'Thank you, you've been very kind. How much do we owe you?' asked Kate. She paid him what he asked and added an extra five-pound note to the tip.

He waved it away. 'Don't like to see a woman in tears and one with a kid, too. Tell her I hope things work themselves out.' He peered around the door as if hoping to see Jessica again. 'By the way, is she anybody famous? I thought I recognised her face.'

'She's an actress,' replied Kate, 'and I'll tell her you recognised her. It will cheer her up.'

He left with a satisfied smile.

Inside her flat, Jessica had knelt down in the middle of the floor and was crushing Thomas against her as if she would never let him go again.

Kate put a hand on Jessica's shoulder. 'What are you going to do?'

Jessica turned a tragic face upwards. 'I don't know. I can't go back there. I was hoping I could stay with you. Just for tonight.'

'Of course,' said Kate promptly, 'but will you excuse me for just a moment?'

Paul had already put his shirt and trousers back on when she went into the bedroom. Kate closed the door behind her and went over to him but he held himself stiffly away from her. 'I'm sorry, Paul . . .'

'I heard,' he said shortly, 'but I thought we'd agreed tonight.'

'We did and I was looking forward to it, but in the circumstances I can hardly leave Jessica alone.'

'I can't see why not. She should go home to her husband. It will probably all have blown over by tomorrow.' He looked in the mirror as he put on his tie, forcing Kate to stand behind him, talking over his shoulder to his reflection.

'Her husband is the problem. She can't go home to him and she has her child to think about. He's had a very traumatic day.'

'All the more reason why he should be with his father.'

Paul turned away from the mirror and went to the bed. He picked up his jacket. 'I'm beginning to understand where I come on your list of priorities, Kate, and it's not very flattering.'

'You're being unfair. Jessica is a good friend and she's very upset. I'm worried that in her con . . .' Kate was just about to say that Jessica was pregnant, but then remembered that Jessica had asked her not to tell anyone. '. . . her state of mind, I think she needs someone to talk to.'

'Those kind of women are always too needy.'

It was Kate's turn to stiffen. 'What kind of women?' she demanded.

'Actresses . . . you know the type.'

'I'm not sure I do, Paul. All *I* know is that a friend has been badly hurt by a man's stupid ego and I consider her pain far more important than dinner and a quick fuck.'

'Well, if *that's* all I mean to you . . .'

'Yes, it is, Paul.' And as she said it, Kate realised she meant it.

He pulled on his jacket and strode past her out of the door. Kate followed him.

On seeing him, Jessica scrambled to her feet and pushed back her hair, forcing herself to smile. 'Paul, I . . .'

'Jessica.' Paul nodded brusquely at her and, scooping up his car keys from where he had dropped them, walked out, leaving the front door open behind him.

Kate closed it and then, taking a deep breath to steady herself, she turned back. 'I'm sorry about that, Jessica.'

'I'm the one who should be sorry. I've ruined your evening.' Jessica was on the point of tears again.

'You've done nothing of the sort. Paul came much earlier and was leaving anyway, he had a prior appointment this evening,' Kate lied. This was not the time to tell Jessica that she had finished with him. 'Now, why don't we put Thomas to bed? He's too young to understand what he's seen, but if he sees you so upset he'll know something bad has happened.'

Jessica nodded her head and slowly released Thomas, whom she had been clutching to her side. Whatever was going on inside his head, he bore no outward signs of being upset. He gazed up at Kate.

'Hello, Thomas. You and Mummy are going to stay with me tonight. Won't that be nice?'

He stuck his thumb in his mouth and continued to gaze silently at her.

'You remember me, don't you? My name is Kate.' This elicited no response either. Kate looked at Jessica. 'Will he be hungry?'

'Ice-cweam.' The thumb had come out of his mouth.

'Oh, no, Thomas, darling, no more ice-cream today. It made your tummy nasty, didn't it? Remember the poor little girl in the park?' begged Jessica.

'Ice-cweam.' The tone was more insistent this time. Jessica looked helplessly at Kate.

'I'm afraid I don't have any ice-cream, Thomas, but I have some very nice yoghurt,' said Kate, rapidly trying to remember what she had in her fridge that might be suitable for consumption by a small child and still be within its 'consume-by' date.

'He doesn't like yoghurt,' said Jessica apologetically. 'In fact, he doesn't like much of anything. At the moment he will only eat fish fingers or jam sandwiches made with white sliced bread, not even wholemeal.'

'And ice-cream,' prompted Kate.

'He doesn't normally even *eat* ice-cream, but all the other children at the puppet show had one, so he insisted on one too, even though they always upset his tummy. He can be so stubborn, sometimes, that I just don't know what to do.' Jessica sounded on the edge of tears again.

Kate regarded Thomas, who had replaced his thumb in his mouth. He was less than half the size of the two adults standing over him, yet he had them both at a disadvantage. 'You can share my bed with Thomas and I'll sleep on the sofa.'

'You don't happen to have a rubber sheet, do you?' asked Jessica. 'He's usually very good, but after all that's happened today he might just have a little accident. He sometimes does when he gets over-excited.'

'An accident?' Kate was puzzled. The child gazing unblinkingly up at her did not appear over-excited. Then she realised what Jessica was referring to. 'Oh.'

'If you've got some thick towels instead, I could put those under him. They would help to soak up some of the damage,' ventured Jessica.

'Thick towels,' repeated Kate.

'Me no go to bed. Me want Mawia.' The thumb had been removed again.

'No, darling, no Maria, not tonight. She's . . .' Jessica stopped.

'Had to go to visit her mummy a long way away?' suggested Kate.

'A *very* long way away,' finished Jessica gratefully, taking Thomas's hand and leading him towards the bedroom.

'But me *want* Mawia.' Thomas stood still. Jessica pulled his hand but he refused to move. She tried again but he still refused, stubbornly shaking his head.

'Oh, dear,' wailed Jessica, 'what am I going to do?'

Kate considered the disparity in their sizes again. 'Carry him?' she suggested.

'But that's using force. The books say you have to reason with them. If you use force you'll teach them bad habits.'

It crossed Kate's mind to point out that Thomas appeared to have acquired quite a few bad habits already, but while it was possible to discuss just about any form of sexual behaviour over the dinner-table, it was still taboo to be thought to criticise the behaviour of other people's children. Anyway, what did she know about child care? If millions of parents found bribery worked, who was she to say they were wrong?

She held out her hand to Thomas. 'If you're a good boy and go to sleep in my lovely big bed, tomorrow I'll buy you the *biggest* ice-cream in the world.'

He took his thumb out of his mouth and smiled happily, then placed a wet trusting hand in hers. She led him through to the bedroom, Jessica following behind.

Leaving a big pile of towels on the bed, Kate went into the kitchen with the intention of putting on some coffee. She had a feeling they were going to need it. She would normally have reached for a bottle of wine, but given Jessica's condition, she did not think this advisable. Since she had gone with Jessica for her amniocentesis test that week and watched the monitor while she was scanned, Kate was feeling quite proprietorial towards the tiny little creature she had seen curled up inside Jessica's womb. But as she searched for the coffee grinder the telephone trilled. Before Kate could pick it up, Jessica came running through from the bedroom.

'If that's Hugo, tell him I never want to see him again.'

Kate picked up the receiver. 'Kate Daniels.'

'Kate, it's Hugo. Is Jessica with you?'

'Yes, but she doesn't want to speak to you.'

Hugo groaned. '*Please*, Kate, get her to the phone. I must speak to her.'

Kate looked over at Jessica, but she waved her hand. 'I'm afraid she won't speak to you, Hugo.'

'Can you talk to her for me? Tell her it was just one of those stupid things. It meant nothing.'

'Then why did you do it?' Kate had not meant to get caught up between Jessica and Hugo, but she was angry on her friend's behalf.

'I dropped by the house to pick up a script. Maria wasn't expecting anyone until later and she had just got out of the bath and was wandering around naked. I got carried away and didn't think.'

'You just let your prick do the thinking for you as usual.'

'Okay, okay, I deserve that. But I love Jessica, I really do, and the thought of losing Thomas is driving me crazy. *Please*, Kate, get her to come to the phone or shall I come round? That's a much better idea – I'll come round.'

'No, Hugo. You and Jessica need to talk, but not tonight. Anyway, Thomas has already gone to bed and he's had quite enough to cope with for one day, don't you think?'

'I love that little tyke, do you know that, Kate. I really love him. He's the best thing that's ever happened to me and the thought of never seeing him again, oh, God . . .'

Kate could hear that Hugo had been drinking. She didn't like the man, but yelling at him would not help. 'I'll tell Jessica what you've said but I can't promise she'll take any notice.'

'And will you tell her I love her and tell Thomas that his dada loves him too?'

With a promise to this effect, Kate put down the phone. She turned round to see Jessica's stricken face.

'What did he say? No, don't tell me, I don't want to hear. This time I'm leaving for good.'

'Why don't you go and settle Thomas down?' suggested Kate. 'Tell him a story – it'll calm you both – then we can have a long talk.'

'Thomas does like my stories,' said Jessica hopefully, turning to go back into the bedroom.

She returned after only a few minutes.

'How's Thomas?' asked Kate, looking up from the newspaper she had just started to read.

'He fell asleep almost immediately.'

Kate got up. 'Shall I make that coffee? I don't know about you, but I could do with some. I think it's going to be a long night.'

Jessica wiped her tear-stained face with the back of her hand and managed a watery smile. 'It'll be like when we were back at university. Just us girls.'

Twenty-Five

• • •

'You were always the one I wanted, from the first moment I saw you at university,' said Max, gazing intently into Kate's eyes.

For one brief, wild moment, Kate found herself almost wishing to believe him. When she'd walked into the club ten minutes earlier and had seen Max's familiar broad-shouldered figure standing at the bar, the intensity of her physical reaction had taken her by surprise. He had been holding court with one elbow propped up on the bar, his large frame dominating the laughing group around him, just as he had the first time she had seen him in the student union bar. Then, as now, she had stood watching him from the doorway and then, as now, he had caught sight of her and given her that slightly crooked smile of his.

She had not wanted to meet him, but since Cambridge nearly a month ago, Max had been calling her almost every day, begging her to see him. Harriet's baby had been born nearly two weeks before, although Max had not mentioned it. She had heard the news from an ecstatic Sheena who had been present at the birth. Kate had eventually agreed to meet him only because she thought that if she saw him face to face she could convince him that their affair was really over. She was also worried that he might say something to Harriet, something she could not afford at that moment. The plans for a pilot show for the series had already gone into pre-production, although Harriet would not be taking an active part for another month, and Jordan already had his marketing team planning the autumn relaunch of the Channel around the series.

She had drawn the line at Max coming to her flat, however, so instead he had suggested that they meet in the Soho club where he, and just about every person who worked in the media except for Kate, was a member. She had never liked joining anything and she particularly disliked this place. It seemed to her that it suffered from false-memory syndrome. In its former incarnation it had been a strip club; now it masqueraded as a country house, with faux marbled walls, swagged curtains and over-stuffed armchairs and sofas. However, on reflection, she could not help thinking that it rather suited its members, coming as they did from the television, film and advertising worlds, all industries noted for their manipulation of the past. Just as Max was trying to do now, leaning towards her across the table, his bulk creating an intimate space between them and the rest of the room.

'I used to watch you at a distance and lust after you when you came into the student union bar, but you were the original ice maiden, so cool and unapproachable. You looked so serious, too, always carrying a pile of books like a mute protest against the rest of us. I know it sounds crazy, but I didn't dare ask you out because I was scared shitless I would make a fool of myself. So instead I used to have the most incredible sexual fantasies about you.' He leant so close that his lips were grazing her cheeks and Kate could feel his hot breath. 'Just the thought of you could make me go hard. It still does. It's doing it right now.' Under the table Max's hand sought her thigh and found its goal. 'Don't tell me something similar isn't happening to you,' he murmured.

Kate wanted to say no but, like an unreformed drug addict, she could feel the old familiar craving like a dull ache between her legs. She slid along the seat, taking herself out of Max's reach. 'I never noticed that you had any problems getting women into your bed when we were at university. In fact, I seem to remember quite the opposite.'

Max looked amused. 'So the walls of your ivory tower were transparent enough for you to notice me, then?'

'If you *really* wanted me, why did you marry Marianne and Harriet?' retorted Kate and immediately hated herself. She sounded like a jealous woman.

Max put both his hands on the table. 'You know how it is.' He shrugged. 'Marianne was a very forceful person and so is Harriet in her own way. She's more the passive-aggressive type, not that I knew it then. I mistook it for being intriguing. Women like Harriet seem to expect men to understand some sort of invisible code about what they want or don't want, but they never give us the key so how are we meant to break the code? It was exciting at first, rather like being a kid again, trying to decipher some message left by another gang. We had this big thing about being spies in our neighbourhood and we were forever leaving secret messages for each other.'

He launched into a long anecdote about his childhood, a favourite topic of his, and Kate found her attention wandering. She used to enjoy lying beside him after they had made love, listening to him talk about his working-class Glaswegian childhood, imagining him as a tough, grubby-kneed, snotty-nosed little boy. But what was it one dissenting critic had said after his third film? 'Gordon has trodden and retrodden the cobbled streets he so picturesquely evokes with such regularity in his films that the groove worn by his particular brand of barefoot philosophy has for me become as tattered and thin as the clothes sported by his beloved street-wise urchins. This is the rose-tinted nostalgia of the professional Scotsman who prefers to sport his kilt in warmer climes, where the lack of any substance under it will not be put to the tough questioning of the working-class Glaswegians whose lives he claims to portray.' Kate found herself smiling and she held her glass up in front of her mouth. Max was at last coming to the end of his anecdote. It was funny, but she had never noticed before how much he liked the sound of his own voice.

'. . . but more often than not, when you found the key to the code, the message was usually something mundane and not worth all the trouble, like wee Jock hates Willy's guts, or in Harriet's case, you left the toilet seat up again.'

He waited for Kate to laugh, but when she didn't he carried straight on.

'However, there was no mistaking Marianne when she didn't like something, she told me so in no uncertain terms. She didn't become silent and wait for me to ask if something was wrong, then reply "nothing". It drives me wild when Harriet does that and she does it all the time. I seem to spend half my life walking on eggshells trying to guess what I've done wrong and it's even worse when she's pregnant. How am *I* meant to know how she feels? I'm a man and men don't get pregnant.' He looked aggrieved, as though he had suffered some grave injustice.

'Now don't get me wrong, I *love* Harriet and of course, it goes without saying that I'd give up my life for my kids if I had to, but Harriet and I don't really have a lot in common. We can't talk, not like you and I do. I'm not saying she's stupid, but she's not Einstein either. Sometimes I think she gets all her opinions from the *Daily Mail*. How can I be expected to have a sensible conversation with her? She's not like you, babe, you're so stimulating.' His voice dropped nearly an octave. 'In *every* way.'

His hand sought Kate's thigh again, but she crossed her legs and pulled down her skirt.

'I think you're being unfair to Harriet. Apart from bearing *your* babies, she's a very successful writer and, if I have anything to do with it, will be a very successful television presenter too.'

He looked pained. 'I'd hardly call what Harriet does writing. *I'm* a writer. And as to presenting television programmes, you can train monkeys to do that and I sometimes think you have. But let's forget about Harriet. I want to talk about us.' He leant across the table towards her. 'You're still angry about the baby, I understand. But there's no reason why it should come between us. It has absolutely nothing to do with you and me ...' Max gestured as though brushing a troublesome insect aside. Kate tried to speak, but he placed his hand over hers, stilling her. 'Kate, *babe*, before you say anything, I want you to know that I really care about you.' With his forefinger he traced the course of a vein on her forearm. 'Please say we can take up where we left off. I *need* you, babe, I really do. And if the baby thing is so important to you I'll happily give you one. Perhaps we can even talk about getting together. I mean ... things aren't too good with Harriet at the moment and maybe we could come to some arrangement ...'

'Well, now, and isn't this a touching little scene?'

Sheena stood in front of the table, her hands on her hips. She was dressed in a sharply tailored pin-striped trouser suit. 'Harriet's producer and Harriet's loving husband, although I do not use that term to mean he loves Harriet. He keeps his loving reserved for every little bit of skirt that has the misfortune to cross his slimy path.'

310

Max started to get up but thought better of it. 'This is none of your business, Sheena,' he began.

'Harriet *is* my business so that makes everything that affects her my business too.' She looked at Kate. 'I like you, Kate, so I'm going to treat this as a temporary lapse of your good judgement and heaven knows, we should all be allowed one occasionally. But I'm warning you, Max, I know all about your recent replay with Marianne and if I hear that you've stepped out of line once more by even so much as a *look* at another woman I'm going to sit Harriet down and have a long heart to heart with her. Do you get my meaning?'

Max nodded.

'You'll have to excuse me now as I've got a book launch to attend, but first I promised to drop by on Harriet and see how that sweet little baby of hers is getting along. Pity he's a boy, but nobody's perfect.' And with that she had gone.

Max started to signal a waitress. 'I don't know about you, but I think I could do with another bottle of wine to wash the taste of that witch away.'

'No!' Kate caught his arm.

Max looked at her. 'You don't believe what she said, do you? When it comes to winning Oscars for bitching that woman deserves a special lifetime's achievement award.'

Kate was still shaken by Sheena's interruption but she forced herself to smile. 'No, everything's fine, really.'

With a clarity that almost startled her she suddenly knew exactly what she intended to do. She put her hand under the table and found Max's crotch. He gave a little gasp and closed his eyes. She could feel him harden almost instantly.

She leant towards him so that her lips almost touched his cheek. 'I've missed you and I want to show you how much. We could go back to my flat, but I don't think I can wait that long. Let's get a room upstairs.'

Max's eyes snapped open and he fished frenziedly in his pocket. He pulled out a key. A wolfish grin spread across his face. 'I was hoping you would say that.'

Kate suppressed the urge to squeeze him so tight that it hurt. Instead she stroked him gently. He gave a low moan.

'Come on, follow me,' she murmured seductively into his ear and, taking the key from his hand, she slid along the seat and stood up.

Max stayed sitting for a moment or two, an expression almost of pain on his face. Then he drained his glass of wine and got to his feet, carefully closing his jacket. 'You go ahead,' he muttered, lowering his head. 'We don't want to be too obvious.'

Kate walked through the crowded bar, casually stopping at tables to exchange greetings when she recognised people and keeping an eye out for Sheena, but she caught a flash of her pink-striped hair in the street and guessed she was getting into a taxi. Outside in the reception area, the raven-haired receptionist was flirtatiously greeting a well-known actor – her attention focused fully on him. To Kate's relief, there was nobody else about. She pushed her way through the swing doors beside the reception desk and swiftly mounted the stairs, which led to a private dining-room and then on to the third floor. Through another door was a corridor, which led to a dozen or so bedrooms for out-of-town club members to use if they wanted to stay the night in London, and others who had drunk too much to get home safely, or, as in Max and Kate's case, who did not want to go home – safely or otherwise.

It was too early for the rooms to be occupied as there was still plenty of drinking time left in the bar downstairs, but Kate did not want to risk meeting anyone. She hurried along the corridor looking for the room Max had booked. When she reached it she hesitated for a moment, staring at the key in her hand. Then she heard the door at the end of the corridor open. It was probably Max, but it could be anyone. Kate swiftly turned the key in the lock and slipped inside.

The room was what estate agents would have described as compact and its one small window overlooked a dank, dingy well between tall buildings, their brick walls blackened by a hundred years or more of London's polluted air, but it was as opulently furnished as the rest of the club. There was barely any floor space between a kidney-shaped dressing-table, button-back armchair and the double bed. A door led off to a bathroom, which was so tiny that it was necessary to press against the opposite wall in order to close the door. However, this had not stopped it being decorated like a Roman bath house in Pompeii. Kate sat down on the end of the bed and waited.

Whoever it was who had come through the door after her, it wasn't Max. Kate felt stifled. She felt a prickle of sweat under her arms. The room was airless and its plush furnishings seemed to dull every sound except the thud of her heart. She stood up and went to the window. The air trapped between the buildings would not be particularly fresh, but at least it would be air. Several tries later she managed to open the window, then returned to the bed. After what seemed an interminable length of time there was a gentle tap on the door. Kate sprang to her feet, her heart thumping even harder. She took a deep breath, ran a hand through her hair and cautiously opened the door about six inches. A hand holding a bottle of champagne appeared round the door. Max followed. He had two champagne glasses in his other hand.

'I thought we should mark the occasion properly, but

I don't think I can wait for your body a second longer, not even to open the champagne.' He put down the bottle and the glasses on the dressing-table and pulled Kate towards him. His mouth closed hungrily over hers.

Kate found herself responding to him. She put her hands on his chest and pushed him away. 'Let's not rush things,' she said teasingly. 'I want this to take a long, *long* time.'

Max started to tear at her blouse. 'I'm not sure I can manage that, at least not the first time. I'm like that bottle of champagne – ready to explode. Feel.' He guided her hand down to his crotch. It was hard.

Kate began to unbuckle his belt. 'Then we should go in order of readiness.' She unbuttoned his shirt and kissed his chest, looking up at him. 'Do you think that's fair?'

Max didn't answer, he was already pulling off his shirt and hopping on one foot to take off his shoes and socks. Within seconds he was naked.

Kate feigned pleasure at the size of his erection. 'Is that all for me?' she asked in a Marilyn Monroe little-girl voice. 'What a clever boy you are. Now lie down and close your eyes and you're not allowed to open them until I say so. I have a *very* big surprise for you.'

Max clambered eagerly onto the bed and lay spread-eagled, his eyes tightly closed and an expectant smile on his face. 'Hurry, please hurry,' he groaned.

Kate stood looking down at him for a moment. A few weeks ago she would have been aroused by him but no longer. A wave, not just of dislike but of revulsion, swept over her. She hurriedly gathered his clothes up into a bundle and went to the window. She had intended to leave them at reception, but now she had a better idea. She looked down into the well. Four floors below there were several rubbish bins. Their rotten contents made them pungent even at that height.

With a smile she tossed Max's clothes out into space. As she watched them float down, Kate felt a sense of freedom she had not anticipated. Noticing his gleaming and much beloved Patrick Cox loafers on the floor, she lobbed them after his clothes. Turning, she picked up the bottle of champagne, which was still cold. She went to the bed where Max still lay with his eyes tightly closed.

'No peeking now,' she warned. 'I'm almost ready.' She lightly ran the base of the champagne bottle down the centre of his body to the base of his stomach, leaving cold drops of condensation on his skin. She stopped just short of his penis, which had begun to droop. It immediately recovered its earlier stiffness. There was a sharp intake of breath from Max.

Kate went to put the champagne back on the dressing-table but she changed her mind and decided to keep it. It was a shame to let it go to waste. She carefully took the key out of the lock, trying not to make any noise, and gently turned the door handle. 'I want you to count to three, *very* slowly. Then you can open your eyes,' she said loudly to cover any sound as she pulled the door open. 'Right, starting now. One . . .'

'One,' Max repeated obediently after her.

On his count of two, Kate pulled the door shut. On his count of three she turned the key in the lock.

Inside the room she heard her name called, softly at first and then loudly, a note of alarm in his question. '*Kate*! Where are you?'

She walked rapidly down the corridor. At the top of the stairs was a decorative Victorian ceramic pot. It had probably been meant to hold an aspidistra, but now it was full of sand to encourage smokers to stub out their cigarettes in it rather than on the carpets. Kate pushed the key down into the sand among the cigarette butts. They would have a master key at reception, but she wanted to cause Max as much embarrassment as possible.

Then she began to descend the stairs lightly. If she had been able to whistle it would have been a merry tune.

Twenty-Six

• • •

The hangover from drinking an entire bottle of champagne by herself could not be the cause of her feeling quite so ill, Kate had been forced to concede two days later. Her muscles ached, her head felt as though it was swimming against the tide in a whirlpool: one moment she thought she was on fire and the next her teeth started chattering because she was so cold. Ruby had agreed with her and had ordered her in no uncertain terms to go home.

She had croaked something back along the lines that she was Ruby's boss and that she could not be ordered to do anything, but Ruby had pointed out that she was in danger of infecting the entire *Harriet at Home* production team with whatever nasty virus she had picked up and she could not afford to have them all off sick.

Ruby's logic was hard to fault and Kate had felt too ill to try. So she had allowed herself to be put into a taxi with a bag full of flu remedies and throat sweets from the chemist's dispensary that doubled as the bottom drawer of Ruby's desk.

But when she got home, Kate could not even face swallowing a pill. The very thought of it made her want to throw up the breakfast she had not eaten. She barely managed to kick off her shoes and take off her jeans before she collapsed into bed, pulling the covers over her head in the hope that, whatever it was, she could shut it out.

Kate had never felt like this before. Other people got ill, not she. While feeling pity for those who did, she had always secretly nursed the conviction that they were weak and were giving in to their bodies. But now it was not just a matter of giving in – she abjectly and completely surrendered and would have signed anything, just to be allowed to close her eyes and die. However, her body refused to allow her the blessed release of oblivion.

How long she lay huddled under her duvet, her joints aching, the slightest movement making her head swim, Kate neither knew nor cared. It could have been hours, days or even years. She lost all sense of time. The only sense that was still reliably working was the one that told her she felt ill. All she could do was concentrate on surviving each successive wave of nausea as it swept over her, dragging her spiralling down into its dizzying depths.

It was the faint but distinct aroma of freshly brewing coffee piercing the fog of her self-pity that first made Kate aware she might not die after all. Cautiously, using only one finger, she pulled down her duvet and peered out.

To her surprise, her bedroom was still very much as she remembered it – at least the furniture, what there was of it. All her clothes had been collected and folded neatly. The window was open – Kate couldn't remember doing this – but the aroma of coffee was probably wafting in from another flat, as the sunshine seemed to indicate that it was morning. She inched the duvet down a little more. There was the distinct sound of movement in the next room and the faint clink of dishes being moved around.

Kate was past the stage of being able to feel frightened. If she was going to be murdered it couldn't be any worse than the way she had been feeling. Anyway, whoever the intruder was, was very neat and she had not yet heard of burglars who tidied up after themselves, although there could always be a first time.

She opened her mouth and a strange guttural sound flew out, but it was enough for the noises in the next room to stop. She heard footsteps and the bedroom door opening, then more footsteps as someone walked across the floor towards her.

'Well! Glory be! And they said there could be no miracles in this pagan age of ours. Yet will ye be looking at this – Lazarus is rising from the dead!' The accent was Irish, and very bad Irish at that.

Kate pulled the duvet cover down a little further. Liam was standing beside her bed. She opened her mouth again.

'Yes, I know,' he said before she could make a noise, 'my Irish accent is abominable, which is unforgivable with a name like Liam and ten generations of Irish ancestors going as far back as ... well, as Liverpool anyway.'

Kate tried again to speak and once more Liam spoke instead.

'You want to know what I'm doing here? Well, a very nice publisher in London wants to publish my collection of stories so Robert gave me a set of keys so I could stay in his flat for a while. At the same time he gave me your spare set of keys to return to you as he didn't think he could pop round and let you in if you locked yourself out while he was in Majorca. Anyway, I thought – given the circumstances of our parting – that I would drop them in at your office, which is where I went yesterday afternoon. There I met this magnificently Rubensesque creature so aptly called Ruby, who told me how ill you were and how they were all so worried about you as you lived alone, and how they had been calling you but you hadn't answered the

319

phone, and that you needed someone nice to give you a little TLC – by that I think she meant tender loving care by a kind person. From the way she was looking me over I thought she might have meant me. So, here I am.'

Kate tried to speak again. She managed a little croak.

'I got here yesterday afternoon, but you were completely out of it so I thought I'd better let you sleep; it's usually the best remedy. I tried to get some fluids down you but you just knocked the cup out of my hand. It made quite a mess so I had to change your bed.'

Kate vaguely remembered a sensation of thinking she was drowning at some point in the night.

'And once I started to clean, I just got on with it. I'm thoroughly house-trained – in fact, I quite enjoy it. The mindless activity of cleaning helps release more creative thoughts. I might even think about working as a daily while I'm here in London. My publisher is very nice but not very rich and has only offered me a tiny advance as collections of short stories are not considered commercial, but I'm not going to quibble.'

Kate took a deep breath and this time managed several croaks.

'Congratulations? Thank you,' said Liam. 'Now do you think you can manage something hot to drink?'

She nodded gratefully.

'And after that I think it's time to get those clothes off and to step into a soothing bath. I'm a dab hand at scrubbing backs.'

Before Kate could protest, Liam had gone.

He was right, of course. She was still wearing her shirt and underwear from yesterday – or was it the day before? She must look – and smell – awful. She struggled to sit up and slowly began to undo her blouse. She had just removed her bra when Liam came in, carrying a steaming mug. She dropped her bra and pulled the duvet up to her chin.

He grinned at her. 'No need for modesty. There's nothing you've got I haven't seen before.'

If Kate had had the strength she would have thrown something at him. Instead, she let him plump up some pillows behind her so that she could sit up and gratefully cradled the steaming honey and lemon drink he had brought between her hands. Liam perched himself on the side of her bed.

'Robert and Oliver send oodles of love and hope you are better soon. I hope you don't mind, but I used your phone to call them last night to say that I was here with you.'

'That's okay,' after a sip of the lemon drink, Kate had found a whisper of a voice. 'How are they?'

'Robert's applying himself to finishing his book after some threatening letters from his publisher about wanting the inflated advance back and Oliver is still hard at work on the garden, although it's like the Forth Bridge, a never-ending task.'

'I try to call them at least once a week,' whispered Kate.

Liam nodded. 'I know. Robert reports faithfully on how you are and what you're doing.'

Which meant that Liam probably knew she had finished with both Max and Paul, thought Kate. Was Robert trying to matchmake again, even after all she had said?

'Robert asked me to say that he isn't trying to matchmake by giving me your keys. He just thought it was the safest way of getting them to you as I was coming to London,' said Liam as though he had read her mind. 'And no such thought has entered my head either. Cross my heart and hope to die.'

His voice was light as he said this, but had Kate detected a flash of something in his eyes? She laid her head back on her pillows. She was more likely to be seeing flashes; she probably still had a temperature.

'However,' continued Liam, 'I do think I should stay here a few days and give you a bit of that tender loving care the girl in your office said you needed. You might be able to produce ten different television series, but you don't seem to be able to take care of yourself. Just think of me as your old Oirish nurse, here to build up your strength with bowls of chicken soup.'

Kate croaked something. Liam leant towards her so that he could hear. She repeated it. He grinned.

'Jewish, you say? Well, think of me as your multicultural nurse, then, and finish that drink while I run you a bath.'

Kate meekly did as she was told, even though she knew she should tell him to go. Seeing him again stirred up a tangle of confused emotions that she thought she had buried. But she still felt weak and could barely totter to the bathroom without Liam's arm, although she had drawn the line at him helping her into the bath and scrubbing her back. She had banished him outside the door for that. And it felt so good to get back into clean sheets and snuggle down while Liam pottered around in the kitchen, making her drinks and, when she began to feel better later that day, a bowl of extremely good chicken soup. He also answered the telephone and fended off callers, taking messages but refusing to let her speak to anyone, saying she needed rest.

Kate insisted she would be able to get up the next day, but just as Liam had predicted she was still unsteady on her feet and the floor refused to stay still if she tried to stand for too long. So, once again, she allowed him to look after her between the long periods when she slept. It was only on the third day that he finally let her venture into the living-room to sit on the sofa with her duvet tucked around her.

After Liam had settled her down and made sure she had everything she needed within reach, he began to prepare a salad for lunch. He was very competent in the kitchen, Kate observed, much more so than she had expected. She had rather assumed that, because he had given the impression that he did not look after himself very well in Majorca, he would not be very good about the house. But in a couple of days he had made himself very much at home in her kitchen, cooking her simple but delicious meals, which he had also shopped for.

He looked across at her as though he knew what she was thinking and grinned. 'I hope you don't mind, but I've been buying cat food for this old tom who seems to think he lives here. I assume he's just another one of London's strays as I don't imagine you're the sort of woman to have a cat, but I'm rather fond of them myself.'

Even as he was talking, Hemingway appeared at the open window behind Liam and leapt down onto the floor. He rubbed himself against Liam's legs, purring loudly. Liam picked him up and cradled him in his arms, scratching behind his ears.

'Here he is. What do you think? Friendly thing, isn't he?'

Kate began to laugh. It was a strange sound at first, like something that had long been out of use and wasn't quite sure of itself, but it became stronger.

Liam raised a quizzical eyebrow. 'Am I missing something here?'

'Hemingway!' Kate managed at last.

'American writer. Deceased. Known for his terse, much-copied writing style and machismo antics. Yes?'

'No. *That's* Hemingway,' said Kate, pointing. Then she explained.

Over the next few days Kate found that being cosseted could be very addictive. She even gave in without too much of a fight when Liam argued that she shouldn't go back to work and Ruby had agreed, saying Tim and Jenny were coping. Scripts and running orders were e-mailed over and she read and changed them while tucked up on the sofa, with Liam providing constant refreshments and little snacks, as well as comments, and Hemingway curled up at her feet. Several times a day she held three-way conference calls with Tim and Harriet, during which she had to order Liam out of the room as he made her laugh by pulling faces at her while she was on the phone.

There was no need for Liam to stay. There hadn't been after the first two days. But neither she nor he mentioned him going to Robert's flat and Kate told herself there was no problem as long as he continued to sleep on the sofa. If she hadn't been sick she wouldn't have let him walk back so easily into her life, but she was glad he had. She had not been conscious of it at the time, but in Majorca she had thought of him only as a lover. Seeing him again had made her realise that she liked him as a man. Although she had watched him closely, he had never betrayed a hint that he now considered her as anything other than a friend, which was exactly what she had said she wanted. Any feelings she might have thought she had were no doubt just another effect of a high temperature caused by the flu and would disappear once she was back to her old self.

The weather forecast had warned of a possible break in the long hot spell that weekend, but Kate found it hard to believe when she woke up to another gloriously blue sky on Sunday morning. She and Liam had talked about taking a picnic lunch and spending the day in Regent's Park if she was feeling totally recovered – which she was. Liam had been preparing the food since ten o'clock that morning, not allowing her to see what he was up to as he wanted it to be a surprise. He had just packed the last carefully wrapped packet into the hamper, from which he had evicted her underwear and scarves, when the first distant thunder-clap sounded.

Kate looked unbelievingly out of the window. It didn't seem possible that there could be a storm, as the sky was still blue. But, with the suddenness that only summer storms seem to manifest, it engulfed them with a fury that sent her and Liam rushing around, struggling to close windows that the wind wanted kept open so that it could dash great swollen drops of rain in, drenching books, papers and furniture. By the time they had succeeded they were both breathless and laughing, and the storm was announcing its arrival directly overhead with jagged forks of lightning chased instantly by great shuddering claps of thunder.

'I guess that puts paid to our picnic,' said Kate.

'Unless we have it here in oriental splendour.' Liam pointed at Kate's beautiful carpet. 'It has the advantage of meaning that we can have chilled Chablis on tap, unlike in the park, *and*', he added with emphasis, 'I happened to notice that one of my all-time favourite movies, *Now Voyager*, is on the telly this afternoon, so we can munch our pork pies and cry into our Chablis along with Bette Davis.'

Within minutes he had made a bank of cushions and pillows on the carpet and rearranged the television so that they could watch it in comfort while eating the picnic he spread out on a cloth. Smiling, Kate watched him. She loved the way he had the ability to turn everything into an adventure, as though they were characters in some story he was writing. He seemed to do it as though it was for the first time. It had been the same when they had made love, she remembered, and felt her cheeks start to grow hot as she did.

'Would milady care to take a seat?' he asked, holding out a hand.

Kate stretched out on the floor, propped up by cushions. Liam lay on his back beside her. Spotting his chance, Hemingway instantly came and curled up into a purring ball on his stomach. Liam used the remote to switch on the television just as the film was beginning. Kate had a penchant for old black-and-white movies too. She settled back on the cushions and sipped her Chablis.

Neither of them spoke during the film, they just wordlessly offered each other food. It was only as Bette Davis accepted a cigarette from the lover she knew she could never have and uttered the final line, 'Don't let's ask for the moon: we have the stars' and Kate felt a tear run down her cheek, that she turned to look at Liam and saw that there were tears running down his face too.

Kate brushed it away with the back of her hand. Liam offered her a box of tissues and they both sheepishly blew their noses.

'I still love that film, though I must have seen it twenty times,' said Kate, her voice still thick with tears.

'Me too. It's just *so* romantic.'

'And I always cry at the ending,' added Kate.

'Me too.'

For a long moment they looked at each other across the debris of their picnic.

'I . . .' began Kate but was interrupted by the telephone.

Liam slumped back on the cushions. 'Damn!'

'Leave it,' urged Kate, but Liam had already leapt to his feet and picked up the receiver.

He turned. 'It's Jessica.'

Kate waved her hand. She was still irritated with Jessica for giving in so quickly to Hugo's entreaties to return to him. 'Tell her I'll call her back.'

Liam put his hand over the mouthpiece. 'I think you'd better speak to her. She sounds very upset.'

Kate climbed grudgingly to her feet. Jessica knew she was angry with her and had not rung since she had

326

gone back to Hugo. If this was another phone call to complain about how badly he was behaving she wasn't sure that she could contain her ire.

Her voice betrayed her irritation. 'Yes!'

'Kate?' Jessica's voice was high and reedy.

Kate changed her tone. 'Is there something wrong?'

'Oh, Kate . . . I'm so sorry . . .'

'Jessica.' Kate was worried now. 'What's happened? Where are you?' She could hear the sound of traffic in the background.

'I'm in the phone box down the end of your road. I'm a terrible coward. I couldn't face you, but neither could I go without telling you.'

'Go? Go where? Jessica, what are you talking about?' demanded Kate, then changed tack. 'Stay where you are, don't move,' she commanded. 'I'm coming to get you.' She put down the phone and turned to Liam.

He was already clearing the floor. 'Don't worry, I'll make myself scarce before you get back,' he said, dropping empty wrappers into the rubbish bin.

'You don't mind?' she asked anxiously.

'Of course not. Friends in need are really important. I understand. The last thing you want is a spare man hanging around.'

Kate flashed him a grateful smile as she hurriedly pulled on her raincoat. She grabbed an umbrella as she went out of the door. Jessica was in such a state she might not have one and it was still raining.

As it was, Jessica was wearing a trench coat that nearly reached the floor and a wide-brimmed fedora, which made her look absurdly tiny. They walked down the road in silence and when Kate opened the door to the flat there was no sign of Liam's presence. Kate held out a hand to take Jessica's dripping coat and hat. When Jessica removed her hat Kate gasped. Jessica's cloud of pre-Raphaelite curls had been reduced to a short golden-red bob.

'Jessica, your *hair*!'

'I needed a change in my image. The other way was old-fashioned. Big hair isn't in any more.' Jessica's lower lip stuck out defensively. She looked like a child caught out doing something naughty.

'Is this what you were frightened to tell me about?'

Jessica shook her head. Then her face crumpled and she sat down on the sofa. 'You're going to hate me and I deserve it.'

Kate sat beside her and took both her hands in hers. 'I'm not going to hate you. *Please*, Jessica, tell me what's wrong.'

Jessica could not meet her gaze. 'Hugo's been offered a film. In Hollywood.'

'That's wonderful. Isn't it what he wants?'

'I'm going with him.'

'I shall miss you, of course, terribly, but there's always the phone and it won't be for ever, will it?'

Jessica shook her head. 'I don't know.'

Kate sat back. 'Really, it's not such an awful thing and I've always wanted to go to Los Angeles. We can lounge around your pool together and drink martinis. It'll be fun.'

'Hugo says there's a part for me in the film. A good one.'

Jessica's hair suddenly made sense to Kate. 'That's even better. I'm so pleased for you. I know you've always wanted to do more film work and now you'll be living in the perfect place.'

Jessica gulped. 'But Hugo says that now's the wrong time to have another baby and the producers won't want me if they know I'm pregnant and I may never have another chance like this and I couldn't bear to lose Hugo so I've had an abortion.' She gabbled it quickly, without taking a breath.

When she had finished there was a long silence. Kate could hear the rain. It had stopped for a little while —

now it had started again: not a tropical downpour as before, but this time steady and persistent. The air had turned cold and although it was only mid-afternoon it was gloomy enough for lights to be needed.

'I knew you'd hate me.' Jessica's voice was barely a whisper.

For a moment Kate almost did. She remembered the tiny, helpless, *perfect* little being she had seen curled up on the monitor screen. It would have been so much easier to hate, but whom? Hating, like loving, was never as easy as it seemed.

She took Jessica by the shoulders. 'I don't hate you, but even more important, you must never *ever* hate yourself. You've taken the right decision and now you must go with Hugo and become the hottest property in Hollywood. If you don't, *then* I won't forgive you.' Kate forced herself to smile as she said this.

Jessica gave her a watery smile. 'And you promise you'll come and visit?'

Kate nodded. 'I can see us already hanging out at the Polo Lounge and Spago's, and at the very least I'll expect introductions to Mel Gibson and Brad Pitt . . .'

After Jessica had gone, Kate stood by the window in the darkened room, staring out at the rain. She was not sure if Jessica had taken the right decision – how could she be? Poor Jessica. Whatever she did, she lost something that was precious to her, and what she gained by going to Los Angeles could never replace what she had lost. That was irreplaceable.

Kate felt overwhelmed by a sense of loss. She put her hands to her face and realised that her cheeks were wet with tears.

'Was it that bad?'

She swung round, caught unawares. She had not heard Liam coming back. She hastily wiped her face with her hands. Liam was standing at the door, dripping wet. He had neither raincoat nor umbrella. He was just wearing a T-shirt and jeans, not even a jacket. His hair was plastered to his face.

Kate walked over to him. 'You're soaking!'

He shrugged. 'I didn't want to come back until I was sure there was no danger of interrupting you. Do you want to talk about it?'

She nodded. 'But only after you've got out of those wet clothes and had a hot bath.'

'Only if you'll scrub my back.' It was said jokingly, as though he did not expect a reply.

Kate reached up and brushed a wet curl off his forehead. 'I'll scrub your back if you'll scrub mine,' she murmured and kissed him.

His lips hungrily met hers for a moment, but then Kate felt him hesitate and he drew back. 'Are you sure?' His brown eyes anxiously studied her face, his expression a mixture of fear and hope.

In the darkness of the room, Kate was suddenly aware of everything around her: the sound of the rain outside; the silence inside; the proximity of her body to Liam's; the noise of her breathing.

She was also aware that, for the first time in a very long while, she was very sure of what she wanted, although she had not been conscious of it until that moment. Second chances were too precious to be thrown away.

'Yes.'

Twenty-Seven

• • •

'So. Who's the man?' demanded Claire, even before Kate could put the tray she was carrying on the table.

'Man?'

'Yes. *Man*. Twice when I've called you recently a man has answered.'

Kate sat down. She placed a *cappuccino* and a Danish pastry in front of Claire, then took her espresso and fudge brownie off the tray, leaning over to place it on the table next to theirs before answering.

'His name is Liam.'

'*And*?' demanded Claire impatiently.

'I think I'm in love with him.'

It was the first time Kate had said the words out loud and they sounded quite normal, even to her ears. She looked around the National Film Theatre bar – nobody was laughing or looking shocked. They were words other people said every day, but not her. She looked back at Claire. 'He moved in two months ago.'

'I knew it the moment I saw you,' said Claire triumphantly. 'You have this kind of inner glow about you. The one that says that here is a woman possessed by love.'

'That's the problem,' confessed Kate. 'I *feel* possessed and it frightens me. One minute I'm walking around with this silly smile on my face and the next I feel like I've dived head first off a high board without checking to see whether there's any water in the pool below. It's so much easier when you're younger. You're more resilient and you have time to make mistakes. I feel I have too much to lose if I get it wrong.'

'And so much to gain,' said Claire promptly. 'The risk of being hurt is always there and, if you love someone, you live with it daily, hourly even. But if love were so easy the world would be populated by happy little munchkins, which it manifestly isn't.' She looked shrewdly at Kate. 'Sometimes, you just have to trust your feelings, which you've never been very good at. The moment anything or anyone becomes too emotional your shutters come down.' Kate started to protest, but she continued, 'It's true. Think about it. You've always run away from what you can't control so it's good to see that you've finally stopped running.'

Kate looked at her little sister. She was right. That was the best thing about being with Liam. It wasn't just that she felt so absurdly happy, or that she found herself wanting to burst into song at the oddest moments, or the extraordinary sex. It was because she felt as though she had at last come home. There was nowhere else she wanted to go.

She had not thought it would be so easy to live with somebody. Until now, she had been as territorial as Hemingway and her flat had been her refuge – the place she had escaped to when things got difficult; where she could be by herself and shut out the rest of the world. But now she found that she not only enjoyed having someone there to talk to about how her day had been, who fussed over her and made her eat and refused to let her work too late at her computer, but that she looked forward to it. Liam had even got into the habit of calling Ruby for a daily gossip so that he knew ahead of time whether Kate's day had been good or bad. He had become so much part of her world that it was as though he had always been there.

'So, am I going to get any more details about this man other than his name?' demanded Claire. 'I've got to be on the two thirty-three train so I'm home before Matthew arrives back from school. I don't like that little menace being in the house by himself.'

She had come up to London to shop at Peter Jones in Sloane Square and had called Kate to see if she had time for lunch. Kate hadn't, but she had suggested they meet for coffee instead. Claire had to catch the train home from Waterloo, which was just around the corner from the Channel. 'Well? What's he like?' she asked impatiently.

'Totally and absolutely unsuitable,' replied Kate.

Claire shrugged. 'Aren't they all? But that's taken for granted. So how is this one unsuitable? Is he married or otherwise attached?'

Kate shook her head.

'Has he got an eye in the middle of his forehead and do his knuckles brush the ground?'

'No. Actually, he's very attractive.'

'And unmarried?' Claire's eyebrows shot up. 'He sounds wonderful to me.'

'But he's ten years younger than me.'

'Since when does that matter? All the women's magazines say younger men are just the thing and much more biologically sensible. You'll die before him so you won't become a lonely old lady along with the rest of us and, if you want children, a younger man is more likely to produce healthy babies.'

'*That* is not on our agenda,' said Kate, her eyes glinting dangerously.

'Okay, okay. I get the message,' muttered Claire hastily. 'So what does this perfect man do?'

'He's a writer.'

For the first time Claire looked dubious. 'A successful one? Would I have read anything of his?'

333

'Not yet. But I think he is going to be very success-ful,' said Kate firmly. 'His first book is with his publisher now but it's a slow process. In the meantime he's being wonderful around the flat. He cooks and he cleans and he fixes things. He's even putting up bookshelves.'

When she had left Liam that morning he'd been busy with a measuring tape, writing down masses of calcula-tions on scraps of paper. When she had protested that he shouldn't feel that he had to do anything to earn his keep, he had replied with a grin that the shelves were really so that she could display copies of all his books when they were published.

Since that rainy Sunday afternoon in August when she had asked him to stay, Liam had done a lot of things. Almost every day she discovered something he had taken care of – usually something she had been promising herself she would fix for years. He had proved particularly adept at finding what she thought were pieces of junk and transforming them into desirable pieces of furniture, with a patience and attention to detail that Kate had come to admire. She now had a wonderful antique wardrobe and an old limed dining-table. He was working on the chairs, which he was collecting one by one; each different and yet in keeping with the others.

Claire raised an eyebrow. 'Putting up shelves? According to some woman I saw on television yester-day that's male nesting behaviour. It was really inter-esting. She was saying that you can tell by unconscious signals like that when a man is ready to settle down. They're just like birds, they start to feather the nest, so to speak.'

'Claire . . .' Kate interrupted her. 'That was my programme you were watching – *Harriet at Home.*'

Claire looked surprised. 'But it was so awfully

334

interesting. I didn't realise . . .' Seeing Kate's expression, she trailed off. 'Oh, dear. What I *meant* to say was that . . .'

Kate held up her hand to stop her. 'I think, or at least I *hope*, I know what you're trying to say. *Harriet at Home* is not my usual style of programme.'

Claire nodded. 'But it's so *awfully* good, or at least . . .' She floundered again, then recovered. 'Well, you know me. I only watch with one eye on the box, the other has to keep tabs on the boys.'

'You'll be glad to know that your views are shared by millions of others,' said Kate drily. 'It seems that, much against my better judgement, I have a hit on my hands.'

The instant success of Harriet's show had taken Kate by surprise. Harriet's original screen test had not gone well. She had neither looked nor sounded good. But Kate had found an unexpected ally in her agent, Sheena. When Harriet had proved difficult about changing the way she looked, Sheena had convinced her. The Alice in Wonderland shoulder-length hair and velvet hair bands had been replaced by a short, head-hugging style and the little-girl-lost clothes had gone, to be replaced by a casual, fluidly tailored look. The transformation had been suggested by Kate, but it was Sheena who had accompanied Harriet to the stylist and the shops.

Sheena had been tough to negotiate with, particularly over the conversion of the basement of Max and Harriet's London house into a kitchen studio that was now being used for shooting the series. Kate had opposed the idea at first, worried that it would mean she would be forced to deal with Max every time they recorded a show. But she had not seen Max since the evening she threw his clothes out of the window. It was Sheena, rather than Max, who was constantly at Harriet's side and the conversion, although a technical nightmare at first, had proved a great success. In the familiar surroundings of her own home, rather than in a studio, Harriet had visibly relaxed on screen and commercial sponsors were fighting to have their products on show on the set, so the building work had already paid for itself.

It was, as a delighted Jordan had told Kate that morning, an unqualified success. Its high ratings had continued to build over the first four programmes, while its audience appreciation index was one of the highest ever. Jordan's desk had been strewn with the press coverage for the series, much of it provoked by Harriet's decision to breast-feed while she was on screen. It had got her and the series not only onto the front pages of all the tabloids, but had also provoked lengthy articles in the broadsheets. It was the kind of publicity that money could not buy and Jordan was making the most of it. His marketing department were rushing to get two new Harriet cookbooks out in time for Christmas and they were in discussion with three major manufacturers about producing *Harriet at Home* kitchenware ranges.

But the success of the series had been bought at a price: Kate seemed to have little time for either herself or for Liam. Once the series was well-established, she intended to move back into a more executive role, but she still had two others she had to oversee, one about gardening and the other about decorating. Neither was doing as well as she had hoped, but then she had warned Jordan that there was a glut of both types of programmes on other channels, and there was only so much flower seed and wallpaper that audiences would take. She had been considering whether a change of format would help.

'Well, I'm delighted for you and for Liam, but I hope you're not like this when you're at home with him,' said Claire tartly.

Kate looked at her blankly.

'You seem to be off in a world of your own.'

'I'm sorry. It's just that I have so much on at the moment ...'

'It doesn't matter,' said Claire, gathering up her shopping bags, of which she seemed to have about a dozen in each hand. 'I'd better make a run for it or I'll miss my train.'

They both stood up and hugged awkwardly as Claire could not lift her shopping-bag-laden arms.

'You promise you won't tell Mother about Liam, at least not yet,' said Kate. 'She'll want to meet him to check him over and right now I couldn't deal with all the questions. You know what she's like.'

Claire nodded. 'I promise. Cross my heart and hope to die.' As they reached the automatic door it slid open and they stepped out into the chill, late-October air. Claire turned and kissed Kate on the cheek. 'I'm happy for you, Kate, but remember what I said about trusting your emotions for once and don't let your job get between you and him. Think about what happened to me.'

She set off towards Waterloo station, clutching her bags as a gust of wind caught them. Kate watched her go, then turned and headed in the opposite direction, hoisting up her collar against the wind, which sent brown leaves and litter skittering along the concrete open spaces of the South Bank.

She was glad she had taken the time to meet Claire. She couldn't really afford it as there was so much to do and she wanted to try to get home early this evening. Despite Liam's cheerfulness that morning, she was worried about him, although not for the reason Claire had suggested. He did not appear to be writing much. She had brought up the subject several times, but had received a non-committal grunt in reply, so she had not pressed him. He was dispirited, as there had been a delay in the publication of his collection of short stories, so she had suggested he start on something new, but she had seen little evidence of activity.

She did not want to nag, for she knew how difficult it was to write, and that writers needed time and sometimes suffered from writer's block, but Liam seemed almost too happy doing nothing apart from pottering around the flat with a duster or a screwdriver in his hand.

Kate stopped outside the Channel and dialled her flat number on her mobile. After a few rings the answering machine came on: 'Hi. You've reached Kate and Liam, but neither of us can pick up the phone at the moment, so please leave a message.'

Kate smiled. Liam was probably out shopping for wood for the shelves. She'd asked him to put the message on the machine because she wanted him to feel that the flat was his home as much as hers. She loved the sound of his voice, but she especially liked the way he said 'Kate and Liam'.

She repeated it under her breath as she pushed her way through the swing doors into the Channel and gave the young security guard a smile which made him blush, and fall over his feet as he rushed to call the lift for her. Kate was still smiling as she rode up to her office, hugging her briefcase. She felt so ridiculously happy, but best of all, her life was back under control. What more could she ask for?

Twenty-Eight
• • •

'I promise you it *is* possible. It is not the kind of mistake I make. You are nine weeks pregnant.'

Kate stared in shock at the doctor. She had picked a woman gynaecologist on the assumption that they were more sympathetic, but the eyes glinting at her from behind half-moon glasses did not seem very friendly. If anything, they were exasperated.

'But I've only missed one period . . .' protested Kate lamely.

'Really? Are you quite sure?'

'Well, I suppose the one before that was very light, but they often are, and it seemed to only last a day, but I was so busy at the time with deadlines looming that I didn't take any notice of it . . .' Why did she sound so foolish? Kate wondered.

'I thought so.' The doctor was now making notes and spoke without looking up. 'I'm seeing a lot like you these days; busy career women, that is. They convince themselves it won't happen to them because they can't find – what is it they call it these days? – a *window* for it in their diaries, and then boom! It happens.'

'But . . .'

She looked up, a tired smile, which said she had heard it all but tell her again, on her face. 'Are you going to say "but it was only the once"?'

Kate nodded.

The doctor put down her pen. 'A lot of women your age now use condoms as their contraceptive of choice and all it *can* take is for a condom to fail or not to be used just that once. We tell ourselves that it won't matter, just this once. But it can and it does. We run out of condoms or our partners can't be bothered to get out of bed because it's too cold or we are overcome by sudden passion. It doesn't matter what the excuse is, we convince ourselves that just this once it won't hurt.' She picked up her pen again. 'Now, can you recall when your "just this once" was?'

Kate could. It was a Sunday night and they had run out of condoms. They'd had an argument earlier, as she had been forced to work yet another Saturday and part of Sunday. She had promised Liam that she would have the weekend free, the first for two months. It had been their first argument and they had gone to bed and made love all afternoon to make up.

When they woke in the early evening, they'd decided to stay in bed and Liam had phoned for a takeaway to be delivered, so they hadn't even had to get dressed. It was only then that they had discovered they had run out of condoms, each assuming that the other had bought some more. They'd lain in bed, eating and joking about setting up a home delivery condom service. They talked so much about the relative merits of all the different types of condoms they would provide that they had talked themselves into having sex without one – just that once. She gave the doctor the date.

'Uh huh. That would be about right.' She looked up at Kate. 'Most people have a remarkable recall of such seemingly trivial occasions when prompted. I put it all down to hormones. Without them, the human race wouldn't survive. A lot of women, particularly those with careers, think they can ignore them, but they can't. They override everything, even our better sense.

340

We like to think those kinds of basic instincts don't apply to us, they're for fifteen-year-old working-class girls on housing estates who don't know any better, but I invariably find that it's the middle-class women who display the most surprise when they get pregnant after taking a chance and who make the most use of abortion clinics. The girls on the housing estates just get on with it and have their babies, much to the hand-wringing moralising nonsense of some politicians. Now, lecture over. Do you want to discuss whether or not you want to keep the baby with your partner or have you already made a decision?'

Kate hesitated. A million thoughts were going through her mind all at once and none of them made sense.

'Well, I should take your time considering it,' the doctor broke in, 'but not *too* much time. If you decide not to keep it, the sooner the better . . .'

'Yes!' Kate interrupted her. The word had leapt out of her lips with more force than she had intended. 'I mean . . . yes, I want to keep the baby.'

And she did. It was not a rational, thought-out decision. It came from a place deep within her that she did not even know existed, which was just as well. Because if she had thought about it, even for a few moments, her answer would probably have been no. This was not what she had planned. It had no place in her life and yet, without her knowledge, it had already found its place, taken root and was growing. Why, she did not know, but in that moment of acceptance she had never been so sure of anything in her life.

'Good.' For the first time the doctor smiled properly at her. 'There are a few things we need to check because of your age, but I don't think age should ever be a bar to anything, do you? In my experience, there's no reason why you shouldn't produce as healthy a baby as any sixteen-year-old and I'll try to do my best to make sure you do – that's of course if you want to stay with me?'

Kate nodded, grinning. 'Yes, I think I'd like that.'

The doctor smiled back. 'One more thing: if your friends are looking for suitable presents for your next birthday they'll have plenty of scope. Your baby is due on or about your fortieth birthday.'

But Kate's conviction stayed with her only until she reached the pavement outside the doctor's office. Then it turned coward and fled, abandoning her to doubts and to the cold wastes of the Euston Road on a chill January afternoon that dusk was already threatening to overtake, even though it was only three o'clock. Kate began to walk, ignoring the bitter wind which whipped itself into a frenzy around the corner of every tall building, blind to everything apart from the knowledge that her life had just been irrevocably changed.

It took her nearly an hour to walk to her flat from the doctor's office, threading her way through the streets of north London almost by instinct, as her sense of direction, like the feeling in her face and hands and feet, had all but disappeared. She fumbled in her bag for her front door key and her numb fingers could barely guide it into the lock, let alone turn it. But, eventually, she steadied her hand enough to get the door open, only to find the flat in darkness. Liam was not at home.

In a way she was glad. It would give her time to warm up and decide how she would break the news to him. Without turning on any of the main lights, she went through to the bathroom and ran herself a hot bath. The heating was still on, so Liam could not have gone far and, as the steam began to fill the bathroom and warmth seeped into her body, Kate started to feel better.

She stripped off and looked at her naked body in the full-length mirror Liam had hung up on the wall, placing her hand tentatively on her stomach. Inside was a tiny little being, but he, or she, wouldn't be tiny for long. Soon her stomach would be horribly distended and she would be forced to waddle around, like the pregnant women she had pitied. Kate took her hand quickly away and stepped into the bath, immersing her whole body, her fingers and toes painful with the return of feeling.

She soon lost all sense of how long she had been floating in the womb-like warmth of the bath and began to feel almost good again. The day had started so well. They had held the end of the first *Harriet at Home* series party yesterday and everyone had been ecstatic. The ratings and audience appreciation indices had remained consistently high throughout the entire run. Kate had given the production team the day off today, knowing that most of them would have hangovers and not be able to do much work, but she had gone into the office as she had a meeting with Jordan. He, too, had been happy. He wanted another series ready to go on the air by the spring and he wanted Kate to come up with ideas for possible spin-off series. She had agreed, but had argued that she needed to be able to hire a good series producer who could take over the day-to-day running of the show so that she would have more time for long-term planning. It had been a gamble and she had expected him to raise a lot of objections but, much to her surprise, he had agreed without an argument and she had been able to call a delighted Anita and offer her the job that afternoon.

Jordan had also raised the possibility of a much longer contract when her present one ran out that summer. Kate had told him she would have to think about it. She had proved that she could make a success of Harriet's series, as much to herself as to anyone, but it was not what she wanted to do. But the baby had changed that. While she could afford to turn down the offer of financial security for herself, she had someone else to think about now, someone who would be dependent on her for a very long time.

She climbed out of the bath and stood, looking down at her dripping body, trying to imagine the tiny tadpole-like creature inside her as another human being, calling her mother, but it was impossible. Quickly, she began to towel herself dry. One thing at a time. First Liam had to be told.

Although she was so sure about her feelings for him, Kate suddenly realised that she was not sure how Liam would feel. A child changed everything. It was no longer just the two of them. They had talked about the possibility of having a baby, but it had been a light-hearted, almost joking conversation. After only four months of being together it was something they might consider at some undefined time in the future. Liam had been keener on the idea than she, but they had both assumed that they would have time: to make a decision to have a child; to prepare. But now the time they so blithely assumed they possessed had suddenly evaporated. They had a deadline which was less than seven months away.

While she was in the bath, Kate supposed that Liam was shopping. He rarely went out to do anything else. She had tried to encourage him to get around more, but it had begun to cause problems of late. It embarrassed him if she offered him money and even more if they were out together and she paid.

She had hoped that they would have more time to relax together over Christmas and the New Year, as they had been invited out a lot. But, after the first couple of parties, Liam had refused to go to any more. He said it made him feel uncomfortable to be around people who had jobs and made large amounts of money. He had even refused to go to the end of series party the night before and had been distinctly mono-syllabic when she had arrived home late, having had a lot to drink. He had not wanted to make love and that morning had got out of bed before she had even woken up.

Kate knew she had not had a lot of time for him recently. More often than not, she left home early in the morning and arrived back late, sometimes too tired even to talk. However, having Anita back in the team would help and now she was pregnant she supposed she would be forced to slow down. Kate found herself smiling as she dressed. A whole new life was opening up for her, for both of them – for all *three* of them.

She padded barefoot into the darkened living-room. A shadowy figure, outlined against the light from the street lamp, visibly started as she went in. She reached for the light switch.

'Kate!' Liam looked startled. 'I wasn't expecting you home.'

'I decided to take the afternoon off as I wanted to spend some time with you,' Kate lied. 'I've been neglecting you and I know you were upset about me going to that party last night.'

He shrugged. 'It wasn't important.'

'But when I came home you . . . we didn't . . .' Kate was going to say that they had not made love, hadn't even kissed. But that was all in the past. 'I'm sorry if I upset you.'

'You didn't.'

Kate went over to him and reached for his hand. 'I've got something very special I want to talk to you about. We can go to bed and discuss it there if you'd like. We've got the rest of the afternoon and all of the night,' she said huskily.

For a brief moment Liam reached out towards her, then his hand fell to his side and he moved away. 'I'm afraid that's not possible. I've got something to tell you, too.' His voice sounded odd, stilted.

Kate felt the hairs at the back of her neck prickling, like a primitive intuition of fear. 'Is there something the matter?'

'I'm leaving.'

Kate thought she hadn't heard him right. She stared at him.

He put his hands in his pockets and hunched his shoulders. 'I'm sorry to land it on you like this, but I think it's best.'

'Best?' she repeated stupidly.

'I wanted to tell you before, but you've been so busy. I've tried, I've really tried, but I feel so . . . so *trapped*. I thought being here with you I would be okay, but I'm not. This is not for me.'

Kate fell as though the air had been sucked from her body. She had to fight to get her breath before speaking. 'But all this . . .' She waved her had vaguely round at the flat, the nest Claire said he had been building. For the first time that evening she noticed that he had finally finished the shelving unit, which had grown from a few shelves into a complete wall storage system. All her books had been placed there in alphabetical order, and her TV and video now sat on their individual perches, VHS cassettes stacked neatly below them.

'I feel like I've been building a cage for myself and now the bars are closing around me. I have to get away. I can't write.'

Kate felt her legs giving out and she sat down heavily on the couch. 'Why haven't you told me any of this before? Perhaps we could have worked something out . . . I don't know what . . . but *something*.'

'Leave London? But what about your work?' Liam's voice was harsh with emotion. It had not been a question. Both she and Liam already knew the answer.

'In Majorca you were just Kate. But here you've become someone else, this *television* person.'

'It's important to me, Liam. I enjoy it.'

'I know. That's why I can't ask you to stop doing it. I'm not into all that stuff about demanding you make a choice – television or me. I know I couldn't give up my writing for you, however much I love you, but I'm sure you wouldn't ask, which is why I won't ask you to give up your work for me.' He looked at her. 'I do love you, Kate. Please believe me. But if I stay here . . .' He looked broken.

Kate nodded, then looked away. She could not speak. She sensed, rather than saw, him going into the bedroom and returning carrying a suitcase and some plastic bags. She was still sitting on the couch when she heard the front door close behind him. It was only then that she realised she had never told him that she loved him.

347

Twenty-Nine

• • •

'But *who* is the father and *why* won't you tell him about *le bébé*?' Kate's mother Cissy always reverted to her native French when under stress.

'Because if I tell him, he'll come back and want to marry me,' said Kate. Of that she was certain. But as much as she wanted Liam, she did not want him back just because of the baby. Not that the question would arise. Since he had left a month ago she had not heard from him.

Cissy stared uncomprehendingly at Kate. She had come up to London alone, insisting that Kate's father stay at home as this was women's business. However, Kate would far rather have had her father visit. He had understood her decision when she had explained it to him on the telephone, but advised that she should explain it to her mother herself, so she was – or at least she was trying to.

If she was not going to be allowed to organise a full white wedding and play the proud mother of the bride, Cissy at least wanted to be able to play the outraged mother of the daughter abandoned by her feckless lover. But Kate was refusing to allow her either part, determined that neither she nor her child should be cast in the role of victim, or that Liam should play the title role of the villain.

Although there were moments when Kate wanted to

hate Liam for leaving she could not. How could she blame him for wanting to be free when she had been running away from commitment for most of her life until now?

Her mother shrugged with Gallic expressiveness. 'And how will you support this child? No doubt you will abandon it to some woman you do not know – a stranger – to look after while you continue with this career of yours?'

It was Kate's turn to shrug. 'I'll find a way.'

And she would because she had to. But not right now. It was all she could do just to keep going at the office while dealing with coming to terms with being pregnant and alone. There were times when she felt like one of those jugglers who spun plates on the ends of sticks. She could manage to keep the plates spinning if she kept rushing up and down, but if one more were added they would all come crashing to the ground.

Her mother brushed an imaginary speck of dust from the skirt of her smart plum-coloured suit. It was one of her 'shopping in Sloane Street' suits. It had a black, Persian lamb, detachable collar with a matching pill-box hat, both of which she was wearing as it was a crisp February day.

'You could come home and live with us. I would look after *le bébé* while you worked. *Naturellement*, it would force your papa and me to make a lot of changes . . .' She shrugged again.

'No!' Kate's voice was sharper than she had intended. She put her hand over her mother's and used the term she had used in childhood: '*Maman*, it's very sweet of you to offer, but I will be fine.'

And she would be. Nothing could ever be as bad again as the despair that had encircled her, threatening to squeeze the breath out of her body the moment she had heard the front door close behind Liam. How long she sat on the couch she did not know. It could have been hours or maybe only minutes, but eventually it was Hemingway's warm body which had pierced her despair. He had leapt up beside her and nosed his way onto her lap, where he lay purring, refusing to be ignored.

On autopilot, she had got up and fed him. The smell of the pilchards, which he had now decided that he liked, had forced her to run retching to the bathroom where, gazing down into the toilet bowl, she had realised she would live because she had to. She still had to deal with the terrible and, at times, almost overwhelming pain of Liam's going, but it had begun to be dulled by the knowledge that she was carrying his child and slowly, bit by tiny bit, the yawning emptiness she felt was being filled by the baby growing inside her.

Her sister had also suggested Kate come and stay for as long as she wanted and had offered her help with looking after the baby. Claire had been the first person Kate had confided in after Liam had left. She had immediately abandoned Roger and the boys to defrost some frozen pizzas and come straight up to London. This time it was Kate who had wept on her sister's shoulder and, since then, they had talked to each other daily.

It was not so much the physical changes in her body that Kate found she needed to talk about, but the illogical fears that crowded in around her when she was alone. She had at first tried to brush them away as ridiculous, but they hung around in the dark corners of her imagination, waiting to catch her out at the least opportune moments. Voicing them out loud made them real, but also diminished them, and she could talk about them to Claire without feeling foolish. Anyone else, even her doctor, might dismiss them as just one of those things that pregnant women had to deal with, but Claire listened patiently and understood.

'What I can't understand is why, when I'm giving life to a child, all I can think about is death,' Kate said hopelessly during yet another long session on the phone to her sister. 'If pregnancy is always like this, all I can say is that I'm sorry for not being around for you to talk to when you were pregnant, particularly with Matthew. How on earth did you survive? I think I would have gone mad.'

'Actually I think you're the brave one, having a child now,' declared Claire. 'I have a theory that there's a reason nature wants us to have children when we're young and it has nothing to do with our physical state. It's because when we're young we don't know anything, even though we think we know everything, and we certainly don't give much thought to the consequences of what we do. We just get on with it – right or wrong – and, if we feel any fear, it's only vague and can be pushed away until some time in the future. But when you're older and have lived, and you know what damage life and living can do, *then* you can be frightened about what life can do to the child you're bringing into the world. Young parents raise children in ignorance, older parents raise them in fear. If I had known when I was eighteen that once you decide to have a child it means that, from the moment they're born until the moment you die, you live in fear, I might not have had any children. But I'm still glad I did and I know you'll be glad too, Kate, believe me. It's just a question of hanging onto your sanity for dear life for the next eighteen years or so. But, having said that, I'm dreading them leaving. So if you want someone to look after the baby you only have to ask, you know. It would be lovely to have a baby around again,' she had ended wistfully.

Claire had agreed to break the news to Cissy as Kate

could not face it although, at Claire's suggestion, they had waited until she was three months pregnant. Cissy had immediately demanded to know who the father was, but Claire had kept her promise and not told her, much to Cissy's annoyance. It was amusing to them both that, after years of complaining that they never behaved like proper sisters, now that they were finally doing so, she complained that they were keeping secrets from her.

Cissy sighed and stood up. '*Alors*. I go now. There is nothing more I can do,' she announced, carefully adjusting her hat on her head. 'You independent women, you think you need nothing. Even the man, he is now superfluous. But your mother, you cannot lose her so easily as a man and soon you will discover what it is to be a mother. Then you will understand.'

Kate hugged her tightly, knocking her hat askew. 'I know, *Maman*, and I love you. I really do.'

Cissy tut-tutted and went to the mirror to straighten her hat, but she looked mollified. 'As long as my independent daughter does not forget that she has a family who will stand by her. We are not so narrow-minded as perhaps she thinks.'

The one person whose reaction to her pregnancy Kate had not been sure of was Robert. It was not that she thought *he* was narrow-minded, far from it, but he had often been disparaging about people who had children, declaring that they had them either to avoid having relationships with other adults, or to try and mend what had gone wrong in their situation with their own parents. According to him, most people spent their lives either trying to earn their parents' love because they felt they had not received enough, or attempting to escape from the consequences of having had too much and feeling suffocated by it. Either way, they ended up damaged and, when they had children, the circle began all over again, as they inflicted too much or too little love in their turn.

But Kate needn't have worried. When she called Robert in Majorca to tell him the news he was so excited that a casual eavesdropper might have assumed he was the father. He had called Oliver to the telephone and, despite their shock at Liam's departure, they had both shed tears of happiness. Robert had wanted to catch the next plane back to London, but Kate had convinced him to wait until he had finished his book. However, he now called her daily, demanding every tiny detail of what it felt like to be pregnant, and carried a photocopied picture of her first scan in his wallet. According to Robert, it was the ultimate fashion accessory of the Nineties.

Kate decided to keep her pregnancy a secret for as long as possible at the Channel. Her expanding waistline was easy to conceal under winter clothes and the second series of *Harriet at Home* had already been on the air a month when, in early April, she called Ruby and Anita into her office and closed the door.

Ruby's scream of joy had threatened to give away the secret, while, despite her previous dire descriptions of giving birth, Anita had almost lifted Kate off the ground as she hugged her in delight.

Between them they had conspired to make sure that Kate kept doctor's appointments and that her diary never became too overloaded with meetings, or that she left the office too late in the evenings.

Grateful though she was for all their concern, Kate was determined not to take too much of a back seat in the office. There were moments when only work kept her sane. She knew with every passing day that she had made the right decision to keep the baby, but equally her fears about being a mother grew. It was absurd, but she both wanted her baby and yet didn't want to become a mother.

At times she could laugh at herself. She was going to be a mother whether she liked it or not. But there were moments when her whole being rebelled against it, and it was at times like these that she was glad that she had the distraction of work.

Harriet at Home was proving as popular in its second series as it had been during its first. Not that Kate had much to do with its day-to-day running – she now left that to Anita and Tim. Harriet had taken a keen interest in her pregnancy, constantly offering advice and telephone numbers for an assortment of gynaecologists, homeopaths, aromatherapists and natural-birthing specialists.

The series ended in June, by which time Kate was six months pregnant. Despite her protests, after the last programme was recorded Harriet insisted on throwing a baby shower on the set, presenting Kate with a signed copy of her mother and baby vegetarian cookbook, while the rest of the production team gave her an assortment of baby clothes and fluffy toys.

Feeling embarrassed by the speeches and uncomfortable in the heat, which she was beginning to feel as the baby inside her grew heavy, Kate tried to slip away as soon as possible, but Sheena caught her as she reached the front door and drew her into Harriet's main living-room.

It was much cooler than downstairs where the party was still taking place. Kate dropped the two large carrier bags full of the presents she had been given on the floor and thankfully sank down into a chair. She wanted to get away, but a few minutes' rest wouldn't hurt. Sheena sat opposite. Today she was dressed in a full-length white kaftan trimmed with gold braid. It was theatrical, but Kate could not help envying how comfortable it must be. She spent most of her days in leggings and oversized shirts.

Kate had a feeling that she knew what Sheena

wanted to talk about. They had had a number of discussions about the third series of *Harriet at Home*, which Jordan wanted for the next schedule, but nothing had been agreed. She did not feel much like discussing it now, but it looked as though she had little choice. She waited for Sheena to begin.

'Kate, there is no easy way to say this, but I want you to be the first to know. There won't be another series of *Harriet at Home*, at least not on Channel 22. We've signed a deal with another channel.'

'Another channel . . .?' Kate felt stunned.

'Jordan has become too greedy. We wanted greater control over the use of Harriet's name in marketing products, but he refused, so we went elsewhere. They've offered us much more money up front, a better deal on marketing, plus more artistic control. Harriet has become a very saleable commodity and we don't want to cheapen her name by allowing it to be used on the wrong sort of product. We'd have loved you to come with us, of course, but a pregnant woman is hardly the best recommendation to a new employer. You do understand, don't you?'

Kate nodded wordlessly. She waited a few minutes after Sheena had left before heaving herself to her feet. She could hear the voices of the production team floating up from the garden where the party was still going strong. The rest of the house was quiet. She picked up her carrier bags and let herself out into the street.

Three months to go and it looked as if she was not only going to be a forty-year-old single mother, but also a forty-year-old unemployed single mother.

Thirty

* * *

The decision to stop work for the last two months was easier than Kate had thought. Her contract was due to finish a week before the baby was born and the Channel had lapsed into its normal schedule of repeats for the summer, so there seemed little point in making the hot and increasingly uncomfortable journey to the office every day.

Before she left, a much chastened Jordan had offered her another contract, but she had told him she wanted time to consider it. Although she had been shocked, indeed angered, by Harriet's departure, in a way it had been a kind of release. She had even been able to laugh when Anita called her with the news that Harriet had thrown Max out and moved Sheena in.

Harriet and Sheena had given an exclusive of their story to *Hello!* magazine, which had rewarded them with a three-page colour spread about their new life together. However, the tabloid newspapers had taken a more sensational line, one of them leading with the banner headline: TV'S MRS PERFECT IN LESBIAN LOVE NEST SCANDAL.

Either Anita or Ruby called every day to keep Kate in touch with the office gossip but, increasingly, it all seemed to belong to a past life. She found that she was quite content pottering around her flat or going to the local shops. After years of just dashing into the corner shop or the local deli in the evening on her way home after work she had discovered that she lived in a small but multinational community of shop owners, most of whom she quickly got to know by name, stopping to chat whether she was making a purchase or not.

Kate had expected to feel resentful at her ballooning body but, towards the end, she found that she just wanted to give herself over to it and to concentrate solely on the being growing inside her. In the early stages of pregnancy she had voraciously read books and listened to music, as though she was trying to store everything up inside for the time when the baby was born and she would no longer be able to sit for hours without interruption. But now she could no longer concentrate on the words on a page for long stretches at a time and she wanted to do nothing that would use any of the energy that was so precious to her baby's well-being. Instead she found herself talking to the baby about Liam, recounting every detail she could remember about him. There would be a time when she knew her child would want to know about its father but by then, some of the details might be blurred, so she wanted the baby to be told them now, while they were still fresh in her mind, even though she smiled at her own foolishness.

At times Kate almost had the sensation she was a foetus herself. It was as though she was floating in warm fluid, suspended inside a protective shell, building up strength for the struggle she knew was to come. Even Hemingway had sensed the change in her and stopped his nightly forays in search of sex and fights, and instead dozed at her feet in front of the television.

Her mother now contented herself mainly with phone calls, although she occasionally arrived on Kate's doorstep, loaded down with things she had bought for the baby. Such visits were always accompanied by the announcement that she was sure Kate would not have thought of buying them herself — which was true. There were also deliveries of a pram and other large nursery equipment from Peter Jones. When she rang to thank her mother, she would invariably receive a lecture on not letting herself go just because she had no man and was pregnant. The best remedy for pregnancy blues was a facial and a visit to the hairdresser, according to her mother, and if she let herself go now she would never get a man.

It was left to Kate's father to enquire about Kate's health and to make secret trips to London to see her. He couldn't let Cissy know, because she would have wanted to come along and he did not want to hurt her feelings by saying that he and Kate liked spending time together without her.

When Kate had asked him how he explained his absences, he told her he had said he was playing golf and that several of his partners had been primed to say he was with them. They, of course, thought that he was having an illicit affair and now, when he went to the club, he was greeted by knowing smiles and was clapped on the back and bought drinks. All of which caused much laughter when Kate recounted it to her sister.

In July, Robert and Oliver came back to London. Ostensibly, it was for Robert to see his publisher as he had at last finished his book. As for Oliver, he claimed it was too hot to do much work on his garden during the height of the summer, but Kate suspected it was because they wanted to see her. Claiming they needed to catch up with what was happening in London, they had taken her out on a whirlwind of shopping, restaurants, theatres, exhibitions and films, until she had been forced to beg for mercy. They also brought with them the first news she had had of Liam since he had left. It was a postcard they had received from the Florida Keys. Liam had scrawled a short message on it:

'Am in search of the other Hemingway' and at the bottom he had added: 'Tell Kate I love her.'

As Kate read it, her eyes filling with tears, Oliver quietly put his arms around her, but Robert could not contain himself.

'I've got friends in the Keys who'll be able to find Liam. You've *got* to tell him. He does love you, he really does, and if he knew he'd come right back.'

From the beginning, Robert had taken the same view as Cissy that Liam should be told about the baby and it had almost precipitated a serious quarrel between him and Kate. 'But you two are *made* for each other,' he had protested when she had threatened him with instant excommunication from her life if he so much as breathed a hint of it to Liam without her permission. 'Oliver and I knew it the moment we set eyes on Liam. You're both just too stubborn to see it.'

'Stubborn or not, you must promise me, Robert,' she demanded and Oliver had backed her up.

He eventually gave his word, but only after she had sworn he could be present at the birth. According to Robert, he had always wanted to stand at someone's bedside shouting 'breathe, breathe' as he had a thing about men in gowns and masks, having been desperately in love with Dr Kildare when he was a teenager.

Laughingly, Kate had agreed, although she had pointed out that he was so squeamish that he couldn't bear the sight of his own blood, so he would probably faint, and that her bedside might be a bit crowded, as both Claire and Anita had already staked out their places.

'That's nothing,' he had drawled in his Southern accent. 'Down home, we throw a big party and invite the whole neighbourhood to watch while the band plays "Take Me Back to Old Virginie" to drown out the screams.'

However, in the end it was not Robert or Anita, or

even Claire who was with Kate, but her nephew Jonathan.

He had come to stay with her during the Easter school holidays as she had promised him, and she had allowed him to dog her now much slower footsteps from the office, to edit suites and to the studios. He had been wide-eyed with wonder as he took in what was going on around him and had made himself useful, running and fetching things whenever asked, which had made Kate's life much easier. Her increasing bulk made the kind of dashing backwards and forwards that she was used to when in production not only tiring but also ungainly.

His visit had stretched from three days into a week and Claire had been worried that he was overstaying his welcome, but Kate liked having him around. He asked intelligent questions and his enthusiasm made even the more cynical members of the production team willing to give him some of their time so he could learn. Jonathan had also proved a hit with many of the women in the office. His physical awkwardness was beginning to fill out into a promise of startling good looks and Kate found herself being eagerly questioned about him, as he looked nearer to twenty than the seventeen-year-old schoolboy that he was.

After that first visit, he had taken to calling her and asking whether he could stay the night whenever he came up to London, and Kate was more than happy to say yes. She liked having him around. He did not expect to be fussed over and made himself easily at home, which suited Kate who gave him a front door key and told him to use it whenever he was in London.

According to her mother and just about everybody else, first babies were invariably late. According to her doctor, this was an old wives' tale and they were no more likely to be late than any other baby. No one mentioned the possibility of it being early.

It was a Saturday night and Jonathan had rung to say he was coming to stay, having been to a film with some friends in the West End. Kate tried to ignore the pains at first, telling herself it was a false alarm. But by the time Jonathan walked in just after eleven thirty they were coming faster and faster. With some difficulty she was trying to pack her overnight case so that, if it was not a false alarm, she would be ready. But, as she weakly reassured Jonathan, she was quite sure that was what it was.

Jonathan took one look at her and called an ambulance. He rode with her to the hospital, holding her hand as she continued to insist – between spasms of pain – that all this was really not necessary. When they arrived, still holding her hand, he used her mobile phone to call his mother, although Kate was insisting that he shouldn't bother anyone, as she was all right and it was too early – but she sounded less convincing by the minute.

It was only when the midwife looked up from between Kate's legs and said sternly, 'Early or not, this one's anxious to arrive and no amount of holding your breath is going to keep it in, my girl. Now, we remember all those lessons about breathing properly, don't we?' that Kate finally gave in, closed her eyes and took a deep breath.

Thirty-One

● ● ●

Kate cursed softly as she heard the doorbell ring. She had only just got the baby off to sleep and was desperately in need of some herself. She checked the cot. Jonathan had not stirred. She marvelled yet again at how one moment he could be screaming, his whole body convulsed with fury, fists and feet flailing as she tried to change his nappy, and the next be a rosy-cheeked cherub, soft and sweet-smelling.

It was at moments like this that she felt completely happy in a way she had not thought possible, and she would simply sit and look at him, sure that he was quite the most perfect thing ever born. But then, the next moment, she felt overwhelmed by grief. It was as though her life was over, which in one way at least it was, for it could never be the same again.

Since Jonathan had been born it was as though layers of hardened skin had been peeled back, leaving her emotionally raw and vulnerable. Yet at the same time she had felt filled with a kind of fierce, overwhelming love, which made her sure she could fight anyone or anything.

Jonathan Robert Oliver Daniels. It was quite a mouthful, but somehow it seemed right. They had all been wonderful. Jonathan had stayed with her all the way through her labour. At times he had closed his eyes and gripped her hand more tightly than she was gripping his, but he had stayed by her side, his astonishment and delight at the birth finally overcoming his squeamishness. And Robert and Oliver had come round every day since she had come home from the hospital. Oliver looked after the baby so she could grab an hour or two of much needed sleep while Robert had turned into a regular housewife, shopping and cooking so there was always delicious food for her to eat – something she was often tempted not to do as she was so tired.

She had not been short of other visitors. Claire phoned every day and came whenever she could, as did her parents. Even Jessica had come over from Los Angeles. Her part in Hugo's film had ended up on the cutting-room floor, but the movie was being talked about as a great success, even before it had been released.

Jessica had gone blonde, and looked tanned and very fit. Her days seemed largely to be occupied with attending one Californian exercise class or another. She had made pilots for two soap operas and, although neither had as yet been picked up by the networks, she was still optimistic.

'English actresses are all the rage in Hollywood. Everyone wants one on their show. They think we have class. It started with Joan Collins and she was already past a "certain age" when she became a big star. Not that I ever tell anyone my real age, of course. Age is the last great taboo in Hollywood. *Nobody* grows old there.'

She claimed that she was divinely happy, but when she held Jonathan in her arms the look of longing on her face had been almost painful.

A second ring on the doorbell broke into Kate's reverie; this time it was more insistent. Whoever it was did not intend to go away. They had probably seen that her lights were on, as she had not closed the shutters.

Kate glanced at her watch. It was only just after six but it was already dark. The November nights were closing in.

With a last check that Jonathan was still sleeping she went to the door. She was very grateful for all her visitors, but there were times when she just wanted to be alone. She pressed the intercom. 'Hello?'

'Kate?'

'Yes?'

'It's Liam.'

Kate felt her knees buckle. She put her hand to the wall to steady herself.

'Kate? Are you still there? I know you probably don't want to see me again, but there's something I want to give you.'

Kate hesitated, then she took a deep breath and buzzed the front door open. As she did, she caught sight of her reflection in the window. She looked appalling. She quickly pushed her hands through her hair, but nothing could hide the baby's sick on the shoulder of the baggy T-shirt she was wearing.

Opening the flat door six inches, Kate peered out. For a moment she thought that she had waited too long and that Liam had changed his mind, but then he was striding towards her. The hall light usually made people look ill, but Liam looked sunburnt and healthy, although a little thin. His hair was much longer than she remembered. He was wearing a thick fisherman's sweater over faded cord trousers.

He reached the door and she opened it another two inches. Their eyes met for a moment but then Liam looked down. 'I prepared a speech. In fact, I prepared several, but none of them seems adequate. So I just want you to have this.' He thrust something at her.

Kate opened the door and looked at his outstretched hand. He still had the most beautiful hands of any man she had ever met.

'Please. Take it,' he urged.

It was then that she saw he was offering her a book. It was his collection of short stories.

'They took their time publishing it, but it's doing okay,' he said as she turned it over in her hand.

'I'm glad for you, Liam,' she said at last.

They looked at each other again, neither knowing what to say next.

'Well, I'll be getting on my way, then. I didn't mean to disturb you,' said Liam, hunching his shoulders and putting his hands into his pockets. He turned and walked to the front door.

As he did, Kate opened the slim hardback volume. The dedication page read 'For Kate'.

'Liam . . .'

He was already at the front door, but he turned.

'Would you like to come in for some coffee?'

Inside the flat, Liam stood uncertainly in the middle of the room, looking around. Kate started to pick up the toys, which were scattered on the floor where she had earlier lain, playing with Jonathan. Then she noticed that she had left his dirty nappy on his changing mat. She grabbed it and swiftly stuffed it into a plastic bag.

'I'm sorry about the mess,' she apologised, 'but you know how it is with babies.'

Liam looked at her. 'Did Jessica have a baby after all?'

Her arms full of toys, Kate turned and stared at him. Robert and Oliver had kept their promise – they had not told him about Jonathan.

'No. He's my baby.'

It was Liam's turn to stare. The expression of shock on his face slowly turning to one of realisation. 'You . . . but does that mean . . .?'

Kate nodded.

'But why didn't . . .?'

'You left. He was – *is* – my responsibility.'

365

'What is . . . I mean, is it a boy or a girl? Can I see . . .?'

'Jonathan. He's asleep in there.' She indicated the bedroom.

Still looking stunned, Liam went in. An instinct she did not understand held Kate back. She remained where she was, holding the toys.

When Liam came back he was crying. He made no noise but tears glistened on his cheeks. He went and sat down on the sofa and put his hands over his face, his shoulders heaving.

Kate dropped the toys, and went and sat next to him. Gently she pulled his hands from his face and, placing hers on his cheek, turned his face towards her. 'Liam, please. It's all right.'

'He's so small, so perfect . . . how could I have left you . . .'

'You didn't know.'

'If I had known I would have stayed. You do understand that?'

She nodded. 'I know. That's why I didn't tell you.'

He pulled away from her and, standing, began to pace up and down, his hands thrust deep into his pockets. 'I just can't believe how stupid I've been. I should have been here for you, for him.' He stopped and looked at Kate, a frown of puzzlement on his face. 'If you knew I would come back, why didn't you tell me?'

'You said you felt trapped. I thought a baby would make it even worse.'

'How could you think a baby, *our* baby, could be a trap?' His voice was accusing.

Kate felt stricken. 'I'm sorry, Liam, I really am.'

He quickly came and sat down beside her, taking her hands in his. 'No, I'm the one who should say sorry. I left, but I've done a lot of growing up since then. If I stay in London, will you let me help with the baby? I mean really help. Look after him when you are at work. I could write as well, he's got to sleep some time.'

'What do you know about looking after a baby?' demanded Kate.

'Not much apart from what goes in messily at one end comes out even more messily at the other. But I'm a fast learner. Anyway, how much did *you* know?' he countered.

Kate couldn't help smiling. 'Not much.'

'Well, two incompetents are better than one, don't you think?'

'I don't know . . .' began Kate.

In the rare moments between exhaustion and stupefied happiness she had slowly and painfully begun to learn a lot about herself. Questions that she had long been able to avoid now demanded answers as insistently as Jonathan's cries required her attention. Her life could never be the same again, of that she was sure – not just on account of Jonathan but because she didn't want it to be.

According to Anita, who kept her in touch with what was happening at the Channel, Jordan was having such problems that he would consider anything Kate suggested to him. She could virtually write her own contract and she both needed and relished the challenge. Kate knew herself too well not to recognise that. But it was different now. In the past she had been driven by her ambition to succeed. It had seemed the only thing that mattered. Now she had a purpose for her ambition and a reason to succeed.

It was as though all the pieces of the jigsaw were falling into place, but they could only too easily come apart again. Yet if she did not take the risk, how would she ever see the complete picture?

'*If* I agree,' she said slowly, 'it would only be for a three-month trial period. We both have a lot of thinking to do.'

Liam held out his hand. 'Agreed,' he said as they solemnly shook hands.

'There's just one more thing,' said Kate. She took a deep breath. 'I love you.'

A grin spread over Liam's face and he leant forward to kiss her, but as their lips touched a loud wail erupted from the bedroom.

Liam stood up. 'I guess this is where my first lesson begins.'

MADDY GOES TO HOLLYWOOD

Maureen Martella

At thirty-three years of age Maddy O'Toole is stranded on Cold Comfort Farm, deep in rural Ireland, with a monosyllabic husband, two children, and her mother. The only bright spot in her week is the American television soap she's addicted to.

Then she discovers that her long-lost sister Gloria is living in Hollywood. No sooner has Gloria invited Maddy – and sent the ticket – than Maddy's on the plane. But what she envisages as a short break ends up changing her life.

For when she arrives at Gloria's hopelessly luxurious Bel Air home she falls helplessly in love with her sister's gorgeous and gentle actor boyfriend, Carlos, none other than the star of her favourite soap.

It's not going to endear her to her sister, but Maddy can't bring herself to contemplate going home ...

Warm, entertaining and indulgent, *Maddy Goes to Hollywood* is a gloriously escapist romantic comedy with an unforgettable heroine.

READING BETWEEN THE LINES

Linda Taylor

When she chucked in her safe job and raced up the M40 to read English at Oxford, Julia Cole didn't give a thought to the future. But now she's thirty, newly graduated and it's pay-back time – at least as far as the bank is concerned. Living in a one-room flat with a cat providing her only male company, *Blind Date* her only regular Saturday night engagement and her last relationship further in the past than a pay cheque, she can't help wondering if she's missing the point.

Until the tall, handsome and only slightly younger Rob strides into the class she teaches. And then his alarming brother Leo, a barrister with a penchant for cross-examining, strides into her friend Maggie's party and puts Julia in the stand. Suddenly, Julia's life is hotting up.

But is she taking both brothers at face value? And is she overlooking the obvious? Perhaps Julia should try reading between the lines ...

'Funny, original and thought-provoking' Katie Fforde

'Take the phone off the hook and pull up your favourite chair. This book is unputdownable' Christina Jones

LOVESICK

Sally Brampton

Harry and Martha had been together for seven years and met at the restaurant every Friday evening which, Martha had once calculated, amounted to three hundred and fifty Fridays if you allowed twenty-four days off for Christmas, New Year, bank holidays and their annual summer holiday. She had been thinking a lot about her life recently, which was unusual for her, but just lately the weeks had started to stretch into a grey sameness which made her feel as if she'd somehow got on to a motorway which had no exit lanes. That evening she calculated that, by her reckoning of three hundred and fifty Fridays, she had sat for a whole year of her life and listened to Harry order prawns.

Bored of Harry's steadfast dependability, Martha leaves him in search of a more exciting and passionate life. But as her life and the lives of those around her begin to unravel the pitfalls of reckless passion become all too obvious.

A bitter-sweet, contemporary novel about friendship, love, the fun of a little danger and the danger of a little fun.

'Sally Brampton's *Lovesick* deals with the complexities of marriage, loyalty and friendship. A moving story that builds slowly to an explosive climax' *Woman's Journal*

'A story of love in the nineties. Full of entertaining characters and heartbreaking events' *Options*

POLLY

Freya North

Polly Fenton loves her job teaching English in London, and she's mad about Max Fyfield. But she's leaving both behind to embark on a year-long teachers' exchange to Vermont. Swapping Marmite for Hershey bars and cornflakes for Cheerios is one thing. Trading lives with her American counterpart Jen is quite another.

But the minute Polly's feet touch down, she's swept off them altogether. She's dazzled by new experiences, wooed by the brave new world; her letters become shorter, then less frequent. When she meets Chip Jonson, school athletic trainer, home thoughts from abroad cease altogether.

Meanwhile in London, her boyfriend, his brother, her best friend and her replacement are forming quite the cosy foursome. If, by the end of the first term, a certain amount of bed-hopping seems inevitable, who is it to be ...?

Spanning three terms and two countries, this is a sparky and sassy story of New England and Old England, fidelity and flirtation, receiving one's comeuppance – and making amends.

Acclaim for Freya North

'A breath of fresh air ... fresh and witty' *Daily Express*

'A runaway success ... destined for bestsellerdom' *Options*

OTHER TITLES OF INTEREST IN ARROW